given to me
from Julie Boss
ta very
much

Tick Tock

www.penguin.co.uk

Tick Tock

Simon Mayo

doubleday

TRANSWORLD PUBLISHERS
Penguin Random House, One Embassy Gardens,
8 Viaduct Gardens, London SW11 7BW
www.penguin.co.uk

Transworld is part of the Penguin Random House group of companies
whose addresses can be found at global.penguinrandomhouse.com

Penguin
Random House
UK

First published in Great Britain in 2022 by Doubleday
an imprint of Transworld Publishers

A CIP catalogue record for this book
is available from the British Library.

ISBNs
9780857526618 (hb)
9780857526625 (tpb)

Typeset in 11.5/15 pt Palatino LT Std by Jouve (UK), Milton Keynes
Printed and bound in Great Britain by Clays Ltd, Elcograf S.p.A.

The authorized representative in the EEA is Penguin Random House Ireland,
Morrison Chambers, 32 Nassau Street, Dublin D02 YH68.

Penguin Random House is committed to a sustainable
future for our business, our readers and our planet. This book
is made from Forest Stewardship Council® certified paper.

In memoriam

Alan Mayo, 1925–1926
'Our wee man'

Mary Bird, 1929–2021
'It's another page-turner, Mary!'

'God omnipotent
is mustering in his clouds on our behalf
Armies of pestilence, and they shall strike.'
Richard II, Act 3, Scene 3

The spore was shaped like a ball, dull grey and seventeen microns in length. That is to say, seventeen thousandths of a millimetre. It spun as it drifted. The spore cloud of which it was a part was buffeted by eddies of breath, draughts from the open window and the heat of nearby human bodies. The cloud floated past two mouths, then spun faster as breath was exhaled, blowing the spores away. Then a third mouth opened, breathing in sharply. A sudden intake, and the air was sucked inside at a speed of two metres per second. The spore was pulled in through the mouth, through the fibrous muscle of the pharynx and past the open epiglottis. In the larynx it was bounced further by the tens of thousands of identical spores in the cloud, all of which had made the same short journey. The ball spun faster.

At the end of the inhale, the spore was pulled down the trachea, a straight drop to the bottom of the windpipe. As it fell, the cloud rotated anticlockwise and the spore funnelled through the tubular branches of the left lung. It slowed as the tubes constricted then stuck on the wall of one of the smallest. There, it waited for germination.

Programmed.

Coded.

Under orders.

In twelve weeks, its hard keratin shell will break and its bacteria will be released. They in turn will release auto-inducers – tiny molecules that signal to each other. Once they message that they have the numbers, the bacteria will attack.

Until then, the spore cloud's cargo of lethal toxin will have to wait.

The driver of the Freightliner X7 bus flicked his tired eyes to the mirror. At 6.37 a.m., it should have been busy. Three quarters full at least. Commuters and returning, sleeping nightshift workers in the main. But he had nine passengers – only nine – and every one of them was silent.

The ID swinging from his neck showed a man happier and heavier than the image in the mirror. He drove slowly, with just one eye on the road. His passengers were nervous; *he* was nervous. He wouldn't have shown up for work at all if his girlfriend hadn't called him a pussy.

Another glance in the mirror.

Bolt upright, the nine were watching each other, their eyes darting from passenger to passenger. Nervous, watchful, *listening*. Above all, *listening*. When the bus was moving and its 600 h.p. diesel engine was clattering noisily, deafeningly, the relaxation was visible: an exhaled breath, a drop of the shoulders. But whenever it slowed down, or spent any time at traffic lights, the delay was greeted with wider eyes and tighter lips. No one was wearing headphones.

Two white men sat at the back, the only passengers sitting close enough for a conversation, but they too had fallen silent. There was colour in their cheeks from the cold outside but otherwise their faces were pale, strained. In front of them, a grey-haired black woman, her handbag clutched to her chest like a shield, stared resolutely ahead. Only her slightly cocked head revealed her alertness, her awareness of possible danger. A muffled and swathed schoolgirl sat three seats in front of her, hands gripped around a book she manifestly wasn't reading. A young black Salvation Army officer

3

stood in the aisle, trying and failing to smile, her gloved hand holding tightly on to the back of a seat. The other four passengers wore white face masks that covered their mouth and nose; one stood by the driver, and the other three sat alone, as far apart as the bus allowed. On one of the misted-up windows, a previous passenger had written 'Silence', the letters now running with condensation.

The bus slowed as it approached a stop. Nine heads whipped left to see who was waiting. *There's someone else?*

It was a middle-aged man, fifties, salt-and-pepper beard, rough working jacket, a scarf wrapped loosely around his neck. An icy blast blew in and the driver punched the doors closed behind him. The man was waved through without paying and immediately sized up his fellow travellers. He pulled the scarf away from his face.

'I'm fine. No need to worry on my score,' he called. Londoner. A ragged voice. A smoker, probably. His cheery tone aroused nothing but suspicion in the nine. Shrugging, he sat down next to one of the passengers wearing a paper mask. His new neighbour flinched, then, recovering, slowly bent his head closer. After a few seconds, he nodded and gave a thumbs-up sign.

The bearded man harrumphed. 'Like I said,' he said, and pulled his scarf back over his mouth.

There was a stretch of dual carriageway ahead, a clear road for maybe half a mile – the only time a bus driver was ever likely to hit 30 mph. The winter light was the usual combination of weak sun and bright neon. The driver thought it made everyone look sick. *Maybe everyone was sick.* If there was no one at the Radcliffe Road stop, he knew he could maintain his speed all the way. Pick up some of his lost time.

The bus shelter looked empty, and he began to move into the middle lane, but at the last minute a gloved hand shot out from behind a full-screen advert. For a fraction of a second, he considered driving on – that hand was late – but then his instinct kicked in and, with the smallest of sighs, he indicated, then slowed. The owner of the gloved hand stayed partially hidden behind the eight-foot-high perfume ad, then the driver made out a dark-coloured parka and a cream hoodie pulled low. Stooped, head down, light brown skin.

In the mirror, the response was immediate. All ten passengers were straining to see who number eleven might be. One of the men in the back row was half standing, peering through the fogged-up window. He wiped away the condensation and pressed his face to the glass, straining for a view.

'Hood's up!' he shouted. 'The bastard's got his hood up!' One of the men in a mask pulled the fabric away from his mouth.

'He takes it down, driver!' he yelled. 'Make sure he takes it down!'

There was an unmistakable edge to the man's voice. The driver got the message. His new passenger would have to take the hood down or there were ten other passengers who would do it for him. Or her. He still couldn't tell.

The bus came to a halt and the doors were opened. Ten strained faces in the mirror; one nervous girl on the steps. Hands deep in her pockets, she stabbed a glance into the bus, then moved towards the driver. Most of her hair was pushed under the hood, but a few loose, dark strands fell in front of her hooded eyes. She cleared her throat. Offered a £10 note. The driver held up his hand.

'Wait,' he said. 'It's not that simple.' He waved it away. 'Don't need your money,' he said through the protective glass. 'But I do need you to remove the hood.' She screwed her face tighter, shook her head then reoffered the banknote.

'Please. To Castle Lane.' There was a rattle in her voice, a phlegmy-bubbling in her words, but that wasn't what had made him shudder.

She was too loud. Her voice was much too loud, and everyone had heard.

'Hood down,' he said, his voice raised now. 'And you can keep the money.' The driver didn't need to check the mirror; he knew he had an audience. The girl scanned the passengers' faces. Ten, all turned to her, all bar an old lady now standing. A man with a paper mask around his neck stepped forward.

'Take off the hood or get the fuck off this bus.'

She took off the hood. Black curls fell to just above her shoulders. The driver caught a glimpse of small ears, no headphones.

'Now kill the engine!' A voice from the back. The driver looked at the girl. Fourteen, maybe, but only just. She hadn't moved from the top step. Whether she was frozen with fear, indecision, sickness or all three, he couldn't tell, but he knew she was in trouble.

'What's your name?' he asked.

'Rose.'

Still too loud. He was grateful for the partition between them.

'Rose, are you sick?'

She shook her head.

Another shout behind them. 'Kill the engine.'

A different voice. 'Yeah, kill the engine. And the heater. We need to hear her!'

The driver sensed the danger. He could see the passengers edging closer. He hit the mic.

'This is my bus.' His voice was amplified so loud his words were distorted and the passengers jumped. 'I will decide who gets on and when the engine gets turned off.' Looks of surprise in the mirror. 'And the heater stays on. Please sit down.'

Most did, but two remained standing. The bearded man and one of the men wearing a mask. The driver cut the mic.

'Rose, Castle Lane is the hospital.' Rose stared at the floor. 'And if you're sick like I think you're sick, you need to get off the bus now.'

The girl began to sway, and he knew he wouldn't catch her in time. She closed her eyes, took a step back and collapsed, falling down the steps, slumping against the automatic doors. There were shouts of alarm from behind and before he could unlock the driver's cabin, one of the passengers had blocked his way. The Salvation Army woman had fallen to her knees, her gloved hands reaching forward and brushing Rose's hair away from her ears. She leaned closer, performed the briefest inspection, then scrambled back to lean against the reinforced glass of the driver's cab.

'Earplugs?' he asked.

The Salvationist nodded.

'Small and pink-skin-coloured,' she said, her words clipped, her breathing rapid. 'Pushed in deep.' He nodded.

'We need to get her off. Now.'

Three of the men rushed forward. 'Just open the doors!' yelled one, a stabbing finger pointing at the driver. 'Get her off before she infects us all.'

The driver shook his head. 'If I open the doors, she'll fall into the gutter—'

'Where she belongs,' said the man, his words only slightly muffled by his mask. 'Open the fucking doors.'

The Salvationist leaned towards the driver. 'Let me out by the back doors,' she said. 'I'll stay with her.' He mouthed a quick 'thank you' and opened them. He watched as she ran to the front, crouched down ready to catch the girl, then raised her arm. 'Ready!'

He hit the door release. There was a hiss and the door began to open, but then, sensing an obstruction, shuddered closed again.

'Jesus Christ,' muttered the driver.

'Try again,' demanded the masked man, and the driver obliged, although he knew it was pointless. Until Rose moved, or was moved, the door would stay shut.

'OK,' said the masked man. 'I've had enough of this. Ready?' His words were aimed at the driver, who shrugged.

'For what?'

The man made a show of holding his breath, then swooped towards the stricken girl. Squatting on his haunches, he reached into the stairwell and grabbed hold of her coat. With a noisy exhalation he hauled her to her feet. Rose's head rolled.

'Hey!' The driver jumped from his seat. 'You can't do that.'

'Open the door! She's not blocking it now. Do it.'

The driver hesitated. He needed the girl off his bus, but not like this.

'We do this gently,' he said. 'Hand her to the Sally Army lady, OK?' The man nodded and the driver opened the doors. The man held the girl by the lapels of her coat, adjusted his grip, altered his stance, then threw her from the bus. She landed on top of the Salvation Army officer and they both hit the ground, hard.

'Drive on,' he said.

Four days earlier

7.50 a.m.

'YOU DON'T GET the next bus.'

'I know.'

'Or Tube.'

'I know that too.'

'And you don't leave for five minutes.'

'Rose, *I know*. We agreed the rules. They were my idea.'

'But you never keep to them, Dad, do you?'

The irate fourteen-year-old girl with light brown skin, grey sweatshirt and black skirt was pointing. A series of finger-stabbing motions punctuated her shouting.

'The rules never apply to you when you don't want them to, do they?' she said.

The irate thirty-nine-year-old man with darker brown skin, jacket and tie held up his hands. A surrender. His next words were spoken softly.

'Rose, the principal has called me into her office. What was I supposed to say? "Sorry, I can't come in just yet because my daughter has this rule—"'

'*We* have this rule.'

'". . . because *we* have this rule that says I can't leave until five minutes after she has slammed the door behind her?"'

The volume kicked up a notch. 'Yes, that's *exactly* what

9

you should have said! You're always saying you can't pick and choose which rules you follow and which you don't.' She raised accusatory eyebrows.

Christ, she's good at this, he thought. If he pursued the argument much longer, he would be late. It was time to go. He never won these spats anyway. He sighed, and retreated.

'You're right,' he said. 'I do say that. I'll try to stick to the rules in future.'

Rose glowered at her father, her large green eyes narrowing, then hoisted her school bag over her shoulder. Slammed the door. He let out another sigh.

'Bye then,' he said to the empty hall. 'Hope you have a good day too.' He stood for a few seconds, staring at the door. He could hear her jumping the steps down to the front door. He shrugged. 'Could have been worse,' he said.

The walk to the Tube took eleven minutes, the scrum to get on a train was usually five and the journey less than ten. Kit Chaplin would be late, but Rose had forced the argument, so there was no use fretting. Once she had gone, he speed-tidied the kitchen, re-checked his work bag, set the alarm. On his way to the station he listened to the news on his headphones, switching to music when he got there. His preferred pre-school playlist was jazz and soul, in the main, Miles Davis, John Coltrane, Michael Kiwanuka, Benjamin Clementine. 'Old grooves,' his partner, Lilly, called it, so that was the name he'd given it. He liked the phrase; it made him an old groover. The playlist now had more than six hundred tracks, and counting. It would take him through the change at King's Cross and up to his exit from Great Portland Street. But first, the platform squeeze. His least favourite five minutes of the day.

The platform was three deep, the next train a minute away. He stood as he always did, one pace to the left of the waste bin, his back to the oncoming train. When he heard it arriving he stepped forward, shoulder first, and when the doors slid open he wheeled and pushed – an old rugby manoeuvre. With his height and broad shoulders, it rarely failed. Short, quick steps, a low drive, and he was on.

Kit grabbed a strap, closed his eyes, tried to concentrate on the sweet sounds in his ears. But it was a battle. He could feel at least three bodies pressed against him. He felt breathing against his neck. A bag pushed into his ribs. A woman's elbow glanced his ear. God, how he hated this. Even with noise-cancelling headphones the carriage sounded like an overflowing doctor's waiting room. A trumpeting sneeze nearby made him shiver; he imagined countless particles of saliva and mucus drifting his way. The Covid memories were strong, but he, like most commuters, had no choice. The bus was no better. Everyone had gone back to everything they were doing before. He wished he could afford the stream of taxis Lilly used. Maybe one day. Kit covered his nose and mouth with his scarf and prayed for King's Cross.

The walk to the connecting train at least had the benefit of a cold blast of winter air blowing through the walkways and escalators. It might be the usual soup of London street air, but to Kit it felt like litres of pure oxygen. At least, he assumed, it didn't come pre-loaded with germs. The second train was more comfortable, less of a flu-incubator than the first. No one dug him in the ribs, no one coughed over his face. Two stops and he was done.

Kit ran up the steps, exited the station at speed.

This was always the cue for pocketing his headphones. Students could arrive at school with beats pulsing and leaking from their headphones, but, Kit thought, not staff. And certainly not the head of English.

Six minutes from Tube exit to staffroom, four at a jog. Kit wrapped his scarf tightly around his neck, hoisted his bag over his shoulder, shoved his hands deep into his coat pockets. The Marylebone Road was as nightmarish as ever. Nose to tail, parallel lines of slow-moving rage and frustration. The most polluted road in London, and he still walked it every day. There was a detour, but he was late already. *Thanks again, Rose.* He pulled his scarf up again. A pointless gesture, he thought. What kind of particles would be filtered out by a wool and polyester scarf from Marks and Spencer? He caught his reflection in a shop window. His wife had always said his face was half elegant, half crazy. Today, that seemed particularly true. His shock of black hair corkscrewed straight up, his amber eyes fierce. He looked like he was about to rob a bank, not take a class on First World War poetry.

Marylebone College School was tucked into the warren of roads that ran between Harley Street and the High Street. Two grand Regency houses had been knocked through to form an impressive double-fronted four-storey school. To the casual passer-by, it could have been a small hospital or consultants' waiting rooms. Creamy-grey Portland stone, large bay windows and a polished-wood double-door entrance. At break and home time, however, its transformation from sedate house to chaotic college was complete. Milling pupils, yelling teachers, hovering parents. Tribal gatherings spilling from the school's steps on to the pavement, then the road. Cars stopping, others double parked, engines running.

Transferred from the private to the state sector in the 1970s, MCS still retained some of its reputation for academic rigour and discipline. For those in the catchment area, it had become a popular choice for parents who wanted a state school with small classes. When Kit had last looked at the statistics, the school's waiting list was eye-watering. Rose had been admitted as they had both attended the local church with sufficient regularity to tick the boxes on the relevant forms. Their attendance had then lapsed, until Kit had started working at the school two years ago.

Rose still hadn't forgiven him. Everyone, she had explained to Kit a thousand times, had an embarrassing dad, but she had an embarrassing dad who was also an embarrassing teacher. She was embarrassed 24/7. There was no escape. Although Kit loved the school and loved being head of English, he knew his daughter had a point. He hoped she would calm down, had always assumed she would. From their first date, Lilly had been reassuring. Said everything would settle. But there was no evidence of that so far. It was quite possible that taking the job had been the wrong choice.

Rose was sitting on her desk.
Lilly was re-reading her father's suicide note.

12.10 p.m.

Kit had two poems displayed side by side on his computer screen, the same two each student had on a sheet in front of them. He had asked them to read both, twice. He had given them ten minutes. Kit knew them by heart but read them again anyway. 'Dulce et decorum est' by Wilfred Owen and 'Gas Attack' by Choman Hardi; 1917 and 1988; First World War, and Iraq's war against the Kurds. Both have a chemical attack; both have a horrified narrator.

'Gas! GAS! Quick, boys!' in the first and 'a chalky-yellow powder settled on your skin' in the second. He preferred the Hardi – it was newer, less familiar. It updated the terror for a generation who had grown up on and were used to *War Horse*. Plus, the poet was Kurdish. The curriculum was more diverse than the one he'd grown up with, but when he came across new voices – voices in different colours – he delighted in placing them in front of his students. Even the grim ones. Hardi's line, 'He groaned like a calf faced with the knife', moved him every time.

He sat back in his chair, his head against the wall. It was a small room, used mainly for tutorials. Plastic chairs, metal and wooden desks, fierce radiators that you couldn't turn down. Kit always opened a small window so that he wouldn't be overcome with the smell of sweat, deodorant and cheap perfume.

The seventeen students in his Year Twelve group read silently. The sound of a shouting match next door was temporarily distracting. A few heads lifted, then returned to the texts. The noise quietened. He heard a clicking from some-where, then a pupil dropped her pen.

'Sorry, sir,' she said, bending to retrieve it, her face disap-pearing behind a curtain of mouse-blonde hair. Kit nodded, said nothing. Jess Slater was a smart girl, a keen student. Then he had gone and spoiled it all by dating her mother. Which complicated matters. Dating the parent of one of your pupils wasn't exactly against the rules, but the principal had made it clear she was 'concerned'. Said she would keep the situation 'under review'. Whatever that meant. Quite how she had found out wasn't clear, but most of the school seemed to know the day after their first date. Rose was mortified. Jess was mortified. Everyone else thought it was hilarious. In class, Jess had clammed up. She blushed furiously, then writhed with discomfort, whenever he spoke to her. So he didn't, unless he had to. Christ, what a mess, he thought. Maybe starting this relationship had been another wrong choice.

The ten minutes of reading time was up. A tall boy with a shock of red hair was desperate to speak. His hand was up, waving. He was smiling broadly.

'Wait, Neil, please,' said Kit, his hand raised. Neil slumped slightly. In the last drop of silence, Kit had heard the noise again. Two clicks, one after the other. He scanned the room, expecting to see a lit phone screen or some leaking head-phones. He saw nothing.

'What is it, sir?' The class were looking at each other, shrugging. Blank faces.

Kit shook his head. 'It's nothing. So. Neil. Tell me what you thought about these poems.'

Rose was playing netball and scored three times.
Lilly was writing a report on antibodies and immune cells.

15

6.10 p.m.

By the time Kit had tubed home, he'd vowed never to do it again. He would run it next time. The commute back had been worse than going in. More faces, more coughs, undoubtedly more germs. He'd had enough. It wasn't far – he guessed four or five miles. He'd been running well until recently, even completing a few half-marathons. But that was before he'd started at MCS, and since then he'd struggled to find the energy. Tomorrow, definitely tomorrow, he thought.

He dropped his bag on to the kitchen table, slumped on to one of its wooden and metal chairs. Resisted the siren call of the Chardonnay in the fridge. If he was going to run tomorrow, he certainly didn't need a hangover.

One floor up, he could hear Rose clattering in her room. Door shut, headphones on. He could hear her half of a conversation. He messaged her.

Pasta? He waited.

Again? came the reply.

You wanna cook?

Not what I meant.

So pasta?

No reply.

'Pasta then,' said Kit out loud.

He dragged himself to the fridge, took out some cheese, a few tomatoes and a bag of fresh pasta. He boiled water, dropped in the pasta, grated some cheese. Put the rest of the cheese back in the fridge. Poured some wine.

It had been a newish maisonette when he and Jody had

16

bought it ten years ago. Money had been tight. He'd sold his Honda motorbike, she'd sold her Mini Traveller, but they had loved the place. Life had been good. Rose was three and, at last, sleeping through the night. They had a kitchen and lounge that were functional, modern. Jody had chosen all the decor. Cool Scandinavian, he'd thought; lots of steel greys and charcoal blacks. When she was alive, he had seen it as minimalist and functional. After she died, he found it miserable and puritanical.

Her cancer had come fast. She was gone in three months. Kit still became breathless thinking about it.

He and Rose barely spoke about her for two years; now she asked questions about her mother all the time. He wished she didn't, but she did. A few years back, they'd gone to see *Mary Poppins Returns* together without knowing the whole dead wife and mother storyline. Kit remembered the gut-churning horror of it all. How he had gripped the arm of the cinema seat so hard the fabric split. How the 'Where The Lost Things Go' song had made him weep so hard Rose had held his hand until he stopped. And on their way home, when she asked him where he thought 'lost things' went, he had answered, truthfully, that he didn't think they went anywhere. Then he'd apologized. She'd said that she thought that was what Mummy had thought too. The rest of the journey home had been silent.

Kit dished out the pasta, called up to Rose. Seemingly between calls, she'd heard and crashed her way down to the table. She'd ditched the school uniform for her usual bright orange dungarees, white tee and blue bucket hat. He'd given up asking her to take the hat off indoors and, anyway, he'd decided he liked it. It suited her and sat well on her curly bobbed hair. That, she got from him. She had her mother's large oval green eyes and small, upturned nose. Her skin was hazel, or possibly caramel. Two small gold studs in each ear. She sat opposite Kit.

'Headphones out, Rose.' She removed the single earbud. 'Thank you. How was school?'

'Fine.'

It was always 'fine', even when it wasn't. She shovelled food into her mouth, tomato sauce painting her mouth and chin scarlet.

'In a hurry?'

She stopped chewing, fork hovering midway between her plate and her face. She shrugged.

'Oh. No. Just hungry.' She smiled. 'And I got you something,' she said. She took her phone from the front pocket of her dungarees, then swiped the screen. 'The bus today,' she said. 'That's Harriet.' She held the screen up. It showed a close-up of a girl's head. Strands of blonde hair hooked behind a pierced, studded ear. The camera went in close, the contours of the girl's ear lobe coming into sharp focus.

'What is this?' said Kit, feigning disgust. 'It's putting me right off my food.'

'Wait,' said Rose, pressing the volume up. 'Listen!' She pushed the phone closer to him, grinning broadly. She was clearly very pleased with her film.

'What?' said Kit.

'Wait!' said Rose again, impatiently. There was some engine noise, more distorted conversations, and then he had it. A click. Then another. Then two more.

'Hear it? That's Harriet's ear, Dad! That sound is literally coming out of her ear!'

Kit frowned. 'Ears don't make noises, Rose,' he said. 'They . . . they receive them. They hear them. I'm not that stupid.'

On the phone's screen, the ear went out of focus, then sharpened. Another click, like an electric spark snapping between terminals.

Rose was indignant. 'Dad! I'm not making this up. My

phone, Harriet's ear. She is making that noise. Honest truth. I was sitting right up close. My head was right next to hers and I heard this noise, this clicking. Or ticking or something. I don't know. Took me a while to realize it was her. Then I asked her and she said she could hear it too.'

'Wait,' said Kit, still sceptical. 'You're sure it was coming *from her ear*?'

Rose was enjoying the stage. 'Yup. Her left ear. Not her nose, her mouth or her right ear. Just the left one. She said that it started earlier in the day.'

'Did anyone else hear it?' he asked.

'Mickie said he could. Then Jason pretended to be interested, leaned in close and licked her face.'

'What?'

'Licked. Her. Face,' said Rose. 'Because he's a dick.' She put her phone back in her dungaree pocket. 'Wild, huh?' She finished her pasta. Wiped her mouth with her hand. 'How's your girlfriend?'

Kit winced. He hated being asked for updates and he hated that Rose always said 'girlfriend' rather than 'Lilly'. Rose had even called Lilly 'girlfriend' to her face. Kit had been furious. Another row. It was true that Lilly Slater was his 'girlfriend'. It was the first relationship he'd had since Jody died and he was enjoying her company very much. Even if he could have done without the whole school knowing. He understood Rose's indignation. Having your father teach in your school was one thing, but to have him 'shagging Jess Slater's mum', as she had screamed it, was something else altogether. His honest denials had fallen on deaf ears. Rose had wanted to take him down, so she had.

Recently, Kit had wondered if Rose was softening towards Lilly, but he still felt . . . well what did he feel? Guilt, definitely. That he was dishonouring his wife's memory in some way by seeing someone else. Fear, also. Fear that he would get 'involved' again and then that Lilly, too, would die. What a dumb-ass idea that was.

Rose knew that Lilly's father had just died, so this time her query had been delivered with less venom, even some warmth. Kit bit down a reply, forced himself to eat some more pasta. Chewed. Swallowed. Shrugged.

'Not sure,' he said. 'It's been pretty bad, I think.'

'Bad how?'

Kit wondered how much to say. Lilly had been brief on the phone, curt, even. 'I'm not sure, Rose, to be honest. She sounded pretty upset though.'

Rose nodded. 'OK,' she said, and stood to drop her plate into the sink. At the top of the stairs, she called out, 'Tell her I said sorry about her dad.'

The door slammed and she was gone. Kit downed the rest of the glass. 'Progress,' he said.

Ten minutes later his phone pinged. Rose had messaged a link and added *OMFG*. He was annoyed at her casual cursing but clicked on the link anyway. There were fourteen videos on it. He watched the first two. His mouth went dry.

7.45 p.m.

Kit grabbed his phone and slumped on to the battered black two-seater sofa. The kitchen and lounge were essentially one room, with two steps separating them, the kitchen higher and larger. The lounge offered a sofa, the battered armchair with its embroidered cushions and a small television on an old wooden crate. Large blue-and-white Matisse prints hung on each of the three walls. A south-facing window gave the room its only natural light, but tonight its wooden-slatted blind was pulled closed against the winter's dark. Tall ferns stood in each corner. An overloaded bookcase teetered on the brink of collapse. Poetry, art history and a whole shelf of Toni Morrison. A small speaker system played Marvin Gaye. The room was, by default, his space, as Rose rarely ventured far from her bedroom or the fridge.

Kit watched the last of the videos again. Up until this one, number fourteen, they all appeared to have been shot in the UK. The language spoken was English, in a variety of accents. This last one, though, had been shot in Central Park. Kit recognized the Onassis Reservoir railings and walkway; he had been there a couple of summers ago. He had watched each video with an increasing sense of disbelief. Now, with a New York scene playing out, Kit laughed out loud.

The UK clips had all shown variations of Rose's film: laughing teens, close-ups of ears and a soundtrack of clicking. Lots of clicking. Some of it was barely audible, but occasionally they were like beats, coming in rhythmic pulses. Like messages in Morse code. Or bursts of static from outer space.

In the American one, a man was sitting on a park bench, breathing fast, clouds of steam billowing from his mouth. He was sweating profusely. A runner, Kit assumed. Thirtyish, Latino, orange-and-black Islanders hockey top. The unseen camera operator sits next to the man, says hi. A woman's voice. The man nods and smiles, coyly, as though embarrassed. The woman says, 'D'you know your ear is makin' a scene?' The man nods again, then the camera does an extreme close-up of his ear, lingering for thirty seconds.

Initially, Kit heard nothing, just the sounds of the park: the wind and distant shouting; ducks and geese slapping and flapping. Then the ticking starts. Four clicks from, presumably, the man's ear, a gap of around a second between them.

After that, it is hard to work out what is real and what is manufactured. The clicks get louder – digitally amplified, Kit assumes – and the music begins. A track has been mixed into the clicks, the ear 'popping' coinciding with some frantic beats, and a cheap filter laid over the scene, turning the image into a photographic negative that pulses with the clicks' rhythm. The water is red, the sky is green and the man has turned a silver-grey. As the screen fades, words appear, as though written on an old typewriter. They say, 'What is this crazy shit?'

'Well, exactly,' muttered Kit.

Rose's voice over his shoulder. 'It's objective tinnitus.'

Kit spun round; he hadn't even known she was there.

'It's what?'

'Objective tinnitus. I looked it up.'

'That's a thing?'

She handed him a tablet. The page on the screen was from an online medical dictionary. It showed two diagrams of an ear. The first was labelled 'Subjective Tinnitus', the second 'Objective Tinnitus'. Kit knew about tinnitus – he'd had it himself after a couple of Metallica gigs an age ago. His ears had rung for days, but he had known that the sound in his head was just that. It was in his head and wasn't really a sound at all; it was just the perception of sound.

The first diagram showed a cross section of an ear, and the text read, 'You perceive a sound that's not there. The perception is caused by abnormal nerve activity in the auditory cortex.' The second diagram showed the outer ear, the middle ear and the inner ear, nerves running from the inner ear to the brain. Pulse waves had been drawn around the middle ear, indicating movement. Or vibration. The text read, 'Caused by a physiological process near the middle ear, like a muscle spasm. A sound is made.'

Kit read the words again. Rose repeated them.

'A sound is made,' she said. 'That's what this is, Dad. The crazy shit in New York and in all those other videos is objective tinnitus.' She pulled her hat from her head with one hand, rubbed her hair with the other. Something she only ever did to emphasize a point. 'The ears are *making sounds*.' She took her tablet back.

'And that's lots of ears making lots of sounds,' said Kit. 'Where did you find all these videos?'

Rose rolled her eyes. 'Just searched for them.' Her phone vibrated in her dungaree pocket. She glanced at the screen and sprinted up the stairs.

Kit felt the sleep-inducing powers of the wine creep through his body. He thought about closing his eyes but knew that would be a disaster. He'd wake at three when the heating had been off long enough to chill him to his bones. Then he'd realize he had a headache. Then he wouldn't get back to sleep. He hauled himself out of the armchair. From his bag, he pulled his laptop and headphones, then sat back down at the kitchen table. 'What's Going On' played for the second time that evening.

'That's the right question,' said Kit aloud, 'but it won't get these essays marked.' Occasionally, he was aware of quite how often he talked to himself. He wondered if he should be concerned. It had started as a way of talking to Jody. He said the things he would have been saying to her. Now it was just thinking aloud. When Rose overheard she would usually call out, 'Someone is seriously losing it down there!' and he would try to stop. Which he did, until the next time.

He opened his laptop, uploaded the essays from his Year Twelves and Thirteens, read one, poured some wine, then googled 'objective tinnitus'.

He woke, frozen, just after 3 a.m.

Rose was asleep, in her room.
Lilly was asleep, in her room.

Three days earlier

5.10 a.m.

LILLY SLATER'S FIRST waking thought was Kit. That hadn't happened before. She made a mental note – that had to be significant, didn't it? It wasn't her newly buried father. It wasn't the pile of work she'd need to dive into as soon as she got to her office. It was of Kit Chaplin. Her daughter's English teacher. It had been seventeen months but was just starting to feel normal.

She had five minutes before she needed to be in the shower. She reached for her phone, texted him. He'd get it when he woke up. She knew he never took his phone to bed so there was no danger of waking him.

Sorry didn't call. Grim day. Talk later?

She added an X then deleted it. Unnecessary. Too much.

She was showered and dressed by five thirty. Blue-and-white block-print dress, black tights, boxy cardigan. One black coffee from the machine, one slice of toast with a no-peel marmalade, one banana. She loaded the dishwasher, added all Jess's take-out containers, swore briefly. She'd noticed the state of the kitchen when she got in late last night, but she had been too tired to clean anything. The only thing she had checked, apart from the window locks, was that Jess didn't have company. If you leave your teenage daughter on her own for a day and a half, it was all to be expected. They'd exchanged texts last night and Jess seemed to understand what was happening. She'd never met her grandfather – knew almost nothing about him – but understood the process her mother was obliged to follow. She got process. Lilly left a box of porridge and an orange on the table. Just in case.

She checked the charge on her laptop and phone, then zipped them both into her bag. Dogtooth wool coat, charcoal-grey scarf, and she was by the front door before six. She ignored the mirror. Patted her coat pockets for keys and gloves. Her Tube pass was in her top pocket, her work accreditation for GSL, Global Shield Labs, in an inside pocket.

She was ready to leave, but she hesitated by the door. Dropped her hand from the deadlock. Took a breath.

'What am I doing?' she whispered. She rested her head against the door. The red matte paint was cold against her skin. She closed her eyes. 'What am I actually doing?' Take the day off. Take the week off. That's what she'd been told, but here she was, dressed and on her way to work. As though nothing had happened. As though her father hadn't just been cremated. As though she didn't really care very much. 'Well?' she asked herself, as if there were a clock running. If she stayed, she would see Jess, could tell her what had happened. If she left, she would be able to collate the new test results. Her indecision surprised and annoyed her. Kit would say she was in shock, but she doubted that. The work was important. Her role was important. The final thirty tests had been filed and she needed to finish her analysis. No one else would do it. No one else would go near it. Lilly exhaled heavily, briefly fogging the paint. She would take a half-day. She would see Jess later. Maybe make her supper. Problem solved.

Lilly patted her pockets again then left the house. She pulled the door shut quietly behind her and headed for the station.

Kit was getting dressed.
Rose was getting ready to leave the house.

7.40 a.m.

Rose was early, but not early enough to get a seat. She leaned against one of the bus's metal support poles, angling her weight to avoid the red 'Stop' button. Rucksack between her feet. DMs, black tights, black pleated skirt, hooded parka over her grey MCS sweatshirt. Hood over headphones. The inside of the bus was only a few degrees warmer than the freezing streets outside; her hood stayed up.

There were two stops before Harriet, three before Millie. She texted both. Harriet was waiting. Nothing from Millie. She pocketed her phone and tried to look through the window. The streetlights were on, the sky still dark. The bus window was a clouded mirror reflecting huddled ghosts. Rose turned away.

At each stop the overcrowded bus somehow absorbed more passengers. Rose clung to her post, positioned her legs around her rucksack. The stop before Harriet, she retrieved her phone. Watched the clicking video of Harriet one more time. Its soundtrack in her headphones made her laugh out loud. This time the sound coming from Harriet's on-screen ear sounded more like a pop. Like a tiny bubble bursting. Followed by more bubbles, more bursting.

The bus slowed and Rose looked up. Montreal Road. Harriet's stop. On this bus you entered at the front, exited midway, just where she was standing. Rose grabbed hold of her bag as departing passengers squeezed past. She turned her head to avoid contact with a flushed and sweating woman in an ancient stretched-to-bursting tracksuit. The woman was finding it difficult to exit the bus but she sucked in her lips and pushed until the scrum gave way. She coughed twice as she passed, her hip brushing Rose's back. Rose shivered. Harriet appeared, as if in the coughing woman's slipstream.

'Hey,' said Rose. She smiled.

'Hey,' said Harriet. She tried to smile.

'What's up?' said Rose.

Her friend's face was almost lost under a thick blue hood, only a few strands of her yellow-blonde hair escaping its fur trim. She grabbed the metal pole, stood at right angles to Rose. Identical height; both five foot two. Their eyes met only briefly, just long enough for Rose to clock the tears. Harriet looked away, stared at the floor. Said nothing.

'Harri.' Rose dipped to catch her eye then reached a hand into her friend's hood. Lifted one ear of her headphones. 'Harri, what is it?' Harriet whispered something, but Rose missed it.

'What?'

'Put it back, Rose,' said Harriet, more clearly now. 'Please.' Rose dropped the headphones to her ear.

Harriet turned to face the window, her back to Rose. They rode for a minute like that; Rose behind Harriet, both with a hand on the pole. When Harriet's shoulders started to tremble, Rose slid her hand over hers. Harriet let it stay there.

As the bus slowed then stopped Rose shifted as much as she could to accommodate the passengers lining up to exit, pushing her closer to Harriet. This was Millie's stop. In front of her the exit doors fizzed open; another icy blast from the street. Rose turned to scan the new arrivals; Harriet didn't move. Rose checked her phone again. No message. No Millie. She messaged Harriet, standing just in front of her, instead.

Talk/not talk?

Two seconds later, Harriet hauled her phone from an

inside pocket, checked the screen, typed a reply. Rose's phone buzzed. A one-word reply:

Scared.

The bus's entrance and exit doors were still open, the last of the new passengers climbing aboard, swiping their passes. Rose grabbed Harriet's arm, pushed her down the steps, off the bus. As they stepped on to the pavement the bus doors closed. Harriet turned to Rose, her pale blue eyes wide with astonishment, her mouth open. She pulled off her large pink headphones. Rose cut across whatever it was she had been about to say.

'We'll walk from here.' She linked arms with Harriet and they set off. There were black railings running along the narrow path, scrappy grassland running to tarmac on the other side. The traffic was busy both ways but downhill to the city was jammed already. Nose to tail, as far as they could see. Hardworking car-heating systems fought their iced and steamed-up windows. Diesel and petrol fumes hung in the air.

After twenty paces of silence, Harriet took a deep breath.

'I'm a freak, Rose.'

'You what?'

'My brother said it as I left just now. He heard the clicking and started laughing.'

'You're still clicking?' Rose glanced at Harriet, who bit her lip then nodded.

'Carl's like, "Put her in a circus! She's an actual freak."'

'Yeah, well, Carl is a dick,' said Rose. 'You've said so yourself. And anyway, he's basically a fifteen-year-old child. He doesn't know shit.'

Harriet snorted then wiped her nose with her hand. 'You got that right. You've always been right about Carl.' She gave a little tug on Rose's arm. 'But he's correct this time, Rose. My head's making noises. Listen.' The two girls put their heads together as they walked.

'Same as yesterday then,' said Rose. 'But you saw those clips I sent you? You're not a freak at all, Harri. Seems like loads of people are clicking.'

'Then we're all freaks,' said Harriet.

Two buses passed. Harriet glanced at them.

'We'll be late,' she said.

'We will,' said Rose. It was a statement of fact, delivered flatly. An expression of comradeship. Ten more paces in silence. Harriet pulled Rose closer.

'I'm so scared, Rose.'

'Did you tell your mum?'

Harriet nodded. 'She said she'd get me an appointment at the doctor's. But I'm scared *now*, Rose. I don't want to wait ten days, or however long it'll take.' They crossed a five-way junction, running to catch the lights. The sky was brightening at last, but most of the light here came from the street's coffee bars and sandwich shops. The pavement was flooded with a warm glow and the smells of breakfast. The queues snaked out of the doors.

Rose swapped sides, threading her other arm through Harri's. 'In which case,' she said, 'when we get to school, we go straight to Nurse Mac.'

'You always say she's useless,' protested Harriet.

Rose smiled. 'I do, and she is. But we might get lucky this time. And we get to miss English.'

Rose and Harriet walked on. They were forty-five minutes from school.

Lilly was at her desk.
Kit was walking into the staffroom.

8.05 a.m.

Kit was old enough to remember smoke-filled staffrooms. In his first year of teaching he had provided a lot of it, his ten roll-ups a day adding – so he thought – swagger to his bookish, scholarly image. When the asthma appeared he had, eventually, ditched his beloved tobacco tins, though with considerable reluctance. Now he realized he had been an imbecile, but every time he pushed open a staffroom door he still thought of lighting up. Even now, with the hangover he had feared and the sure knowledge it would make him wheeze all day, he felt the familiar nicotine tug.

The MCS staffroom had been the school dining hall until the 1960s, when it had been repurposed by the then headmaster. It still felt like a refectory to Kit, with four long dining-style tables placed two and two, with plastic chairs of all colours tucked haphazardly around them. Laptops and piles of exercise books indicated places in use or reserved. Beaten-up old armchairs were scattered around the periphery, most of them occupied. Of the thirty-one staff, Kit was still one of the newest. Turnover was lower than average for a London state school. The 'Outstanding' grade in the last Ofsted report was certainly part of the explanation. The nearby John Lewis store's generous teacher discount explained the rest.

Kit dropped his bag on the first table, made for the coffee tray. It was vile stuff, but it was there and it was free. He took a brimming paper cup back to his chair. He needed at least half of it before he could be sociable. He felt the scorching liquid all the way down to his stomach. Now he could look up. He nodded as members of staff caught his eye.

'Hi, Aisha. G'morning, George,' he managed eventually. Behind him in the easy chairs were head of science and deputy head Aisha Khatri and George Hall, Games. Or 'Athletics', as he would have it. Both were slumped under a hardworking noticeboard. Kit was sure they were having an affair, but they were both married, just, and had three kids between them, so he didn't pry. He dragged his chair around to face them. It was Aisha he had been hoping to see. He was about to jump straight in with it but instead forced out some pleasantries.

'You guys OK?' he said, then wondered if that sounded like he assumed they were a couple. He winced and stumbled on. 'If I remember, Aisha, you're not a fan of Tuesdays.' Now it was her turn to wince.

'You remember correctly,' she said. Late thirties, loose-fitting crimson dress, black woollen cardigan, long black hair piled high on her head and tied with an elaborate black cord. She closed her eyes. 'My two worst classes back to back. Destroys me every time.' George's phone rang and he hauled himself out of his chair.

'Scuse me,' he said. 'Better take this.' He shuffled off towards the coffee station, trainers squeaking on the wooden floor. Kit heard him say, 'Hi, darling,' then the rest was lost. Kit leaned in.

'So, Aisha. Question for you. Have you heard of objective tinnitus?' He said the words with a peculiar emphasis, as if they were in an unfamiliar foreign language. She pursed her lips.

'Tinnitus I know,' she said. 'Objective tinnitus I do not. That implies there is a subjective tinnitus . . .'

'It does,' said Kit. 'And if I've read it right, there is. That's the normal ringing-in-the-ear stuff. Headphones too loud, Metallica, Earls Court, 2003, you know.'

'Okaaay.' Aisha managed to frown and look amused at the same time.

'I know,' he said, hands in the air, palms towards her. 'Maybe not what you'd expect from the English department first thing. But look at this. My daughter recorded it last night. It's her mate on the bus home.' He took out his phone and played Rose's video of Harriet's noisy ear. Aisha's expression changed.

'This is for real?' she said.

'Wait,' he said, then he played three more videos, finishing with the American one.

Aisha shook her head. 'Nope. No idea,' she said. 'Never seen it before. But when my Year Eights are kicking off, asking about the human reproductive system *again*, I'll think of them with strange noises coming out of their ears. Maybe it'll help.' She strode to the door. Kit and George, who had finished his call, watched her go.

Kit mixed up another coffee. He sipped it slowly and read his Tennessee Williams notes until the bell went.

Lilly was studying germ manipulation.
Rose was knocking at Nurse McKay's door.

8.50 a.m.

Rose and Harriet had hung their coats up, stowed their bags under their desks and walked the length of the building to get to 'the San'. It was just a room at the end of a corridor with medical equipment and a nurse, but it said 'Sanatorium' on the door, so 'the San' it was. The girls were side by side on a low bench, backs to the San wall. It was in a far corner of the building usually referred to as 'Old School', as it was, by some measure, the most dilapidated. The heating system had been installed many decades ago, the windows and doors were warped and draughty, and the painted walls Rose and Harriet were staring at were chipped and scuffed. Aisha Khatri's biology lab had the misfortune to be the closest classroom to the Old School. It gave the corridor its distinctive, never-fading rotten-fish smell. Harriet was impatient, her fingers tapping her phone screen.

'This is crazy, Rose,' she said, her voice hushed. 'What am I going to say to her anyway? She'll think I'm mad.'

'You say you're scared. And you tell her why.'

'Really?'

'Really. It's what she's here for.'

'Or not here for,' said Harriet. 'When does she get in?'

Rose shrugged. 'Presumably now?'

'We could come back at break?' suggested Harriet.

'No,' said Rose. 'We're late for English because we're at the San. No one will argue. We could be here for anything.'

Harriet nodded. She stopped tapping. 'Shit,' she said.

'What?' said Rose, head snapping right.

Harriet had gone pale. 'It's faster, Rose. The noise. It just got *faster*.' Her voice tailed off, the last word barely a breath. Rose leaned closer, their heads touching. She frowned as if struggling to hear, then her eyes widened.

'OK. Got it,' she said. Nodded. 'Faster is right.' She held her friend's hand.

Harriet squeezed hers back. 'OK, now I *do* want to see Nurse Mac.'

'Just 'cos it's faster, it doesn't mean anything. Doesn't mean it's worse.' Rose didn't sound convinced.

Harriet noticed. Her grip tightened. 'What do I do, Rose?' Small staccato sobs interrupted her speech.

Rose checked her phone. 'We'll give Mac two minutes,' she said, 'then we go to Whitlock.'

'Really?' Harriet turned to Rose, wiped her eyes with a sleeve.

'Really.'

'So you *do* think it's worse.'

A beat.

'I suppose. Yeah.'

There was a bustling sound from beyond the dog-leg turn in the corridor. A running, tripping woman in a tracksuit and with wild ginger hair came bowling towards them.

'What a state,' muttered Rose.

Joanne McKay bellowed as she ran. 'Sorry, girls! Just give me a moment, will you?' She flew past them, unlocked her door. 'One minute,' she called, pushing the door closed with her foot. The girls exchanged glances.

'Is this even worth it?' said Harriet. 'Maybe go straight to Whitlock?' The San door flew open again. Nurse Mac was now, somehow, dressed in a white tunic and black stockings. Like a real nurse.

'Come in!' she said, all smiles. The girls entered the San, both of them noticing the pair of tracksuit bottoms that had been kicked into a corner. 'Sit down then.' She gestured at two chairs against an unadorned cream wall, then sat behind an old school desk. 'Er, Rose Chaplin, I know. And . . .' She raised her eyebrows at Harriet.

'Harriet Teale,' said Harriet.

Nurse Mac wrote on a pad. Fired up an ancient computer. She stared at the screen, clearly waiting for some information to appear. There were a few seconds of silence in the room. Nurse Mac cocked her head, looked at the girls. Frowned.

'Can you hear clicking?' she said.

9.05 a.m.

Kit knocked twice on the principal's door, heard Whitlock's summoning call. He took a breath. This really didn't feel good. He had barely started his Year Ten lesson when he got the message. The head wasn't a woman for trivia. The timing was all wrong. It must be Rose. Or maybe Lilly. *Shit.*

He pushed the door open. Two enormous sash windows filled the office with a thin, watery sunlight. Kit saw the principal and the nurse first, then Rose and Harriet, next to each other on two chairs. Rose flicked her eyes to Harriet. Kit guessed the rest. Jan Whitlock was typing furiously into her laptop. Late-fifties elegant, greying auburn hair held back with a slide. She peered over large pewter-grey glasses.

'I spelt "tinnitus" wrong,' she said to the screen. She hit enter, read from a fresh page. 'Ah!' She glanced up. 'Kit. Come in. Rose says you know about this . . . clicking noise?' It sounded like an accusation of negligence. Nurse McKay, just behind Whitlock, folded her arms. Her freckled face was impassive.

'Take a seat. Please,' said Whitlock. She gestured to a wooden dining chair. Kit perched awkwardly. He took a breath. Smelled coffee and wood polish.

'Well,' he said, 'I only know what I looked up last night. There are' – he waved his arms and shrugged – 'there are several videos online, all posted in the last twenty-four hours, all showing, or appearing to show, people with noise coming *out* of their ears. Rose told me about Harriet Teale.' He glanced at the girls. 'Naturally, I was curious.'

'And you call it what?' The principal's eyes were back on the screen. Kit sensed that Rose had been about to speak but was holding back. He frowned. Whitlock had made it sound as though he'd discovered this strange condition.

'Well, the medical sites call it objective tinnitus.' A quick look to McKay. 'But obviously I have no expertise here. I'll happily defer to Joanne on this.'

The nurse coloured. 'Hmm,' she said. 'Well, if I'm honest, I'd never heard of it until Rose told me about it five minutes ago. Tinnitus, yes; objective tinnitus, no. I'm sorry, Dr Whitlock.' She looked embarrassed by her lack of knowledge. 'I've been a nurse twelve years and I've never come across it.' A rally of sorts, thought Kit. The principal swivelled in her chair to face McKay.

'So no other pupils have come to you with this?'

McKay shook her head.

Whitlock turned to Kit. 'And were any of the videos you watched of MCS pupils? Apart from Harriet's, obviously?' Her words were crisply spoken, business-like. Not overly concerned then, thought Kit. An ass-covering exercise. He relaxed a little.

'Not that I saw, no,' he said. 'But I'll send you the link, just to be sure.' Then, startled, he remembered his lesson on war poetry the day before. The dropped pen, the silence. And the clicks. 'Actually, there was someone else,' he said.

All heads turned. McKay's eyebrows arched. Whitlock's eyes narrowed slightly.

'I'm sorry,' Kit went on. 'I'd forgotten. But yesterday, towards the end of a Year Twelve lesson, I think I heard a couple of clicks. Very similar to Harriet's and the ones in the video clips. It was a strange noise, which is why I noticed it. I thought it was music from someone's headphones. Something like that. But it wasn't. Then the bell rang and I forgot about it.'

Kit sensed the mood change.

'And you don't know where, or who, it came from?' asked the principal.

'No. It wasn't loud enough,' said Kit.

Whitlock stood suddenly. Brushed her high-waisted skirt flat. 'In which case,' she said, 'find all of them. Talk to all of them. Before break, please, Kit. Soon as you can. I'll get someone to check Harriet's classes. Back here at eleven.'

A nod, a brief smile, and he was dismissed. Kit glanced at Rose, but she wasn't looking.

He jogged to his Year Tens. He ignored their desk-sitting and phone-messaging.

'OK, listen up,' he called from the doorway. Twenty-three pupils returned to their seats as if it was Musical Chairs and the music had stopped. 'So, I have a job to do for Dr Whitlock. Please read the Cecil Day-Lewis poem on the sheet, then write at least five hundred words on the language he uses and the structure. In silence. Please leave the door open.' He made eye contact with any pupil that was looking at him. 'So that's in silence. And no phones.'

A faster jog to the deserted staffroom. There were seventeen in his Year Twelve class; he had to track them all down. 'Track and trace,' as Lilly would say. He had the register, and the school database would tell him where they were now. Or where they should be. He accessed the school's information management program then searched for each in turn. He scribbled the results. Seven were in DT, six in history, and the rest had a free period. He sighed. This would take longer than he wanted it to. Longer than Whitlock wanted it to.

It had taken most of his first term to learn how to navigate the labyrinth that the school had become. But now he had 'the knowledge', he was outside the Design and Technology room in thirty seconds. He knocked, entered. The DT teacher, a willowy Glaswegian called Jim Sutherland, glanced up.

'Mr Chaplin!' The smile was unforced. The two men had shared many a post-school pub visit. 'To what do I owe the pleasure?' Kit leaned in, turning his back to the class. His words were as quiet as they needed to be.

'Apologies, Jim. I need a word with seven of your students. No time to explain.' Kit caught the beginning of a frown, but his next words were for the class. 'Those of you in my English set, outside, please. And don't worry, it's nothing bad.' He gave the best smile he could manage, then waited for the seven to trudge outside to the corridor. Kit nodded his thanks to a bewildered Sutherland, then followed them out. He pulled the door shut behind them. Seven puzzled faces.

'I'm sorry to interrupt, but I have an urgent health enquiry.' Now they looked even more puzzled. 'I know this is weird,' Kit said. 'I'm an English teacher, not the school nurse. Trust me here, and please be honest. Are any of you having . . .' He searched for the right words. 'Are any of you having hearing issues?' Seven blank faces. 'Anything unusual? Anything at all?'

'What sort of thing, sir?'

'Yeah, how d'you mean, sir?'

Time was counting down and Kit felt his pulse ticking up a notch.

'It's very simple,' he said. 'Is your hearing the same now as it was, say, last month? I need an answer from each of you, loud and clear.' He realized he was sounding crazy. Kit got seven yeses. 'Thank you. You can go back into class.'

Kit walked off, leaving the students staring after him, bemused. As soon as he turned the corner, he started jogging again. History was first floor. He took the stairs three at a time. And checked his watch.

9.55 a.m.

His visit to the history class yielded one more confused teacher, six more puzzled students, and no hearing problems. Zero. Maybe this would all turn out to be nothing. Eight more students to find, all on a free period. He'd try the library, but the truth of it was that some might have left the building. The top two years had privileges, the most precious of which was being allowed to leave the school premises. Misuse was rife but for now, he just had to hope they were in school.

Kit jumped down the stairs. The library was ground floor, near the front entrance. It was one of the reasons he had fallen in love with the school. The library was the first room you came to on entering MCS. It was a bold statement. To Kit it said that without books, we are nothing. He was surprised how often he had had to fight that particular corner, even in a school.

He pushed at the double glass doors. Greeted the librarian. Spotted four of his class sitting together around a table. Two girls, two boys. Bingo. He pulled up a chair. They shuffled theirs to accommodate him.

'Guys, I'll be brief.' He looked from one confused face to the next. 'Straight answer, please, to a straight question. Are any of you experiencing any problems – any issues at all – with your hearing?'

The four looked dumbstruck. Two put hands to mouths. One of the boys pushed his chair back, turned away from

Kit. The boy nearest to him frowned. Lanky, short, high-fade hair, brown skin. His school ID said Marcus Graham.

'We have actually, yeah. We were just talking about it, sir.'

Kit sat up straight, looked around the four.

'We?' he said. 'How many is "we"?'

Marcus glanced at the other three. 'Well, all of us.' His voice was hushed and questioning. 'What's going on, sir?' Kit noticed Marcus reach for the hand of the girl next to him.

'Honestly, I don't know,' said Kit. He made eye contact with each in turn. 'But Jon, Eve, Ellie, Marcus, I think we should find out, don't you? How would you describe . . . what's happening? At the moment. In your heads.' Opposite Kit, Eve Brewer, whom Kit normally thought of as the haughtiest, most entitled girl in the school, looked like a terrified twelve-year-old. She bit her lip, blinked hard.

'It's like having a clock inside your head.' She sounded exhausted, her voice thin and reedy. 'Just, like, all the time. Twenty-four/seven.'

'So it's like a ticking?' asked Kit.

They all nodded. *Christ*.

Marcus unhooked his hand from Ellie's and leaned in.

'Did you hear us or something, sir?' he said. 'It's just, we ain't told anyone yet, so . . .'

Kit shook his head. Saw no reason to hide anything.

'I heard one of you yesterday. In English. Don't know which one. It was a definite click but I saw no reason to be interested. But it's not just you,' he said. 'A Year Ten girl has it too. And it has a name . . . hang on.' He fished out his phone, found the page he'd saved. Held the screen out in front of him. 'It's called objective tinnitus.' The four students bent forward and read in silence. Kit heard two clicks, one after the other. A double shot.

'Who was . . .' began Kit. Two hands, first Eve, then Jon, next to her.

They all carried on reading his phone screen. Marcus finished first. He sat back.

'I feel better now,' he said. 'It's called something. I've got . . .' He peered at Kit's phone again. 'Objective tinnitus. It's got a name.' Ellie and Eve exhaled slowly. Jon was still reading.

'But *why* have we got it?' said Jon. 'Says here it's very rare. And that old people get it.' He looked up at Kit. He had pale blue eyes, unkempt, shoulder-length, mouse-blond hair. 'Also, sir, you don't *catch* it. It says here "emotional stress, ear wax and brain tumours". You can't catch them, can you? We can't all have that shit. That would be mad.'

Kit raised his eyebrows.

'Sorry, sir,' said Jon.

Another click, quieter this time.

'Mine,' said Marcus.

Kit had no idea what this was about and no understanding of the anatomy of the ear either. But he did know he didn't like any of it. Jon was right. Tinnitus was not contagious. It wasn't even an illness. It was a condition. A symptom. He had another thought. 'Have you all been to a concert together? Or a club maybe? That's the only thing I can think of.' Four head shakes. He'd done all he could here. 'OK,' he said. 'Principal's office at eleven. All of you.' He stood to go. Two more clicks. 'I'll tell Mrs Whitlock you're coming.'

He stepped outside the library, texted Lilly.

10.20 a.m.

No.

Lilly texted just the one word. She hadn't heard of whatever Kit was asking about. Strange question. Her phone buzzed again.

There are five cases in school, she read. She exhaled sharply. Kit was asking for medical information and clearly hoped for an answer. She was his personal hotline, the fount of all knowledge. All medics had to deal with it. You have a 'Dr' in front of your name, so you can obviously diagnose anything. Answer every question about a friend's illness. Recommend the best local GP. She knew that Kit tried hard not to do this, and he had told her so many times. Then she had a thought.

Is this Jess?

She waited for a reply. Typed 'objective tinnitus' into her online medical dictionary. She scanned the text, the diagrams, the photos. Wondered how she hadn't come across it before. Her phone buzzed.

Not Jess, not Rose.

Child hysteria? wrote Lilly.

Quite the opposite, came the immediate reply.

Lilly hesitated before putting her phone away. She dealt with pathogens. Bacteria, viruses and protozoa. Things that cause disease. She researched and made vaccines, then tried to predict how viruses might evolve. Since her Ph.D., then Glaxo SK and the Jenner Institute, this had been her world. For most of her professional life, she had trained immune systems to defend themselves. She worked with pathogenic micro-organisms to create antibodies and immune cells. Then, when the disease arrived for real, it lost. That's what she did. That's what she had always done. Tinnitus wasn't an infection so there was no pathogen. No pathogen, nothing to vaccinate against. That's why she hadn't come across it before. So move on. She could catch up with Kit later. Lilly put her phone away.

She shut down the tinnitus page and started to read the test results that had come in for a new mosquito-borne virus from Taiwan called Tembusu. It had started on a duck farm last December and the Animal Health Research Institute people were worried about transmission to humans. They had asked for her opinion by midday. She read fast, H2 pencil in hand, A4 notepad turned to a new page. Her attention drifted. She touched her phone's screen, read Kit's message again. Five cases. She didn't trust gut instinct. It was dangerous ground for a scientist. She trusted only in peer-reviewed evidence. You thought with your head. There was no such thing as thinking with your gut.

But her crowd had got it wrong too many times. Wrong on Ebola in 2014, when it crossed the Atlantic. Blindsided by the novel swine flu virus in Mexico in 2009 which killed hundreds of thousands. And the fallout from Covid-19 continued. Too many dead, too many variants, not enough vaccine. As a student, she had studied the 1976 American swine flu fiasco, where millions were vaccinated for a virus that didn't exist. She had written extensively on the 1947 smallpox vaccination campaign in New York that caused more harm than the disease had. 'Groupthink' was real, for government and scientists. The experts had been looking the wrong way. Old generals trapped into fighting the last battle, not seeing the new threat. She spent as much time as she was able with new techniques, tracking which virus was where, then predicting how it might evolve.

So if this wasn't gut instinct she was feeling, it was her education and experience suggesting that she make sure that Kit was fussing over nothing. And suggesting it so strongly she felt it in her gut.

Speak at lunch? she wrote, then returned to the virus from Taiwan. She had a deadline. She detested lateness. She had ninety minutes.

Kit was with the principal, in her office.
Rose was with Harriet, outside the principal's door.

11.02 a.m.

Jan Whitlock's office was close enough to the school's entrance to have street views. From the chairs either side of her door, cars and taxis could be seen crawling past, pedestrians stopping occasionally to peer in through glass doors. Rose stood; Harriet sat. The smell of mass catering filled the corridor. It was the start of the morning break; small groups of students drifted past, a few asking the girls questions. Harriet kept her head bowed; Rose waved them away.

'Worse?' she said.

'Worse.' A whispered reply.

'Faster?'

'So. Much. Faster.' Harriet put both hands over her ears then started rocking slowly. Forwards and backwards, like she was praying. 'Distract me,' she said. 'Tell me stuff. Any old crap is fine. Just . . . talk.'

Rose rested a hand on her shoulder. 'What's the largest WhatsApp group you're in?' she said.

'The netball one, I think,' said Harriet. 'But the drama one is pretty big too. Maybe it's that one.'

'Fine,' said Rose. 'Post on both. Ask if anyone else has got this shit going on in their heads.'

'You do it.' Harriet thrust her phone at Rose. 'The password's my birthday.'

Rose typed the six digits, then wrote the same message on both chat pages. 'I'm saying *Hey. Has anyone got some kinda weird noise in their head. Or just me?*' She looked at Harriet. 'That OK?'

46

Harriet nodded once, head still in her hands.

'Drama group has thirty-six contacts, netball has twenty-four,' said Rose. 'Some crossover, but that's decent numbers.' She sent the message. Handed the phone back. 'Well, we asked.'

Another group wandered towards the principal's office. Two boys, two girls. They hesitated in front of the door, looking at Rose and Harriet.

'Are you . . .?' began the long-haired white boy.

'Before you? Yes, we are,' said Rose.

'Fair,' he replied, to Rose's obvious surprise. The four stood in a line next to Harriet. A queue of six for the principal. None of them spoke. Other pupils glanced at the group, then moved on. A delivery man in biker gear was buzzed through the main doors. Dropped a large envelope at reception then left. Behind Rose and Harriet, the rumble of an unintelligible conversation came through the principal's door. Half a Year Thirteen sports team jogged past, studded boots in hand, calling to each other as they went. The pungent menthol aroma of muscle relaxant drifted along with them. For a few seconds, the corridor fell quiet. Rose was still standing, one leg pressed against the wall, one hand on Harriet's shoulder. Harriet was still sitting. The other four were standing, two and two. Boy girl, boy girl. Marcus with Ellie; Jon with Eve.

Then, in rapid succession, seven audible clicks. A stream of irregular, electric snapping noises. Maybe it was the corridor's harsh, reflective surfaces, maybe it was their close proximity, but they all heard the sounds. Harriet's head jerked up. Rose pivoted to face the four. They all stared at each other in disbelief.

The principal's door opened. She smiled.

11.06 a.m.

Kit looked up. Rose was framed in the doorway, hesitant. She glanced in, then glanced away. Kit caught her eye. She ignored him. She had one thumb hooked under her rucksack strap, and there was something about her stance, chin high, upturned nose in the air, that reminded Kit so strongly of Jody he felt his stomach flip. This happened a lot at school. He rearranged the pens in his top pocket, tried to focus.

'Come in, come in!' called Whitlock. She beckoned with one hand, a phone pressed to her ear with the other.

Rose and Harriet entered, Rose steering her friend to the first chair, then resting a hand on her shoulder. Behind them, Marcus, Ellie, Jon and Eve shuffled in. There weren't enough seats, so they hovered awkwardly just inside the door. Kit thought they seemed agitated, distressed even. They hung on to each other as though a storm might toss them overboard.

Principal Whitlock waved her free hand in a circle. Finger raised. She was wrapping up. Nurse Mac arrived at a trot, shut the door, then leaned against it. Kit stood opposite her, his back to the window. He waited for Whitlock to end her call.

The principal hung up. Took a deep breath.

'So, Mr Chaplin,' she said, 'what have you discovered?'

Kit stepped forward. Eyes on the four. 'I have discovered,' he said, 'that in my Year Twelve class, Jon Norris, Marcus Graham, Eve Brewer and Ellie Howard here all have the same tinnitus as Harriet. Each of them has a clicking noise that is coming from their ears. I spoke to them in the library. I could hear it clearly.'

'And you spoke to everyone? Everyone in that class?'

'I did, yes. I spoke to the last ones just now. The others are fine.'

Whitlock held up her hand. 'Can we just pause then? I

would like to hear this . . . clicking before I take it further.'
She held her hands up for silence.

Kit squirmed. *Dance, monkey, dance*, he thought. *Poor bloody
kids*. He stared at the floor. The silence was painful. He stole a
glance at Rose. Her face was burning with resentment, lips
pressed furiously together. He was about to say something,
aware his daughter would only keep silent for a brief period of
time, when two clicks sounded. The first made Whitlock gasp,
as if she'd burnt her mouth. The second followed almost immediately. She exhaled slowly. 'OK,' she said. She looked along
the line of four, then at Harriet. 'How often does this happen?'

'All the time,' said Harriet.

'Really. So non-stop?'

Harriet shook her head. 'Every minute, I suppose.'

'And you, Marcus?'

The boy shifted his weight from one foot to the other.
'About that, yeah, miss.'

'And is that the same for all of you?' Whitlock aimed a finger at the remaining pupils.

Three nodding heads. Three mumbled voices.

'Yes, miss.'

'And who was that just now?'

Eve and Marcus slowly raised their hands.

'I see,' said Whitlock. 'And when did it start? Each of you,
please. Harriet, you go first.' Whitlock picked up a pen and
waited for an answer.

Harriet closed her eyes. 'A week ago, I think. A bit longer,
maybe.'

Whitlock wrote on her notepad.

Marcus next. 'Friday, miss. Lunchtime.'

'Same,' said Ellie.

Whitlock wrote again, looked up at Jon and Eve.

Jon shrugged. 'I don't know for certain, miss. Think it was
Thursday maybe.'

Finally, Eve, to Jon. 'I messaged you on Wednesday. It had just started for me. You didn't have it then though.' She nodded at the principal. That was her answer.

'I see,' said Whitlock. 'One final question.' She tapped the pad three times with the pen. 'Normally it's none of my business, but now maybe it is.' She put her pen down. This was unofficial. Kit suddenly knew what she was going to ask. They're couples, he thought. Of course they are.

'Are you ... going out together?' said Whitlock. 'From what I've read, tinnitus isn't contagious, but it still seems relevant. Certainly, I'll be asked.'

Kit thought she'd made a pretty good job of not making it sound like a criticism, but there was still a suggestion of it hanging in the air. All four nodded. Marcus indicated Ellie. Eve pointed at Jon. Whitlock nodded. Kit could see that Harriet knew it was her turn. She brushed each sleeve, then spoke to the floor.

'Well, I'm not with anyone,' she said. Rose tugged her friend's arm, whispered in her ear. Harriet looked at her, indignant. Rose shrugged. Harriet folded her arms.

'OK, I was seeing Deacon James for about five seconds. A few weeks ago. If that's relevant. Which Rose says it is.' She glared at her friend again.

Whitlock nodded again, wrote on her pad. 'Thanks, all of you. Really. I'll be in touch as soon as I know anything more. If there is anything more. Now. Do any of you feel as though you need to go home?' She looked at them in turn. Marcus, Ellie, Eve and Jon glanced at each other, shook their heads. Harriet nodded. 'Very well,' said Whitlock. 'You may go, Harriet. The rest of you, back to your lessons.'

They filed out, Rose and Harriet close behind. Kit watched Rose go. Rose didn't look back. Whitlock waited a few seconds. Checked her notes.

'I spoke to three colleagues. Two are heads, one is a deputy.

One in London, one in Cardiff, one in Manchester. I told them about Harriet. About the clicks. London and Manchester said no, they had nothing, but Cardiff . . .' She allowed her head to drop. 'Christ, Cardiff. Chris Black is the head there. He was at university with me. He said he had just had a staff meeting about pupils with hearing trouble. Noises. Clicks. All of it.'

Kit felt his skin prickle. Neck and shoulders. Nurse Mac put her hand up.

'I spoke to an audiologist in Harley Street. Said she'd come in if we wanted. But she was quite dismissive, really. She said in twenty years she'd seen a handful of objective tinnitus cases. She could recall three, though she said she might have more on file. She had watched the YouTube videos I sent her. Said they were either fake or, and I'm quoting here, Dr Whitlock, there is "something fucking weird going on". That's what she said.' Nurse Mac blushed. 'Sorry, Dr Whitlock.'

The principal brushed her apology away. 'Well, Nurse Mac,' she said, 'thank you for confirming what is becoming obvious.' She flicked her eyes between Mac and Kit. 'Something "fucking weird" is indeed going on.'

Kit blinked; Nurse Mac blushed a deeper shade of crimson. A moment's silence, then a knock on the door. It opened without an invitation from Whitlock.

A tall black-haired boy tried a smile, then stopped. Both hands clasped a bag to his chest. There was a sheen of sweat on his forehead. His cheeks were flushed. He saw Nurse Mac, then Principal Whitlock. 'Mr Sutherland told me to come and see you, miss,' he said, a tremor in his voice. 'I was looking for Nurse Mac. But he said to come here instead.'

The boy was Deacon James. He said he had the strangest headache.

Rose was on the bus home with Harriet.
Lilly was researching the mosquitoes of Taiwan.

51

Midday

Her peppermint tea was weak and powdery but she'd had her fill of caffeine. Lilly inhaled the steam rising from the mug and sipped absent-mindedly. She was about to stab at the enter key. Her report was ready. She had merely confirmed what the in-field microbiologists had suggested – that the virus wasn't avian flu but it could be zoonotic. Transfer from duck to human was possible but not likely. Also, that if it did jump, humans wouldn't be able to replicate the virus. We were the dead-end host. How she loved those words. It meant game over. Bad news for ducks; good news for us.

The document was saved, the covering email finished. But she hesitated, finger over the mouse. From somewhere outside, a distant, clanging alarm bell. Just behind her, the clicking of a warming radiator. Lilly ran a finger over one eyebrow then the other. She felt the need for a second opinion, she had Weibo on her phone and the Chinese social media app had helped before. There was a Beijing-based medical researcher she knew called Heidi. They had exchanged messages back in 2019 when the World Economic Forum had run a pandemic exercise, modelling an imagined virus called CAPS. Coronavirus Associated Pulmonary Syndrome. Lilly shivered at the memory. The model had the virus jumping from bats to pigs and then to Brazilian farmers. Over eighteen months, CAPS 'killed' 65 million people. Terrifying numbers, she had thought back then. Lilly had been shocked, but no one had been interested. Different times. Ancient history.

'Heidi' could be anyone, of course. The name didn't sound

Chinese. She could be a government stooge, but she had shared research before. Maybe she would again. She had certainly been across the Chinese stats and, given that her government claimed Taiwan belonged to them, Lilly assumed she'd be across the reports of the virus too.

Lilly opened the app, tried to ignore the feeling that a thousand Chinese bots were instantly mining her data. She kept her communication brief.

I hope you are well. Are you following the Tembusu ducks in Taiwan? Lilly wondered if mentioning Taiwan might be a trigger word but sent it anyway. Beijing, she knew, was eight hours ahead. If Heidi was in China, it would be the middle of the evening. So, a long shot. She tapped a pencil. Wiped dust from her keyboard. Centred it again.

Her phone buzzed. Text from Kit.

Lunch?

Lilly's eyebrows rose. He'd never suggested that before, not on a school day.

Wait, she messaged back. Her phone vibrated again.

Sandwich. Fifteen minutes.

She smiled, briefly, at Kit's spelling-out of the number. An English-teacher thing for sure, but she enjoyed the fussiness and the formality of it. She was typing her reply when a Weibo message popped on to the top of the screen. Lilly sat up straight. Pulled some strands of hair back behind her ear. Tapped the box. Which opened.

Hi, Lilly. Yes, we know about the TEMBUSU. Many dead ducks, maybe a million. That is all. H.

Lilly nodded. An affirmation. Then, on a whim, she messaged back.

Thanks. Any interest in objective tinnitus? The cursor in the message box flashed on and off. Lilly shook her head, not quite believing she was asking a presumably eminent Chinese scientist about Kit's videos.

Ha ha! In ducks? Nothing here, Lilly. Thank you. H.

Lilly shrugged, smiled sheepishly. Worth a try. From her laptop, she submitted the Tembusu report to the Animal Health Research Institute. Filed it to her firm's viral evolution database. From her phone she texted Kit.

Pret A Manger. 12.50.

She shook her head, smiled. Added a circumflex.

Prêt A Manger. 12.50.

Pressed send.

Twenty months earlier: MCS Big Hall

TEN MINUTES AND *it will all be over. The ordeal of parents' evening was only ever tolerable with the prospect of alcohol. It could be a pint of Ghost Ship or a glass of Sauvignon, it really didn't matter. Kit can almost smell the inside of the Lord Stanley. He glances at a departmental colleague next to him. Her table is a few metres away. A handful of parents hover, waiting to grab some final minutes with their child's English teacher. He watches their faces. They are, he thinks, only pretending to be interested in each other's conversation. What they really want is to talk up their child's potential to star in this year's production of* The Crucible. *He smiles. Almost done.*

In the Big Hall, which, puzzlingly, seems to be the same size as the Small Hall, fifteen teachers are sitting at tables. Eight sit in front of the gym wall, facing seven along the far wall. The high rectangular windows are wide open but there is little breeze and the room is too hot. Parents zero in on the tables when their slot with the teacher is due, seizing seats as soon as they become vacant. Everyone fans themselves with the school newsletter they've been handed. Earnest parent–teacher conversations are everywhere. One table is empty. The games teacher has already gone home. No one needs to speak to the games teacher, thinks Kit.

The last parent he has to talk to is Jess Slater's mother, but she's late. He glances again at his watch, gathers up some papers, folds his hands together. Maybe a half of Ghost Ship, then the Sauvignon.

55

Kit is suddenly aware of a woman walking towards his table. She is bustling in, clearly trying to make up for lost time with every stride. He has met Lilly Slater just once before, remembered her as a striking woman. Now she is glowing. Flushed cheeks, wide face, shoulder-length dark blonde hair.

'Dr Slater,' he says, standing. She shakes his hand then sits in one of the two chairs opposite him. And takes charge.

'I know I'm late,' she says, leaning in. Both hands on Kit's table. 'Apologies. This happens a lot.' Then, without pausing, 'Jess enjoys English, Mr Chaplin, she told me to be quite clear about that.' Eye contact. A blueish green. No make-up that Kit notices. 'She has always enjoyed reading but has struggled with the rigour and application needed to write the essays. But this year, so far, has been different.' She pauses. Kit wonders if she's finished, smiles. Waits. She raises her eyebrows. 'Sorry,' she says. 'Your turn.' She hooks a loose strand of hair back behind her right ear, sits back in her chair. Smooths her linen dress. Kit feels suddenly nervous. On trial.

'Well,' he says, returning her full gaze, smiling. 'That's very good to hear. I enjoy teaching Jess, and you're right, her written work has been impressive this term.' He runs a ruler down a lined sheet of paper in front of him until he gets to Jess's name. 'Three As, one A minus and two Bs is a great tally,' he says. 'She struggled a bit, I think, with the contemporary poetry but, to be honest, a lot of it can be . . . quite dense at times.' He smiles; it is not returned. 'I do encourage her to speak up more in class, Dr Slater,' he says, 'but she does sometimes retreat behind her laptop. It would be good to hear her voice more. When she does contribute, it is always worth listening to.'

She looks away, considers his words. 'Yes, that is fair,' she says. 'She's quiet at home also. It's just the two of us now, and I think she struggles with that sometimes.' A pause. He waits. She leans in again. 'To be honest, she spends most of her time in her room. She comes out to eat. And even then, if I didn't ask her questions, she might not say more than few words.' She leans back. 'I'm sorry. I don't know why I'm telling you that. It's not your concern . . .'

'Actually, it is,' he says. 'I have a daughter too . . .'

'Jess did tell me that.'

'And what you say sounds very familiar. It is just the two of us too. And it's difficult, no doubt about that. And when we're both at home, I still seem to have the place to myself.' He smiles, surprised to be talking about his home life. 'I hear her clattering around in her room. She does most of her talking there, on the phone or her laptop. So I honestly think your situation with Jess sounds very normal.' They both smile. She sits up straighter in the chair.

'Thank you,' she says. She sounds relieved.

'As for friends,' he says, 'well, I'm not Jess's form teacher. But my guess would be that she is possibly an introvert and seeks out other girls like her. She won't be the centre of a large gang, but she will have a small circle of good friends who will watch her back. And when I say I want to hear her more in class, I don't mean I'm trying to draw her out of her shell. I mean I want her to know that what she says is interesting. And well observed.'

She drops her head, smooths her skirt again. 'Thank you so much,' she says. 'That's the most helpful thing I've heard all day.' She looks around. Most teachers are packing up. 'Now, I must let you go.' She stands, offers her hand.

He stands, shakes her hand. 'Thank you, Dr Slater.'

'It's Lilly,' she says. 'Please call me Lilly.'

He nods. 'Thank you, Lilly.' He watches her leave, then sits. He smiles briefly, then clears his desk.

12.50 p.m.

Lilly was there first. One high circular table was free, with two stools, in the far corner. She perched on one, placing her bag on the other. Both table and seating had clearly been designed to maximize turnover. She was uncomfortable in seconds. A woman in a vast padded winter coat balancing a tray of sandwiches eyed the table as though it were a rare treasure to fight for. Lilly looked away. The woman drifted off.

The café was running at a furious pace. Rows of refrigerated baguettes and sandwiches were surrounded by the hovering hungry. By the tills at the far end, multiple queues formed and dissolved, depending on which assistant made themselves available. The tables and long breakfast bars were all full and the café was humming with the sound of coffee machines, unwrapping cellophane and snatched phone calls.

A kiss on her cheek, a face full of black hair, and Kit was opposite. Lilly surprised herself by not being annoyed. He grinned, reached over, gave her a salad in a box.

'Hi, you,' he said.

'Hey,' she said.

He was wearing a black silk tie she'd bought him a while back and his white shirt looked fresh and pressed. She was pleased to see him. He noticed. The grin widened to a full-on smile. He squeezed her arm then pulled away. Handed her her bag. Perched on one of the stools, he unwrapped his sandwich. A moment of awkwardness, maybe. He spoke quickly.

'Well. How'd it go yesterday? Was thinking about you.'

She dropped her gaze.

'It was pretty bad, I suppose,' she said, working out what she actually did think. 'Maybe we can talk about it tonight?'

'Of course.'

'Pret isn't the best place to talk funerals.'

'No, you're right,' said Kit. 'I'm sorry.'

She shook her head. 'Not at all. Thanks for being so concerned. And thanks for not coming. The bastard didn't deserve anyone else there. Not even convinced I should have gone, to be honest.'

'Was it just you?'

'A couple of old guys. No idea who they were. They didn't want to talk to me and I sure as hell didn't want to talk to them.' She laughed, briefly. 'And now here I am, actually talking funerals in Pret a Manger.' She shook her head in disbelief. 'But later is better. Tell me about this tinnitus. I know you haven't got long.' She produced a wooden fork from her bag, opened the salad box.

Starting with the videos Rose had shown him, Kit told Lilly what had been happening over the last twenty-four hours. The whole story in ninety seconds. Her eyes never left his.

When he'd finished, she nodded, started her food. She digested his words and her salad together. She loosened the grey scarf around her neck, her hair still tucked under its folds. He could see the tiredness in her face, the exhaustion that only funerals bring. But he knew without checking that she was, by some margin, the best-looking woman in the room. Pale skin, blue eyes ringed with shadow, high and handsome cheekbones. A delicate mouth, lines around its edges. Straight blonde hair to the shoulders, both sides hooked behind small ears.

Her eyes focused mainly on her food, occasionally flicking to Kit. She ate faster than anyone he'd ever known. Food was just fuel to her, and to hell with the taste. If he hadn't bought her lunch, she probably wouldn't have eaten at all. Lilly seemed to survive on biscuits and tea. A small cardboard box containing some grilled chicken, avocado and tomatoes was a considerable triumph. She ate systematically, in a clock-wise spiral, circling the final, central piece of avocado. He knew she worried far more about cutlery than food, not trusting anything that could have been handled by anyone else.

Kit glanced at his watch. Ten minutes and he needed to be gone. The funeral conversation had been postponed, as he'd thought it would be. A brief, targeted conversation – Lilly's favourite kind – would happen next. He started to eat his sandwich. The café noise came from all sides but their table was shrouded in an intense silence. He knew Lilly was think-ing. Analysing. Sifting. Quantifying. She finished the food, cleaned her fork with a disinfectant wipe from her bag. Placed the wipe in the now-empty salad box, the fork back in the bag. Her lab rituals transferred to the sandwich shop. Now she looked at Kit.

'What happened with the check on Harriet's friends?' she said. The cool, efficient tone wasn't a surprise; the question was.

'What?'

'You said that the principal was going to trace and check Harriet's contacts. What happened with that?'

Kit felt a flicker of annoyance. He masked it by chewing for longer than he needed on the bread and cheese. She was right, of course. As far as he remembered, there had been no comeback on Harriet's contacts. but was that the main issue at stake here? How about the noises actually coming out of students' heads, for starters.

'I don't know,' he said. 'An old boyfriend of hers came into the principal's office saying he had a headache, but I'll chase it up when I get back. Which will need to be soon.' Urgent, but not too urgent, he thought. But for Christ's sake, Lil, hurry up. Two students from MCS walked past his table, arm in arm. Joined one of the queues. The girl kissed the boy on the cheek. Kit wondered if they might be clicking, but the relentless lunchtime cacophony masked everything. The boy kissed the girl back. Kit tried to remember their names.

Eventually, Lilly said, 'How many clicks have you heard yourself? Not on video.'

Kit shrugged. 'Six or seven maybe.'

'Did they all sound the same?'

'Pretty much, yeah.'

'Describe them.'

'They were just like on the videos I sent you, Lilly.'

'In words.'

A brief pause. Kit wiped his mouth on a paper napkin. This was Lilly working. This was how it happened and it was pointless to protest. 'Somewhere between a tick from a small clock and the snap of an electric spark. Something like that.' Lilly nodded. The MCS couple walked out of the shop. 'And,' said Kit, 'most of them are couples.'

Lilly frowned. 'Explain?'

'My four students are two couples. And Harriet's ex has it too. They must have infected each other.' He could tell she wasn't impressed. 'OK, got that wrong,' he said. 'Jumping the gun?'

Lilly had no idea. What Kit was describing was like nothing she'd heard before. Objective tinnitus she now understood. But an 'outbreak' of it made no sense.

'Kit, they can't infect each other if there is no germ to do the infecting,' she said. 'You can't infect someone with tinnitus. There's no virus, no bacteria, no nothing. It must be something else.'

'So . . . a coincidence?' said Kit. 'Really? What about the

Cardiff head saying he has the same thing going on at his school?'

'I don't know, Kit. Honestly, I don't know and I'm just reacting to what you're telling me. It sounds and looks like a type of tinnitus, agreed. But that's it. If it's an infection, it has to be something else. Maybe there's another condition or illness that causes the human ear to emit sound.' She shrugged. 'Not my field. As you know.'

Lilly watched Kit prepare to leave. He folded his wrapper neatly in four, buttoned his coat, returned his phone to one of its outside pockets. She sensed some disappointment. He had obviously hoped for more.

'Sorry,' she said, knowing she had nothing to apologize for. 'I'll try and find out more this afternoon.'

'Hey, Lilly, this is my thing, not yours.' Kit put his hand on her arm. 'So thanks for listening. Come round tonight at seven? I'd like to hear more about yesterday.'

'Need to see Jess first,' she said. 'I left before she woke up this morning.'

'Of course.'

Her phone buzzed and she peered at its screen. Her eyebrows shot up. A Weibo message. Heidi again. Kit had got up to go.

'Wait,' she said. He sat down again. She opened the message.

Found this on ProMED. H.

Lilly clicked on the link embedded in the message. While it was connecting, she told Kit about Heidi. 'And ProMED is the Program for Monitoring Emerging Diseases. A site that trawls the web looking for chatter about unexplained illness, disease outbreaks, that kind of thing.' Her phone was still connecting. Kit glanced again at his watch. Shuffled impatiently in his seat. 'And it's where we picked up the first documented reports of Covid-19.'

Kit sat still.

A connection. Lilly read fast. Spun the phone.

Kit read fast. Swore briefly. 'Send me the link?' he said.

Lilly nodded. 'I need to call California. Talk later.'

Rose was watching Harriet sleep.

Principal Whitlock was at her desk.

Seventeen months earlier

LILLY IS DRESSED *down. New black jeans, white T-shirt, an agnès b grey V-neck sweater. Her hair is loose; she is not wearing make-up. She has arrived first and ordered sparkling water. She chose the venue. A gastro-pub seemed right. Not too formal or pressured. Not too juvenile or loud. She'd eaten there once before and remembered it as a modest success. Businesslike and discreet. She would rather no one else saw them, but if they did, it could look like a business meeting. Even if Saturday evening (six until eight thirty) was an unusual time for business. A date night designed not to look like a date night. Jess is with her father for the weekend; Kit had said that Rose would be at a friend's but that he would need to pick her up around ten. This is not going to be a boozy evening. Which suits Lilly fine.*

Their daughters had been the connection. She had been so reassured by Kit's analysis of Jess, she wondered why no one else had said anything like that to her before. Of course her daughter was an introvert, and how liberating to be told that Jess didn't need to be coaxed out of her shell or be the centre of attention. That she would have friends anyway. And that when she did speak, people listened. After that parents' evening Lilly had smiled all the way home.

They had had a further brief conversation at a school event (engineered, she was sure, by Kit) and then again at a Year Twelve charity evening just a few days ago. She had shocked herself by reminding him that her phone number was on the class contact list, 'should he need to discuss anything further'. She had clearly shocked him too, as Kit had blinked rapidly, then stammered his thanks. He had called the following day.

Kit arrives, clearly flustered and nervous. 'Am I late?' he says.

She pours from the water bottle, hands him the glass.

'Not at all,' she says. 'I was early. Wanted to check the booking.'

'We're fine till eight thirty?' he says. He has on a white shirt and grey jacket over blue jeans. She thinks she recognizes Issey Miyake aftershave. He sits opposite her, his back to the other diners.

'That's what they said. I hope that's OK,' she says.

'Yes, yes, that's great.' He twists, looks around the room. They are upstairs in a corner of a room with eight tables; six are occupied; fifteen diners in total. He glances at each face in turn, then looks at Lilly. She is smiling.

'I did that too,' she says.

'Did what?'

'Checked to see if there is anyone here I know.'

He laughs. 'Was it that obvious?'

'It was. And there wasn't. You?'

He shook his head. 'We're in the clear, I think.' He leans in close and, for one dreadful moment, she thinks he's going to kiss her. But he's still speaking, conspiratorially now. Flicks his head to the right.

'Unless that guy has only recently grown that beard. In which case it could be anyone. Including some of my Year Twelves.'

She laughs a little. He relaxes. They both look at the menu.

'I haven't done this for so long,' he says to the table.

She's done the calculation. 'Eighteen years for me,' she says.

'The same for me.' He seems to enjoy the coincidence. He talks about Jody; she talks about Liam. He talks about her cancer; she talks about his affairs. They both talk about their daughters. Under pressure from the waiter, they both order the risotto. They talk without a break until they're brought the bill, which they divide between them.

Outside, it's almost dark, but the air has kept some of the warmth of the day. They linger.

'How long till you need to pick up Rose?' she says.

'She's expecting me at ten,' he says. 'I was planning to let it slip a bit. But not much. Thirteen years old is still thirteen years old.'

'Does she know about . . .' She swings a finger between the two of them. 'This?'

He grimaces. 'She does not,' he says. 'And Jess?' He pulls a face – a comic rictus grin. Expecting the worst. She reassures him.

'No chance,' she says, enjoying the reassurance she is bestowing. He wipes imaginary sweat from his brow. They both laugh.

Opposite the Tube station, they decide on coffee from a cart. They sit, side by side, on an old bench. She likes his company. When he reaches for her hand, she doesn't pull away.

1.55 p.m.

Kit was flushed, breathing heavily. He explained the ProMED site to Whitlock, the forwarded post open on his phone. She held his phone in one hand; the other was palm out. In front of Kit's face.

'Let me read it,' she said. 'Then you can mansplain it to me.' She scanned the message. 'OK, I get it. Sixteen mentions of this tinnitus in the States, fourteen in California, two in New York. And' – she pointed at the screen – 'dozens of other mysterious diseases.' She scrolled. 'The West Nile virus. Epizootic haemorrhagic disease. Invasive mosquitoes.' She handed the phone back. 'The whole world is sick, Kit, and I'd rather have the tinnitus than any of those.' She pointed at his phone, as though it contained the West Nile virus, epizootic haemorrhagic disease and invasive mosquitoes. 'Is it really such a big deal?'

Kit was puzzled at her change in tone. He opened his mouth to speak but she answered her own question. 'I just spoke to the Academy's CEO, you see. I think you've met him. He didn't think it was anything to panic over.' Kit had indeed met the CEO and remembered the staffroom assessment of him as, to quote Jim Sutherland, 'an annoying little shit'. 'In fact,' said Whitlock, 'he found it all rather amusing.'

'Did he indeed?' Kit felt suddenly very tired.

'He did, yes. Are we overreacting here, Kit?' She peered over her large glasses, eyebrows raised. 'Might that be possible?'

Kit bit back a sharp response. Took a breath.

'Of course, it's possible,' he said. 'I'm just the head of

English.' He stood with his hands behind his back, hiding his clenched fists.

'Go on,' said Whitlock. 'I sense there's more.'

Kit took stock. Maybe he *was* overreacting. Maybe it was more funny than scary, and maybe it was better than the West Nile virus, but right now, he couldn't be sure. 'I am . . . concerned. That's all. We have it. In the school. Your head-teacher friend in Cardiff says his school has it, sixteen Americans have it. We don't know what "it" is, but Harriet Teale has gone home sick with it.' He folded his arms. 'So no, we are not overreacting.'

He had a lesson in two minutes, though he couldn't remember what or where it was. That usually meant it was Chaucer. His laptop was in the staffroom. He was going to be late, but this was important. He remembered Lilly's question. 'Did we trace Harriet's contacts?'

The principal frowned. 'Sorry?'

'You said you'd have someone trace her classmates,' said Kit. 'I wondered if that had been done.'

Whitlock rocked back in her chair, rolling a fountain pen between her fingers like a cigar. 'It has not,' she said. 'I forgot.' She rocked again. 'So let's take this up one step. The CEO won't like it, but . . .' Her words faded away. Kit filled in the blank for himself: *He can do one.* 'I'll email the parents this afternoon. A precaution. An advisory.'

She tapped the pen on her pad. The meeting was over. Time for Chaucer.

3.30 p.m.

Harriet's bedroom was small and boxy with a slanting roof. A small steamed-up window above a single bed, a longer steamed-up window above a grey self-assembly desk. An open laptop with a rainbow screensaver sat at one end; three unopened Asos packages were at the other. An unlit candle, headphone buds and assorted make-up boxes filled the rest of the space until nothing of the surface was visible. An overflowing wardrobe's doors were wide open, clothes and schoolbooks scattered across the floor. The room was toasty, a radiator under the desk firing hard. Rose had removed her sweatshirt, her white shirt was hanging loose over her skirt. She leaned against the bed, Harriet lay on top of it. Her eyes were closed.

'Thanks for staying,' she whispered.

'No worries,' said Rose. 'Someone needs to be here. And if it's me, you get the added treat of hearing me calling your brother a dick. To his face. Whenever he gets here.' The tiniest of laughs from Harriet. 'I could always leave a message in his room, I suppose. "Dear Carl. Stop being such a dick." Signed "Everyone you ever met".'

'Sweet,' said Harriet.

Rose had no need to ask about the tinnitus. In the quiet of an empty house, the only sounds were the occasional gurgling from the radiator and the ticking from Harriet's ear. Rose had taken to timing them and making notes. She had readings from nine per minute to sixteen per minute. The trend was upwards.

'Can we watch something?' said Harriet.

'Sure,' said Rose. 'Your phone's bigger. In your bag?'

Harriet nodded. 'Side pocket.' Rose stretched to reach. The rucksack was under the desk and she pulled it closer, retrieved the phone.

'Hey,' she said. 'Sixteen WhatsApp messages. Can I look?' A nod from the bed. Rose scanned the replies. 'Netball first. Seven messages. Phoebe says she has a headache, Meera has her period, Natalie sends sympathy. So does Gen. Also Becky.' Rose read on in silence; Harriet opened her eyes.

'And? What else?'

Rose took a breath. 'Faith says *Fuck! You have this too? Call me* and Mariella says *Thought I was going crazy. Where are you?*' She looked at Harriet. 'Wow,' she said.

Harriet propped herself up on her elbows. 'And drama group?' Rose scrolled again. 'Jokes, mainly. Stupid-ass comments. Apart from Deacon James, who says to message him. And Kirstie Thomas.'

'What did she write?'

'Tick tock,' said Rose.

'Is that it?' said Harriet.

'That's it.' Rose spelt out the letters. 'So that "tick tock". Does that mean she has it, or is she trying to be funny?'

Harriet slumped back to the bed. 'What do I do, Rose? Is it better that there are lots of us?' Rose didn't answer; she was back on the screen.

'Another message from Deacon. Just now. Says to watch the new *TrashMask*.'

'Really?' said Harriet. 'Gave up on him when he went batshit-crazy last year. Became just another whiney, entitled white American.'

Rose was still holding the phone. 'Agreed. But do we watch?'

Harriet shrugged. 'S'pose,' she said.

Rose clicked the link. Harriet shuffled over; Rose lay next to her. If they lay on their sides, there was just enough room for two. Rose rested the phone on her thigh. The screen showed a twenty-something man, shaved blond hair, wide nose, high cheekbones, mauve-tinted glasses. An extreme close-up. His face and shoulders were the only things in shot. His nostrils flared as he spoke.

'Not the usual message from me today,' he said. His eyes looked down the lens. His Tennessee drawl stretched the words to their limits. 'Nothin' 'bout movies. Nothin' 'bout fitness and nothin' 'bout make-up.'

'He's not wearing any!' whispered Rose.

'I can't hear it,' said Harriet. 'Turn it up.'

'Y'see, I think I'm sick.' A long pause. Silence. The man who called himself *TrashMask* looked at the camera. Harriet clicked. The phone clicked. Twice.

'You. Are. Kidding,' whispered Rose.

The man tried to smile. 'I got this noise in my head. And I'm told you can hear it too. Which don't sound right to me. So I'm gonna take me a short vacation to see if I can sort this out.' Rose handed Harriet her phone back. 'There really are lots like you, Harry,' she said. Rose glanced at her friend. Harriet's eyes were wide, her brow creased and sweating.

'What did he say, Rose? I . . . I couldn't catch it all.' She completed the sentence, but only just, her words slurring and fading. She covered her mouth with her hands. Her eyes brimmed with tears.

'Harry, what is it?' Rose sounded startled, scared even. She took her friend's hands from her mouth, held them in hers. 'Harry! Talk to me.'

Harriet shook her head. Gripped Rose's hands tight.

'Harriet! Talk to me! Say something!' Rose was shouting now. Harriet opened her mouth, closed it again. She squeezed her eyes shut, forcing tears down her cheeks.

'One,' she said, as though she had never said the word before. Her breath was short now. 'Two,' she tried. Panic filled her eyes. 'Three.'

She gave a despairing gasp. Then screamed.

4.40 p.m.

Kit slumped into one of the staffroom armchairs, his bag on his lap, his phone in his hands. He closed his eyes. The staffroom was busy and getting busier. It was the most social time of the day. Gossiping, bitching, arguing, flirting, laughing. Like a pub before closing. But Kit figured that closed eyes meant 'do not disturb'. The email to parents had been the model of understatement. To Kit's eyes, it read like the standard headlice warning that went out every term. 'Someone in the school has an ear infection,' it said. 'If your child's hearing has altered in any way, please contact the school.' It listed Nurse Mac's email and school phone number, then the school's main office number. The only clue to any underlying concern was the fact that it had been signed by the principal. All the MCS health emails originated from Nurse Mac. Kit was sure many of the parents, experienced in reading the coded language of school reports, would realize something was up. He took a deep breath. Opened his eyes. He had company after all.

Aisha Khatri pulled up a chair. Coat on, scarf loose around her neck, in a hurry. She finished reading from her phone's screen, then looked up. She appeared agitated, twisting a silver ring on her thumb, working it one way then the other. She tapped the screen with a long fingernail.

'This your tinnitus thing?' she said. He thought of protesting that it wasn't 'his' but didn't have the strength. He knew what she meant. He nodded.

'It certainly is, yes. We have a number of cases now. Two Year Twelve couples have it. Harriet Teale went home with it. Her ex-boyfriend has it too.' He saw her begin to protest, raised his hand. 'And I know tinnitus isn't infectious,' he said. 'So . . . no, I don't know what's going on.' He tried a smile. He managed a shrug.

'Well, whatever it is,' said Aisha, 'I got a call from my childcarer saying she was sick and couldn't look after my son tomorrow. Something wrong with her ears, she said.' Kit leaned forward.

'Did she say any more?'

'No. Not really. But she sounded pretty freaked out, to be honest.' She stood, pocketing the phone. 'I need to go.'

'Thomas is OK, though?' asked Kit.

'Apparently,' said Aisha, pulling gloves on. 'But the chances of finding alternative childcare at this notice, I'd say, are thin. So might not be in tomorrow.' She buttoned her coat.

'Can Ben not help?' he said. Kit knew her husband wasn't the most modern of parents, but surely even he could step up here.

'Conference,' she said. It was obvious she was unimpressed.

'Understood,' said Kit, nodding. 'Good luck.' Aisha pressed her lips together and left.

Kit checked his watch. He should check on Rose. Or maybe he shouldn't, as she hated it so much. She had grown wise to the sleight-of-hand texts he sent. Even if he was asking whether she wanted pie or pasta, Rose had realized it was just her father's way of finding out what time she'd be back. She'd left school to take Harriet home, but he had heard nothing since. He messaged, *How's Harriet doing?* Even Rose couldn't see that as 'passive aggressive', her favourite complaint. He wondered how Jody would have handled it and, for the third or fourth time that day, considered how tough it was for Rose to negotiate her teenage years without a mother. Maybe Lilly would, given time, fill some of the gaps, but certainly not while Rose insisted on calling her 'girlfriend'.

His phone rang. It was Rose. He frowned.

'Hey,' he said. 'Something up?' The pause was just long enough for Kit to know that there was.

'I'm at Harry's,' said Rose, 'and we're in her room.' Another pause.

'OK,' said Kit, then stuck a finger in his ear to lose the

staffroom. He thought he could hear muffled sobbing but wasn't sure. 'Rose, what's up?'

'Hang on!' said Rose. Too loudly, he thought. He heard rustling and muffled words – Harriet and Rose. With Harriet shouting. Then the phone was grabbed again. Kit's stomach flipped.

'Dad! Dad!'

'I'm here, Rose!' Now it was Kit shouting. Staffroom heads turned. Kit stood. His bag dropped to the floor.

'Rose, what is it?' He heard a short, panicked breath.

'Dad. Harriet's gone deaf.'

Rose was with Harriet.
Kit was leaving MCS.
Lilly was calling California.

5.15 p.m.

Lilly had ignored five calls from Kit. She'd messaged him that she was on a call, but he had stayed on it. Most times, she would have cut short her conversation, but Professor Linda Harris, an old Glaxo colleague now at the University of California in San Francisco, was late for a meeting and then would be unavailable for a while. And her information was extraordinary. The fourteen 'clickers', as she had called them, were all students, and each had presented in the last few days. There were five couples out of the fourteen; the other four were single but were friends. Nine were clicking from one ear but five were clicking in both. The clicks varied in frequency and tone but were averaging six or seven clicks a minute. None of the students was in pain and only two of them had had tinnitus before.

Lilly had written down: '5 couples, 4 friends.'

'That's a classic infection pattern, Linda,' she said, her tone flat.

'Agreed,' said Harris. 'Which isn't possible. Either that, or they have the tinnitus with something else.' She paused, before adding, 'Or it *is* something else.'

'Like what?' said Lilly.

'Well, that's just it,' said the professor. 'There is nothing else.'

Lilly's mobile buzzed again. The text, from Kit, said *Emergency*. To Harris, she said, 'I'm sorry, can you hold a second?' She stabbed at the screen of her mobile, hitting the speaker button. 'Kit, what is it? Brief, if you can, and I'll get back to you.' She heard the sounds of a car interior, then Kit's voice. He was brusque.

'Harriet Teale, Rose's friend, has gone deaf. Rose is with her. I'm heading there now. That brief enough?' She knew he was annoyed, but she'd manage that later.

'OK, I'll call you back.' she said. She picked up the land-line receiver. 'Sorry about that—'

The American cut her off. 'Did he say deaf? That guy on the phone there? Please tell me that's not what he said.'

'That's what he said.'

'Who is he?'

'He's my, er, partner. A teacher. Head of English at a school in town. He has some "clickers", as you call them, at his school.'

The professor's tone dialled up a notch. 'And one of them has gone *deaf*?'

Lilly's tone remained neutral. 'So it would appear.'

She'd need to call Kit soon. She needed to tell him about this conversation with the professor. And if Harriet really had gone deaf and it had anything to do with her tinnitus, *and* if it was remotely contagious, everything was about to go bad. Very quickly. She started to compile a list of colleagues to call, then realized there was silence on the other end of the phone. Lilly thought the line had gone dead. Then she could hear furious typing sounds. They were still connected.

'Jeez,' said Harris. A long pause. More typing. 'So. Just the one?'

'As far as I know, but I haven't really been looking at this until today. I was just helping out, to be honest.' More typing. 'Look, do you need to go?' said Lilly. 'You sound like you might have . . . you know, people to speak to.'

'Sure,' said Harris, only slightly calmer now, 'but we need to stay in touch. Because if you put my stats from California with yours from London . . .'

Lilly waited for the professor to finish her sentence. She tried a prompt. 'We have a problem.'

Sharp laughter on the other end of the line. 'You could say that, Lilly, yes. If there is just the one deaf kid, we can live with that. But if there are more, if the tinnitus, or whatever it is, leads to deafness in other patients, and it's . . . contagious . . .'

Lilly finished that sentence too. 'Then there'll be a riot,' she said.

'You got that right,' said Harris. 'We'll talk soon.' She hung up.

The phone rang instantly. Harris again.

'Maurice Hilleman,' she said.

'What about him?'

'The Hilleman prediction?' said Harris. She sounded breathless.

A beat. 'Christ. You think so?' said Lilly.

'Just a thought. Gotta go.' Harris hung up again.

Lilly spun her chair. Ignoring the bleakness of her reflection, she stared out at the already dark London skyline. So much for the half-day she had been going to take. So much for getting back to see Jess. So much for making her daughter dinner.

She reached for her mobile, scrolled to Kit's number. Her finger hovered above the send key. Everything suddenly felt so fragile. Kit and her. Jess and her. Everyone and her. The implications of a deafness that you could *catch*, a deafness you could infect someone with, made her hands shake. She would explain to Kit what the professor had told her. She would get a cab home and make Jess a hot chocolate. But she couldn't ignore the evidence. She couldn't pretend everything was all right. And if the University of California's most eminent epidemiologist was talking about the Hilleman prediction, it most certainly wasn't.

Lilly eased on her coat. She checked her ID and ordered a cab. She'd be home in twenty-five minutes. She realized she hadn't thought of her dead father for hours.

6.15 p.m.

Lilly sat at her kitchen table, still wearing her coat and scarf. The lights were on full. The hall and lounge lights were on full. A small black-and-silver radio on top of the fridge played a Brandenburg concerto. She needed brightness, she needed warmth, she needed music. The kettle had boiled for a tea but had switched itself off, still full. A cup with a teabag in stood next to it. With the exception of a laptop, the table was bare. As Lilly's hands poked and tapped, its screen filled up with overlapping research papers and old emails. She found her Hilleman notes.

Maurice Hilleman was the grand old man of vaccinology. He was responsible for making mumps, measles, rubella, chickenpox, hepatitis A and hepatitis B preventable. As a student, Lilly had studied his research and had almost met him at a Washington dinner back in 2003. It was Hilleman who had realized that the three viruses that cause influenza pandemics were H1, H2 and H3 and that they returned to America in a strict rotation: H2, H3 and then H1. Not only that, but each one triggered a pandemic every sixty-eight years. Exactly sixty-eight years. She had highlighted a quote: 'A sixty-eight-year recurrence ... would suggest that there may need to be a sufficient subsidence in host immunity before a past virus can again access and become established as a new human influenza virus in the population.'

Lilly exhaled long and hard. The H2 virus had last struck in 1957 so the maths didn't quite work. But Covid-19 had, according to some studies, reduced average life expectancy by eighteen months. If Hilleman was right, they were due an influenza pandemic very soon.

She had spent the journey home recalling all the emerging pathogens she had ever researched and whether any had included tinnitus or deafness as a symptom. She doubted it, certainly not with any strain of influenza, but now she was pulling up every document she could find to test her supposition. She found a paper she had submitted in 2016 called 'R and D Blueprint for Action to Prevent Epidemics'. She located an article she'd written for the Coalition for Epidemic Preparedness and Innovation. She scanned it and saw the same parade of villains. Severe acute respiratory syndrome, Middle East respiratory syndrome, Ebola, Lassa fever, Marburg virus, Crimean-Congo haemorrhagic fever, Rift Valley fever and Nipah virus. Among the symptoms she found headaches, pneumonia, vomiting, diarrhoea, bleeding, liver failure, loss of sight, confusion and seizures. She didn't find tinnitus or deafness. Lassa fever caused hearing loss in some survivors, but it had always come after fever, muscle pain and vomiting. And all the Lassa fever cases had been in West Africa. The clickers in the UK and US did not have Lassa fever.

Her phone buzzed. The taxi was outside.

In the Uber, she checked her messages. Jess had asked if she could eat at a friend's. Lilly had been about to protest but then thought better of it. Having left her daughter alone the previous night, she was hardly in a position to complain. She told her to be back by ten, to get a cab home. Lilly got a double-thumbs-up emoji in reply, which counted, she thought, as wild enthusiasm. The driver glanced in his mirror. 'You mind the radio?' he said.

Lilly shook her head. 'Go ahead. Whatever you like is fine.'

He nodded, turned up a news station. She tuned out. She

pushed away the proteins, the clickers and the Ebola stats. Her immediate concern was food with Kit and Rose. The three of them hadn't eaten together often, but each time had been excruciating. Maybe it would be better now. Maybe the funeral, and what had happened with Harriet, would change the dynamic. At the very least, she didn't want to be called 'girlfriend'.

Lilly knew she was totally ill equipped to deal with this new dynamic. Since her divorce, it had been just her, Jess and the job. And she had been quite happy with that. She hadn't dated, hadn't even thought about it for years. Liam and his aftermath had been quite enough chaos for one lifetime. Their relationship had been a failed experiment for sure, but they had Jess as a glorious, unexpected consequence. Lilly's uncontested custody of their daughter had led her to Marylebone College School and that had, in turn, led her to Kit. Smart Kit. Funny Kit. The increasingly irreplaceable Kit, who came with the always unpredictable Rose.

Lilly exhaled slowly. She watched her breath fog up the window then it slowly cleared. The roads were wet and dark, the traffic stop-start. She would be later than she'd said and texted Kit to warn him. In reply she got a message saying *Watch this. See you soon*. She touched the link embedded in the page. A three-minute video played. A quick-cut sequence of student-age faces appeared. Commentary in Spanish. Each face smiled, bowed then clicked. After a dozen or so, the clicks ran together and formed a beat track. Each of the faces now 'danced' to the rhythm, nodding, eye-rolling and twitching. At the end, the faces all appeared to laugh, then it faded to black. Lilly's screen offered 'play again', but she'd seen enough. 'And they think it's art,' she muttered.

She drummed her fingers on her leg. If this thing had reached Spain, or Latin America, as well as the UK and US, it was already too late, already irreversible. After 2020, there had been much grand talk of global health experts working together to transform disease forecasting. The epidemiologists said they'd talk to the ecologists; the economists said they'd talk to the agriculturists. Everyone said they'd talk to the vaccinologists. It hadn't worked out that way. After paying out on vaccines and bail-outs, governments everywhere ran out of money and everyone went back to their silos.

At least her new company, GSL, was doing its bit. Fighting a new fight. Pathogen prediction was expensive – they were, after all, trying to keep pace with viral evolution – but the start-up had found a venture capitalist flushed with success from coronavirus vaccine production. And their aim – to program immune systems against future pathogens – had unlocked plenty of funding. It turned out that setting up a 'biotechnology incubator' had been a smart move. But for all their yeast cells, receptor proteins and genome sequencing, no one had seen the new deafness coming. No one.

Lilly felt a prickle of sweat down her back. Was this another spillover event? Had another bat caught a cold? She knew the Chinese wet markets were running again because she'd seen the videos. When she'd queried the wisdom of this with 'Heidi', she'd been accused of being a colonialist. Most academics she knew had shied away from difficult conversations about 'cultural differences'.

Lilly chewed at a nail. She had a sense of time draining away. Circling the drain. She fidgeted against the seatbelt. Glanced at her watch. Maybe this meal was a bad idea after all. The driver retuned to an oldies station.

'Sorry about the traffic,' he said. He glanced around, then waved with one hand at the streaked image of headlights behind him and tail lights in front. 'We're stuck. Should have turned off at the roundabout back there. When we had the chance. Kinda committed now.' He glanced at her in the mirror.

Lilly shook her head. 'I get it,' she said. 'It's fine.'

Kit was keeping the pizzas warm.
Rose was crying on her bed.

7.35 p.m.

They sat around the kitchen table. Rose, her usual dungarees, tee and hat, to Kit's left, her pizza demolished. Lilly to his right, pizza just two slices down. Rose's eyes were bloodshot and wild. Lilly played with her cutlery.

Rose and Kit talked *at* her. They spoke fast, in tandem, their words overlapping.

'The cab took for ever. Thought it'd be quicker. Mistake.'

'I rang Dad. I rang her mum. Then waited. Her mum arrived first. Gave her some tablets.'

'When I got there, Rose was on the stairs. Said I shouldn't go up.'

'It seemed like a private thing, Dad. That's why. That's all. Harriet was terrified, she wanted her mum.'

'I get that. Just wanted to help.'

'You know she went deaf, right? We were just in her room – she was clicking like crazy – and then she said she couldn't hear anything, and then . . .'

'So, anyway, I called up. And Tilda – that's the mother – she says she'll deal with it.'

'And thank you. She said thank you.'

'Yes, she did. She said that.' A breath.

'Then what?' said Lilly, judging the moment.

'Then nothing. Then we came home. And here we are.' Rose chased some crumbs around her plate. Swallowed hard. 'All safe and sound.' Her voice caught, her eyes filled. Kit put a hand on her shoulder.

'And Rose has been trying to message Harriet, haven't you?' he said. It was a statement, not a question.

'Last I heard,' said Rose, 'her mum was on the phone to the NHS or something. Nothing since.'

'What were the tablets?' asked Lilly.

Rose shrugged. 'Dunno. They were out of her bag. Paracetamol, maybe? Antibiotics?'

'I've called the principal,' said Kit. 'Left a message.'

'She doesn't know?' said Lilly, incredulous.

'If her mobile is off . . .'

'You should call Nurse Mac,' said Rose.

'Left a message there too.' Kit was exasperated. He knew the college had to make a call on this, knew he had to pass on the news of Harriet's deafness as soon as possible. 'Hopefully Tilda has done that already,' he said.

'I wouldn't count on it,' said Rose.

'Isn't that what any normal parent would do?'

Rose raised both eyebrows. Kit sighed.

'OK. Of course.' To Lilly he said, 'Tilda thinks the school has gone downhill since her day. She's an old pupil. One of many who disapproves of—'

'Everything,' said Rose. 'Pretty much everything.'

Kit smiled. 'That's about right. She disapproves of everything and everybody. Especially since Whitlock arrived.'

'Has Harriet told anyone else, Rose?' asked Lilly.

Rose shrugged. 'I only know there's nothing on the Whats-App groups.'

'Have *you* told anyone?' asked Kit.

'No. 'Course not.'

Kit nodded. He looked at Lilly, saw the dark rings around her eyes, the tightness around her mouth. He winced at his forgetfulness. 'I'm so sorry, Lilly. The whole point of this was to find out about the funeral. We got kind of . . . overtaken.' He shook his head. 'So sorry,' he said again.

Lilly tried a smile. 'Honestly, it's fine. I can't just tell you like that anyway. It can wait. Harriet is the issue here.'

Rose stood, took her plate to the sink. 'Can I ask a question?' she asked, her back to the table.

'Hang on,' said Kit, arm raised. 'Wait. We can't just move on.'

Rose turned round, leaned against the sink.

'You buried your father yesterday, Lilly,' said Kit. 'I know you didn't want me there, but still . . . It seems wrong there was no one there for you. I wish—'

'Kit, stop,' said Lilly. 'Please. It was a formality. A ritual. For me, he died years ago. Decades ago, even. I've lived almost all my life without him. It was an event to mark his death. I attended that event. That's it.'

Rose opened her mouth, hesitated. Kit did the same.

Lilly managed a half-smile. 'I know. And the answer is no. His suicide is actually irrelevant to how I feel. That might make me sound heartless, but really . . .' She'd said enough. She shut her eyes. Pressed her lips together. She saw his note again, now folded away in a drawer at home. Opened her eyes. Rose was watching her, her large eyes staring. 'So. Now you can ask the question, Rose,' she said. She exhaled slowly.

'OK,' said Rose. 'With Harriet. Maybe this is just an infection. That's all. I had an ear infection once – could hardly hear a thing out of one ear. Might it just be that?'

Lilly heard the hope and pain in her voice. She knew she couldn't help much. Knew too that this was the longest, most 'normal' conversation she'd had with Rose.

'Honestly, I don't know,' she said. 'This isn't my field. But it's possible, of course it is. We just need to find the infection that causes the clicking. In a way, that's more mysterious than the deafness. Harriet needs to get checked out as soon as possible.' She shifted in her seat, already thinking about getting home.

'I spoke to a colleague in California this afternoon. They have it too. And that video you sent, Kit, suggests that Spain, or maybe Latin America, has it. There may well be an innocent or comparatively harmless explanation for all of it, but we need to know what that is now. Tomorrow, at the latest.'

She checked her watch.

'You need to go?' said Kit.

'Just getting twitchy,' she said. 'I haven't seen Jess yet. Need to be back before her. She's at a friend's.'

'Right,' said Kit. 'Of course.' He leaned back on his chair, arching his back until it clicked, then rocked forward again. 'So what's the deal in California then?' he asked. 'This is the guy you were speaking to when I rang?' His tone was neutral enough, but Lilly thought she detected a hint of 'you-should-have-taken-my-call-earlier' about it.

'This "guy",' said Lilly, 'is Professor Linda Harris, top epidemiologist at the University of California, San Francisco. I knew her at Glaxo. She has fourteen "clickers", as she calls them. Five couples; the other four are friends.'

'But five couples?' he said.

Lilly nodded.

'It's couples at school too,' said Kit. 'Pretty much, anyway. Whitlock made a point of it.'

Kit and Lilly exchanged glances, then they both looked at Rose.

'I'll order that cab,' said Lilly.

The ProMED site was logging new tinnitus reports in France, Ireland, Germany, Denmark, Canada and Sweden.

Eight UK hospital Accident and Emergency departments were registering patients with unexplained hearing loss.

In Mexico City, a care home was announcing that all eighteen residents had gone deaf.

Two days earlier

4.38 a.m.

COFFEE AND TOAST already. Kit sat in the silent kitchen, lit only by the strip light above the stove. He hadn't slept. Or didn't think he had slept; he couldn't be sure. He'd got up twice, gone back twice, listened to the radio, tried to read. His head, thick with tiredness, had momentarily confused the drip, drip of rainfall in the guttering outside his bedroom with tinnitus clicking. He knew he was wasting time. He got up.

Couples were a problem and he was in two of them. One with Rose; another with Lilly. The thought of contamination, the idea of infection, filled him with horror. He knew, because others had told him, that he still blamed himself for not, somehow, spotting Jody's cancer before it was too late. It had made him, he had thought, hyper-vigilant, seeking some kind of atonement through diligence. He had been ferocious in his policing of the Covid rules back in '20 and '21, and the thought that he might have been lax now made his flesh creep. He needed to play catch-up. And if, in time, it became clear he had been over-reacting, then he could live with that. So be it.

He finished the toast, swilled it down with the last of the coffee. His phone buzzed. Whitlock, at last. *Sorry to miss your messages. I'll be at school at 6.* He thought of calling but knew this was a conversation – almost certainly a series of conversations – that had to be had in person.

Kit checked his watch. The first Tube train was in forty minutes.

5.30 a.m.

As far as he could recall, Kit had never caught the first Tube. He stood on the freezing grey platform, head down, bag slung across his back. There were a dozen or so other bleak-looking travellers spread out across the length of the platform. Four stood together, occasionally muttering to each other. Kit found his space and waited. Ray Charles played in his earbuds.

It had been too early to wake Rose. He had left her a note on the kitchen table, sent her a text also, apologizing and leaving some cash in case she needed it. 'See you at school,' he'd written, already hearing her reply: *Not if I can help it.* He smiled briefly. A second lift-load of passengers arrived. A woman with a green woollen hat pulled hard over red hair walked to within a metre of him and stopped. *Really?* he thought. *You have the whole platform and you choose to stand here?* The air started to move. A stale, cold wind, driven by the approaching train. Green-hat woman stepped forward; Kit moved a few paces away.

As the first carriage passed, his music cut out. A second's pause, a beat of annoyance and his phone rang. Another carriage passed. He rummaged deep in his coat pocket with gloved hands. He was briefly startled. Who would be ringing him now? Surely Rose wouldn't be up. It could be nothing good at this hour. MCS maybe, or Principal Whitlock. The train was almost stationary. He had seconds.

The phone screen showed an unknown number. Not school. Not Rose. He took the call.

'Hello?'

'Kit Chaplin?' A cheery woman's voice, twenty-something.

'Yes. Who is this?'

The train stopped, the doors rumbled open.

'Mr Chaplin, my name is Felicity Wiman. I'm a researcher at *Good Morning Britain*. I'm calling about this new ear-clicking noise, which I think you've witnessed.' Green-hat woman had sat down. Kit stepped into the train, lingering by the open door. Three carriages from the front. The TV researcher was still talking as the doors closed. She was still talking when the signal dropped. Kit put the phone back into his pocket. Ray Charles picked up where he had left off.

He stayed standing by the door. There were plenty of seats, just green-hat woman in front of him and the four friends talking beyond the next set of doors. They sat two and two, leaning in to continue their conversation over the train noise. Two of them shared a flask of coffee. The smell reached Kit. He resolved to grab an espresso if the coffee shop at Great Portland Street was open.

The TV woman had been talking about the YouTube videos of clickers when she was cut off. Kit had no idea how she had found him or his number, but he had been grateful for the tunnel blackout. Her tone had been jarringly whimsical. They were obviously after a 'quirky' story, and he had no intention of telling it. But if one researcher was on to the story, others would be close behind. The news was out. He needed to get to MCS as quickly as possible. He'd skip the coffee.

The train slowed. He slung his bag over his shoulder. Green-hat woman was on her feet. King's Cross was thirty seconds away. The train slowed some more, harder this time, then came to a sudden, unexpected, screeching stop. Kit lurched into the carriage wall. Green-hat woman, off balance, went sprawling, crying out sharply as her chin hit the floor. From the four companions, cries of alarm and spilt-coffee curses. Muffled shouts from the other carriages. Kit went to help the woman, offering his hand. Blood ran from her mouth. There was a nasty-looking graze on her chin.

'What was that?' she managed through damaged lips. She rummaged in her bag, finding a tissue.

'Emergency brake,' said Kit. He knelt on a seat, cupped his face to the nearest window. They were still in the tunnel, but some light seeped from the platform ahead, turning the black walls to a grimy grey. 'Though just as we are arriving in the station is a strange time to pull it,' he said. He stood to peer through the window into the connecting carriage.

'What's going on?' called one of the four men. Through the filthy glass, Kit could see a number of passengers doing what he was doing – staring through to the next carriage. Towards the front of the train. One of them yanked the door open and ran through.

'They're getting forward,' said Kit. 'Heading to the first carriage.' The woman appeared at his side, still pressing a bloody tissue to her mouth.

'Can we open it?' she asked, still struggling with her damaged boxer's lips. The door had a slidable window and a large recessed steel handle. Kit tugged it downwards. The locking mechanism clicked. The door gave an inch. Another pull on the handle and it swung open. Kit strode through an empty carriage. Discarded newspapers littered the seats. Coffee cups rolled on the floor.

At the front of the train, a crowd, Kit guessed, of around twenty passengers were gathered by the driver's cab. Some were knocking on the door, calling out.

'Hey, what's happening?'

'You OK in there? Is something on the track?'

Green-hat woman again. 'Maybe that's it,' she said. 'Some-one must have jumped. Shit.' Then added a hasty 'Poor bastard'.

Most of the passengers sat down. There seemed to be a general acceptance that a suicide was the most likely explanation and that they would be stuck for a while. Kit paced and checked his phone. If the signal had been strong enough to give the television researcher a few metres of tunnel to work with, maybe it could grant him the same privilege. But no dice. No bars. No wifi. Kit walked to the driver's cab, then stepped right. Through the window he could just make out the first few slabs of the platform. He held his phone to the glass. Slid it to the top-left corner. Still nothing.

There was never a good day to be stuck on an Underground train, Kit thought. But when the principal has called you in for an early meeting and you've just realized that you want to argue for school closure, today would be the worst. 'Not now,' Kit muttered to himself, his breath briefly steaming the glass. 'Please, not now.'

The train's engine shuddered to a stop. Kit shut his eyes and exhaled slowly.

5.45 a.m.

There was a raised voice from the driver's cab and the carriage fell silent. Kit spun round. Two men who had been leaning against the cab door turned to face it, one putting his ear to the gun-grey metal. For a few seconds there was quiet, then the shouting started again. The words were indistinct, rapid-fire, jumbled. A disembodied, metallic, female voice squawked a reply before the shouting interrupted her. When he stopped, she tried again. It sounded like a negotiation of some kind. The only words Kit caught were from her.

'Twenty metres,' she said, then repeated it a number of times. 'Twenty metres! Twenty metres!' A request or a suggestion that he should pull the train forward, Kit assumed. The train didn't move. The man with his ear to the door knocked twice. Hard. The whole carriage watched him.

'Hey, buddy! How about pulling into the platform? You know? Like, it's your job?' No reply from the driver, but from the cab the metallic voice blurted more words, all of them incomprehensible. Kit strained to hear a reply. He thought he heard the driver move, but that was all.

'Maybe he's sick,' said green-hat woman. 'Collapsed or something.'

And maybe he's gone deaf, thought Kit, the idea dropping like a depth charge. Then the correction. In reality, almost anything else was more likely. He needed to get a grip.

There was more shouting now. Different voices, just a few metres away. From the platform, presumably. Three, maybe four men. Short, staccato sentences. Kit thought they sounded bizarrely cheerful. Using the kind of tone you'd use to encourage a small child to do something they didn't want to. It worked. The train's engine started again. The coach shuddered briefly, edged forward. Kit didn't know a train could move so slowly but, as the platform inched into view, he could see the shouting men. In a line, two transport police, two London Underground officials and two paramedics, all staring into the driver's cab. Pointing, waving him in. The train stopped again. The engine cut again. Kit was standing at the first door of the front carriage, which was now clear of the tunnel. The nearer transport police officer held a finger up and mouthed, 'One minute,' then pointed to the driver's cab. Kit nodded.

'The copper says one minute,' he called to the carriage.

The Tube staff stepped forward to the platform edge, keys in hand. They had eye contact. They summoned the paramedics. Behind Kit, more passengers had walked through the train and were now pressing their faces to the glass. Straining for a view. Straining at the leash.

'Come on, guys!'

'Get us off now!'

Gruff morning voices. Impatient, stressed. Kit watched the first Underground staffer open the driver's cab, disappear inside, then step out, to be replaced by the paramedics. Underground man leaned back in.

'Driver must be sick,' called Kit, his head half turned. 'Medics in now.' Mutterings throughout the carriage were silenced by the tannoys crackling into life.

'Ladies and gentlemen, we'll be getting you off as soon as possible. Just the front door will open for now. If you can make your way forward . . .' Shouts from the cab, and someone killed the mic. Through the glass, the crowd on the platform had been pushed back. Behind Kit, everyone was now standing. Pressing closer. Some banged on the windows.

'Just open the bloody door!'

The door opened. Kit was first out, pushed forward by the scrum. The platform air felt fresh, cold. He twisted left to glimpse inside the cab, peering over a crouched medic and past the two Tube staff. He briefly caught sight of the stricken driver. He was bolt upright in his seat, his hands over his face. One of the transport police officers stepped forward, blocking his view.

'What happened?' asked Kit. 'Is he going to be OK?' The man looked blank.

'You just need to leave the platform, sir. Quickly as you can.' Kit nodded, returned to the throng, checked the time. He was already late for his Whitlock meeting. He took the steps two at a time, ignored the coffee shop at the station entrance and sprinted for the college.

Rose was asleep.
Lilly was trawling Californian newspapers.

6.35 a.m.

Three hours' sleep wasn't enough, but it would do. Lilly had operated just fine on much less than that. When her brain was firing, she had no choice. She wasn't cold, but she pulled the cord of her dressing gown tight, pulled the lapels together. Repositioned her water flask. Straightened her laptop.

For the last two hours she had been searching for more reports of the clickers, starting on the medical sites, then the online news. She hadn't found much more than the Californian professor had told her. There was a half-page in the *LA Times*, and some local news sites had cut and pasted the same story. A Canadian site carried the headline 'My mother-clicking headache' and a story about a student who had filmed his mum taking painkillers. Another video to add to the collection. More ill-judged whimsy to regret later.

The sound of the shower let her know Jess was up, and she kicked back from the laptop. Now she felt the ache in her shoulders and neck. They hurt, like they always did. She arched her back, rolled her shoulders, then stood. She walked around the kitchen table four times, windmilling her arms. In the medicine box by the microwave she found the paracetamol, took two. She switched on the radio and the kettle. She stared into the fridge, rubbing her neck with her hands. Orange juice and bacon would be her peace offering to Jess. She took both, poured oil into the frying pan.

If couples were a defining factor in both Professor Harris's results and in Kit's observations of the students at MCS, then it had to be an infection. And as that ruled out tinnitus, objective or otherwise, she needed to look elsewhere. But the results of her research were clear – only objective tinnitus caused the ears to *make* sounds. Nothing else. She needed help, but Jess needed breakfast. Lilly fried the bacon to a crisp, cut the bread slices thick, put the ketchup on the table. Jess's bedroom door slammed and Lilly put the coffee machine on. Jess's hairdryer roared and Lilly frothed the milk. When Jess appeared, grey T, black high-rise mum jeans, top knot, she gaped at the table.

'I mean, I smelled bacon . . .' she said, reaching for the orange juice. 'Guilt offering?'

'Something like that,' said Lilly. Jess pulled up a chair, sat in front of her bacon sandwich. She was taller than her mother, darker haired and broader shouldered, but they shared the same blue eyes and delicate mouth. Three earrings in each ear, two studs and a small silver hoop. She finished the juice and the sandwich in under a minute.

'You want another one?' asked Lilly. 'There's plenty more.'

Jess shook her head. 'I'm good.'

'And I really am sorry about not being here,' said Lilly. She sat opposite, sipped on a tea. She wondered how much to say about Kit. It was never Jess's favourite topic.

'I get it,' said Jess, now starting on the coffee. She sipped noisily. 'Tell me about the funeral.'

Lilly was caught off guard. Felt herself crashing through several gear changes.

'Well . . .' She tailed off. Sighed.

Jess glanced up. 'If you don't want to . . .'

'No, it's fine,' said Lilly. It was far from fine, of course, and Lilly could see that Jess knew it. 'Well. Thanks for asking. It was horrible, actually. Grim from start to finish.' She paused. Jess waited. 'I was probably only in the crematorium for half an hour.' She sipped her tea, spoke to the mug. 'But it felt like a week.' More tea. 'And a week in the company of two old guys who didn't speak. At all. Not to me, not to each other. Also, a know-nothing priest. And my dead father.' She swallowed hard. 'I resented every minute I was there.'

'What did the priest say?'

Lilly paused, trying to recall. A small shake of the head.

'I have no idea,' she said. 'But I'll take a guess at platitudes. Something meaningless and routine. Then the curtains were pulled and that was that. I told them I didn't want the ashes and to dispose of them any way they saw fit.' Now she looked at Jess. 'That I didn't care either way.'

Jess nodded. She let her mother's words settle. She finished her coffee. Chased some breadcrumbs with her finger.

'And what did they say?' she said. 'When you said that.'

'Again, I honestly don't remember,' said Lilly. 'And they can think what they like. I called a cab, got the first train home.' She smiled. 'It was completely rammed. Everyone squeezed in. Crying babies, shouting students, smelly food. Everything was mad. It was everything I hate. But actually, it felt good. Good to be done with it all. To be leaving all the . . . mess behind.'

A strident solo piano played from the radio. Lilly didn't notice. The feeling of release that had flooded her on that journey home was the only good memory of that day. Recalling it now was cheering. She raised her mug. 'And it was good to get home.'

Jess nodded, raised her mug in reply.

'What happens to his house?' she said. 'Do we get it?'

Her daughter's bluntness didn't surprise her. It was a trait Jess had inherited from her. Lilly shrugged. 'Maybe. Depends if he had a will. Could have left it to anyone. The police gave me a set of keys, so . . .'

'And if there isn't a will?'

'Well, unless there's any other next of kin I don't know about – which is quite possible – then I suppose it'll come to me. And if so, I'll sell it to the first person who'll take it off me.'

97

'Fair,' said Jess. She wiped her finger around the mug, then sucked the froth from it. 'Is that—' She broke off, eyes to the table. 'Is that where he . . . died?'

Lilly hadn't been sure how or what to tell Jess, but now the moment had come it seemed obvious. Over breakfast, and everything. She pulled at the lapels of her dressing gown again.

'The house is where he killed himself, yes. Shot himself, actually. Gun to the head.'

Lilly's words seemed to ricochet around the kitchen. Jess placed her hands over her mouth. They sat in silence, staring at each other. Too late to go back now. Everything on the table.

'Under the chin, to be precise,' she said. 'And there's a note. He left a note.' Jess's eyes filled with tears. One hand stayed on her mouth; the other she placed on Lilly's arm.

'Oh, Mum,' she said.

On the radio, the concerto faded away.

'What does it say?' said Jess, her voice a horrified whisper. Lilly reached into her dressing-gown pocket, produced a folded sheet of lined notepaper. Pushed it across the table.

On the radio, the seven o'clock news.

Jess took the paper. It was a piece of A5 torn from a spiral-bound pad. She hesitated, then unfolded it, placed it on the table. Black, scrawling biro over three lines. Lilly watched her read the words, three maybe four times.

On the radio there was a sudden burst of noise. A sound like the tapping of a fingernail on a tooth. Or an electric spark. Clicking.

Lilly spun in her chair. Stared at the radio.

'Mum?' said Jess.

The Tube driver was in hospital.
Rose was sitting on her bed.
Kit was in Principal Whitlock's office.

7.05 a.m.

'And who was the second caller?' Jan Whitlock peered over the top of her glasses. Hair and make-up just so, buttoned-up jacket. 'You said there were two?'

Kit nodded. 'A journalist from LBC. Wanted to know what was happening here. What I'd seen. Told him I couldn't comment on anything and hung up.' He watched Whitlock as she took notes. She was behind her desk, laptop open on a news site, a second computer showing emails and notifications. All the lights were on. Some street neon seeped through the lace curtains. The strange pooling of the light drained Whitlock's face of colour. She looked as exhausted as he felt. A tracksuited Nurse Mac sat, hands on lap. Phone on her knee. Kit paced.

He needed more coffee, more breakfast, but all he had was a cup of tea from Whitlock's flask. It was already cold.

'How on earth did they get your number?' asked Whitlock.

Kit shrugged. It was hardly the issue of the moment. 'No idea,' he said.

Whitlock checked her watch. 'OK. Well, the CEO's calling in five. Let's assume he's been following the news . . .'

'In which case,' said Kit, 'he'll want to close the school too. No one wants to be late to this. No one wants to mess up again.'

The three of them had been there since just after six thirty. Kit had explained the drama on the Tube and what he'd seen of the stricken driver. Whitlock had said, 'Poor man,' but had not jumped to any of the conclusions Kit had. Nurse Mac's open mouth and surprised eyes had said it all, though.

Whitlock checked her watch. Glanced at the news site, sat up, clicked her mouse twice. 'Kit, look at this.' He strode to her side of the desk. The screen showed the CNN home page, the second video offered was the Central Park one. The 'what is this crazy shit?' one. 'One of yours,' she said.

Kit bent to read the headline. 'Film-maker: "Mystery clicking video not a fake."' He scanned the page. '"Carla Michaelson, 27, said the man in the video is her partner and that the noise coming from his ears had begun the day before it was filmed. Michaelson revealed that her boyfriend, 29, had suffered from tinnitus in recent years but that she had never been able to hear it until now."' He straightened, stepped away.

'Except,' said Whitlock, 'you say that's wrong.' She turned to Kit.

'Not me,' he said. He gestured to Nurse Mac. 'It's just not possible.'

McKay nodded. 'That's true,' she said. 'Sounds like tinnitus, feels like tinnitus, but it can't be tinnitus. However, we do have to assume for now that Harriet's deafness is connected to the clicking in some way.'

Whitlock leaned forward, steepled her fingers. 'Do we? Have we heard from her parents? Her GP or the hospital?' McKay shook her head.

'Not yet,' said Kit.

Whitlock shuffled papers. 'I need something solid,' she said. 'Something confirmed. If I'm going to close the school, I need something in writing.' She glanced between Kit and McKay. 'Never mind the CEO. I'll call UKHSA now.'

'But the possibility—' began Kit.

'The procedure,' cut in Whitlock, 'is that, in these

circumstances, you call the UK Health Security Agency. I'll let you know.'

7.22 a.m.

Kit stepped out of Whitlock's office, rang Rose. It was quite normal for her not to pick up, but he got lucky. Street noise in the background.

'You checking on me?' she said. 'What's up?'

'Oh, just trying to persuade the principal to shut the school, that's all.' He tried to keep some of the exasperation from his voice. 'Where are you?'

'Five minutes away,' she said. 'Harriet texted me. Woke me up.' He jumped at the news.

'Where is she, Rose?' he said. 'How is she? We have no information.'

'Hospital. As from early this morning. And I'd say she sounds as scared as she looked when we left her.'

'Rose, listen,' said Kit. 'I need to talk to her parents. They haven't told us anything. It's really urgent.'

'I'll message her. Also, Dad . . . so school's still open, yes?'

'Yes, it is. For now.'

'OK,' said Rose brightly. And hung up. Kit frowned. That had sounded all wrong, her sign-off completely at odds with the rest of the call. He shrugged. Another call to make.

'Lilly, it's me. MCS is still open. I'm trying to persuade Whitlock to close, but she's insisting on calling UKHSA first.'

'Still, her call, surely,' said Lilly. Kitchen clatter in the background.

'So tell Jess to come in. If she hasn't left already.'

101

'I will. Oh, and Kit? I'll call at lunchtime. Might have some information for you. Just checking something.'

'OK,' he said. 'Sure. Thanks.'

He killed the call, opened the door back into the principal's office.

'Did the CEO call?'

Whitlock shook her head. 'He did not,' she said.

'UKHSA?'

She pointed at her phone. 'On hold,' she said.

7.40 a.m.

There were just five of them to begin with. Rose sat in the middle of the MCS front steps, rucksack at her feet, A3 art pad in her hands. She had written in large black capitals 'SCHOOL STRIKE' and perched it on the steps, facing the street. On another page she had written 'NO SCHOOL' and on another '#NOT SAFE'. She was holding them up either side of her face. The four friends she'd messaged overnight were sitting in front of her, two and two. They also held signs, reading 'SCHOOL STRIKE', '#forharriet' and '#shutthe-school'. As more pupils arrived, the numbers of protesters swelled quickly. Within five minutes, they filled the pavement and were spilling on to the road. Passers-by took photos. Drivers slowed to gawp.

By seven forty-five there were more pupils outside MCS than inside. Cheers and applause greeted each pupil who joined. A man, face red raw from the cold and with a blue scarf wrapped around his neck, crossed the road. He scanned the crowd, called out, 'Hey! What's going on here?'

Rose jumped up, walked over. 'School strike,' she said. 'There's an ear infection in the school. My friend has gone deaf because of it, but they won't close. We think that's wrong.'

He nodded at one of the makeshift posters with the hashtags. 'And that's the Harriet you're talking about?'

Rose nodded. 'Yup,' she said. 'Harriet Teale.'

'What's your name?' said the man.

'What's that got to do with anything?' she said, suddenly on her guard.

'Oh,' said the man. 'I'm a reporter. Rob Clarke. ITV News. Interesting story. That's all. What are your teachers saying?'

'Well . . .' began Rose.

A braying boy's voice from behind Rose interrupted. 'And her dad's head of English, if you must know!'

Rose spun, gave the boy the middle finger. She mouthed, 'Fuck off, Jonah,' then, 'I need to go,' to the journalist.

'What does your dad think?' he called after her, but her phone was buzzing. Harriet had sent her mother's number. She forwarded it to her father.

7.50 a.m.

Kit hit the number as soon as it appeared on his screen. He'd been watching the protest from the window, Rose at the heart of it. He managed to be both furious and admiring at the same time. He felt horribly compromised with Whitlock, but at least he knew he and Rose were on the same side here.

On the line, he counted seven rings before a scrambled answer. A tired woman's voice at the other end. Speaking close to the mouthpiece.

'Yes. Hello.'

Kit walked as he talked. 'Tilda, it's Kit Chaplin, Rose's dad. I'm calling from MCS. And we were all wondering how

Harriet is doing.' He started walking towards Whitlock's office at pace.

From the phone, a long sigh and a silence. Kit already knew it wasn't going to be good news.

'We've been here since three this morning. She's in isolation, Kit. They're running all kinds of tests – no results yet. I know they've given her painkillers for a headache that came on after you left. But that's all.' Kit knocked and entered Whitlock's office without waiting for a reply. The principal looked up, startled. He pointed at his phone.

'Tilda, I'm putting you on speaker so Dr Whitlock can hear what you're saying.' He placed his phone on her desk. 'Go ahead. Just say again what you told me.'

'OK. One more time.' Another breathy sigh. 'Harriet is in isolation and they're conducting all manner of tests. She still has no hearing. And she has a headache. That's it, really.'

'Mrs Teale, it's Jan Whitlock. I'm so sorry to hear about Harriet. Can you tell me what they are testing her for?'

'No, I can't. But everyone's masked up. Full PPE, and she's in isolation. That's all I know. I'm sorry, but I need to go.' And she was gone.

Kit retrieved his phone, let the silence hang.

Whitlock stood, walked to her window then turned. 'OK,' she said. 'We close. Thank you, Kit.' She walked to her chair, rested her hands on its back.

'I'll update the website myself. It'll trigger the emergency text system. We'll take it from there. And call those journalists back. Start with the *Good Morning Britain* woman, then LBC. Tell them what we're doing.' Kit was surprised. This was quite a turnaround. His eyes narrowed.

'Really? Of course I can, but . . . to be honest, I think they'll want to talk to you. The head of English is hardly the voice of authority, is he?'

Whitlock considered that. 'Call and see what they say,' she

said. 'And you can tell those bloody strikers, or protesters, or whatever they are, they can go home.'

Kit nodded, left the room.

8.35 a.m.

Good Morning Britain and LBC did still want to talk, and both wanted to talk to the principal. Kit had assumed that *GMB* would be on the phone, but they had insisted on a FaceTime, in-vision conversation with Whitlock. A brief tech-primer with an engineer, and they were ready.

Kit sat by the door. His head was swimming with the implications of what was happening. He had a long list of questions and no answers. How long should the school shut for? How many were infected? Might he be infected? What advice should he give to worried parents? Might Harriet's deafness be caused by something else, and was all this a huge over-reaction? He took a deep breath. One thing at a time. Whitlock's television interview first.

Despite a bright sunrise, all the office lights were on. Whitlock had placed some school trophies behind her on the windowsill. Kit recognized the Creative Writing Cup, as he had judged the competition, but the others – two shields and three more motley unpolished cups – were unfamiliar. If Whitlock had asked his opinion on her newly curated backdrop, he would have said it looked a little needy. But she hadn't. So he didn't.

He could tell she was tense. She sat staring at the screen, waiting for the presenter to come to her. She shifted in her chair, poked and prodded her hair, licked her lips. She tilted the screen towards her, adjusted the laptop's position on the desk. From its speakers, a conversation about the weather, some incoming high pressure and the Gulf Stream. Kit assumed they would come to Whitlock next. He felt his stomach churn.

Then the clicking started to play on the laptop, and they were on. Kit sat upright: another adrenaline surge. The presenter, male, Scottish, summarized the content of the clicking videos. His tone was one of mild amusement. Kit couldn't see the screen but he could almost hear the raised eyebrow in his voice. Whitlock fidgeted in her seat, tried to smile at her screen. The presenter was now speaking to her.

'Dr Jan Whitlock is the principal of Marylebone College School in London, where some students have reported experiencing this extraordinary phenomenon. She joins us now. Good morning, Dr Whitlock.'

Whitlock nodded, tried a different smile. 'Good morning.'

'Tell us what you saw yesterday. Did you have students clicking, like we saw in that film just now?'

'We did, yes.'

'Tell us what you heard.'

Whitlock folded, then unfolded her arms. 'So,' she started, 'yesterday a student had a clicking noise coming from her ears. She was, understandably, worried. We asked around the other students and discovered five more also making this clicking sound.' She opened her mouth to say more, then appeared to change her mind and closed it again. She pressed her lips together.

'Can you describe the sound?'

'So it's the same as in the clip you played earlier. A tapping sound. A snapping, maybe – like an elastic band. Something like that.'

'Was it rapid-fire, Dr Whitlock, or just an occasional sound?'

'What I heard was occasional. Two or three a minute, something like that.'

So far so good, thought Kit. Just the facts, ma'am, just the facts.

'And what's going on, in your opinion?' asked the presenter. 'Have you ever come across this before?'

Whitlock shook her head. 'Never. No. But I am told that there is a rare type of tinnitus that is audible to others nearby. It could be that.' Her expression said that she was out of her depth and was willing the interview to be over.

'And how are your pupils and staff reacting? I understand you had a protest outside the school this morning. A strike. Is that correct?'

'Oh,' said Whitlock. 'There was a brief misunderstanding, but it has all been cleared up now. We have closed the school. The students are doing OK, but we took the decision to close as a precaution.'

Kit's insides turned to water. He could hear the surprise in the presenter's voice. What he'd clearly thought was a quirky health item had taken a different turn.

'You've closed the school?' he said. 'You must be worried about infection to take such action?'

Whitlock's eyes were glassy. 'As I said, it seemed a safe, precautionary measure to take.'

The presenter sensed he was on to something. Blood in the water. He circled closer. 'In case anyone else starts experiencing this clicking?' he said.

'Yes, of course.'

'Might other students and staff be experiencing it already?'

Kit shook his head, mouthed a big 'no'. Whitlock wasn't looking.

'It is possible, yes,' she said.

'So what should parents be thinking, Dr Whitlock? And should other schools also close?'

There was perspiration now on Whitlock's upper lip. 'Well,' she said, 'they should consult . . . they should contact . . . I can't really advise other schools, I'm afraid.' Her tone had a finality to it, clearly indicating that she had nothing else to add.

'Dr Whitlock, thank you,' said the host.

'Thank you,' said Whitlock.

A pause.

'And our best to your students,' said the man. 'Actually, before you go, one last thing. I should have asked how they're getting on. How is that first student? Is it true she's in hospital?'

Kit shot to his feet, waving his arms. How on earth did he know that?

Whitlock was wide-eyed with shock. She hesitated, swallowed hard. 'Yes, I'm afraid she is.'

Kit clenched his fists. He considered slamming the laptop shut. Etiquette, manners and deference held him back. It would be the wrong choice.

'And, Dr Whitlock, is it true she's gone deaf?'

Whitlock said nothing.

'Dr Whitlock? Has one of your students who was experiencing this clicking gone deaf?'

Kit thought Whitlock was going to faint. She glanced, unseeing, at Kit, then back at the screen.

'Yes, I'm afraid she has.'

Within minutes, the panic began.

8.50 a.m.

For the next hour, Marylebone College School was the centre of the storm. The first journalists arrived in minutes, the first television crew soon after. The first news site to run the story gave it the headline 'Deafness: the New Contagion'. It had been updated within minutes with a question mark at the end, but the damage had been done. The tone on social media sites pivoted from whimsy to catastrophe in minutes. The clickers had been reported in eight countries, but now that one of them had gone deaf, hashtags declaring #deafepidemic #deafpandemic #newpandemic appeared everywhere.

In the staffroom, small groups of teachers huddled around laptops and coffee.

Lilly rang first. Kit hesitated, then answered.

'I know,' he said wearily before she had a chance to speak. 'Trust me, I know.' He was slumped on one of the old, dilapidated staffroom armchairs.

Lilly was incredulous. 'How did they know about Harriet?' she said. 'Who would have told them? Also, it seemed like the presenter changed course midway through. As if someone gave him that information *during* the interview. If he'd known about Harriet going deaf, he'd have started the interview with it, surely?'

'One of the hashtags at the protest was "for Harriet",' said Kit, 'so presumably it was from that. And Whitlock says she thought the interview was over because he said thank you. Then, when she realized it wasn't over, that it was still going, it was too late.'

Across the room, Kit saw McKay take a call, then slowly stand.

'And,' continued Lilly, 'most importantly, where is Harriet? Which hospital did she go to? Because they need to put out a statement pretty damn fast.'

Still on her phone, McKay sat down again, seemingly drained of strength and colour.

'All we know,' said Kit, 'is that she's in isolation and everyone is in PPE.'

Lilly's reply came in a low whisper. 'You. Are. Kidding.'

Kit had hauled himself to his feet. 'Sadly, I'm not. And I

need to go, Lil. Call you straight back.' He hurried across the staffroom. McKay had her head in her hands. Her shoulders were trembling. Kit crouched at her feet. Heads turned, conversations paused.

'Joanne, what is it? What's happened?'

McKay dropped her hands to her lap then wiped her eyes with a sleeve. She struggled for words. Kit prompted her. 'Who was that on the phone?'

She took a deep breath. 'It was Marcus Graham's father,' she said. Her voice was thin, fluttering. 'Marcus has gone deaf. Ellie Howard too. Her mum had called him. Obviously extremely upset. Actually, he said she was hysterical.'

Gasps and strangled cries from around the room.

'Where is he taking him, Joanne? Did he say?' asked Kit. McKay shook her head. 'Sorry, no.' He hung his head briefly, then forced a reassuring smile. Stood up. He glanced at his colleagues. 'Anyone else think we should all go home?' he said.

A moment's silence as everyone looked at everyone else. 'I mean, clearly we don't know what's going on here, but if three students have gone deaf, who's to say there won't be more? And who's to say we won't be affected?'

A few nodding heads. Some gathering of coats and bags.

Kit watched as his colleagues' worry bloomed into outright fear. The genie was out. Startled eyes, nervous words. A stepping-away. A separating-out. Suddenly, everyone was two metres apart, then laughing self-consciously about it.

'Well, where have we seen this before?' muttered Kit. One of the new teachers raised a hand. 'Shouldn't we wait for Dr Whitlock to close—'

McKay spoke from her chair. 'In Aisha's absence, Kit is the most senior member of staff here. Take a vote. Then tell Whitlock. That's it.'

Kit couldn't argue with that. 'Agreed.' He already knew

what the vote would be from the buttoning of coats and the drift to the door, but a vote would give him some cover. 'Who wants to go home? Hands . . .'

Everyone raised a hand.

'. . . up.' Kit shrugged. 'OK, I'll tell Dr Whitlock. Use the back entrance, unless you want to be on the news. Stay in touch. Watch the WhatsApp.'

He strode from the staffroom. He needed to get home, needed to talk to Rose and Lilly. His phone vibrated constantly, but he ignored it. One more talk with Whitlock and he should be out.

As the corridor turned towards the principal's office, the school's glass entrance revealed a solid line of reporters, their heads pressed to the door, like children in a nursery. Phones, cameras, microphones. When they caught a glimpse of Kit, they hammered on the glass with their hands and yelled incomprehensible questions. He knocked quickly on Whitlock's door and entered.

For a moment he thought the study was empty. Her desk was deserted, the computer screen dark and the laptop gone.

'Oh,' he said, hesitating.

Whitlock's voice from somewhere: 'I'm here.' Kit walked the length of the room to a small alcove behind a pillar he'd never noticed before. She was perching on a chair, open laptop on her knees. Handbag at her feet, phone on the floor. Her hair had flattened, her shoulders slumped. She seemed diminished. 'They appeared at my window,' she said. 'This is the only place I can't be seen.'

'Well, they're at the front door now,' said Kit. 'It's like a scene from *The Walking Dead*.'

'Maybe,' said Whitlock, 'but we need to say something. To make a statement. And I . . .' She pressed her lips together. Exhaled through her nose. 'I can't do it. So I was wondering if you could, Kit.' The weakest of smiles. 'It would be so hugely appreciated.'

He was dumbfounded. 'To say what?'

'To say that we have closed. Briefly. While health needs are assessed. A precautionary measure. That kind of thing.'

'They'll tear me apart,' said Kit.

'They'll be fine,' said Whitlock. 'You'll be fine. Treat them like your Year Elevens.' Another humourless non-smile. 'Please, Kit. For me. For the school.'

9.20 a.m.

Jim Sutherland had the keys; Kit had the statement. In front of them, a glass wall and what looked like thirty, maybe forty reporters, spilling all over the school steps. A TV truck had parked at a bus stop, its side doors open. An engineer spooled out cable. Kit decided to take Whitlock's advice. He shouted through the glass. 'Off the steps, then I come out!' He could see a few reporters pass on the message, but others carried on pushing, carried on shouting.

Kit caught the eye of the blue-scarfed man he'd seen talking to Rose earlier. Kit beckoned him closer. 'You all have thirty seconds to get off the steps. Or no statement.' The reporter pulled a face. Exactly like a Year Eleven kid, Kit thought. 'Anyway,' he shouted, 'how close do you really want to be to me anyway?'

He saw the light dawn in the reporters' eyes. They backed off. The steps were clear.

'Genius,' said Sutherland. 'Ready?'

'No,' said Kit.

'Off you go then,' said Sutherland.

As the door opened, cameras were hoisted, microphones

and phones held aloft. Kit clutched the statement he'd written with Whitlock and stepped outside. Bright sunshine, biting wind. A barrage of questions was fired his way, but he answered none of them. He stood on the top step, waiting for silence.

Year Elevens.

There were more reporters now, spilling off the pavement, between the parked cars and on to the road. Two men were standing on a car bonnet. Three police officers appeared. The men hastily climbed down.

Kit had their attention. It wasn't going to get any quieter. He looked around, found the reporter with the blue scarf, addressed the comments to him. 'I have a brief statement,' he said, his words producing clouds in the cold air. 'And I won't be answering questions.' He dropped his eyes to the text. His hands were steady. 'Marylebone College School has this morning taken the decision to close the school temporarily. A number of our students – we think no more than six – have an unexplained hearing condition.' He could hear his voice bouncing off the buildings opposite, hoped he wasn't shouting. He wondered about looking up but was afraid he'd lose his place in the statement. He kept his eyes down. 'This morning, three of the six reported that they have lost their hearing altogether.' Kit heard many of the reporters repeat the number. He sensed a mood shift, a hushed silence now. He had argued with Whitlock for full transparency on the numbers and had won. 'We do not know what has caused the hearing loss, we do not know what is causing the clicking noise. So, as a precaution, and with the safety of our students and our staff as our priority, we will be closed until further notice.' Now, he looked up. He remembered the last part. 'Our message to concerned students and parents is this. If any of you experience this clicking noise – a sound that is coming *from* the ear – please seek medical attention as soon as you can. Thank you.'

Kit turned, Sutherland opened the door. Three shouted questions followed Kit inside. 'Should all schools close?' 'Are you going to isolate?' and 'How's your family, Mr Chaplin?'

Instinctively, Kit turned to see who had asked the last question, but Sutherland hauled him in.

'What the fuck,' said Kit. 'How did he—'

'You're on the MCS website,' said Sutherland. 'And your daughter was manning the barricades earlier. As you know.'

'"How's your family, Mr Chaplin?"' Kit repeated. 'Of all the questions to ask . . .'

Sutherland pushed him along the corridor. 'Maybe it's the only question anyone's going to ask,' he said. 'How are your family, Kit?'

Kit pulled up, turned. Irked with his friend. 'If you mean Rose, she's fine. If you're including Lilly, she's fine too, and at home with Jess. But the other two questions need answering. Should all schools close? Yes, I think they should. Are you going to isolate? Yes, I suppose I am. Until we know what the hell we're dealing with. Don't you think?'

Sutherland was thinking about his reply when the principal's door opened. Whitlock looked out, beckoned both men in. Her face was ashen, eyes watery. She led them over to the alcove then faced them. It was clear she'd been crying.

'Are you OK?' began Sutherland.

Whitlock raised a hand. 'Wait, Jim,' she said. 'Wait.' She was summoning her strength, Kit realized. She cleared her throat. 'Aisha just rang. She's looking after her kid, as you know, but in the night she heard an unusual clicking sound . . .'

'Oh God,' said Kit, heart sinking fast.

More tears pooled behind Whitlock's glasses. 'Her son is clicking. And, as of one hour ago, so is she.' She straightened, regained some poise.

'Go home,' she said. 'Walk. Take a cab. Cycle. Avoid Tubes and buses. Just like before. You know the drill.'

CNN was interviewing two of Professor Harris's students. They both click live on TV. The governor of California calls Harris for a briefing.

In Cardiff, the First Minister of Wales was calling headteacher Chris Black. Black advises immediate school closure.

Rose was on the number 253 bus.

Lilly was climbing out of her cab.

9.40 a.m.

Lilly was relieved to be out of the Uber. She'd opened the windows and pulled her scarf over her mouth, but still she was edgy. She'd seen Kit's statement, then followed the reaction. She'd seen reports of at least twenty schools and colleges taking MCS's lead and closing 'as a precaution'. It was a reasonable assumption, she thought, that the majority of other schools would follow suit as soon as they could.

Kit had messaged, *Closing school. Heading home.* Standing on the corner of Baker Street and the Marylebone Road, she messaged him back.

Meet outside Gray's ENT Harley St 5 minutes? Something you need to hear.

She ran across the double zebra crossing, jogged right into Harley Street. The pavement was almost clear of frost but in the shadows, where the sun was yet to reach, smudges still glistened. Watching her step as she weaved her way through the usual throng, she almost ran into the familiarly gaunt figure she had come to see.

Jeremy Casey, senior consultant at the Gray's Ear, Nose and Throat Hospital, was standing, steaming coffee in hand, outside the main entrance. He was white-haired and stooped, wire-rimmed glasses, Crombie coat, black scarf. They shook hands.

'I can give you five minutes, Lilly. We should walk around the block. Stop us catching our death. How is life at your shiny new biotech company? GSL – is that it? Have I got that right?'

116

He was teasing, but she thought he was still impressed. 'It's fine, thank you. You should drop by some time.'

He smiled. 'Of course. One day. When things have calmed down.' A glance at his watch. 'Where's this teacher friend of yours?'

She bristled but let it go. 'He's round the corner, at MCS. You know it?'

Casey nodded. Eyes narrowing. 'Of course. My daughters went there. Back in the day. When it still counted for something.'

'And he's my partner, Jeremy,' Lilly said. 'I should have said. His name is Kit Chaplin.' The white, wiry eyebrows arched.

'Ah. Well. Forgive my poor manners, Lilly. How long will he be, do you think? I really am up against it in there. The whole world wants to talk tinnitus.' Lilly caught sight of Kit running up the road, an easy, loping stride, and closing fast. She raised her hand, and Kit his in reply.

'As do I. As does Kit.' She nodded over Casey's shoulder. 'He's here now.' They watched as he cut over to the pavement, pulled up a few metres shy of them.

'Hi,' he said, breathing hard. Nodded at Lilly and Casey. 'I should keep my distance,' he said. 'We've just closed the school. Unknown infection. Just playing it safe.' He looked between Casey and Lilly. Lilly did the introductions.

'Jeremy Casey. Senior consultant here.' She gestured at the imposing red-brick Edwardian building they were standing in front of. 'Jeremy taught me at UEA and we worked together on biotech at Glaxo. Jeremy, this is Kit Chaplin.'

Casey nodded. 'Pleased to meet you.'

'Likewise,' said Kit. He looked at Lilly with an 'over to you' expression.

'So,' said Lilly. 'I rang Jeremy after hearing the radio reports this morning. He had something to say but he couldn't talk about it at the time. He said to meet here. I thought it would just be me, but school's out, so here you are too.' She turned to Casey. 'You said you have a theory, Jeremy?'

Casey sipped his coffee. 'We are talking, I think, about SOAEs. Spontaneous otoacoustic emissions. They're almost always tones that are emitted from the ear. The clicking is very unusual and is caused by a spasm in the inner ear muscles. But I've never heard it like this before, and never heard so much of it before.'

'But it isn't infectious,' said Kit.

'Definitely not,' said Casey.

'But MCS has six cases,' said Kit. 'And three have gone deaf. So . . .' He spread his arms. 'I'm heading home to isolate with my daughter because there is something seriously terrifying happening. If it's not tinnitus, I'll wait with everyone else to be told what it is. And what to do about it.'

Two women walked past them, greeting Casey as they walked up to the hospital. He raised a hand in reply. Waited for them to disappear inside.

'Have the three who have lost their hearing gone to hospital?' he asked.

'I know one has,' said Kit. 'But that's all I know.'

'OK.' Casey glanced at his watch, then at Kit. 'I should say – if I may – that I was expecting just to be talking to Lilly here. She messaged about you coming along, Mr Chaplin, and I said it wouldn't be a problem.' His eyes narrowed. 'However, sharing a medical opinion beyond academic and professional circles is not usually . . . encouraged.'

'Is that right?' replied Kit. His tone was neutral, but Lilly sensed danger ahead.

'That is right,' said Casey. 'A professional colleague understands context, perspective and emphasis.' Kit folded his arms. 'Civilians,' continued Casey, 'if I may use that term, can often get the wrong end of the stick completely, causing untold problems.'

118

'Well, Mr Casey,' said Kit. 'If *I* may. If you can help me, great. If you can't, you can spare me your patronizing consultant bullshit. Keep it for your patients. I'm sure you're absolutely terrific at your job and, if Lilly rates you, so do I. But my students are going deaf. And I need to find my daughter. So, if you'll excuse me . . . ' Lilly held his arm as Kit made to go past.

'Rose is missing?'

Kit frowned. 'She's just not answering her phone, that's all,' he said. 'I'm sure she's fine.' He sighed. 'But I need to go.' He glanced at Casey. 'I'm sorry. I don't have the capacity for small talk, for hedging, for caveats. If you have something to say, please say it.'

Lilly touched Casey on the arm. 'Two things, Jeremy. One, you can trust him. Two, you did sound like a pompous arse.'

Casey smiled in acknowledgement. 'A weakness of mine. Apologies. Well. My hunch – and that's all it can be without an examination, and blood tests, imaging tests, spinal taps, and so on – is that we will find that what we are dealing with here . . .' He dropped his voice conspiratorially, glanced around, leaned in towards Lilly. 'What we are really dealing with here is a form of meningitis.'

10.25 a.m.

Lilly jumped. 'Really? Meningitis?'

Kit's mouth was open. 'Does that make you go deaf?'

Casey's brow furrowed. 'Hearing loss is sometimes a complication with meningitis, but it never comes first. Never. So this really is just a theory.' He drank the last of his coffee. 'It's an infectious disease of the brain. A swelling of the meninges, the membranes around the brain and spinal cord. There are many strains of meningitis but I haven't come across one that behaves like this before. So, I may be wrong, but it's the closest I can get.' He smiled his consultant's smile. A default setting. 'And now I must go. Forgive me, Lilly. Mr Chaplin, good to meet you.' The slightest of nods.

'One more thing,' said Lilly. 'If it is a strain of meningitis, what might the reproduction number be?'

'That's what I was checking when you called me,' said Casey. 'Last report I could find was in the *American Journal of Epidemiology*. It said that the R number for the usual meningitis strains would be around 1.42.' That smile again. 'But this ain't usual. Anyway. Talk soon.' Casey disappeared through the hospital's glass doors. Lilly and Kit didn't move. The silence was broken by Kit, his throat tight.

'One point four two isn't good, is it?' he said.

'Could be worse. It means it's spreading, for sure. Anything above one . . .'

'I remember,' Kit said, checking his phone. 'Should . . . should I get tested, Lilly?'

'No one will test you if you're not displaying any symptoms,' she said. 'But if Casey is right, then things will move pretty quickly from here.'

Kit put one hand to his forehead. Squeezed his eyes shut. 'Shit,' he said.

They stood frozen for a few seconds, reeling from Casey's theory.

'He could be wrong,' said Lilly. Kit said nothing. 'He could easily be wrong. Walk with me to Bloomsbury?'

'OK,' said Kit, checking his phone again. 'Tell me about meningitis. I used to know a bit about it, and now I don't. Apart from the rash thing. I remember that.' He hooked his arm through hers then pulled away. 'Sorry. I don't know how I should be behaving here,' he said.

Lilly shrugged. 'Let's just walk,' she said.

A metre apart, they walked past chemists', cafés and bars. The two lanes of congealed traffic were of no interest to them. They barely noticed the fog of diesel they were walking through. Hands pushed deep into her coat pockets, Lilly was thinking fast. Playing catch-up again. Meningitis as a diagnosis hadn't occurred to her, precisely because any hearing loss – if it developed at all – came later. She tried to reconcile the jokey, clicking videos with the horrors of bacterial meningitis. She failed. It wasn't making any sense.

'Talk to me,' said Kit.

'Wait a minute,' said Lilly.

'Talk to me,' said Kit, 'or I'll head home.'

'OK,' she said. 'What was the first jab Rose had?'

Kit was wrongfooted. 'What? Oh, I honestly can't remember. Why? Would it have been for meningitis?'

'Probably. At eight weeks, normally. The Hib, it's called. The haemophilus influenzae type b vaccine. It's been a huge success. A triumph for medicine. One of the four major causes of bacterial meningitis in children has become a memory. It was always a real fear for parents and GPs, but it's slipped from our consciousness. You won't be the only one who needs a refresher.'

They reached the Georgian elegance of Portland Place, waited for a gap in the traffic, then crossed by the monolithic Chinese embassy. Lilly glanced back at the two armed policemen who guarded its doors.

'What?' said Kit.

'Just thinking about my contact in Beijing. If indeed she is in Beijing.'

'You think she can help?'

They turned right on to a wide pavement, lined on one side with listed, white-grey limestone buildings and on the other with parked cars.

'Depends what this is,' said Lilly. 'But let's assume that bats weren't involved and that it didn't originate in a wet market in Wuhan. So, there are many different types of meningitis. Viral, bacterial and fungal are the most common, but bacterial is the most deadly. There's a whole range of symptoms, but among them are fever, muscle pain, headache, stiff neck, a dislike of bright light and a rash . . .'

'That's the stuff I remember.'

'Right. But you probably didn't have it on a poster in your bedroom when you were thirteen,' said Lilly.

'Sorry, what?' said Kit. They glanced at each other. He sported a wry smile. 'You had meningitis symptoms *on a poster?*'

Now Lilly smiled. 'Yup. And causes, treatments and complications. With cartoon illustrations to go with it. I was a weird kid.'

'Not movie stars or pop stars?'

'Sure. A few.'

'Like?'

'Can't remember, I'm afraid.'

'But you remember the symptoms, causes and treatments of meningitis?'

'Ingrained,' she said. 'And now rather useful, as it turns out.'

They paused as scores of schoolchildren ran across them, pooling by the edge of the pavement. Year Fives, guessed Kit. Nine- and ten-year-olds. They had turned to see who was joining them, their backs to the cars. Many more pupils came running, a few yelling as they went. There was a panicked urgency to them that Kit recognized.

A warning.

Something wasn't right.

122

10.50 a.m.

'They look proper scared,' muttered Lilly.

'And no staff in sight,' said Kit, walking over. They had blue sweatshirts and black trousers or skirts, pupils of a small prep school. They stood in groups, the girls with arms clasped around each other. Many had hands over their mouths. All of them had turned to face the doors they had just run through. As though they were scared of what was following.

'You guys OK?' asked Kit. 'You got a teacher in charge?' Three turned, one shook her head. A child's scream from inside, and Kit had heard enough. 'I'd better check,' he said to Lilly.

'Go,' she said, waving him inside.

He'd just reached the school entrance when the heavy wooden double doors were flung open, crashing with force against the stone walls. A boy no more than ten flew past Kit, hands over his ears. Black, curly hair, the palest of skin. He screamed as he ran. The other children screamed back.

The boy ran straight through them.

In between two parked cars.

Into the path of a white SUV.

From thirty miles an hour, it stopped in twenty metres. Behind it, a parade of savage braking and desperate swerving. The horrified driver of the SUV leapt out. Looked around, then under his car.

Then vomited.

Kit ran towards the car then pulled up short. He could see the driver, the car and the body. A horror tableau. Blood ran like black motor oil between the rear tyres.

The twenty or so pupils on the pavement scattered. A few went straight back inside, the rest split left and right. Crying, shouting, screaming. A woman with a teacher's lanyard chased north; Kit chased south. He overtook them in a few strides. Stretched his arms wide. Removed the dread from his face.

'OK, whoa there, guys!' he shouted. 'Just hang on.' Eight terrified faces stared at him. Two moved to swerve around his fingertips, but he stretched and reached.

Kit knew that the driver, the car and the body were clearly visible now, just a few metres to his left. Two boys started to look. Kit moved to block their view.

'My name is Kit Chaplin. I'm a teacher at Marylebone College School, over the way. Just stay with me. Look at me, guys! Eyes to me, that's right.' In the road, a sprinting police officer.

Kit glanced up. Lilly was on the phone. A line of onlookers. Three running women, lanyards swinging. Two looked at Kit, one at the crash. He held up his hand. Eyes back to the pupils.

'And here are your teachers now!' He leaned left then right, arms out again. Like a goalkeeper preparing for a penalty. The first of the running teachers arrived, breathless. Mid-thirties, black, hair pinned high. With panicked eyes.

'Thank you, thank you,' she shot at Kit. She and her colleagues enveloped the traumatized children.

'Just passing,' said Kit, relieved to step away.

He walked back to Lilly, heart racing, legs weak. He leaned against a parked car. Shouting, police radio chatter and sirens wailing. Powerful motorbikes arriving fast. Faces at windows. He wanted to cry. Lilly was talking.

'I called 999,' she said, 'but that copper ran from the embassy. He was there almost straight away.'

Kit nodded, closed his eyes. Saw the black-haired boy running again. Saw him disappear under the car.

'Do we need to stay?' said Lilly. 'Make a statement?' She

answered her own question. 'I guess we do.' Kit, eyes closed, felt her hand on his arm. He anticipated her.

'I know it's not my fault,' he said, his voice thick, his throat dry. 'It's not even my school.' He opened his eyes, fixed them on Lilly. 'But he ran *past* everyone, Lil. Ran *through* everyone. No one stopped him.'

A paramedic, an ambulance and two police cars arrived in quick succession. Officers with tape hurried to secure the scene. The last of the children were ushered inside. The doors slammed shut behind them.

11.10 a.m.

Rose was perched on a bollard outside Outpatients reception. Leg bouncing. Agitated. Wired. She checked an address on her phone, looked around her, then entered the building. The fierce lighting matched the heat for intensity. Rose pulled her hood back, undid her coat. The reception area was like a small airport terminal. Bright, functional, designed for passing through. It was lined with grey plastic chairs, all facing a semicircular reception desk. A bored security guard showed no interest in her or anyone else. Blue information boards hung from the ceiling. They signposted accident and emergency, anaesthetics, cardiology, neo-natal, obstetrics, oncology and urology. They directed her left, right, straight on and back outside. She shrugged and approached the desk.

The receptionist's badge said 'Gina'. 'How can I help?' Late forties, rosy-cheeked, bottle-blonde. 'You look lost, love,' said Gina. Londoner, old-school.

Rose stepped forward, pulled out her earbuds. 'I'm looking for a friend of mine.' She glanced left and right. 'And I'm not sure what to do.'

Gina smiled. Flushed-pink lipstick. 'Does this friend work here, or are they a patient?'

'Oh, she's a patient,' said Rose. 'Harriet Teale. She's fourteen. Like me. She's a school friend, you see.'

'Right you are,' said Gina. 'What unit is she in, do you know?' Rose looked at her phone.

'She says ICU. Is that a department?'

The briefest of frowns from behind tortoiseshell glasses. 'That's the Intensive Care Unit, love. You wanting to see her?' Rose nodded. Gina smiled, removed her glasses. 'It's unlikely they'll let you in. That's why it's intensive care, you see. I can ring, if you like. See if anyone answers. They're very busy.'

Rose nodded again. 'Yes, please.'

'Take a seat,' said Gina. 'I'll see what I can do.'

Rose walked back to the plastic chairs. Six rows, a dozen in each. About a third were occupied. She perched on the end of a row, next to a mother with a baby in a sling and a toddler asleep. In front of her, three students were talking in hushed voices, one glancing round to check who the new arrival was. Rose stared back. She glanced right. The security guard was outside, smoking. Glanced left. Lifts to all floors. A large 'London Central Hospital' sign in blue and white, tall plants and flowers on either side.

Rose watched the receptionist make calls, the telephone handset wedged to her ear with a raised shoulder as she used both hands for typing. She checked her own phone, scrolled through WhatsApp and other messages. A nudge from the mother sitting next to her, who pointed at the reception desk.

'I think she wants you,' she said. A brief smile.

Gina was holding her hand aloft. When Rose looked up, the receptionist used it to beckon her over. Rose scrambled back to the desk.

'What did they say? Can I see her?'

Gina shook her head. 'They said no visitors. Like I thought,

126

love. I'm sorry. She's in isolation. What was she admitted for, do you know?'

Rose blinked a couple of times. She spoke to the floor. 'She'd gone deaf, I think,' she said.

Gina's eyebrows rose. 'Oh, I see. One of them. You'd best go home. I know I would. There'll be no visitors allowed in for a while.'

But Rose, eyes fit to burst, had put both hands on the desk. 'Them?' she said. 'You have others? Others like Harriet?'

Gina backtracked. Adjusted her spectacles. 'I couldn't say for sure, love. Just what I've heard, that's all. Why don't you call tomorrow? Save yourself the journey.'

Gina's phone rang. Rose was dismissed.

Sky News was reporting a schoolchild's death in a traffic accident. Jeremy Casey was examining a new patient who wouldn't remove his hands from his ears.
Kit was in a cab, heading home.
Lilly was at her kitchen table.

12.35 p.m.

Lilly had sat without moving for fifteen minutes. Jess was out. The house was silent. A smell of toast lingered. Eventually, she reached for the glass of water in front of her. A small sip. A slight tremble. She took the glass in both hands, rested her arms on the table.

They had stayed until the police had taken their details. She had called an Uber for Kit, then, realizing she wanted to go home too, ordered one for herself. She had offered to return home with him, but he had said no. Most of her was relieved.

She sipped some more water. She didn't think she was in shock, but her hand tremor suggested otherwise. The (presumably) dead child, the conversation with Jeremy Casey and the conversation with Jess over breakfast had unsettled her. She felt raw. Exposed. Like layers had been peeled back. She had fought all her life to avoid feeling vulnerable again, but this accumulation of events had left her feeling, at best, unprotected.

Lilly could see her old meningitis poster now, as clearly as if it were stuck to the fridge in front of her. A3, creamy-yellow, large black-and-red lettering, black-and-white photographs. 'MENINGITIS! KNOW THE SYMPTOMS!' it shouted at the top, with headache, fever, stiff neck, rash, nausea, vomiting, light sensitivity and confusion all picked out in a livid red ink. The four types of infection – bacterial, viral, parasitic and fungal – were in italics. And along the bottom, the warnings, numbered. 1. Get treatment early. 2. Don't confuse it with flu. 3. It can be transferred through coughing, sneezing or kissing. She'd stuck it to a cork noticeboard with drawing pins, one in each corner. It had had a small rip in the bottom corner.

Kit had found it extraordinary that this was the poster she remembered, and now she thought about it, so did she. She knew that other posters came later. That they would have replaced the meningitis one and been more colourful, more glamorous. It was just that she didn't remember them. Maybe she'd kept it as a memento of a time when her father had still visited. A final, desperate souvenir of a family life that had disappeared when she was two. Maybe she'd liked the starkness of it, the lividness of its message and its brutal practicality. Maybe all of the above. She wondered where Jess was. Sent her a text.

When her phone rang, she assumed it would be Jess, but the screen said 'Number withheld'. She killed the call. It rang again. 'Number withheld.' Killed it again. Salesmen. Scammers. Hoaxers. They were the 'number withheld' crowd, and she had learned to ignore them. But when it rang again – 'Number withheld' – she remembered that she had given her details to the police in Great Portland Street. At the scene of the accident. She took the call.

'Dr Slater?' A man's voice.

'Yes. Who is this?'

'My name is James Appleby. I'm a detective sergeant with Wiltshire Police.'

Lilly frowned. Sat up straight. 'I'm sorry,' she said. 'Where?'

'I'm a DS with Wiltshire Police. Based in Salisbury.' Now she got the accent.

'Oh,' said Lilly. 'Sorry, I was expecting . . . someone else. Anyway, how can I help you?'

The DS cleared his throat. 'You are Dr Lillian Slater, daughter of the late Edward Slater?'

'Yes,' said Lilly. 'What of it?'

'Well, I'm sorry to have to tell you that there has been a break-in at his house. Last night, we think.'

She stood up. 'What?'

'Yes, I'm afraid so. It's been ransacked, Dr Slater. Maybe a burglary. We were wondering if you could come down here to assist with our investigation. Tell us if anything has been stolen.'

Lilly's head was spinning. 'Well, I'd have no idea, I'm afraid. I hadn't seen him in decades. I haven't been back to the house either, apart from when you guys took me there. After his body was discovered. Sorry not to be more help. Presumably someone knew it was an empty house. Took advantage.'

The DS ignored her speculation. 'Are you the next of kin?' he asked.

'As far as I know.' Lilly caught the weariness in her own voice.

'Well, we can board up the house temporarily,' said Appleby, 'but you should get it done properly or you'll end up with squatters. And if you're wanting to sell it, you might want to see for yourself what needs to be done, Dr Slater. It's in a bit of a state.'

Lilly paced the kitchen, one hand clasping the phone to her ear, the other tangling her hair into a loose plait. Her father had been an irrelevance to her for so long, yet now he was dead the old bastard was clawing his way back. She heard the front door open and the sound of Jess kicking off her shoes.

'Sorry, DS Appleby,' she said. 'I just can't. I'm sorry.' She hung up. Slumped into a chair.

'Hey,' said Jess, walking to the sink. She filled a glass with water, drank half. 'You OK?' She drank the rest. 'Sorry, dumb question.' Pulled up a chair. 'Did the kid die?'

Lilly nodded.

'Sorry, Mum,' she said. 'You want some tea?'

Lilly shook her head. 'Had some earlier, thanks. And the police just called. Said the house in Salisbury has been broken into. They wanted me to go down.'

'Your dad's place?'

'Yes. They wanted to know if I could help them. I said no.'

'Really?' said Jess. 'Well, it's a crime scene twice over. And in the space of a few weeks. So maybe you can see their point?'

Lilly said nothing. She wasn't sure that she could.

Jess tapped at her phone. 'You could be there in a couple of hours, Mum,' she said. 'Just go. Why not? I'm sure Mr Chaplin will cope without you.'

Lilly nodded. The 'Mr Chaplin' tag had come up many times. Jess had said he had been 'Mr Chaplin' in their house long before he was 'Kit'. Which seemed fair enough. 'So that's the way it is,' said Jess. 'And before you think of some other excuse, I'll go stay with Dad. School's cancelled, so being in Dorking is no big deal.'

Lilly had no desire to return to Salisbury, least of all to her old house. But the policeman on the phone had been right. There *was* a mess to clear up. She had probably been using Jess as an excuse to not go. Now that had been removed by Jess herself.

'Mum,' she said. 'It's the twenty-first century. You can be there and back in no time.' Jess held up the train times on her phone. Lilly didn't need to see them to know Jess was right. 'You can go first class,' said Jess. 'Work all the way.' Her daughter knew her too well. 'I'll call Dad,' she said.

Two miles short of Durham station, a London to Edinburgh train had stopped. The driver had reported hearing loss. The east coast rail line is blocked.

At Abbey Road Studios in north London, all recording was
  halted as two sound engineers are hospitalized. The other staff
  walk out.
Kit was at home, asleep on the sofa.
Rose had walked home, had her key in the door.

4.55 p.m.

The green-and-yellow minicab turned into the dark and neon cul-de-sac. The police car was parked in the drive, underneath the furthest streetlight. Everything was as DS Appleby said it would be. Lilly had found his number on an answerphone message. Told him she'd changed her mind. She'd caught the first train. She had travelled first class. She had worked all the way.

Lilly wanted to get this over with. To work fast. To get home. She didn't mind Jess staying at her father's, but the never-far-away bad-mother guilt trip had kicked in immediately. She was away *again*. It was another clock that was ticking.

She paid the taxi driver, stepped outside. Salisbury in the dark felt warmer than London in the daylight, and she tugged at her scarf, loosening it slightly. Lilly walked slowly, reluctantly, over the familiar tarmac. Clayton Drive had been her home for almost twenty years. In the way that a child remembers, she knew every one of its sixteen buildings, its thirty-two semi-detached homes: 1930s mock Tudor, pale red bricks, bay windows top and bottom. Short drives at the front, large gardens at the back. Lights shone from all of the properties, a few illuminating the original stained-glass panels in the front doors.

One house was dark. Numbers eleven and twelve were at the end of the left side of the drive, before the turning circle. Eleven was lit, twelve was not. Eleven was where the Batley family had lived (together with their dogs and annoying twin boys); twelve was hers. Hers and her mum's. Her dad too, before he left. The three of them for one year, two of them for eighteen years. Appleby got out of his car as she approached. He was older than he'd sounded on the phone. Mid-fifties, stout, cropped white hair under a grey Harris tweed cap. Button top, press stud peak. He tapped it briefly as Lilly approached.

'Good evening, Dr Slater. DS Appleby.' He held up his ID, then folded it away inside a voluminous black coat. Lilly felt a flicker of amusement. Old school. She found herself reassured.

'Good evening,' she said. She offered the keys from her pocket. 'Do we need these?'

The policeman nodded. 'The damage is at the back. We've sealed it as a crime scene so front door would be best. Thank you for coming down. This shouldn't take long.'

Yellow police incident tape stretched across the side path that led to the back of the house, looping from a drainpipe through a patterned breezeblock wall. Lilly peered around the corner. The thin wooden door sported a broken lock but had been pushed shut.

'First point of entry,' said Appleby.

Lilly took a breath, unlocked the house. She smelled the cleaning fluid first, then the musty accumulation she still recognized as her father. She preferred the cleaning fluid. She popped the lights.

The hall was clear, a small table under a tall mirror being the only ornamentation. It was warmer inside. Lilly felt the small radiator. The heating was still on. Three closed doors, two on the left, one at the end. Lounge, dining room and kitchen.

'Maybe the kitchen first,' suggested Appleby, his cap now in his hands.

'Sure.'

He opened the door, turned on the light. She walked past

him. This was the source of the solvent smell. A reminder, should she need it, that this was the place of her father's suicide. Blue tarpaulin and hardboard covered the damaged door where entry had been forced.

'Second point of entry,' he said. The drawers and cupboards below the sink were open, their contents littered on the floor and on the small wooden kitchen table. Rubber gloves, dishwasher detergent, cutlery, wooden spoons, old metal tins labelled 'Nails' and 'Solder'. Nothing remarkable. One wooden chair lay on its side; the others stood in the middle of the room. The larder had been ransacked, almost every tin and jar lying scattered on the floor. A pickle jar had broken, the vinegar smell cutting through the chlorine.

'I'm sorry you had to return here,' said Appleby.

'It's fine,' muttered Lilly. A ludicrous thing to say, she thought. She pushed on.

In the dining room, plates, mats and tablecloths had been pulled out of the sideboard. On the wall, a framed painting of a steam train was askew. Lilly had no recollection of ever eating in here. It was a room she had always been slightly scared of entering. Its only purpose seemed to have been to provide a place for her mother to write letters. And occasionally to drink with a friend. In the lounge, the sofa and easy chairs had been upended. The hundreds of books from the shelves above the fire had been swept to the floor, falling into toppling piles on the carpet.

Lilly looked at Appleby. 'I don't know what you're expecting from me,' she said. 'Or what to say, really. I don't know if there was anything of value here, so who knows if anything is missing? Certainly not me. Is there no one else who can help you?'

Appleby smiled his understanding. 'It's a formality, really, Dr Slater. Did your father have any hobbies? Any collections, as far as you know?'

'None that I recall,' she said. They moved to the hall and she glanced to the front door, its green-and-red glass still endowing the house with a surprising elegance.

Lilly felt suddenly overwhelmed and placed a hand on the wall. Two decades ago, she had stood here, screaming at her father on the doorstep, blaming him for her mother's death. She had called him a cold-hearted, evil fucking monster. She saw no reason to change her opinion. If she'd had the nerve, she would have repeated the charge at his funeral.

Appleby paused behind her, hovering. 'Are you OK, Dr Slater?'

'Not really,' she said, though her voice was level enough. 'This isn't easy, as you can imagine. But let's get it over with. Upstairs?'

The DS nodded.

'You should understand, if you don't already,' Lilly said, hand on the banisters as they climbed, 'that my father took no interest in me. So I, eventually, took no interest in him. That's how it was.' She climbed. 'He left when I was two. My mother died in 2000. That's when he moved back in. He still owned half of it, apparently.' She felt the rage as though it were yesterday.

'And you?' said Appleby.

'I'd moved out. To university,' she said. 'Otherwise, I'd have boarded the place up. Anything to keep the bastard out.'

On the landing, three more closed doors. Bathroom, large bedroom, small bedroom. Or bathroom, what became her father's bedroom and her bedroom.

She stepped into her father's bedroom, heartbeat kicking up a notch. She pressed the light switch. An unmade double bed. Drawn curtains. The churning smell of sweat, musky, stale aftershave and shoe leather revolted her. Her stomach churned. She put her hands over her mouth and nose. Held her breath. Sheets, blankets and pillows had been ripped from the bed and lay in heaps around the room. A bedside table had been toppled, its lamp smashed. Magazines and books covered the floor. There was nothing else. She hurried out.

On the landing, she exhaled.

Just one room left.

5.15 p.m.

Lilly's bedroom door still bore the scars. She could see where she had stuck 'LS' in ceramic letters, only to pull them off two years later. There were pin holes and BluTack stains dotted over most of it. The new additions were a chrome rim-cylinder keyhole just above the handle and two heavy-duty bolt locks, top and bottom.

'That new?' asked Appleby.

'Certainly is,' said Lilly. 'I had a lock on the inside, but nothing like this.'

'Serious locks,' he said. Lilly checked the keyring she'd been given. Two keys, but neither fitted the new keyhole. Surprisingly nervous, she tried the handle. The door swung open.

'Huh,' she said.

Of all the rooms, it was the only one that had changed beyond recognition. Every sign of her had gone. It wasn't even a bedroom any more. Beneath a curtained window a desk sat squarely, an office chair tucked neatly under it. A wooden chest stood to one side, each of its three drawers pulled out and empty. In one corner, a small fridge, also empty. Cheap grey office carpet. Wires for a router ran along the floor, but there was no router at the end of them. And no computer or laptop either.

Redecorated. Recarpeted. Redesigned.

She felt liberated. Not her room, not her house. Her bedroom had been her haven, her sanctuary. With its disappearance, the emotional hold that 12 Clayton Drive had had loosened. Her heart felt lighter.

'So,' she said, turning to Appleby, 'I think we're done here. Presumably, the computer stuff was taken. That's what's missing. I can't tell you if anything else is gone and, in truth, I don't really care. I'll arrange for new doors at the side and in the kitchen. When the legals are complete, I'll clear it out and sell it. Soon as I can.'

Appleby nodded, played with his cap. 'Understood. So.' A brief, apologetic smile. He spoke slowly, as if for his own benefit. 'As far as you know, there's no jewellery, no art or anything of that nature that you were expecting to see, and haven't?'

Lilly was getting tired of this now. 'Correct,' she said. 'He was an under-employed, impoverished supply teacher. He wrote to me once, asking for money. If he'd had anything of value, trust me, he'd have sold it.'

'Might he have kept anything of your mother's?' suggested Appleby. His tone was tentative, as though he knew he was encroaching on sensitive ground. Lilly winced, turned away. Her mother had died more than twenty years ago, but she still grieved. Her father, she knew, hadn't merely accepted her death, he had welcomed it. And had barely pretended otherwise. She had seen him, soon afterwards. Grinning. Strutting. She had felt taunted by his happiness.

'He took everything,' she said. 'But kept nothing.'

The silence in the room lasted many seconds. Appleby, head bowed, spoke first.

'Dr Slater, I'll leave this, if I may. In case anything occurs to you.' He offered his card, and she took it. 'Can I drop you anywhere?' he said. 'I need to get back . . .'

She waved him away, unthinking. 'No, it's fine,' she said. 'Thank you. I have the taxi number.'

When he left, Lilly sat at the desk where her bed had been. She listened to Appleby exit the front door, drive away. She turned his card over in her fingers, placed it on the pine top. Bottom-left-hand corner. Her old table had been where the router should have been, her drawers where the open fridge stood. Her noticeboard, complete with meningitis poster, on the wall behind her. She wheeled herself over the thin carpet tiles, stood up. Her hands ran over the wall. Her fingers found the tiny indentations the drawing pins had left. She saw the warning again.

'Meningitis!' she said aloud. 'Know the symptoms!' She allowed herself a smile. What a strange child I was, she thought.

Clayton Drive was silent. Her room had never been silent. If it wasn't her music, it was the Batley twins next door. Arguing, fighting, shouting through the wall. She remembered that she had welcomed the noise. Sought it out. It came from another world, an alternative way of life that one day, she hoped, would be hers. And she had been right.

She stood to leave. She reached the door. The sound of the blue tarp downstairs suddenly flapping loose made her pause. Then there was the sound of the hardboard giving way. She stepped on to the landing, peered over the railings. She was about to call out Appleby's name but stopped herself. It clearly wasn't the cop this time. But someone was there. She heard steps in the kitchen. Steps in the hall. She saw a darkening at the bottom of the stairs and crept back into her old room. Closed the door as silently as she could manage. The brass sliding bolt was still there.

Footsteps on the stairs.

Her hand tremor was back. She couldn't grasp the knob. The closer her fingers got to the lock, the more they shook. She cursed silently.

Footsteps on the landing.

She pressed her right palm over the lock then steadied it with her left. She pushed, feeling the brass hard against her skin. Using both hands, millimetre by painful millimetre she guided the barrel home.

The bedroom-door handle began to turn.

She stepped away.

Grabbed Appleby's card.

5.34 p.m.

'Miss Slater? Miss Slater?'

The man behind the door knew who she was. The handle turned again.

Lilly's hands could barely hold her phone, let alone press individual keys. The more she concentrated, the more she shook.

'Miss Slater?'

She'd typed six digits.

'Miss Slater? It's Leon Kerridge.'

Something about the absurdity of the situation, combined with her inability to key the next number, made her pause. A moment of silence.

'Leon Kerridge,' said the voice again. A Wiltshire voice, a flat delivery. Comedically matter-of-fact. As though she would, of course, know who he was. The house was silent again. Lilly's heart jackhammered in her chest. She'd never heard the voice, never heard the name. But she decided to speak.

'I'm calling the police.' She mirrored his tone. A simple statement of the facts.

'Why are you doing that?' he said. The man sounded genuinely puzzled.

'Because,' said Lilly, 'you're in my fucking house. That's why.'

'But I'm trying to help,' said the man.

'I'm ringing them now,' she said, hesitating before pressing the final digit in Appleby's number.

'But I'm Hugh Kerridge's son,' said the man. 'I'm trying to find him.' His puzzlement had turned to indignation. Lilly sat on the chair. She typed in the last digit then hovered over the send key.

'OK,' she said. 'You have ten seconds to explain what you're talking about. Then I call the police.'

Silence.

'Starting from now,' she added. Some shuffling from the other side of the door.

'Well,' he said. 'My dad worked with your dad. Back in the day. Now he's disappeared. And what with your dad being dead and everything, I thought I'd ask you.' More silence. 'Oh, and sorry about the mess,' he added.

'That was you?'

'No.'

'But you're apologizing for it.' This was surreal. She felt calmer. He didn't sound like he was about to stave the door in.

'Yes, I'm sorry about it. That's all.'

'Do you know who did it?'

'Yes.'

Lilly shook her head slightly. She'd been slow on the uptake.

'And who did it?'

'The Mackies and the Allens.' A specific answer to a specific question.

'You know them?'

'Yes.'

Lilly was certain this man – perhaps Leon Kerridge, as he said – was on a spectrum somewhere. She phrased the next question differently.

'Do you think you should tell the police about them?'

A pause. 'Maybe.'

His voice was coming from a different direction. Sitting down, maybe. She began to wonder how she was going to get out of this.

'So, Leon, I'd like you to leave now,' she said. 'Walking into someone else's house uninvited is wrong. I have locked the door because I am scared. I am sorry to hear about your father's disappearance, but this isn't the way to discuss it. Please leave by the front door and walk away from the house. Go back to your home.'

She listened at the door. He was standing up again.

'Can I come back tomorrow?' he said. Lilly stared at the floor. What was this madness? Negotiating with someone who had just broken into your father's house – even if the breaking-in bit had actually been the 'Mackies and the Allens' – was ridiculous. Kit would be furious. But Kit wasn't here.

'Ten o'clock tomorrow,' she said. 'And ring the doorbell. And wait for the door to be answered. And please leave by the front door now.'

She heard him go down the steps, a steady, deliberate descent. Almost certainly holding the banisters. The door latch opened and seconds later clicked shut. Lilly unlocked the bedroom bolt, ran into her father's room, peered through the curtains. The man calling himself Leon Kerridge was ambling away from the house. He rolled slightly as he walked. Short puffa jacket, baseball cap, overweight. Middle-aged, certainly, maybe pushing fifty. He didn't look back. Lilly watched him until he was out of sight.

She called a cab.

Radio station Z100 in New York was reporting that its breakfast show hosts had been hospitalized with hearing difficulties.
At Charles de Gaulle airport in Paris, twenty-six flights were cancelled when 'unwell' air crews failed to report for work.
Jess was eating pizza in Dorking.
Rose was watching YouTube.
Kit was being doorstepped.

6.10 p.m.

'You should back off.'

'Excuse me?'

'Two metres. Preferably more.'

'Really?'

'Anyway, I have nothing to say.'

The reporter had told Kit she was from the *Mail*. He hadn't caught her name. White, early thirties, platinum cropped hair. She was still too close.

'The boy's name was Craig Roberson,' she said. 'He was ten. I thought you might want to know.'

Kit stood in the doorway, one hand on each jamb. 'First, please move back. Second, I knew that already. And third, what you actually want is my account of what happened at the school today. So that you can add some prurient detail to your story. True?' He raised his eyebrows, raised his head too. She stared back at him, phone in hand. Kit had no doubt she was recording their conversation. He started to shut the door.

'One other thing, Mr Chaplin,' she said. 'You know that your daughter shut a lot of schools today?' He hesitated, opened the door again.

'I'm sorry?'

'Your daughter. That school strike she ran? It's been copied everywhere.' She accessed the photos on her phone, held up the screen. Even from two metres, Kit could see the images of pupils outside school gates. 'Belfast, Manchester, Truro,

Cardiff, Ipswich and Coventry,' she said. 'That's just a few of them. Impressive work, don't you think?'

Kit shrugged, uncertain what to say. 'I didn't know that,' he managed.

'The signs they're holding up say "No School" and "Not Safe". Exactly what Rose wrote. She's quite the influencer.'

Kit nodded. 'If you say so.'

The reporter tried a smile. 'Is she in? Any chance of speaking to her?'

Kit tried a smile in return. 'None at all,' he said. Shut the door.

'I think you'll be busy tonight,' she called. He turned off the hall lights. Through the frosted glass, he watched the still-illuminated figure of the reporter tap a few words into her phone then walk away. Kit hauled himself back up the stairs to their apartment. It was the reporter buzzing on the front door that had woken him; he still felt woozy from sleep.

He opened his laptop, found the six o'clock news, played it from the start. The child's death was the lead story, followed by the strikes.

'Hey, Rose!' he called. He poured a glass of wine. 'Hey, Rose!' Louder this time.

She opened the door. 'Food?' she said.

'Watch this,' he said. She took the stairs three at a time.

'You were snoring when I came in.'

'I don't snore. Watch this.'

'Dad, you've got thirty-five unopened emails,' she said, pointing at his phone. 'Eleven texts and sixteen missed calls.'

'Later. Watch this.'

She stood at his shoulder. He smelled crisps and tea, of course, but sweat also. Fear, maybe.

'You OK?' he said.

She pointed at the screen. 'I'm watching. Let's see it.'

He played it from the start. Pictures of the school in Portland Place, a school photo of the dead boy, grinning under dishevelled hair. A school statement. Flowers left on the steps. The on-screen reporter didn't speculate about why the boy had run out, but the next item was the school strikes. A few seconds of footage of the MCS entrance was followed by coverage of the walkouts around the country, then two in Denmark, one in Germany. Kit hit pause.

'Did you know about this? About all these other walkouts?'

Rose nodded. 'Sure,' she said. ''Course.' She rewound to the section on MCS, paused it. 'Especially this one.' The freeze-frame showed Rose on the school steps, art-pad pages held aloft. 'But Cardiff was the big one. When that school came out, it spread fast. All went crazy after that. Play the rest.'

The report went back to MCS, showed the clip of Whitlock getting flustered, then a photo of Harriet with a graphic of three silhouetted faces. The caption read, 'Harriet Teale, one of three pupils to "have gone deaf".' An audiologist explained the different types of tinnitus and why it wasn't possible to catch it. A statement from the Department of Education said schools should open tomorrow as normal.

'Well, that's not going to happen,' said Rose.

'You think?'

'I know.'

'Because?'

Rose gave him that look. The multipurpose look of assumed authority she had acquired at the age of five. 'Because we're scared, Dad. I'm scared.' She shuffled away from the laptop. 'You should have been there when Harriet screamed.' She sat on the bottom stair. Kit let the silence run, knew there was more. 'I realized the only screams I've ever heard are fake ones,' she said. 'Or the ones you get in horror movies when you know someone can turn on the lights. And that everything will be OK. But this one . . .' She stared into her hands. 'It went on for ever.'

Still Kit said nothing. He had learned to detect the few moments when his daughter wanted to tell him something. To keep quiet when his instinct was to fill the void with 'fatherly wisdom'.

Rose took a deep breath. 'I didn't know what to say. Then I realized she couldn't hear me anyway. And now it's Marcus and Ellie. And Deacon. And Mariella. And Faith. And . . .'

Now Kit spoke up. 'Wait. Who did you say? After Marcus and Ellie . . .'

'Mariella Keeble and Faith Anderson.'

'Deaf?'

Rose nodded. 'So that's why we're scared. And who knows who else is infected? Maybe *we* are, Dad, maybe *we'll* both go deaf.' Her voice wobbled, eyes filled with tears. 'Have you thought of that?'

Kit scrambled over, sat on the floor, back against the base rail. Side by side. Rose hadn't been a hugger since she was eleven. He held back. Hoped the physical proximity worked somehow, sent the right message of support. The appropriate manifestation of love.

'Yes, I have thought of that,' he said. 'And I'm scared too.' He felt her head on his shoulder. Kit held his breath. Felt his eyes prickling. He didn't move. Then she sat up again, the moment gone.

'Whether the other strikers are scared . . .' Rose said. She shrugged. 'Maybe striking is just more fun than maths. Who knows? But when everyone finds out about what's going on at MCS, everyone's gonna strike.'

The entry phone buzzed. Kit ignored it.

'I reckon you're right,' he said. 'We should probably stay put here for a while, don't you think?'

Another buzz. Rose was answering before he could get up.

'Some reporter from the *Mail*,' she said. 'Says you spoke earlier?'

'We did.'

'Says she wants to talk again. Says she's got more stuff.'

'Hang up, Rose. Tell her no. Enough already.'

Rose listened to the phone.

'She's gone. Or someone's let her in.'

8.45 p.m.

The hotel boasted four stars, which Lilly thought generous. The room was functional, the room service passable. She lay on the 'Junior Queen double bed', a small whisky in a tumbler beside her, Sky News muted in front of her. Jess had sent a video from a Dorking pizza restaurant. Lilly had run the shower hot. Used both shower gels and the shampoo. Her skin still tingled. Now, when she inhaled, she smelled the citrus tang of the soap, not the sour traces of her father.

Her laptop was perched on her knees. The screen showed an image of what looked like two blue balls stuck together. They were surrounded by a complex mesh of spaghetti-like strands. There were no words, no explanation.

It had arrived in an email from Jeremy Casey, subject: 'I'll ring!' That had been half an hour and one whisky ago. She had guessed it was a colourized image, probably from a scanning electron micrograph, of a single meningitis bacterium. A meningococcus. Strictly speaking, a diplococcus. *Diplos* for double, *coccus* for round. Why Casey would send her what appeared to be a stock image, she didn't know. She would wait to be enlightened.

Two hours later, she jumped, startled, from sleep. A moment of orientation, then a scramble to find her buzzing, vibrating phone. Jeremy Casey. She woke up her sleeping laptop, took the call. By the time she had put the phone to her ear, he was already in full flow. No greeting, no pleasantries.

'So, this is just between us, Lilly. I most certainly shouldn't be sharing anything. With anyone. I sent you an image from our team downstairs. It's a meningococcus from the cerebrospinal fluid of one of the kids in isolation. It's bacterial meningitis all right – the white cell count and protein is high, the glucose is low. So much we know.' He took a breath. 'But is this one different, Lilly? If you look at the picture, I'm wondering if the cell surface is enlarged in some way. Stretched, maybe? Might be nothing. Might be my fevered imagination.'

She enlarged the image, stared as closely as her tired eyes permitted. 'First reaction?' she said. 'No obvious changes for me. Would need to look at the gene sequence. Sorry.' She pushed the screen away.

'Yes, that's happening,' said Casey. 'The lab's on it. To be continued. But it's a nasty fucker for sure.'

'And any idea where this "fucker" has come from?'

'Well,' said Casey. 'Here we go. Meningitis has, as you know, multiple causes. This particular bugger is a bacterial cause. Meningococcal bacteria. It has multiple strains, and they can all evolve over time. The meningococcal bacteria reproduce fast and are constantly mutating and swapping genes with each other.'

'Yup, got that.' Lilly thought she'd remind him that he wasn't addressing his students.

'So, the usual process,' he said, not missing a beat, 'is that one of those changes gives a strain an advantage. It might make it more able to survive and reproduce within the host. To *invade* more efficiently.' He somehow gave 'invade' three syllables. 'This is now a new substrain, and it can spread rapidly. You've heard of a clonal expansion?'

'Studied it way back,' said Lilly. Again, *hello*.

'Well, if you're unlucky, that is what happens next. And that is what *has* happened next. It might not have seen the light of day or, as has happened here, its expansion has amplified massively.'

'That's the usual process?'

'It is.'

'Is this the "usual process"?'

Casey paused. Took a breath. 'Don't know yet. Nature can be a bugger like that. I've checked it with our library and I can't find a match. Nothing. I worked on a new strain back in '18. It killed at least twenty thousand in Nigeria and Niger. Bloody awful, it was. But the symptoms were traditional. Totally orthodox. As were the cells. This time, the CSF says it's meningitis, but the symptoms are saying *pay attention*.'

Lilly was fully awake now. She paced the room. 'As I remember, Jeremy, you don't like change,' she said.

'Half right, Lilly. From my *patients*' point of view, I hate change. I want an infection I know and understand. An infection that behaves the way it has always behaved. That way, sick people get better. And with this bacterium, we certainly need to know what we are dealing with. That it'll respond to the antibiotics we're pumping into these poor kids. It should do, but it might not.'

Lilly put him on speaker, walked the phone into the bathroom, wiped a wet flannel over her face. From the minibar she took a mineral water, chugged half of it. Casey didn't notice.

'But professionally?' he said. 'I'm buzzing. Most folk don't give meningitis a thought – it's all sorted. Civilians think this, but health professionals are lazy in this regard too. So, the guard is down. Our eyes are off the ball. Our attention is elsewhere. Even – I have to say it – even your guys, Lilly. When you're all trying to predict which pathogens are going to evolve and how, do any of you think of meningitis?' Lilly knew the answer was no, knew too he wouldn't wait to hear her say it. He thundered on. 'Of course you don't! Vaccines and antibiotics have it licked, yes? Well, we have just discovered that the answer is, categorically, no.'

She stopped pacing. Head clearing. 'So what are you saying, Jeremy?'

Casey harrumphed. 'I'm not saying. I'm merely speculating, Lilly, as you know. But my *speculation* is that it *is* a new strain. But no one is going to say that for quite a while.'

The TV was showing more pictures of school strikes, interviews with audiologists, diagrams of the inner ear.

'Someone will need to say something soon, Jeremy,' she said. 'I assume a statement from the hospital must be imminent.' She could almost hear the shrug.

'Not my call. But you'd imagine so. Anyway, got to go. Please don't share that image just yet – they'll hang me out to dry. Goodnight, Lilly.'

He hung up before she could reply.

Twenty minutes later, she looked up from her laptop, her attention caught by flashing lights from her television screen. A hospital press conference was about to start. She texted Kit.

'Here we go,' she said.

11.05 p.m.

'You watching this?' called Kit. Rose's door was open, an invitation to conversation.

'Yup,' she called.

'Come down,' he suggested.

'I'm in bed,' she replied.

His screen showed a white woman in a blue skirt and jacket and a black man in a white hospital coat with blue scrubs visible underneath. They sat at a desk beneath a large London Central Hospital sign, tall plants either side. Two microphones on stands. They both leaned in, arms on the table. The woman spoke first. Late forties, short, layered blonde bob, shiny skin.

'Good evening, I'm Bella Miller, chief executive here at the LCH, and this is Dr Trevor Obi, clinical director of infectious diseases and part of our team here dealing with the new infections. I have this evening declared a major incident at LCH.'

Kit rested his head on the fingers of his left hand. 'Dear God,' he muttered.

'What does that even mean?' called Rose.

'Wait,' he said.

'As you may know,' said Miller, 'this means an occurrence that presents a serious threat to the health of the community. We are satisfied the conditions have been met. I'll tell you what happens next after Dr Obi has explained the situation.'

'That's what it means,' called Kit. He glanced up the stairs as the volume from Rose's laptop shot up.

On screen, the doctor sipped from a glass of water. Bald, brow-line glasses, tight, nervous smile.

'Good evening. Here at LCH we are currently treating twenty-eight patients, all of them presenting with hearing-related issues. All reported a tinnitus-style clicking noise coming from their ears, and nineteen have lost their hearing altogether.'

'Nineteen?' yelled Rose. She appeared in the bedroom doorway, an old T-shirt of her mother's falling to her knees. 'Nineteen, Dad!' He waved her down to join him. On the screen, Dr Obi was rattling through his account.

'Subsequently,' said Dr Obi, 'twelve are now suffering from headaches and stiff necks. As a result of blood tests and lumbar punctures, we can confirm that we are treating an outbreak of bacterial meningitis.' The doctor took a large breath. 'However, the tinnitus and loss of hearing is not a recognized symptom pattern of this or any other known type of meningitis.'

Next to Kit, Rose was agitated, tugging her hair. 'This is not OK, this is not OK,' she muttered on a loop. Kit reached out a reassuring arm, but she stepped away.

'Also, the pre-symptom infection period,' said Dr Obi, 'appears to be a lot longer than we have seen before. There is much about this situation that gives us cause for concern. Given how long this outbreak has gone undiscovered, we expect there will be many others who develop these symptoms.'

Kit and Rose glanced at each other, then back at the screen. A phone number had appeared in white numbers across the bottom. Kit hit pause, grabbed a pen.

'You gonna call?' asked Rose.

'No,' he said. 'Or maybe yes. I don't know. All of MCS will be tested, I'm sure. I'll talk to Mrs Whitlock first. I'm sure they don't want the whole school turning up at A&E.' Rose played with the neckline of her T-shirt. Stared at the freeze-frame.

'Harriet wants me to go in,' she said. 'She wants to see me.'

'I'm sure she does,' said Kit. 'I'd want to see you too. But she'll have to wait.' He gestured to the screen. 'They won't be allowing visitors, Rose. You heard what they said. And anyway, don't you want to keep away? At least for a while?'

He recognized her expression. The glaring eyes, the clenched jaw. Head tilted upwards. It was a look her mother had given him many times. He used to be defenceless against it but had learned some new moves.

'She can still message you?' he said. Rose nodded. 'Can you tell me what she's saying?'

She pursed her lips. 'No.'

'OK.'

Rose climbed the stairs. Paused by her door. 'But she did say the only thing she can hear is the train in her head. That's it.' She went inside, closed the door.

Kit sighed deeply, pressed play.

The rest of the press conference was about how the hospital was setting up a large-scale clinic, retraining the staff and making the hospital safe. The final words went to Dr Obi, who addressed the camera. Straight down the lens.

'Do not ignore these symptoms,' he said. 'Bacterial meningitis can be fatal. Especially if not treated in time. If you have these symptoms, or think you have been in contact with someone who has them, you must call this number.'

Kit picked up his phone.

Engaged.

He tried again.

Engaged.

He speed-dialled on repeat for twenty minutes, then texted Lilly.

Trying to ring that number.

Me too, she replied.

Not enough lines, he wrote.

No reply.

He messaged Whitlock.

No reply.

'Too late, too late. Go to bed, old man,' he said. He undressed, read some Toni Morrison.

Fell asleep.

When Rose came down the stairs twenty minutes later, he didn't stir.

When she left the flat, he slept on.

*Charles de Gaulle and Heathrow airports announced a
    'temporary' closure.*
*The British Airline Pilots' Association said their members will not
    work 'for the foreseeable future'.*
Lilly was asleep.
Rose was on a night bus.

The day before

1.30 a.m.

ROSE GOT OFF the bus at Goodge Street. She walked fast and purposefully, eyes peering anxiously from under an enormous hood. Her earbuds were in, but silent. A small queue at the twenty-four-hour pizza bar ignored her. The customers at an all-night coffee shop didn't even see her. Hands deep in her pockets, her left clutched her phone, her right the keys. Like she'd been told.

A cloudy night had kept the temperature above freezing, but her short, rapid breaths still turned to billows of steam. A car slowed as it drew alongside. She didn't look up. Walked faster. She looked as though she knew where she was going. The car pulled away.

The ten floors of the London Central Hospital shone from across a tree-lined, iron-railed square. Rose kept close to the railings until she saw the bollards she'd sat on the day before. A row of six, lined up in front of the reception entrance. Lights on, door revolving. It looked busy. She counted six people who ran up to the door, slowed just to navigate the rotation, then disappeared inside. They were followed by a row of men in orange bibs.

Rose crossed the road, perched on the same bollard. Through the steel-edged glass walls and revolving door, she

studied a maelstrom. More rush-hour railway station con-
course than hospital reception. A snaking queue had formed
in front of the reception desk, curving around the seating
and out of sight. Rose slid off the bollard, pressed her face to
the glass. All of the chairs were occupied. Agitated men and
women, most on the edge of their seats, studied the queue
and each other. One security guard stood by the sole receptionist, another by the door in front of her. Both men were
speaking into their radios, then both began filming on their
phones. She waited for the next arrivals, then swung through
the doors behind them.

The temperature jumped by at least twenty degrees. She
unzipped her coat, pulled its hood down, followed the new
arrivals to the back of the fidgety, restless queue. After the
heat, it was the noise that hit her. This wasn't the respectful
buzz of patients waiting for an appointment, more the sound
of angry demonstrators pushing against police lines. Everyone spoke at once. Some were shouting. Conversations
overlapped and competed with each other. Phones and tablets played rolling coverage from the news channels, and
played it loud. A fraught couple with a young baby were trying and failing to stop the child crying, a hungry wail slicing
through the bedlam.

In a brief lull, an overwrought woman near Rose yelled,
'Where are the doctors?' Her cry was taken up everywhere.
Many of the seated stood to shout. A crowd was now pressing up against the reception desk. One of the security guards
stopped filming, waved his arms.

'Everyone in their seat or in the queue!' he bellowed. 'Seat
or queue!' His agitation was infectious. The crowd in front of
him picked it up, shouted back, 'We need tests! We need doctors!' The security man spoke briefly into his lapel radio,
then to the receptionist. He escorted her through a door
behind the desk then returned on his own. Rose saw him

spread his arms in a gesture that seemed to be saying something like *See what you did? Now it's just me.*

The queue stayed put. A few peeled away to nearby chairs,
some sat on the floor, but most stood their ground.

Rose glanced left, right, then spun three-sixty. Behind her,
men in orange bibs were dividing the reception area in two.
They worked at speed – evidence of the approaching deluge
was everywhere. The London Central Hospital sign was just
visible above wooden screens two metres high that had been
wheeled together to form a temporary partition. Through the
gap, visitors were hurried out, and medical staff and orange
bibs were hurried in. The main door spun constantly, new
patients arriving, injecting new drama into the old. The 'where
are the doctors?' chant started again. Two worlds in one hospital: left, right. Two responses to one crisis. One was organized,
running to a plan. The other was chaotic, out of control.

The crowd in front of the reception desk drifted away, sat
down, gave up. The receptionist returned to her post. In front
of Rose, the queue became animated again, those seated
clambering back up from the floor. The line looped forward.
Fifty, maybe sixty, anxious, impatient faces. Necks craned to
spot any progress. The most agitated stepped out of the line
to count those in front. A man tried to let two friends in,
waving them forward from their seats. He was slapped so
hard by the woman behind him that he lost his balance, fell
to the floor. One of his friends helped him up; the other
pushed the woman, hard, both hands to her chest. The
woman screamed. The security man vaulted the reception
desk, hauled her attacker away, frogmarched him to the spinning doors. Then, to cheers and applause, sent him sprawling
to the pavement.

Rose hesitated, then, while everyone's attention was on
the street outside, she walked straight up to the desk. A
diameter against an arc.

'Excuse me.'

'Back of the queue,' said the receptionist, glancing up. Grey hair scraped off her face in a ponytail, thick-rimmed glasses, liver-spotted face. The badge said 'Megan'.

'No exceptions. Weren't you looking just now? You saw what happens if you push in. Back of the queue.' Behind her, the security guard turned nightclub bouncer was back. Then the shouts started.

'Hey! She pushed in!'

'Back of the queue!'

'We've been here hours!'

The guard's eyes dropped to Rose. She glanced at her phone screen, swallowed hard.

'I would like to request an end-of-life visit, please,' she said.

Megan's thin eyebrows rose. She wheeled back slightly in her chair. 'And why would that be?' she said, her tone sceptical.

'My friend Harriet Teale asked me to come. She's dying, you see.'

A softening in the woman's scowl. 'Well, now,' she said. 'What's your name?'

'Rose Chaplin.'

'So, Rose.' More shouted complaints. The receptionist held up her hand. An acknowledgement. She understood. And she was dealing with it. She leaned in.

'End-of-life visits are for next of kin. You know what that means?' Rose nodded. Megan took off her glasses, rubbed her eyes. 'So that'll be her mum or dad, I'd imagine,' she said.

More yelling from the queue. The baby started crying again. The guard was getting twitchy.

'You need to queue, young lady,' he said. 'Just like she told you.'

Megan half smiled. 'Join the queue,' she said, 'and I'll find a doctor for you to talk to. How's that?'

Rose held up her phone. 'Look,' she said. 'She says she's dying. She's one of the nineteen who have gone deaf.' Her eyes glistened. 'Your doctor was talking about it earlier. On the TV. Please help me.' Megan's smile was gone as quickly as it had appeared.

'Like I said. Back of the queue. I'll find a doctor.'

The guard stepped forward and Rose was gone. She ran back, to sarcastic applause and jeers. 'Bloody cheat!' called a woman as she passed. Rose kept her head down, rejoined the queue. Three new arrivals appeared behind her. Clouds of alcohol fumes drifted with them. Two men, early thirties; one woman, slightly younger. All white. They eyed the line in front of them, then one called to a friend who'd found a seat. Middle of the back row.

'Nightmare, Kev! We'll be here all fuckin' night at this rate!'

Rose shrunk in front of them, head down, hands in pockets. Phone, keys.

The seated man called back, 'It's a bloody disgrace is what it is.'

Rose pulled her hood over her head, tugging it low over her eyes. The woman behind her sounded distressed.

'We might as well go home, Neil,' she said. She sounded hoarse, exhausted. 'The man on the phone said to come in, but look . . . No one is going to see me for hours.'

'Sit with Kev,' said another voice.

'But he's pissed,' said the woman.

'We all are, hun,' said the man.

'But he's more pissed,' she said. 'And he's a nasty little shit, so no thanks.'

'Well, you're the sick one. Suit yourself. Christ.'

Many heads in front of Rose turned, then quickly turned back. A tap on Rose's shoulder. She glanced behind her. The man grinned. Unshaven, patchy, rapidly receding blond hair.

161

'How long you been waitin' then?' he said.

'Not long,' she answered. Turned back. Another tap.

'You sick too?' he asked. Rose shook her head. Turned back. A third tap, harder this time.

'Unfriendly bitch, aren't you?' He peered down his nose at her. 'I was just makin' conversation.'

Behind him, the woman looked briefly at Rose then at the man.

'Leave her alone, for Christ's sake, Neil. She's just a kid.'

The second man, who managed to be skinny and have a fat stomach at the same time, squinted at Rose, then the woman.

'So what's she doing out at this time then?' He appeared pleased with his own question, because he asked it again. 'How come you're out at this time, little girl? Eh? And take your headphones out when you talk. That's just rude.' He reached out a hand towards Rose; she stepped away.

'I'm visiting a friend,' she said, eyes to the floor. She turned away. Phone in one hand, keys in the other.

'There. She's visiting a friend,' repeated the woman. 'Now leave her alone.' But skinny/fat man had a new toy. He poked Rose in the ribs with his finger.

'Who's your friend then?'

Rose stepped forward, out of range. He followed, jabbed his finger harder this time. 'Is it your boyfriend?' He extended each syllable, making each sound leery and suggestive. 'Or maybe a girlfriend?'

Rose ignored him. The woman pulled the skinny/fat man back. Ten metres in front of them, the man in the furthest row leaned back in his seat. Called to his friends.

'What a fucking shambles this is!' he yelled. He rocked the chair on to its back legs. 'Tell them you're sick, Helen. You're infectious, aren't you? They should . . .' His seat toppled, sending the man crashing to the floor. He hit the ground hard, his head smacking the floor. A few cheers from somewhere, and he was on his feet. He paced a small, unsteady circle then launched a punch at the man who had been sitting next to him. Caught square on the ear, the man collapsed on to the woman in the adjacent seat, then rolled to the floor.

Everyone seated stood up.

The security man by the door ran to the poleaxed man.

Rose was grabbed from behind.

Hands covered her mouth.

2.05 a.m.

It was the woman. She pulled Rose back, whispered in her ear, 'Unless you really need to see your friend, I'd get out of here,' then pushed Rose gently away. Rose glanced back at her, nodded.

In front of them, a mass brawl had broken out. Skinny/fat man and his grinning mate had run to the defence of their drunken comrade. All three of them were swinging at whoever came close, including a security guard. The queue had melted away to the walls. The mother with the baby had had enough, made for the door. Behind the reception desk, the other security guard was sticking to his post, the horrified receptionist standing just behind him. The yells and screams bounced around the room, the hard, reflecting surfaces amplifying the chaos.

Five men in orange bibs pushed past Rose, closely followed by five more security staff. Directed by the security guard at reception, who was now standing, gesticulating, on the desk, they kettled the fighters in the middle of the room. Everyone else moved to the walls. Five injured sat or lay on the floor, two with blood running from head wounds.

163

Rose edged forward. The large, still-sweeping revolving door was on the other side of the melee. She walked clockwise. It would take her past the reception desk, past the external glass walls with the bollards beyond, then through the door into the night. Some of those closest to the door had already spun out. They had walked a few metres but then hung back, watching from the safety of the streets. Rose glanced left and right, then walked towards them.

A splintering sound and, from inside the kettle, chairs flew. The only weapons to hand proved more than enough to break the loose security cordon, metal legs catching eyes, ears and scalps. Skinny/fat man, his male friends and three others were swinging chairs like hammers, throwing them like javelins.

Rose backed towards the reception desk. There were sirens from outside. An alarm inside. A piercing wail filled the lobby, then the low rumble of descending security shutters. The two sides of the lobby fronted by glass windows were being clad in galvanized steel. Rose sprinted for the revolving door. She was three metres away when its wing doors shuddered in their rotunda wall. The locks had dropped. She hit the push bar anyway, but it didn't yield. The hospital was locked.

She called her father.

2.10 a.m.

One ring and Kit was fully awake. A habit from the depths of his wife's sickness. The only light in the room was the digital clock by his bed and the glowing screen of his phone. He registered the time and the caller name. Heart hammering, adrenaline surging, he answered.

'Rose? What . . . where are you?' He could hear bedlam down the phone. An alarm of some kind, people yelling.

'I'm at the hospital, Dad. You need to get me. I'm sorry.' She was projecting over the noise, but he knew she was scared.

'Why are you at the hospital? Are you sick?' He pulled on yesterday's clothes.

'No, it's . . . it's Harriet, she's bad.' He was fully dressed. 'And they've locked the doors. I can't get out.'

His head was spinning. 'They've locked the hospital?' He put her on speaker, hit the Uber app. His cab would be two minutes. 'Why would they do that?'

'Just some fighting,' she said. 'How long will you be?'

A quick calculation. 'Ten minutes,' he said. 'Stay on the phone, Rose. Stay on the phone. Don't disappear on me.'

'Battery is low, Dad. Call when you're near.'

'Wait, Rose, what's that alarm . . .' His phone went silent. 'Shit.'

Kit grabbed his coat and was on the street as the Uber arrived. 'It's an emergency,' he said to the driver as he jumped in. 'Fast as you can, please.' The driver glanced at him in the mirror, nodded. Kit stared blindly out of the window. How could Rose possibly be at LCH? What could have happened to make her leave the house without telling him? For now, the fear was running more strongly than the anger. But that tide could turn.

He had done the middle-of-the-night emergency run to hospital with Jody more times than he ever wanted to recall. They had been desperate affairs, the last ones in an ambulance. Knowing the end would be soon, but just praying it wouldn't be this particular soon. Holding hands. Forced smiles, fake reassurances.

He caught his wild eyes and unkempt hair in the window's reflection. I must have looked like this for months back then, he thought.

Kit glanced at his phone, willing it to flash a reassuring message. He searched for the hospital on Twitter, but they hadn't posted for weeks. He hashtagged 'LCH' and 'London Central Hospital', found six posts. All in the last hour. He sat up straight, felt his scalp prickle.

Queuing at #LCH for #clicking. Been here hours.

Kicking off at #LCH

Crazy fuckers fighting at #LCH. Avoid!

One post had a photo. Kit enlarged it. An interior shot: knocked-over chairs, a man in an orange bib pointing angrily at something. It showed nothing, but Kit felt the fear surge again.

'How long?' he asked the driver.

'Two minutes.'

'Can you make it one?'

The driver said nothing, but his speed remained a solid thirty. Then twenty. 'This really is an emergency,' Kit said, straining forward. 'I know you're sticking to the rules here, but my daughter is in all kinds of trouble at the moment. Please.' At a red light on Tottenham Court Road, Kit gave up. 'You know what? I'll run from here.' He sprinted from the car, slamming the door. 'Asshole,' he said.

Flashing blue lights filled his vision as soon as he turned the corner. They bled down a side road, reflecting off shop windows. Could be two emergency vehicles, could be twenty. He ran faster.

A right turn into a tight alley and LCH was in partial view. A modern high-rise, white blocks, rows of tinted windows. The ground floor had disappeared behind grey shutters and a row of police cars. He ran to the main road and pulled up, breathing heavily. Looked left and right. Quiet and darkened Regency academic buildings butted against the glare of the hospital. He counted seven vehicles backed up to the entrance, light bars blazing. The alarm had stopped. From inside, he could hear a few raised voices but, with the shutters down, he could see nothing.

Kit called Rose.

She picked up.

He saw her.

2.30 a.m.

'Rose!'

She was running at speed when she answered. Two hundred metres and disappearing fast.

'Dad!'

'Behind you,' he said. 'Across from the entrance.' She spun round, saw him, then glanced back to the revolving door. He saw her hesitate, clearly reluctant to track back. He ran towards her. Three ambulances sped past, driving between them. He crossed the road and she set off again, like a relay runner waiting for the passing of a baton. He caught up; they ran together. Her coat was undone, flapping behind her. Her hood had slipped loose. Sweat ran from her forehead. Eyes wide. Face set. Running scared.

A thousand questions.

'Why are we running?' was the one that came out first.

'Just run,' she said. Agitated, panicky.

'Where to?' he said. 'Run where?'

She pointed straight ahead. The glare of Tottenham Court Road. A double-decker night bus had just pulled up.

'We're catching a bus?' Kit was incredulous. He was about to argue, but for the moment this was her show. Until he knew the story, maybe she was right. Maybe this was precisely where they needed to be. He felt himself steered around the back of the bus to its central double doors.

167

Several passengers were disembarking. Kit and Rose squeezed past them, collapsed into the first seats they came to. Rose by the window, Kit next to her. Both breathless, both fighting hard not to show it.

'I haven't got my Oyster card,' whispered Kit.

'No one pays,' said Rose.

'You know that?' said Kit.

Rose just stared ahead. Another question for another time. The bus pulled away and Rose relaxed a little, shoulders dropping. A long exhale. He glanced around. Twenty or so passengers, none of them interested in the new arrivals. The driver in his enclosed cabin also seemed oblivious to their presence.

He leaned over. 'Who were we running from?'

'Everyone,' said Rose.

'Does that include the police?'

She nodded. Stared forward.

'Are you sick? Or injured?'

She shook her head.

'In trouble?'

She shrugged.

'Talk at home?' he said.

She nodded.

At the stop before the Euston Road he spotted a black taxi with its yellow light on.

'Quickly,' he said. 'Let's go. We can get this.'

3.30 a.m.

Once Rose was showered and in her dressing gown, she wanted to talk. Kit had assumed she'd sleep first but instead she asked for food and tea. He went with the flow. Sat opposite her. She spoke as she ate. She didn't look at him.

168

Rose showed him the message from Harriet, said she knew he wouldn't have let her go to visit and described the scenes at the hospital when she got there.

Kit had vowed to himself not to say anything until she had finished. He kept his promise with difficulty. His supplies of adrenaline long extinguished, fatigue was catching him fast. He ate toast, drank tea and listened, with increasing exasperation at his daughter's reckless stupidity. He also marvelled at her ingenuity, but that bit could wait.

'The police arrived just after I called you,' she said. 'They unfroze the door. About six of them came through. Started tasering everyone. Then one guy starts to freak out. The cops are about to taser him too, but he's like, "I've gone deaf! I've gone deaf!" And he collapses. Everyone backs away. No one wants to be near him.' Rose shovelled some more toast. 'Then this creep of a man, dead thin but with a big belly, is all over me. Pissed, he is. Stinks of it. He says he's trying to hear if I've got the clicks.' Kit feels his skin crawl. 'He puts his head near mine. Then he says, "If I get the clicks from you, I'm gonna cut you. Find where you live. Cut you, and your family." All that.'

Kit couldn't hold back. 'Sweet Jesus, Rose. What were you thinking? No wonder you were scared. But the police were there, you said. Didn't you tell them?'

'Everyone is freaking out,' Rose said. 'Thinking they're infected. Demanding tests and shit. The police are struggling, calling for back-up. They didn't look like they wanted to hear from me about a man being a dick. So when one of them left the doors unlocked, a bunch of us got out.' She swallowed half a mug of tea.

'And the creep?' asked Kit.

'Tried to follow me out, didn't he?' she said. 'Door got bolted just in time.'

'Well, thank God for that.' Kit leaned in. If he didn't say

anything now, he knew he never would. Arms rested on the table, hands together. A measured tone.

'I'm mightily relieved you're home in one piece, Rose, but really . . . what the hell did you think you were doing? Of course I'd have taken you in. If Harriet is that sick. I'm not exactly sure that an end-of-life visit is what it would be in this case—'

'And there you go,' said Rose, looking up. 'Exactly like I said. She's dying, Dad! I'm her friend and she asked me to go. It's what friends do.'

'Yes. Maybe. Sometimes. But you can't just go out in London in the middle of the night!' he said, his voice rising. 'You just can't! Please promise me you won't do it again. Ever.'

Rose stood, tightened her dressing gown around her. Thinking about it.

'I was scared,' said Kit. 'That's the truth of it.' He was as surprised to be saying this as she was at hearing it. She sat down again. A long silence. 'Look. It's just you and me, Rose,' he said. 'I have to be a dad *and* a mum here.' Another pause. 'And your mother was a fierce protector. The fiercest. Of you and me. You might not remember that, but she was. So' – he was running out of words, running out of energy – 'so that's why I'm saying this.'

She stared at him. 'You've got Lilly,' she said.

He shook his head. 'No, I haven't,' he said. 'I haven't "got" Lilly. I've only got you. Who knows what happens with Lilly in the future? And anyway, she looks after herself.'

Rose looked as though she was going to say something, then changed her mind.

'OK, well, goodnight then,' she said. Top of the stairs. 'And thanks, Dad, for coming to get me.'

Kit raised his mug to her. 'Of course,' he said. 'Just . . . don't try it again, OK? It was a one-time-only offer.'

Rose disappeared into her room.

He cleared the dishes, took his laptop to bed. Sky News was running the hospital story at the top of its bulletin, then replaying the school strikes, the infection fears, interviews with audiologists, infectious disease specialists and micro-biologists. Kit found himself too tired to undress but too wired to sleep. And with no school to get up for, he watched on. After forty minutes he realized there was nothing new to see, that even the news anchor and reporters were running out of excitement. He was about to shut the laptop when a blue strip appeared across the bottom of the screen. 'Break-ing news,' it flashed, the rest of the bar left empty. The newsreader leaned in to watch an out-of-vision screen, flan-nelling until he had the promised information.

'Well?' said Kit. Whatever the news was, the man on screen was excited again. Whatever he now knew had been enough to spark him back into life.

'We have some breaking news for you,' he said, staring again at his off-camera screen. 'We are awaiting confirmation on this, but Sky sources are telling us . . .' Again he paused.

'You're doing this on purpose now,' muttered Kit.

'We understand that Cardiff General Hospital has also declared a major incident and that they'll be holding a press conference in the next hour.' Another pause, a glance down. A moment to read. 'And, according to the Reuters news agency, hospitals in Bolton, Manchester, Belfast and Liver-pool are declaring major incidents also.'

The news anchor looked up to the camera, adjusted his glasses, then made a show of checking the time. 'I don't need to tell you,' he said, 'that all these announcements, taken with the news that Cardiff General Hospital is calling a press conference *now*, at ten minutes to five in the morning, is quite extraordinary.' The breaking-news strap now filled with the words 'Cardiff: major incident declared. Others expected soon.'

Kit was wide awake again. Whitlock had mentioned her headteacher friend in Cardiff and the clickers in his school. London school, London hospital. Cardiff school, Cardiff hospital. This was not a coincidence. Now, those other hospitals. More would follow, he was sure of it. Falling like dominoes. He wondered if he could stay awake through another hour of speculation. The same guests, saying the same thing, increasingly torn between the rigours of their science and the need for the drama of rolling news. Another strap rolled out across the screen. 'News alert. Cardiff Hospital press conference imminent.'

Kit went for a refill. He wasn't going to sleep any time soon.

The BBC's political editor was reporting an imminent COBRA meeting. It would be addressed by the chief medical officers for England, Wales and Northern Ireland.
In Edinburgh, the First Minister of Scotland was holding talks with the Scottish chief medical officer. A forty-eight-hour closure of schools in Scotland is announced.
Rose was asleep.
Lilly was waking up.

9.55 a.m.

Another cold day, uniformly grey skies. When Lilly's taxi pulled into Clayton Drive, its headlights still on, the puffa-jacketed, baseball-cap-wearing man was already there. Standing by the low brick wall in front of number twelve. He'd said he was Leon Kerridge, son of Hugh Kerridge, and she would go with that for now. She had searched their names online. Barely a trace of either. She found a Salisbury Hugh Kerridge on his retirement from Currys Electrical in 2009 and someone of the same name in a photo of the local railway social club in 2014. She assumed they were the same person, but the photos were too grainy to be certain. There were Leon Kerridges in Singapore, Boston, Stirling and Perth. None was the man now staring at the taxi.

'Hello again,' she said as she approached the gate.

The man nodded. 'Hello,' he said.

Close up, he was a round man. Round in body, round in the face. Unshaven, unkempt. He stood awkwardly, glancing between her and the ground. Lilly hesitated, a few metres away.

'Leon, is it?' she said.

'Yes, it is, Miss Slater,' he said.

'Lilly is fine,' she said.

'OK, Lilly,' he said.

'You say your dad's missing.'

'He is, yes.' Leon was younger than she had thought yesterday, maybe early forties. Short black hair under the cap, lopsided features. A face that had slipped slightly.

173

'And you want my help.'

'I do.'

'And why me?'

He looked agitated, fidgeting with his jacket zip and cap peak. 'Well, he left without his medicines,' he said. 'That's why.'

Lilly frowned. 'Well, I'm sorry to hear this, Leon. But why are you asking me? What can I do?'

'I cleaned up the house a bit,' he said.

Lilly was startled. 'You did what?'

'I cleaned up the house a bit,' he repeated. 'Even if it was the Mackies and the Allens. I still did it.' She scanned the house from top to bottom.

'You've been back inside?'

'Yes. To tidy up.' She noticed now the stains and bits of plaster on his trousers. 'You know it's a crime scene?' she said. 'That's why the yellow tape is on the side gate.'

Leon shuffled some more. 'It had come down,' he said. 'Would you like a cup of tea?'

Lilly frowned. 'Would I like a tea in my dead father's house? Is that what you're—' Before she had finished the sentence he had disappeared around the side. She checked her phone, hesitated. She messaged Kit.

At the old house. Talk later. She then copied the message to Jess, adding an x. They knew where she was. She followed Leon to the back of the house.

The garden there was cracked slabs and wild grass which ran to a battered, high fence and the overlooking houses of Salt Street. Three of them had windows which looked out on all, or part of, number twelve. She remembered faces behind lace curtains and awkward teenage sunbathing. Maybe the current occupants had heard or seen the break-in. She assumed the police had wondered that too.

The back door, now consisting of the old frame filled out

with nailed-down tarpaulin and plywood, swung open. Leon waved her in. Lilly made a show of holding her phone in one hand, then stepped inside. She felt the few extra degrees of warmth, pulled the door shut behind her. The contents of the larder were still strewn across the floor, sugar crunching under feet, but the table had been wiped, the chairs righted. Two cups sat by a kettle, a teabag in each.

'Tea?' said Leon. 'If you like,' he added.

Lilly stood by the sink, memories of hurried term-time breakfasts and birthday-cake surprises swirling. She saw her mother, suited, smiling, exhausted. Now she understood it was a performance. A reassurance for her daughter, who didn't need to know how bad the finances were or what a total shit her father was. Lilly had guessed both of these things, of course, but had played her part in their little show. Sun shone through thin clouds. Lilly wiped the kitchen top with her sleeve.

'Sure,' she said. 'Let's have tea. Then I'll need to tell the police we're here. And find someone to repair all the damage. Clear it all up. Make it safe.' She filled the kettle. Plugged it in. Leon sat on one of the chairs.

'And find my dad,' he said.

'We can tell the police that as well,' she said, leaning back against the counter. 'But first, explain why you think I can help.'

He sat, arms folded, eyes to the floor. 'You can help because they worked together. They talked a lot. And because your dad might have known where he would go.' He raised his eyes to hers. Hopeful, expectant. The kettle boiled, she poured. Served the mugs. Pulled up a chair. It scraped over splinters and shards.

'But you see, Leon, I hadn't spoken to my father for more than twenty years. I know nothing of his life. Nothing at all. I don't even know he knew your father. You said they worked together?' She fished out her teabag, resting it on an old newspaper. Sipped her tea. 'Didn't your father work for Currys or something? I saw a picture of him in the paper.'

Leon shook his head. 'That was later.'

'Later than what, Leon?'

'Later than Porton Down, Lilly.'

10.25 a.m.

Lilly nearly spat out her tea. She swallowed the scalding fluid with some discomfort. 'Porton Down?' she spluttered. 'The defence place?'

Leon nodded, frowning. 'The Defence Science and Technology Laboratory. Yes.'

She stared at him; he looked away. This wasn't right. Couldn't be right.

'You're saying my father, Ed Slater, worked with your father at Porton Down.'

'His name is Hugh Kerridge,' he said. She nodded. Tried again.

'Ed Slater worked with Hugh Kerridge at Porton Down.'

'He did.'

She sipped without tasting. Either this man was a fantasist or she had some facts to change. All her life, she had known just a few things about Edward Slater. That he was a part-time maths and science supply teacher. That he could never hold down a job. That he was always broke. That he had left her and her mother shortly after she was born. That her mother had divorced him two years later. That he fought her for every penny. That he had spread rumours about her health, suggesting she drank away his money. That the crippling anxiety he had caused led to her

176

fatal stroke when she was just forty-one. And he didn't come to her funeral.

That man didn't work at Porton Down. That man *couldn't* have worked at Porton Down.

She remembered that, after he had left, he would occasionally turn up at Clayton Drive. To begin with, her mother had invited him in, but after a massive row, that had stopped. She remembered presents arriving in the post, sometimes for her birthday, sometimes not. A chemistry kit, a microscope, a book about the periodic table. She wondered if her meningitis poster had been part of this erratic gifting. But if so, why had she kept a poster from someone she hated? Why look at something every day that reminded you of why your mother was miserable?

So maybe Leon Kerridge was a fantasist after all.

'I'm not sure I can believe that,' she said. She sipped some more tea, decided to move on. Leon produced a large, folded brown envelope from inside his jacket. He checked its contents then handed it to her.

'I'll need them back,' he said.

'What are they?' she said, taking the package.

'Photos,' he said. 'Of my dad with your dad. In Porton Down. I'll need them back.'

'Sure,' she said. 'I get the message.' She peered inside. Three standard-size photos fastened with a paper clip. She tipped them into her hand, slid off the clip. Each one showed her father, gaunt and grey, his elbow resting on the shoulder of a thin, red-haired man with a moustache. She gasped, put a hand over her mouth. The men's expressions and positions were only slightly different in each picture. They had obviously been taken at the same time. They looked pleased with themselves, as if celebrating a special event or some good news.

But Lilly felt sick.

'This is your father?' she managed.

'Yes,' said Leon, visibly brighter. 'Hugh Kerridge. Have you seen him?'

Lilly's head spun. She *had* met him, once, briefly.

'Not recently, no,' she said. 'But a few months ago, at my office . . .' It had been an upsetting incident at the time. A man had arrived at the reception of the building where she worked, asked to speak to her. He had refused to give his name and security had been alerted. Lilly had been told that he merely wanted to pass on a message about her father, then he would leave. When she had gone down to see the man, he began by saying that her father was depressed and needed help. She had explained they were estranged and that she wanted nothing to do with him. He had become violent, elbowing the security guard and lunging at Lilly. He had grabbed her sleeve but had been pulled away by the security man, who had received a knee in the groin for his trouble. The assailant had run off. The whole episode had lasted no more than thirty seconds. She had no doubts it had been the man in the photo.

She filtered the story for Leon's benefit. 'This man, who you say is your father, turned up at my place of work, wanting to see me. But he refused to leave a name. He said he wanted to tell me about my father, but I'm afraid he started to shout a bit. There was some pushing and shoving and he was asked to leave. But this was last year – November, I think. I haven't seen him since.'

Leon looked puzzled. 'My father was in London?'

'Yes,' said Lilly. 'At my work.' While Leon digested that, she looked back at the photo of her father. She hadn't seen a photo of him for many years. There had been no image of him on the funeral service sheet or at the crematorium. She had kept no pictures at home. And yet here he was, smiling as if he'd won the lottery. The background appeared to be yellow-and-white doors with circular, porthole-style windows. She handed the photos back.

'There you go,' she said.

Leon looked puzzled. 'Oh?'

'You wanted them back.'

'You don't want one?'

'No.' She realized she was being offhand, could see he was deflated. She sighed.

'Look, Leon. It's certainly a picture of our fathers. But they could be anywhere.' She indicated the two-tone doors. 'That could be a toilet at Paddington Station, for all I know. They certainly don't prove they worked at Porton Down.'

He offered one of the photos back to her. 'They're the level-three laboratories,' he said. 'That's what the yellow means.'

Lilly couldn't help herself. 'And what is level three?'

He shrugged. 'It's where they test things.'

'Really?' said Lilly, unable to keep the sarcasm at bay. 'They test things. I see.' She waved the photo away. He flipped it over, held it up again. In black marker pen, the letters 'PD', followed by '2004'.

'See?' he said.

Her turn to shrug. 'Again, Leon, it proves nothing, I'm afraid. What can I say?' She finished her tea. 'I'm sorry your dad is missing. I hope he gets his meds. Please tell the police. I'll tell them he travelled to London last year. But apart from that, I can't help.' She stood up. 'And we should go now.'

He didn't move. 'They were sacked,' he said. 'Just after this photo was taken.' Every time Lilly thought she had an exit out of the conversation, he pulled her back. She felt herself being dragged in again.

'Sacked?' she said. 'Do you know why?'

Leon gathered up the photos, slid them back into the envelope. Brushed down his jacket and trousers. Drank his tea in three gulps. 'Something went wrong,' he said.

12.45 p.m.

After getting the all-clear from DS Appleby, Lilly found a firm to repair the damage to her father's house. They had told her it would be completed in forty-eight hours. Back in her hotel, her one bag was packed, her train ticket placed alongside her key pass on a small coffee table. There was a taxi rank outside. Her train would leave in an hour. She could go home.

But she was staying.

It was only as she zipped up her suitcase that she realized how annoyed she was. Leon Kerridge's photos, together with his wild suggestion that their fathers had both been sacked from Porton Down because 'something went wrong', needed examination. It wasn't the dismissal that surprised her but the fact that he'd worked anywhere near an internationally respected government science facility. It suggested that her assessment of her father as a loser, as merely a venomous, vindictive and bitter old man, might need some re-evaluation. But following the evidence was what she did. If it was awkward, if it made her feel uncomfortable, then so be it. And this had the potential to make her feel very uncomfortable indeed.

She had spoken to Jess, who said she was fine at her father's. They had apparently got a take-out for breakfast and ordered some clothes online. She was annoyed with the lazy parenting but figured she was hardly in a position to complain. Jess had sounded thrilled, so it was a problem for another day. Lilly had bought herself time. She booked the room for another night.

At the hotel's taxi rank, another of the green-and-yellow minicabs waited for custom. She clambered inside. The car's heater was set to maximum. A greenhouse on wheels. The contrast in temperatures made her eyes water. The driver glanced at her in his mirror.

'The crematorium, please,' said Lilly, plugging in her seatbelt. And before I'm incinerated myself, she thought, cracking her window open an inch.

'Right you are,' he said.

They swung into traffic. Lilly closed her eyes. With extreme reluctance, she tried to remember the faces at her father's committal. There had been her, the priest and two others, both men. One white, one black. They had sat separately. They were both sixty-plus. That was it. As far as she remembered, they hadn't spoken to each other. And they certainly hadn't tried to speak to her.

She opened her eyes, wound her steamed-up window down further. The taxi slowed, turned on to a twisty, narrow road running through landscaped gardens. Kerb-side daffodils and snowdrops provided the only colour.

The driver glanced at Lilly. 'Garden of remembrance, or main building?'

'Main building, please,' she said. 'And might you be able to wait for me? I shouldn't be too long. Just need to check something.' He nodded. Looked as though he might chance a conversation, then thought better of it.

They approached a network of buildings that reminded Lilly of every 1960s state school she had ever seen. Functional, sterile, inoffensive. A place with work to do. Somewhere no one wanted to stay long. A small convoy of black cars was parked up in front of them, and her driver detoured into the car park.

'OK here?'

'Perfect, thank you,' she said.

She waited for the mourners ahead of her to go inside, then walked to the main building. Two storeys of glass and concrete, a reception area leading to the chapel on the left and a waiting room on the right. The last time she had been here, her father's coffin had been here too, and some of that day's oppressive, leaden feeling returned to her stomach. She smelled flowers and soap. A woman behind the reception desk smiled.

'You can go in,' she said, indicating the chapel doors. 'They haven't started yet.' Lilly smiled back. 'Oh no, it's not that I came for,' she said. 'I wanted to see the book of condolences for Edward Slater. He was my father. It was three days ago.' The woman kept on smiling. Maybe working with death all the time forced you to be like that.

'One minute,' she said, and disappeared into a small office behind. Lilly heard some drawers opening and closing, then she appeared with a thin black leather-bound book. In a plastic window on the front, an oblong of paper with her father's name typed on it.

'There you are,' said the smiling woman. 'Please, take a seat. Read it at your leisure.'

Lilly walked away, opening the book as she went. There was, as she had guessed, just the one page to read. She perched on a wooden chair, the book open on her lap. Underneath her father's name and dates, two signatures. No messages. No condolences, no prayers, no rest-in-peaces, just two names.

Mark Goddard. Trevor Littlewood.

She flicked through the other pages. All blank. She took a photo of the page, handed the book back. The smiling woman smiled her thanks.

'That was quick!'

'Well, there weren't many condolences, to be honest,' Lilly said. 'But I got what I came for. Thank you.' The opening strains of Frank Sinatra's 'My Way' played in the chapel. She walked swiftly to the doors, suddenly anxious to leave.

The sharp air took her breath and she relished the moment. Outside, it was raw and bitter, but it was silent. It didn't smell of anything. She was on her own. She felt the familiar sensation of freedom she had when leaving a party.

Thank Christ that's over.

She walked a lap of the car park, ignoring the looks from her taxi driver. She was in no hurry to return to his furnace, even if the meter was running. She could walk through the gardens, but they felt fake and theatrical. She'd take the measured concrete this time. She looked at the two names on her phone. She had no idea whether Mark Goddard and Trevor Littlewood could be found or if they would want to speak to her. But they must have known Ed Slater well enough to feel they should attend his funeral, so they knew more than she did. They had sat apart so, presumably, they didn't know one another. They hadn't tried to speak to her, which was odd. Rude, even. Passing on condolences was what you did. At a funeral, it was one of the few things *you were supposed to do.*

She remembered them glancing at her when the priest acknowledged her presence. She stopped walking. Perhaps it had been the first they'd heard of Ed Slater's having a daughter. She wouldn't put it past him.

Lilly walked across to the taxi, now chilled to the bone. She had hurried away at the end of the funeral service, so even if Goddard or Littlewood had wanted to speak to her, it would have been obvious that she didn't want to speak to them. Well, that had changed. She would find the two men, then go home.

The prime minister was saying there were no plans to close schools in England.
The New Zealand prime minister said she was considering closing the country's borders.
Kit was in his kitchen, preparing a fry-up.
Rose was in her bedroom, online.

1.38 p.m.

Cross-legged on the floor, Rose leaned in to her keyboard. Out of bed for barely ten minutes, she was still wearing the pyjamas and dressing gown she'd slept in. Her curtains were drawn, her bedside light was on. It illuminated a floor covered in books, collections of make-up and piles of discarded clothes. Some washed, some not. Three mugs with dried-out teabags were lined up by the door. Some brassy R&B played from a small speaker on her bed. The smell of bacon drifted up from the kitchen.

Her screen was on a YouTube selection of videos posted overnight, paused at the LCH riot report. Phone-shot film footage showed police and ambulance crews ushering the injured, upset and annoyed from the entrance. The time code in the corner of the screen indicated that it had been taken shortly after she and her father had caught the bus out of there.

She checked her phone again. Nothing new from Harriet, fifty-seven messages on WhatsApp, and it looked like many hundreds on Discord. As she watched, twelve more appeared. She skimmed through them. They all were from school strikers, some with images and video of placards and chanting. Most were from the UK and Europe, but she noticed a run of ten from California. Three different high schools and a university, each with their own sit-down protest. Via text, she had approaches for interviews from CNN, MSNBC, Fox, ITN and Sky as well as three from various BBC outlets. Then came the *Mail*, *The Times* and the *Sun*.

Her WhatsApp messages were all from MCS students, each one agonizing over the condition of friends. Marcus, Ellie, Deacon, Mariella and Faith had all followed Harriet into hospital and the ripples were spreading throughout the school.

A new image dropped on to her screen. The headline read, 'Is this school strike leader Rose?' The photo showed Rose in the reception of the hospital, crouched in the middle of a fight, one hand on the floor and glancing left at a man swinging a chair. He was skinny with a fat stomach.

She clicked the link. The *Mail Online*. She read the first paragraph.

> *Rose Chaplin, 14, the girl who started the school strikes which have swept the country, appeared to be involved in a riot at one of London's top hospitals last night.*

'Shit,' she said.

1.45 p.m.

The frying pan spat oil at his laptop, but Kit kept reading. He flipped the bacon, eyes not leaving the screen. The NHS website was clear. The meningitis vaccine MenACWY is a single-dose injection protecting against four strains of meningococcal bacteria – A, C, W and Y – and is offered in schools to Years Nine and Ten.

'You haven't had the meningitis vaccine,' he said, hearing Rose's arrival rather than seeing it. 'And you need to have it.'

'OK,' she said. 'Why haven't I had it?'

'First week of summer term is when MCS does it,' he said.

185

'Letters go out at the end of this term. I rang the GP surgery, but they're not answering. Answerphone message said they had some vaccine.' He hoisted the bacon on to two plates of toast, eggs and beans. 'We'll be grand company too, with all this inside us.'

'We?' said Rose. He looked up at her. Smiled at her dishevelled hair, her bleary gaze. 'I'll drive you. Plus,' he said, 'there are reporters outside. They've been ringing the doorbell all morning.'

'Oh. Hadn't heard.'

'I unplugged it. It was driving me crazy.' He placed both plates on the table. She sat opposite him, showed him her phone. Kit glanced at the screen, saw the photo. 'I saw it an hour ago. Everyone is sending it to me.'

'What have you said?'

'Nothing. To anyone. But it's clearly you.' He was trying not to sound angry.

'The guy with the chair,' she said. 'In the photo. He's the one who threatened me.'

Kit put down his knife and fork. 'Of course he is,' he muttered. He put his head in his hands. 'Jesus, what a mess.' He looked at Rose. 'And now he knows who you are!'

'I'm sorry, Dad.'

'I know, I know.'

'And I'm scared.'

'I know that too.'

Rose ate her food without speaking, then cleared both plates and washed them up. She really is scared, thought Kit.

'Also, everyone wants to interview me,' she said, hands in the sink. 'All these TV companies.'

'They're coming straight to you?' said Kit, appalled. Rose nodded. 'Well, they need parental permission and they know it. Outrageous.'

'But I don't want to talk to any of them anyway,' said Rose.

'So no one will be asking you.' She came back to the table with two cups of tea, put one in front of Kit. An unmistakable peace offering. He couldn't remember the last time she had done that.

'How many reporters outside?' she said.

'No idea. Maybe they've gone, but I doubt it.'

'What do they want?'

'A photo of you and me, I imagine. And some answers about last night, probably.'

'I'll just say it wasn't me,' said Rose. 'They can't prove it.'

Kit thought about that. He hadn't thought of just lying. But why not? He didn't have a better idea.

'OK,' he said, 'let's try that. But we do need that vaccine. Even more than we need to avoid the reporters.'

Heavy steps on the landing outside their front door. Two voices, indecipherable.

Rose sat up, eyes wide, glanced at the door.

'Dad?' she said, just before loud knocking made them both jump. 'Dad!'

Kit, face like thunder, leapt for the door. Opened his mouth, then closed it again. Waited.

More knocking. He peered through the fish-eye. The swollen, distorted image of a young white man with a black beard filled the lens.

'Mr Chaplin. It's Rory Maguire from the *Mirror*. Can we ask you a few questions?' Kit turned to Rose, mimed zipping his mouth shut. Then wrote on a pad. Held it up.

SAY NOTHING.

Rose nodded, walked over, took the pad.

HOW DID THEY GET IN?

Kit shrugged theatrically. A small white card appeared under the door.

'Mr Chaplin, that's my card,' boomed the voice from the landing. 'You can check with my newsroom if you need to – the number's on it. We're writing a piece about the new deafness. Just wanted a few words, if we may?'

LEAVE THE CARD, scribbled Kit. Rose gave a thumbs-up. The reporter tried again.

'Do you know they've started calling the school strikes the "Rose Revolts", after your daughter? My son just called me. Said there's a "Rose Revolt" at his school. Wondered if you might want to comment?'

Kit raised his eyebrows, mimed applause. More footsteps, more knocking.

'Mr Chaplin.' A woman's voice this time. 'I'm the reporter from the *Mail*. I spoke to you yesterday. Can you confirm that it is your daughter in the hospital riot photo?'

On his side of the door, Kit gave her the finger. Rose followed suit. He wrote on the pad.

THEY'RE TRESPASSING.

SO CALL THE POLICE.

Kit reached for his phone. The *Mail* reporter made one more attempt.

'And did you know that Harriet Teale, your daughter's friend, has taken a turn for the worse? Death's door, they told me.'

Rose's face crumpled. Kit wrote fast. LYING. She stared at the word, wiped tears from her cheeks. He tore off a new page. SHE'S PROVOKING US.

Rose turned, ran for her room.

Rose was writing a text to Harriet.
Lilly was getting a taxi to Mark Goddard's house.
Kit was calling the police.

2.40 p.m.

The only place Kit could view the small front garden belonging to the block of flats was from the landing window just outside his door. The space that had been, until a few minutes ago, occupied by the press pack. They had started to drift away when he put Nina Simone records on at high volume so, as the police arrived, most of them were outside anyway. When the fish-eye showed the all-clear, he stole a glance down to the street. He saw the police patrol car, saw the reporters turn to watch. He counted six, one with a camcorder in his hand.

He ducked back inside, ran to Rose's room. Two quick-fire knocks. He didn't wait for a response. He called through the door.

'Rose. If we go now, like, this second, the police are there. The reporters are distracted. We can get to our car, and get to that vaccine. But it has to be now.'

Her door opened.

'Actually, yes,' she said. She grabbed her phone and her bucket hat.

'Different hat?' he said.

She nodded. From a drawer she found an old NYC baseball cap of her mother's.

He smiled. 'Amazing.' If he hadn't been about to escape from his own home, trying to evade reporters to get a vaccine for his daughter, he might have allowed himself the indulgence of reminiscence. But Rose was already jumping the stairs, and he knew they had only seconds.

189

From their second-floor flat, it was twelve steps, a pivot, then twelve more to the first. Twelve, pivot and twelve to the lobby. Rose took three at a time, Kit stuck with two. The elaborate Victorian front door – stained glass with twisted wrought-iron decoration – was a few metres to the left. They turned right. An unlit corridor led to a plain back door. Kit's key took them to the communal courtyard – flagstone paving, a high common-box hedge that ran roadside and an ancient brick wall that right-angled its way around the rest. They paused, breathing steam, as Kit relocked the door. Although sunset was a good ninety minutes away, the afternoon was fading already, heavy low cloud drawing curtains on the day. What sounded like a spirited exchange of views between police and press drifted around the block. A door slam. Maybe they were done already.

'Where's the car?' hissed Rose.

'Other side of the hedge. Behind that van.' Kit pointed to the middle of the hedge, their cornflower-blue Fiesta just visible through the foliage. The hedge was too thick to climb through, but at the top end, where it met the wall, it was falling away and possible to squeeze through. 'If they see us, we say nothing. With the police there, they won't dare stop us leaving. Ready?'

Rose nodded. Kit ran at a crouch, Rose at his heels. Head down, he powered through the gap in the hedge, the sharpness of its branches clawing at his neck. He glanced left. Another door slam. Time to go.

Ten metres to the car. At five he pressed the key fob to unlock the doors. At three the police drove away. At two, the man from the *Mirror* walked round the corner.

2.45 p.m.

'They're here!' yelled the reporter.

Kit and Rose dived into the car at the same time, hit the central locking at the same time. Kit rammed the ignition key home. He knew the car hadn't been driven for at least a week. He could see the remains of the overnight ice still clinging to the corners of the windscreen. The Fiesta was filthy, ten years old, and he hated every clapped-out, under-powered inch of it.

But it started first time.

The man from the *Mirror* and the woman from the *Mail* appeared on either side of the car. They were both shouting questions, tugging at the handles. Kit reversed away from the van, jerking the car free. As he braked, the reporter with the camcorder shoved the lens against Rose's window. She slid low. Kit slammed the gears to first. He roared twenty metres to the top of the road, then slipped into second as he turned into the main road.

'Are they following?' he said.

'You burnt actual rubber, Dad,' said Rose, grinning. 'I've never seen that before. Ever.' An empty Coke bottle rolled against her feet. She threw it on the back seat.

'Me neither,' he said, eyes darting between the road and his mirrors. 'But are they following?'

Rose spun in her seat. 'There are two cars coming out of our road now,' she said. 'So, maybe? Who knows? How long till the surgery closes?'

He shrugged. 'Don't know. At four, maybe? Something like that. I'll drop you off and park up.'

'And, so you know, your old coat and my hockey stick are on the back seat. And two bottles of water. And some cough sweets.'

'I know, I know,' he said. 'The car's a tip. But at least it's still going. I did wonder for a moment . . .'

Kit could feel his heart hammering, his pulse racing. His skin tingled. He felt alert, hyper-vigilant. If he had to do an emergency stop, he felt as if his reaction time would be zero. He drove round a few blocks, turning left and right at random, fighting the urge to do it all at sixty miles an hour.

'Enough already,' he said. He swerved into a parking space, their seatbelts locking as he braked sharply. He took a deep breath. 'What kind of cars came after us?'

Rose shrugged. 'No idea. Both black, if that helps.'

'Not really. But let's assume they're gone. We'll get the vaccine and hope they're not there when we get back.'

He eased the Fiesta back into the road. If the reporters were still outside, he reckoned they would just have to do some sort of deal. Was that how it worked? Give them a quote and they go away? He glanced at Rose, seat almost flat, cap pulled low. Unbidden, the memory of their first drive back from hospital came to him. Newly strapped-in car seat, a swaddled baby Rose, thin woollen hat pulled low. And an exhausted, terrified Jody in the back, demanding he drive more slowly.

'Unhelpful,' he muttered.

'What is?'

'Oh, nothing. You ready to jump out? We're nearly there.' She eased the seat upright as they turned into Arkwright Road. High-rise sixties council blocks on either side, a shiny new-build school on the right and an old single-storey doctors' surgery opposite. And from it, a queue that stretched out of sight. He pulled over again. Put on the hazard lights.

Rose sat up, pulled the seat up behind her. 'You have got to be kidding.'

'No wonder they didn't answer the phone.'

Arkwright Road was on a gentle incline, the surgery at the higher end. From where Kit had stopped, he could see the line snaking out of the reception and down the hill. He guessed around two hundred, maybe more, all wrapped up against the gathering gloom.

'Did all these people really not get the Hib?' said Rose. 'They all need it?'

'Or think they do,' said Kit. 'Not quite the same.'

Children, students, families. All wanting what he wanted but with the foresight to have got there earlier. On closer inspection, it wasn't a continuous line – many were leaving considerable gaps between themselves and the strangers in front. Social distancing was back.

Kit parked in the school car park under a sign that said 'No parking. Clampers in operation.' He wrote a note saying, 'Visiting teacher'. 'Needs must,' he said to Rose.

'Fine with me. But I thought you were going to drop me off?'

'That suddenly doesn't seem such a good idea,' he said. 'And we need that jab. Come on.'

They walked towards the end of the queue, into the car-lined road then on to the crowded pavement. Kit looked for a friendly face, a cheerful nod maybe, from someone who might let them in, but quickly realized that wasn't going to happen. Not only did he not see anyone he knew but the mood was clearly fractious. There were frustrated calls to 'get on with it' and 'hurry the fuck up'. Ahead of them, two men in red-and-white beanie hats were shoved into the road when someone accused them of pushing in. Initially they squared up to their accusers, then clearly had second thoughts. They jogged up the hill.

'I don't like this very much,' said Rose.

'It's certainly not like the Pfizer queue, that's for sure,' said Kit.

When they reached the end of the line, Kit glanced at his watch. 'This is going to take for ever.' He sighed. 'Not that we have much choice.'

The woman in front of him turned. She was frowning. 'You're too close,' she said, eyes darting between him and Rose. 'Don't you watch the bloody news?' Kit was lining up a sharp response. He felt a tug at his elbow.

'Don't say anything,' said Rose, pulling him back a few paces. 'You'll just make it worse.'

He contented himself with glowering at the back of the woman's neck. She shuffled forward a few steps, then glanced behind to see where Kit was.

'We could play Grandmother's Footsteps, if you like,' he said. 'It would pass the time, anyway. Promise we won't cheat.' He smiled. The woman said nothing.

'Shut up, Dad,' hissed Rose. 'You're embarrassing.'

Sleety rain started to fall, gently at first, then with more vigour. A few in the queue peeled away. People shuffled to close the gaps. Kit peered up the hill, then glanced left to where his car was parked. There was movement behind the vehicles. Kit took Rose's arm.

'Trouble,' he said.

She followed his gaze. The men in beanie hats were back, now clearly armed with sticks. Clubs of some kind, or baseball bats. They shouted as they crossed the road, jackets undone, bouncing on their feet. They pointed their weapons at a point in the queue twenty metres up from Kit.

'That's a hockey stick,' said Kit.

'That's *my* hockey stick,' said Rose. She was right. The green-and-blue stripe was clearly visible. Kit's stomach sank.

'They must have broken into the car. Bastards!' Kit was already calculating the cost of replacement when the beanie-hat men charged.

'That's the fucker!' called one, and ran at the queue, his impromptu lance held in front of him. The line split in two. Those nearest Kit and Rose ran downhill and past them. The rest ran uphill, past the surgery. Shouts from everywhere. Kit pulled Rose between two cars. Crouched low. He held tightly to her coat. Raised his head until he could see over the roof of the car in front. He saw the beanie-hat men clatter one man with the hockey stick and catch another with a punch to the head. Both victims scrambled away.

'Should we help?' whispered Rose as one of the victims staggered past them, holding his head. A siren spared Kit answering, blue flashing lights appearing at speed at the top of Arkwright. The police car crunched to a stop outside the surgery. Two officers jumped out, pulling on their caps. Looked north and south. Up and down. The queue of two hundred had melted away, but Kit could see groups gathering again in sixes and sevens further down the road. In gardens, behind walls.

'Come on, Rose,' he said, stepping back on to the pavement. 'Let's get lucky for once.' He glanced at Rose, then at the path to the surgery. 'The queue is gone,' he said, 'but everyone will be back soon. While the police are here, we should try.'

Kit set off, Rose allowed herself to be pulled along. She glanced over her shoulder, noticed the clumps of reassembling queuers.

'I think they're all watching us, Dad,' she said.

'Well, we'd better be quick then,' he said.

3.10 p.m.

When Mark Goddard answered his door to her Lilly realized she hadn't thought through what she wanted to say. She floundered.

'Oh, er, hi,' she said. 'Hello. Is it . . . is it Mr Goddard?' She knew it was, recognized him from the crematorium, but the reticence seemed appropriate. He was black, just under six feet tall, white hair cut close to his scalp. Almost a buzzcut. It gave him a military look and Lilly found herself standing straighter. Bright hall lights shone behind him.

'That all depends . . .' he began, then stopped abruptly. Frowned. 'Wait,' he said. 'You're Ed Slater's daughter. I saw you at the funeral.'

'That's me,' she said, managing a smile. 'I'm sorry to drop by unannounced.'

'How did you . . .' he began.

'The electoral register,' she said. 'And online directory enquiries. It didn't take long.'

'I see,' he said.

'I was, well, I was wondering if I could ask you a couple of questions? About my father?'

He stared back at her through round-lensed tortoiseshell glasses. She felt appraised, assessed. Weighed in the balance.

'What sort of questions?' he said. It wasn't a refusal as such, she thought, but it certainly wasn't a welcome. Lilly tightened her coat, adjusted her scarf.

'Well, how about why did you go?' she said. 'To the funeral. I didn't really get to talk to anyone . . .' Her question faded away. She knew she'd been the first to leave. Goddard hadn't moved since he'd opened the door and didn't look like he was moving any time soon. Thinking about his reply.

'He was a colleague,' he said. She guessed private-school-induced RP. A rich baritone. Almost actorly. She waited for more. Nothing came.

'At Porton Down?' Goddard nodded. 'Did you work together? Was he a friend?' she tried.

'He was a colleague,' he repeated, his tone expressionless. Almost robotic. As if he could keep this up all day.

'And the other man there?' she said. 'Trevor Littlewood.'

'What about him?'

196

Lilly felt a flash of irritation. Tried to disguise it. Tried a smile.

'Was he a colleague too? Maybe I should talk to him?' She could have predicted his reply.

'They were both colleagues,' he said. Lilly stared at the ground, suddenly very tired. She wondered quite how much energy she had to pursue this.

'Of course,' she said. 'Well, thank you for your time. I'm sorry to have troubled you. One more thing. Was my father sacked?' She looked for any reaction from Goddard. 'Maybe along with a man called Hugh Kerridge? Mid-2000s, let's say.'

The first flicker of a reaction from Goddard. They stood watching each other. Then Lilly guessed he was listening too.

'I'm not clicking, if that's what you're wondering,' she said.

Goddard nodded. 'And neither am I. Would you like to step inside?'

And now Lilly hesitated. Did she want to step inside? She suddenly wasn't sure. The house felt remote. It was large, detached and set back from the road. A gravelled driveway, a neat lawn and tubs of glossy, green-leaved spotted laurel framed the front door. It was pretty Victoriana, but she knew nothing of this man, knew nothing of his relationship with her father, knew nothing about any work they might have done together. Goddard raised his eyebrows, as if to say, *Well?* She sensed he didn't care one way or another and was encouraged. She would be briskly efficient.

'Thank you,' she said. 'I won't keep you.'

Goddard waved her in. 'First on the left.'

She stepped inside. High-ceilinged hall led to high-ceilinged lounge. Heavy red velvet curtains, a high-backed crimson sofa and matching armchair. A laptop and a teapot stood on a sixties G-plan Danish wooden coffee table. No photos on the mantelpiece, no art on the walls, save for a small framed painting of an old locomotive. She smelled wood smoke, though the fire was unlit. Also peppermint, maybe from the teapot. He followed her in, gestured to the sofa.

'Please,' he said, sitting in the armchair, closing the laptop. Lilly left her coat on and buttoned. She perched on the sofa. Raised her eyebrows. 'Well?'

'Miss Slater,' said Goddard, 'your father was a difficult man and I did not know him well.' He sat with a neat precision, hands held in his lap. 'There are still limits on what I can say, but I did work with your father and Hugh Kerridge until early 2005.'

'When they were both sacked,' suggested Lilly.

'Something like that.'

'Hmm. What were they working on? Can you tell me that?'

Goddard paused. There was a stillness, a composure about him. He seemed a measured man. 'I can say that Kerridge was quite the geneticist,' he said. 'In his day.'

'Before it went wrong.'

'Something like that.'

'Were you working with them at that time?'

'I was.'

'But you weren't sacked?'

'I was not.'

'Is that why you came to the funeral?' The question hung between them. 'Or something like that?' she said. He nodded. She folded her arms. 'Is there a reason for this ... reticence?' Lilly said. 'Maybe I'm prying into difficult territory here?'

He sat as though posing for a portrait. Upright, hands still clasped, unmoving.

'*Dr* Slater, you are an eminent scientist yourself. The website of the company you work for is clear on the matter. The interview they have online is fascinating. Another time, I would love to discuss pathogen prediction with you.'

Lilly was taken aback. 'You know about me?'

'I looked you up. After the funeral. It didn't take long.'

Lilly felt the conversation slipping. 'Forgive me, Mr Goddard . . . or is it Dr Goddard? I'm sorry, I don't know.'

Goddard unclasped his hands, held them, palms out, as if in supplication. 'Either is fine.'

'So,' said Lilly, struggling to keep her patience, 'Dr Goddard. What point were you trying to make when you mentioned the website?'

He took a beat. 'That there was much you left unsaid.' Another beat. 'And I understand that.' He fell silent again. She altered direction.

'And what of Trevor Littlewood?' she said.

Goddard shifted in his chair. He looked away, as if composing an answer.

'I don't know what you know of Porton Down, Dr Slater,' he said, his eyes returning to hers. 'But between 1949 and 1989 there were, as part of the ongoing research programmes, human trials. Experiments on up to twenty thousand people, if I remember correctly. The "service volunteer programme", it was called. In 1953 a man there died of Sarin poisoning. In '62 someone died from plague bacterium. More recently there was an out-of-court settlement with three ex-servicemen who said they were given LSD without their consent.'

Lilly did know some of this and remembered the LSD story. She nodded. 'I read about the case. Wasn't it thought that LSD could be used to incapacitate the enemy?'

'It was. And that possibly it might have uses as a truth drug.' He paused. 'Which it didn't.'

Lilly was warming up, thought of unbuttoning her coat. Decided not to.

'Is this relevant to Littlewood?'

'The police launched Operation Antler in 1999 to look into it,' he said. 'The possibility of malfeasance at Porton Down's volunteer programme. Eight cases were sent to the Crown Prosecution Service. There were no prosecutions.'

Lilly smiled briefly. 'OK, I realize that you're just telling me things you think I should know rather than actually answering my questions. That you're leaving more things unsaid, I suppose. It's probably an official secrets thing. But thanks for what you have told me.' She stood up to go. Goddard rose too. 'One more thing. Outside, a moment ago, you were concerned I might be clicking.'

'I was,' he said. His lips tightened.

'You know many clickers?'

'I'm afraid I do.'

He did that thing with his eyebrows again. Lilly interpreted it as inviting another question. She frowned.

'Trevor Littlewood? Is he one?'

'I'm afraid he is.'

'How many others?' she said.

'About a hundred or so,' he said. 'Maybe more.'

Lilly's jaw gaped. 'A hundred or so? Really? Where?' Goddard stared at her. Then she answered her own question. 'Porton Down?'

'Somewhere like that,' he said.

3.23 p.m.

The surgery was a complex of low buildings all leading off from the main reception and waiting room. Wide double doors normally opened as you approached, but Kit could see that now they remained closed. A security grille was partially lowered. A man in uniform, a security guard of some kind, presumably, stood on the other side of the glass and grille. Arms folded, in charge. Kit counted ten queuers in front of them, forty or fifty behind him. A police car's blue lights reflected off the glass. Kit hoped they would stay.

The security man cocked his head to take a message from his lapel radio. He walked to the double doors, unlocked them with two keys. Top and bottom, then a latch-bolt mechanism. He tugged the door open. Only his nose and mouth appeared through the gap.

'Twelve only,' he said. A Londoner. A veteran. 'Six to waiting room A, turn left; six to waiting room B, turn right.' He counted them in, Kit steering Rose through ahead of him. 'Eleven. Twelve. That's it.'

Security man was pushing the door closed even as Kit crossed the threshold. The metal strip at the bottom of the door caught Kit's ankle and he stumbled inside. He glanced back at the man but he already had his hands full. The woman behind Kit in the queue was yelling abuse through the door. The security man was beckoning the police over.

Christ, this is going to be close, thought Kit.

Through a deserted reception, the first six hurried left. Kit and Rose, with two women and two girls, filtered right. Ferociously white lights lit a short corridor at the end of which was a small, windowless rectangular room with two doors leading off it. One had a plate that read 'Dr Mellor'; the plate on the other door read 'Dr Ng'. In the middle of the room were ten seats, two rows of red plastic chairs. Everyone stood. Kit eyed an emergency exit next to him, a single door with a metal push bar across its width. He assumed they would leave that way. He tried to work out the surgery's floorplan in relation to the road. He was sure the exit door opened on to a sidestreet at right angles to Arkwright. Also, that it wasn't visible from the queue. And that, for now, made it a safe exit.

He made nervous eye contact with the two women. One smiled; one turned away. Outside, the sound of glass smashing, followed by the staccato blast of a police siren. Rose held on to Kit's arm.

'Shouldn't be long now,' he said.

More shouts from outside, closer this time. Dr Mellor's door opened. A thick-set man in a crumpled suit beckoned the next patient in. Smiley woman and a girl bustled inside, closed the door. Now Dr Ng's door swung open, and a petite woman in blue scrubs stood waiting. The other woman disappeared inside with her child.

'Just us, then,' said Kit.

Rose said nothing. She hadn't said anything for a while. Her expression was set, her eyes fixed on Dr Mellor's door. As though speaking were a distraction. As if any conversation might delay things.

The police siren fired again, but this time it stayed on. Mellor's door opened, the woman and child scurried out. They pushed the bar on the emergency exit, disappeared. Kit pulled the door shut, then followed Rose into Dr Mellor's room. One desk, two chairs and two high rectangular windows. Kit showed Dr Mellor Rose's NHS number and medical record on his phone. The doctor glanced at both. A white polystyrene box the size of a small loaf sat on his table. It had two labels, one bearing the address of the surgery, the other a seal. It was unbroken.

'I won't keep you long at all,' said Dr Mellor. He went to open the box.

There was a sudden thudding noise from outside, then both windows shattered. The doctor howled. A cloud of tiny glass shards flew across the room. Kit and Rose dropped to the floor. Kit felt his skin and scalp burning, saw that Rose was cut too. She had lacerations on her cheek, nose and neck. The doctor was on the move, scuttling out of the room in a crouch. When he reached the waiting area, he used a chair to help him stand, then ran towards reception. He crossed over with the security man, who had appeared in the doorway and helped Rose to her feet. Dr Ng ran in, helped Kit, looked at his cut face. The security man shook his head.

'You need to go,' he said. 'Side door here. The grille is down at the front, but it's not secure any more.' He pushed the bar; the door swung open. 'But wait. Let me check. Stay here.' He exited, turned a sharp right around the corner of the surgery. Kit looked out at the short path and the darkened service road that led away from the surgery. Tarmac and concrete, high walls.

'It comes out at the top of the hill,' said Kit. 'If you follow it out of the estate.' He glanced at Rose, trails of blood running down her face. She nodded.

'He said to wait.'

'I know.'

They ran.

Under Rose's hoodie, a white polystyrene box.

3.53 p.m.

The cuts to Rose's face were superficial. Her left temple and cheeks bled, but Kit's gentle cleansing had revealed the shallowness of the wounds.

'Could have been a lot worse,' he said. He dropped the last of the cotton wool into the bin.

Kit hadn't washed Rose's hair for a decade, but when he had finished a teaspoonful of glass shards had settled in the bottom of the sink. She then washed his, inspecting every inch of his scalp. He could tell she was wired but hoped the process of washing, sifting and rinsing would be calming.

Not quite a ritualistic cleansing but something like it. It worked for him, anyway.

As he expected, there had been more broken glass by his car, the break-in leaving the back seat showered with fragments. It had been a cold journey home. When Kit saw the box Rose had taken from the surgery, it had been a silent one too.

They towelled themselves dry, then regrouped at the kitchen table. In front of them, two cups of tea and a polystyrene box.

'Dad,' said Rose, towel over her shoulders, 'I don't feel safe. I know the reporters have gone, but they could come back any time. And the surgery was nuts. Everyone has gone crazy.'

'Agreed,' said Kit. 'And then you stole this.' He tapped the box.

'Dad!' said Rose, exasperated, rocking back on her chair. 'Yes, I took the box. And if I hadn't, someone else would have. There was a riot, remember?' He reached for her hand; she took it away. 'Seriously, Dad,' she said. 'I thought you'd be pleased.'

He managed a short laugh. 'Honestly, Rose? I am sort of . . . and impressed. Amazed that you had the presence of mind to take it in the first place. Even though—'

'Even though it's stealing,' interrupted Rose. 'OK, I get it.'

Kit picked up the box. Oblong, polystyrene, very light. In printed red letters, top right, the words PERISHABLE. DO NOT FREEZE. REFRIGERATE ON ARRIVAL.

'Put it in the fridge?' said Rose, pointing at the box.

'Of course,' he said. 'Forgetting my vaccine discipline.' He placed it next to some fresh pasta and a can of beer. He boiled the kettle again. Rose was silent, sipping. He topped up both cups. Waited for her to talk. He knew words were coming. He blew on his mug. She looked up, looked away.

'Can Lilly do injections?' she said. Taken by surprise, Kit forced a swallow of hot tea. Then he spluttered and laughed.

'What?'

'It's a perfectly sensible idea,' she said. 'I need a meningitis vaccine. And there's now one in the fridge. We just need someone who can inject it.' She sat back, sipped some more tea. She was clearly pleased with her plan.

'Rose, it's stolen. We need to give it back.'

'We're keeping it safe.'

'But it's still stolen.'

'Is she still in Salisbury?' asked Rose.

'She is.'

'How long to drive there?'

Kit felt as though he was losing control of the conversation, fast. 'Wait,' he said, putting his mug back on the table. Both hands in the air. 'Hang on, Rose. First, about two hours and, second, we don't know it's the meningitis vaccine in there. It could be anything.'

'Like what?'

Kit's mind went blank; he couldn't think of a single other vaccine. 'You know what I mean,' he said. He knew it was feeble.

'Dad, the doctor was about to inject me with this stuff. You saw him. What else could it be?' Kit knew he'd lost. 'And if Lilly can do it, I could have the meningitis jab tonight. Or we could try again at the surgery. Or go to hospital again. Or wait for the school.'

Kit closed his eyes, shook his head. She was so good at this. Her logic was impeccable. And he wished Jody could have heard it. He smiled in spite of himself.

'OK. Here's the deal. Non-negotiable.' Rose's eyebrows arched. 'We open the box,' he said. 'If it is the meningitis jab – we can look it up to check, and I'm sure you're right – we ring Lilly. If she says she can stick a needle in your arm without killing you, we drive to Salisbury.' She smiled. 'And you help me mend the busted window.'

'Fair,' she said.

Rose retrieved the box from the fridge, placed it on the table.

'Like it's yesterday's takeaway,' said Kit. 'Go on then. Open it. Let's see what we've got.'

She slid a fingernail across the seal, pulled at the flap. The box hinged open. Inside were twenty-four individually packed, pre-loaded syringes. She handed it to Kit. 'You read it.'

He stared at the labels. Just two had ones that were facing him and readable.

'Bexsero,' he said. He looked it up. Read aloud. 'Bexsero is licensed in the UK as a meningococcal group B vaccine. For bacterial meningitis.'

'Step one,' she said. 'Now call Lilly.'

Kit put his phone on the table, dialled the number, put it on speaker. Three rings, and Lilly answered.

'Kit, hi,' she said. 'I just walked back into the hotel.' He heard a door closing then the rattling of cups. She sounded busy. Occupied. Distracted.

'Hey,' he said. He leaned in. 'You're on speaker. I'm here with Rose. Listen, a strange question.' He took a breath, still wondering whether to proceed. Took the plunge.

'Can you vaccinate someone?'

A brief pause. He could imagine her stopping whatever it was she was doing to stare at the phone. Taking notice.

'I'm sorry, Kit. Can I what?'

'If you had the right kit,' he said, 'and you deemed the circumstances ... appropriate, could you vaccinate someone? With a syringe and needle.' He shook his head, wondering why he had added the last line.

'Yes, I could,' she said. 'If it was needed.' Her tone was matter-of-fact, but her caution was clear to Kit.

'OK, then,' said Rose, too quietly for Lilly to hear.

'Why do you ask?' said Lilly. 'And who is the "someone"?'

4.05 p.m.

Lilly poured hot water on to a teabag. It was some kind of fruit infusion, her cup filling with a dark red liquid that smelled vaguely of berries. She sipped as soon as its temperature allowed. The steam and the scalding liquid felt good, some deep heat into her chilled body. She wondered if she'd caught something on Goddard's doorstep. Or walking round the cemetery car park. Or talking to Leon.

Still in her buttoned-up coat, she sat at the small table with its leaflets, pen and Post-it notes. She scribbled notes from her day, as much to see them all written down as anything else. One fact per Post-it.

100+ clickers at PD.
Ed Slater worked at PD.
Ed Slater sacked.
Hugh Kerridge, geneticist, sacked.
'Something went wrong.'
Hugh K. missing.
Mark Goddard, 'colleague' of Slater and Littlewood.
Littlewood clicking.

She arranged the notes vertically, the *100+* note at the top. The headline fact out of all of them, she thought. Then, a new, shorter line of notes.

Kit and Rose.
Meningitis vax.
Hotel room.

Lilly had agreed that Rose needed the Men-ACWY as soon as possible, agreed that they had tried to get it done properly. She also acknowledged, when pressed by Rose, that under these circumstances, she would vaccinate Jess if she had to. So therefore yes, they should come to Salisbury. And yes, she would vaccinate Rose. If either Kit or Rose had asked whether she had actually vaccinated anyone before, she would have replied, truthfully, no. But that in her vaccine research at UEA she had practised on dummies. She knew how to deliver it and where to deliver it.

Kit and Rose would arrive by eight o'clock. She booked the adjoining bedroom. Realized she was looking forward to seeing them.

Lilly topped up her tea from the kettle, took off her coat. Back at the table, she rearranged the small oblongs of paper, staring at each in turn. She peeled off the *100+ clickers at PD* note, held it in her hand. Weighed it. It felt heavy to her. Something about the way Goddard had said 'about a hundred' followed by 'maybe more' had given his number greater significance.

She searched on her laptop for 'Porton Down clickers' and 'Porton Down infections'. She found plenty of years-old conspiratorial nonsense but nothing of interest. Then she searched for anything to do with Porton Down in the last week. Again, nothing new. Next she picked up the *Hugh Kerridge, geneticist* note. She thought of Kerridge's bizarre appearance at her workplace, his warning about her father and then him running away. She opened Google Scholar and began to search. After half an hour she had found no published articles or books or any senior positions held by anyone called Hugh Kerridge. Next she targeted the 1990s and 2000s. If he was at Porton Down in 2004, and if he had done anything in genetics, it would have to have been then. She trawled through research papers on genetically modified crops, herbicide-tolerant plants, cloning, glow-in-the-dark fish and the human genome project. She checked footnotes, dates and photos. And then she found him.

She had scrolled past a small colour photo a number of times before she recognized who she was looking at. A team of geneticists studying DNA in the marshes of Santa Pola, Spain, had lined up for a formal-looking snapshot, backs to a large jeep. The only named figure was the microbiologist Francisco Cardoso. He was front and centre, bald, fifties and smiling widely. Lilly had met him once before, knew the significance of his work. And to his right, three along, holding a cigarette, was the equally smiling Hugh Kerridge. Red hair, larger moustache. It was dated 1994. She knew Cardoso had been at the universities of Moscow, Oslo and Alicante and was a significant player in the development of gene editing. A few more clicks and she had what she needed. An Alicante staff list for 1995 showed Kerridge listed as a molecular biologist. Any colleague of Francisco Cardoso would certainly make that known on a CV. Porton Down had obviously been impressed. Her father had obviously been impressed. But quite where he fitted into the story, she had no idea.

She could go back to Goddard but wasn't sure what else he would offer. She could try to find Trevor Littlewood, but he was, according to Goddard, clicking. Maybe he was hospitalized, maybe he was deaf. She replaced the Kerridge note, peeled off the next one. Stuck it on her laptop.

'Something went wrong.'

Things had gone wrong at Porton Down before. Goddard had mentioned the human trials, the Sarin and plague deaths, the LSD experiments and Operation Antler. A quick search revealed the Sarin death had been a soldier called Ronald Maddison. The plague death had been a soldier called Geoffrey Bacon. Was it so ridiculous to think that there were other, unpublicized experiments that were also unethical and had had calamitous results?

Lilly paced the straight line that ran from the table to the bedroom door. Ten steps, brushing the bed, ignoring the television. She had never tolerated conspiracy theories or theorists. She loathed what they had done to public health and the damage to the understanding of vaccines.

'And yet, here I am,' she said out loud.

Her phone buzzed. The screen displayed a news flash.

'BREAKING. HOSPITALS RUNNING OUT OF MENINGITIS VACCINE. Ministers blame sudden surge in demand.'

It was accompanied by a photo of a snaking queue outside an unnamed hospital. She clicked the link, read the report. NHS Supply Chain was reporting dwindling stocks of the vaccine and a lag 'of a few days' before a return to normal. There were also some concerns about antibiotic supplies.

She messaged Kit. Told him about the adjoining room. Told him to drive safely.

The prime minister was announcing the closure of schools in England.

The British Medical Association has asked people not to disguise their clicking but to see a doctor or go to A&E.

Boots and other chemists sell out of ear plugs.

Kit and Rose were on the M3.

A cool box was strapped into the front seat.

6.29 p.m.

The noise from the broken window was what Kit's father would have called 'an infernal racket'. If they had been travelling at twelve miles an hour, it would have been bearable, but anything above twenty and the clattering began. They had pushed all the remaining glass from the frame, then attempted to seal the space shut with thick card and gaffer tape. A double layer of black bin liner – one inside, one out – provided a 'waterproof seal'. It also provided a drum skin for the wind to pummel.

To compensate for the freezing wind that still blew through the gaps, Kit ran the car's heater on full. The radio played Steely Dan. Conversation was impossible.

They had started the journey with Rose in the front passenger seat, the vaccine box in the back. However, they had soon realized she would have to administer running repairs to the window. Rose and the box swapped places. Just as well this was her idea, thought Kit, because if it had been mine, she would be in the foulest mood right now. As it was, she had one hand on the flapping plastic, the other scrolled the contents of her phone. Occasionally, she would use both hands to type a few words and the noise level in the car would explode. She quickly reverted to one hand again, the other flat against the window. Her phone buzzed incessantly.

The tap on his shoulder coincided with a roadside sign for Fleet services. This, it occurred to Kit, could be any trip they'd taken in the last ten years; the long drive, the sign reading

211

'Toilets', the tap on the shoulder. He pulled off the motor-way, parked up in front of the food hall. The bin-bag drum solo came to an end.

'Thank God for that,' he said. The silence was blissful, even though he knew it was just a brief respite. He kept the engine running, kept the heater on. Rose started to get out of the car.

'Wait,' said Kit. 'We need to do this together.' His hand rested on the vaccine box.

'I won't be long,' said Rose. 'I'm not shopping or anything.'

'Would rather you weren't on your own, that's all.'

'Well, it's a toilet, Dad, so . . .'

He nodded. 'OK, you first. I'll stay here. I can wait.' He turned the radio to a news channel, watched her go. She walked fast, baseball cap pulled low. Automatic doors, a quiet food hall, a right at the burger joint and she was out of sight. He checked the central locking, then watched for her return. Nerves jangled through his body. He fidgeted with his seatbelt, talked himself into calm. The chances of anyone recognizing her in the Fleet services toilets was so remote even a paranoid father should be reassured. He wanted to check his phone – he had heard it buzzing as he drove – but refused to take his eyes from the gap in the tables that marked Rose's path to the restrooms. The radio reported growing alarm from European Union ministers of health over rising rates of 'as yet unexplained hearing damage'.

'Well, you sure got that one right,' he said.

He'd counted to thirty-three before she emerged. She was walking more slowly, he thought, eyes everywhere. At one point, she turned one-eighty and walked backwards a few steps. Then she was with him, back seat, passenger side. Slightly breathless.

'You go,' she said.

'Everything OK?'

'Well . . .'

He turned to face her. 'What?'

'It's like a church in there or something. No one's talking. Not that I could see, anyway. And there's no music playing. Not in the toilets, not anywhere.'

'Are they . . . listening?'

'Go see for yourself.'

He took his phone, climbed out of the car. Turned, leaned back inside.

'Central lock as soon as I close the door. Keys are in the ignition. I'll be sixty seconds.' He hesitated. There was no doubting his nerves at leaving Rose and the vaccine box. Maybe he could last until Salisbury. But now he was intrigued by what Rose had told him. 'Call me,' he said.

'Dad, just go.' She held up her phone anyway. 'I'll be fine.'

He slammed the door. She fired the central locking. He walked inside.

The food hall was fiercely lit, an arc of multicoloured outlets serving to a circle of wooden tables and chairs. Twenty seated customers, Kit guessed, mainly sitting in family groups of two and three. A few more queuing at each counter. He glanced back at the car, then walked around the perimeter, following Rose's route to the toilets. And she was right. Where once the hall would have been flooded with chatter and muzak, now he walked through a library. The diners ordered by pointing, ate without speaking. Those at the tables nearest to him looked up as he passed, eyes and ears following until he was gone. The loudspeakers were silent. Kit could hear his breathing and his footsteps, both more rapid than normal. At the burger bar, he glanced right to the car, but all he saw was reflected food hall.

In the toilets a form of social distancing had returned, no one close to anyone else. Someone had unplugged the electric hand dryer and a pile of paper towels sat on top.

Kit was unnerved. He had no doubt everyone was listening to everyone else. Waiting to hear clicking. But then what? Would a clicker be chased out? Asked to leave? Lynched? He was quickly drying his hands with one of the paper towels when he heard a long blast on a car horn.

A Ford Fiesta's horn.

He was outside in twenty seconds. Rose was in the driving seat, one hand on the horn, head twisting right as if following someone. When she saw Kit, she unlocked the car then clambered over the seats into the back. He jumped in; she was already talking. Staring out of the rear window.

'Two guys, big coats, walked past. Then walked past again. Staring in. They looked at me, then the box. One of them shouted that I should turn the engine off. I pretended I couldn't hear. They walked off, but one of them glanced back at me. He smiled and it creeped me out. So I hit the horn.'

'The right thing to do,' said Kit, plugging in the seatbelt. 'Still tracking them?'

'Nah,' she said. 'Lost 'em. Too dark, too many cars.'

Kit pulled the car away, rejoined the motorway. 'Just a two-minute stop. That was all it was. Just two minutes. And it feels like everything has changed.'

'And no headphones,' said Rose, her voice rising to combat the drumming, which had started again. 'Did you notice? No one.' Kit hadn't noticed. 'I saw it on one of the chats,' she said. 'Everyone's just checking everyone else. All the time. Headphones just look suspicious.'

'Really?'

'Like, *what are you hiding?* That's what it said. Take out your buds in company. It's the new rule.'

Kit turned the radio back on. They drove without speaking. Ten miles down the road, there was another tap on his shoulder.

'Again? Really?'

'No,' said Rose in his ear. He could smell her chewing gum. 'Not that. Guess where most of my WhatsApp messages come from?'

'Which group are we talking about?' he shouted.

'The school strikes one.'

'That's a new one then.'

'Yeah,' she said. 'Anyway. Where do you think they come from?'

He shrugged. 'London? MCS?'

'Yes,' she said. 'It's London. Followed by Salisbury.'

7.23 p.m.

Lilly stepped out of the shower as her phone buzzed. She'd run it hot and long. Sometimes it clarified her thinking. The heat, the pounding water and the cascade of sound had the power to block all unwanted thoughts. But not this time. Kit and Rose were on the motorway and their imminent arrival pushed everything else from her mind. She hauled on the towelling robe, wiped the steamed-up phone screen on her sleeve. A Weibo alert. She raised her eyebrows.

'Hello again, Heidi,' she muttered. Hit the link. Which led to another link. She knew she should be cautious. That she, or they, might be leading her on. But there was an urgency to proceedings now. And if 'Heidi' or Beijing or whoever was running the account wanted her to know something, she wanted to know it too.

What she got was a file. It wasn't big; the download took just a few seconds. It was called 'Ceftriaxone'. She frowned. Her finger hesitated above the enter key on her phone. Ceftriaxone was the name of a common enough drug used for bacterial infections. She'd taken it herself for an ear problem a few years ago. Why would a Chinese-delivered document be named after an antibiotic? She opened the file.

Two pages of dense script in a strange font, much of it redacted. Lilly skim-read then went back for the detail. It appeared to be a transcript of a conversation between two, maybe three, unnamed people. They were discussing fires in factories. In China, presumably. KivPharm was one company, SCW Syntpharm the other. They had both reported damaging fires that were severely affecting production. Factory faults appeared to be blamed, and no one seemed to be suggesting that the fires were linked. Who these voices belonged to was anyone's guess. Lilly's was that they were police or state officials of some kind. The last paragraph suggested that the factories were closing for the foreseeable future. It was undated.

And that was it.

As she dressed she googled KivPharm and SCW Syntpharm. They were China's two biggest exporters of antibiotics, particularly of ceftriaxone. There was no news of any fires there or in any Chinese plant that she could see. Which wasn't at all surprising. What she found was far more chilling. Last December, *The Times of India* had reported a blaze at the Popular PVT plant in Bangladesh and had an account of vandalism at the Andhra Company in Mumbai. Both large pharmaceutical companies. Both exporters of antibiotics.

Lilly buttoned her shirt, chose a fine-knit merino-wool cardigan from her case. The news reports online were verifiable; the Chinese file was not. She could well be being manipulated, she realized that. The Chinese fire stories could well be faked. So she might easily be adding two and two here and making five. But right now, it fitted. The problem that the hospitals were having with drug availability was undoubtedly caused by the surge in demand for vaccine and antibiotics, driven by the new meningitis strain. But if the stocks were low in the first place, it wouldn't take much to cause a panic.

She called Jeremy Casey. An answerphone message. She said, 'Jeremy, it's Lilly Slater. Quick one. Is there an international shortage of antibiotic drugs and meningitis vaccine? That's it. Call me when convenient.'

She hung up, then tidied the room.

7.35 p.m.

Kit was tired to his bones. Ordinarily, he'd be concerned about falling asleep at the wheel, but the accumulation of flapping plastic, cold air, the vaccine box next to him and his daughter behind him meant that he was wide-eyed and focused. They were twenty miles from Salisbury and now, it would appear, twenty miles from a host of Rose's new contacts.

'How many are we talking about?' he called above the din. He glanced at his mirror. Rose was counting.

'Fifty-three,' she said.

'Wow,' said Kit. 'What are they saying? Can you read some out?'

'Erm, sure. They're all pretty much the same, but it's stuff like *noticed the guy next to me on the bus was literally crying. He told me to move. He said he'd just started clicking.* Then there's this one. *My dad and my sister are just back from Salisbury General. No vaccine left. Chrissie is actually going crazy upstairs.* There's a couple more like that. You want more?'

He glanced again at the white box strapped next to him. Twenty-four shots of stolen meningitis vaccine. Arriving in a town where the hospital – presumably Salisbury District – had run out. The value of their cargo was increasing by the mile.

'Sure,' he said.

'Went with Sol to the hospital,' she read. *'Intensive care is full and they're treating him in a general ward. And his mate says they're low on antibiotics.'*

'OK, two bad things,' said Kit. He filtered left off the motorway and swung on to the A303. The hammering plastic eased slightly then picked up again. Two lanes of traffic, fast-flowing. Maybe thirty minutes to Lilly. 'Intensive care being full is obviously one bad thing. But "my mate says" is how the worst of the internet runs. The fact that "his mate" has said something is of no use to anyone. And should be of no interest to anyone either.'

Rose sat back in her seat. Switched off. It was one of his speeches, he knew that. She'd heard it a hundred times – why would she choose to hear it again? But he wanted to keep talking.

'How many in this WhatsApp group?' he said. 'Sounds like you're getting messages all the time.'

'I am,' she said. 'It was full at two hundred and fifty-six. That's the max you're allowed. So it went local. There are ten altogether, I think, all pretty full.'

'And are you in all of them?'

'I am.'

'The original school-strike leader.'

'I guess.'

'No wonder your phone buzzes all the time.'

She didn't reply. Typing, scrolling, typing again. Then she leaned forward again.

'But what if he's right?'

'Who?'

'Sol's mate. Whoever he or she is. That the hospital has actually run out of antibiotics. What then?'

Well, then we're fucked, is what he thought.

'We can ask Lilly. We'll be there soon,' is what he said.

In the back seat, Rose messaged Harriet. *Hey, girl. Hope today is OK and the food doesn't suck too bad. Rx.* She attached a vomiting emoji, pressed send. She waited. She texted Harriet's dad. Waited. No replies. She messaged all her Salisbury responders, invited them to her Discord server. *Better there than here*, she wrote. Now her phone was buzzing. One by one they joined up, started messaging. Rose wrote, *Why so many clickers in Salisbury?* It didn't take long to find out.

In fifteen minutes she had thirty-seven posts, almost all of them from users who said their parents worked at Porton Down. Rose did a quick Wikipedia check and carried on reading. Most told of a parent or parents who had started clicking, of family jokes and quirky videos, then concern as the 'tinnitus' spread. In most of the cases, there was one or more hospitalization due to deafness. When the meningitis diagnosis was confirmed they had all gone to Salisbury General Hospital. Rose counted twenty who had been admitted. Eighteen were writing from the hospital. One written by Sanjeev04 read, *My mum is somewhere here. I think she's gone deaf. I'm hooked up with antibiotics on a drip. Pretty scared tbh. Before she got bad I heard her say to my dad that they all assumed something had leaked. Some testing had gone wrong. They all mentioned Maddison and Bacon then got told to say nothing. Thanks for setting this up. That first strike you ran was amazing!*

Five of the other posts mentioned Maddison and Bacon. Rose posted, *Maddison and Bacon?* She got instant replies. Geoffrey Bacon had died in 1962 from a Porton Down plague experiment. Ronald Maddison had died in 1953 from a Porton Down Sarin nerve agent experiment. Sanjeev04 added, *Maddison and Bacon is another way of saying fuck-up.*

Rose again. *So you think all this clicking, deafness, meningitis, whatever, is a PD fuck-up?*

Thirty-six yeses.

So why is London worse then? she wrote. *Why are there more cases there?*

One reply. Sanjeev again.

You tell us.

8.10 p.m.

The final stretch of the drive Kit found interminable. The A343 took them through villages which, he was sure, would be charming for a pub lunch or to cycle through, but as the car was still generating a constant, overpowering torrent of sound, he was desperate for the journey to end. The drop in speed on the narrower roads helped, but not much. The drummer still drummed. The wind still blew.

He had given up on the radio, given up talking to Rose. Kit felt as though he had taken a pounding. Eighty miles that had felt like eight hundred. Two hours that had felt like two weeks. But the end was in sight, literally.

The sign read, 'Welcome to the medieval cathedral city of Salisbury.'

'Hallelujah,' he said.

He dropped his speed to thirty. 'If you see a sign for the Godolphin School, shout,' he said. 'Lilly says the hotel is two minutes from it. Near the centre, apparently.' He glanced in his mirror. Rose, headphones on, had her eyes closed. 'Fair enough,' he said. 'As long as I don't get lost. He followed the signs to the city centre. As the bin-liner bedlam eased, noise seemed to erupt from everywhere else. The Fiesta's engine's revs sounded high, the tyres rattled on the tarmac, the glove-box shook in its casing. Even the heater seemed to be blowing harder.

Kit reached back, tapped Rose on the leg, waited for a response. She removed an earbud.

'What?' she said.

'We're here,' he called to the back seat. 'Need your eyes on this.'

She closed her eyes. 'I'm asleep.'

'You can sleep when you're in a nice bed, but you need to get me there first.'

'I need pizza.'

'Deal.'

Rose put on her cap, leaned forward. She peered through the windscreen. The car stopped at some traffic lights. A roundabout, second exit, city centre.

'And garlic bread.'

'Sure. As long as Salisbury does Dominos, you can have your pick of the menu.'

The engine was idling. The tyres and glovebox were silent. The radio was off.

Click.

The lights were still red. Kit started drumming his fingers on the dashboard.

'Stop that,' said Rose.

'What?'

'Stop it. Stop with the fingers!'

He caught her urgency, turned to face her. She was over his shoulder. Their heads inches apart.

Click.

Kit felt his insides churn. A prickle of sweat broke out on his back. His heart raced. There was a chance it was some-thing else, of course. An engine clicks as it cools. There were so many moving parts in a car, so many noise-generating components, that a clicking sound could come from absolutely anywhere.

Click.

But not like that. Kit heard it, felt it, understood it. It was inside him. He owned it. He made it.

He was clicking.

Rose opened her car door and ran.

8.15 p.m.

Kit froze, hands glued to the wheel. His mind flooded. A torrent of images and words cascaded into his head. Tutti and Frutti, the sisters in *To Kill a Mockingbird*. They were deaf. He remembered that one had no hearing at all, the other used an enormous ear trumpet.

Rose had stopped running.

Also, Dickens. He wrote a short story in which his narrator, Dr Marigold, taught adopted, golden-haired and deaf Sophy how to read and write. Wilkie Collins had written his Madonna. Another vulnerable, angelic deaf girl.

Rose had turned to face the car.

And wasn't it Daniel Defoe who had written the first deaf character in an English novel? Or was that disputed now? Kit wasn't sure.

Click. A spark between his ears. He winced.

Rose was screaming at him.

The traffic lights were green.

Behind him, two short blasts from a car horn. Kit put on his hazard lights, wound his window, waved them past. The car overtook, a broadside of invective coming his way. Kit didn't notice. More panicked, tumbling thoughts. He knew a number of things had to happen, but he wasn't sure in which order to do them. So he did none of them. He stayed in his car. His car stayed at the traffic lights. The lights changed again.

He should run and get Rose. Then call Lilly. If there's nothing else you're doing, call her. But get Rose first. Obviously, don't do anything without her. Drive to the hospital, tell them you have meningitis. Call 999. Tell them. Obviously, you might be the only one in the county with any meningitis vaccine, so tell them that too. But get Lilly to give Rose the jab first, as that's why you drove all this way. It was too late for him. But maybe he could have a shot too, just as a booster? It couldn't do any harm. Go back to London, better facilities there. But don't drive now. You're not in a fit state.

Click. A snap of static through his head. He winced again.

A figure in his headlights. Rose. Shivering, sobbing, hands on the top of her head. Looking all around. Agitated, animated. Bereft. Inconsolable. She started to shout. At last he got out of the car, held out his arms.

'Rose! I'm so, so sorry.' Kit's voice cracked. 'Christ, I don't know what to say.' He gripped the top of the door for support. 'And I don't know what to do either.' He felt the tears come but dug his nails into his palm. Deep breaths. Great clouds of steam shone green then red as the traffic lights changed again. Two cars pulled up alongside him, faces staring from the windows.

'Dad, what do we do?' Rose yelled.

'OK. OK,' he said, grabbing some thoughts together. 'So. Get in the car. Yes? We'll call Lilly. Tell her what's happening and where we are. Come on.' He started to climb back into the car.

'But you've got it, Dad!' Rose's voice was desperate. 'I can't get back in the car with you now.'

'Rose. We've been in the car for hours. We live in the same

house. A few more minutes won't make any difference. And you really need that jab.'

'Unless it's too late,' she said, her face crumpling again.

She swayed like a drunk and he thought she was going to collapse on to the road. 'Come on, get in and get warm, anyway. It's just a few minutes ...' She nodded. They both scrambled back into the car. Rose opened her window. The lights changed again. The traffic continued to flow, detouring around their drama.

He called Lilly. Placed the phone on the armrest. Put it on speaker.

8.35 p.m.

Lilly stood on the steps outside the hotel, glancing left then right. A narrow street, hanging on to its elegance by a thread. High-end shops, overflowing bins, rubbish in the gutter. Lilly was lit by both the lobby's own spots and a flickering streetlamp. Her coat collar was up, a grey wool scarf hastily wrapped around her neck. Depending on where they had parked, Kit and Rose could appear from either side. Another look left and right. In her hand, two room keys.

Kit had sounded in control – just – but Rose was with him. Being strong for her was who he was. She knew that. And Kit was most likely going to go deaf. She knew that too. She wrapped her coat tightly around her but shivered anyway. She messaged Jess, said she hoped to be back tomorrow. Even as she sent it, Lilly wondered who she was kidding. A feeling of profound dread had settled in her stomach.

Rose appeared first, sprinting. Coat unbuttoned, flapping like a cape. Cap in hand, hair wild.

'Rose! Here!'

A moment of panic. They had never embraced before, not even shaken hands, but Rose didn't stop. She flew at Lilly, arms thrown tightly around her. No words. Lilly hugged her back. No words. Jess hadn't hugged her since she was ten. She felt unprepared. Unrehearsed. It ran its course. Rose pulled away.

'I need the vaccine,' she said. She wiped tears from her eyes with her coat sleeve.

'I know,' said Lilly.

'Dad has it. In this box thing we have.'

'I know.'

'Will it save me? Will it stop the disease?'

'And that I don't know.'

Kit appeared around the corner, the white box held in both arms. Lilly gasped. He was walking as fast as he could, which was not very fast at all. In fact, he was struggling to stand. A passer-by would assume he was a drunk taking more bottles home. She ran to him. Took the box. He backed away.

'I'm taking myself to the hospital,' he said. His eyes were stricken. 'Please vaccinate Rose. Then call me.'

'Wait, Kit, no. You have to stay here. They're out of drugs. It's just temporary, apparently, but they've been deluged.'

He shook his head. 'A hospital does not run out of anti-biotic drip.'

'This one has. So have others. At least let me get you a cup of tea. Some food. I'll explain. I'll vaccinate Rose. Then you decide.' Lilly felt overwhelmed with sadness. Maybe her heart was breaking.

When Kit left the car, he had made his mind up. He knew that he couldn't stay with Rose or Lilly, not like this. But now he hesitated. He was cold, exhausted and in shock. Tea and a sandwich sounded amazing. A warm hotel room with a sofa sounded amazing.

Click.

His eyes said, 'Did you hear that?' Her eyes said, 'Yes, I did.'

'The offer stands,' she said. 'Rooms 208 and 209. I've checked you in. You just go to the room. Follow us up.' She waited for a reply. He seemed lost. 'Kit? Is that OK? Room 208 or 209.'

He nodded. 'Got it,' he said.

Lilly strode back up the steps and into the hotel, the box now under her arm. Rose was just inside the door, agitated. Bouncing from foot to foot. She opened her mouth to speak, but whatever the intended question, it was answered by Lilly's determined stride. Rose fell in behind her. They walked past a deserted reception desk, over creaky ancient floorboards. The smell of the burning log fire followed them up the stairs to the second-floor landing. They followed a sign and rooms 208 and 209 were at the end of a short, gloomy corridor. Lilly held the door to 208 open.

'I think your dad is following us up. But let's see what we have here first.' She placed the box on the bed, lifted the lid. A bubble-wrapped sheet of six sealed and loaded syringes, stoppered, plunger-out, sat in a shaped cardboard tray. Lilly felt down the side of the box. Four trays, twenty-four jabs. She inspected each of them. All the same dose, all the same needle size.

'Let's do this then,' she said. The unmistakable jangle of nerves. She didn't think it showed. She washed her hands in the bathroom, pulled some cotton wool from her toilet bag.

Rose sat at the table with the Post-it notes. She'd already removed her coat and jumper and was rolling up the left arm of a long-sleeved T-shirt.

'Dad's going to go deaf, isn't he?' she said. A small, stricken voice. It was a statement, not a question, spoken to the floor. Lilly boiled a cup full of water in the small plastic kettle that came with the teabags, sugar and UHT milk. She knew only honesty was going to work here.

'There are so many unknowns at play here, Rose. And I'm not a GP. So I can't possibly give you a proper answer. However, based on what has been observed elsewhere, yes, that has to be a possibility.' The kettle came to the boil. The door swung open. Kit stood in the doorway. Looked at Rose, looked away again.

'Next door is unlocked,' Lilly said. He didn't move. 'And I really don't need an audience for this.' He nodded, disappeared. She heard the door to room 209 open and Kit slump on the bed. She poured water from the kettle into a cup, then dipped a swab of cotton wool.

'It's not an alcohol wipe, but it's not a bad alternative.' She cleaned an area on Rose's arm – a few square centimetres – then reached for the vaccine. She lifted the first sheet of syringes, then tore along a perforated line to release one. She punctured the plastic, held it up close. Checked the name of the drug, checked the expiry date.

'Wait,' said Rose. She reached for her phone, unlocked it, handed it to Lilly. 'Take a photo of it.' Lilly obliged. Handed back the phone.

'Your hand's shaking,' said Rose.

8.55 p.m.

Lilly put the phone and the syringe down by the Post-it notes. She looked at her hands. Both were trembling. She clenched, then unclenched them. They stilled. She sat on the bed, clasped them in her lap. She caught Rose's expression. Lilly interpreted it as disappointment.

'It happens sometimes,' she said. Honesty still the best policy. 'It is possible to know what you're doing but still be nervous.'

'Scared?'

'That too,' said Lilly. 'But I know how to do this, Rose. There's point five millilitres of meningitis vaccine in that syringe and it'll be in your arm in sixty seconds. Then your immune system will learn to defend itself to fight the meningitis bacteria if it meets them for real. You'll have all the antibodies and immune cells you need to win the battle. And that'll be it.' She managed half a smile. 'Then we'll talk with your dad.'

Rose nodded. 'Do it,' she said. 'It's what we came for.'

Lilly squeezed a syringe from the pack, twisted the plastic stopper from the tip. Ten centimetres from needle to the plunger thumb rest. Clear liquid in the barrel. The rubber plunger head sat at the finger flange. Locked and loaded.

Her thumb pushed lightly, and clear liquid dribbled from the tip. She was aware of a slight tremble in her hands, but Rose wasn't watching any more. Head turned, her eyes were closed. Lilly took a breath, took Rose's arm in her hand. She felt her tense, saw her jaw clench. Rose started to hum.

The injection had to go straight into the muscle. Rose's arm was scrawny, honey-coloured against Lilly's pale fingers. She brought the needle to the muscle. She started to shake. Took it away again.

Heaven's sake, she thought. This isn't difficult. Rose hummed louder.

Lilly held the syringe like a pen. Thumb, and first two fingers around the middle of the barrel. She'd revised the details: ninety degrees to the arm, a quick thrust, through the fat, into the muscle, depress the plunger. That's it. She ran the sequence in her head again, repeated it like a mantra. A routine. A deep breath. Needle to the muscle. She followed through.

Rose winced. 'Shiiiit,' she whispered.

Lilly pushed until two centimetres of needle had penetrated Rose's arm, then adjusted her grip so her thumb could push the plunger. She watched as the rubber plunger head pushed the fluid out of the barrel and into Rose's muscle. Her hand was steady enough. When the syringe was empty, she eased it out. A bead of blood appeared on Rose's arm and Lilly reached for another piece of cotton wool.

'Hold this here,' she said, pressing it to the blood. 'Sorry if that hurt.'

Rose turned her head back, held the cotton wool. 'It was fine,' she said, sounding like it wasn't. 'Can Dad have some?'

Lilly shook her head. 'He's already got the infection, Rose. So it's too late for the vaccine; he needs to be hooked up to some antibiotics. In hospital.'

The interconnecting door opened. Kit appeared, laptop open in his palm.

'If you're talking about me, I should probably be here,' he said. Lilly caught the sound of running water.

'Bath first?' she said. 'I'll chase the food.'

'Jab done?' he said.

Rose nodded. 'Jab done. But Lilly says you can't have one, Dad. Says you need to be in hospital.'

Kit came in, put his laptop on the bed. He slumped next to it. 'I know. Just been reading all the details.' He hesitated, wondering how much to say. Decided he'd say everything. 'Guess how long I have?' He glanced between Rose and Lilly. They stared back, aghast. 'Before I go deaf,' he added. He stared at the carpet.

'Kit—' began Lilly.

'No one knows,' interrupted Kit. 'That's the answer. It could be anything. Some people say a week. Some have only had an hour.'

Rose's eyes filled. 'One hour?'

Click.

All of them winced.

'I also learned,' said Kit, 'that the hospitals are out of

antibiotic drip. They're saying stay put if you get infected. Not to turn up at A&E just yet.'

'So you just . . . what?' said Rose. 'Do nothing?'

He nodded. 'Seems so.' He stared at the curtains. Lilly and Rose stared at him. The moment stretched. The bath filled.

'Does it hurt?' asked Rose. A timid voice.

He shook his head. 'I ache all over from the journey. My head hurts from that bloody window we fixed. But the clicking is just . . . clicking. I hear it. You hear it.' He forced a smile. 'That's it,' he said. 'For now.' He closed the laptop. 'I'll have my bath.'

Lilly still stood; Rose still sat. The empty syringe lay next to the Post-it notes.

'What happens now?' said Rose.

'Any chance of a drink?' said Kit.

9.05 p.m.

> *I know that I shall meet my fate*
> *Somewhere among the clouds above;*
> *Those that I fight I do not hate,*
> *Those that I guard I do not love . . .*

The hotel bath was better than his own. Kit stretched, uncoiled. Even fully submerged, his feet didn't touch the end. He'd filled it, squirting in whatever it was the hotel had provided. The bathroom filled with pine-laden steam. Condensation ran down the mirror, the walls and his whisky tumbler. His eyes were closed.

> *I balanced all, brought all to mind,*
> *The years to come seemed waste of breath,*

A waste of breath the years behind
In balance with this life, this death.

Christ, he hated First World War poetry. Read too much, taught too much. And yet here he was, reciting it. Incanting it, as if it was some kind of meditation or prayer. If that was all the wisdom he had, he should give up teaching now. Which, he realized with a numbing certainty, he was about to be obliged to do anyway.

The muscle pain Kit could deal with. The headache would ease. But the knowledge that he was desperately sick – he wasn't sure what he could do about that. He wasn't even sure where he should be. Or whose room he should sleep in. All that he knew for certain was that he was a burden. Worse, he was a source of infection. And, on top of everything, he had failed his dead wife. He had promised Jody he would protect Rose. Now that looked a shaky, unwise, unkeepable promise.

He submerged himself below the bubbles. His ears filled with water, the world disappeared. His school taught mind-fulness, explained to the students the benefits of 'living in the moment'. Well, here he was, and this was his moment. He hadn't held his breath for years, but while his lungs allowed, he relished the power of the heat and the whisky. They worked well together. His muscles relaxed, his brain fogged. He heard a voice coming from somewhere in this envelope of deadened sound, but he had a few more seconds to himself. He counted them. He managed twelve.

When he resurfaced Lilly was sitting on the floor of the bathroom. She had refilled his glass. He wiped his face with his hands.

'You absolutely shouldn't be here,' he said.

'That's probably right,' she said. 'But I'm here anyway.'

'You can't get this too, Lilly!' Kit's voice was desperate.

She clicked the door shut.

'Kit, we've been together plenty of times in the last few weeks,' she said. 'We have slept together five times since Christmas. If I'm catching this thing, it's likely I've caught it already.'

He reached for the flannel, wiped soap and sweat from his eyes. Sipped some of the whisky.

'You were counting?'

'No,' said Lilly, 'but I *have counted*. We need to decide what we do next. And we need to decide together. Rose was asking.' She told him about Leon and Hugh Kerridge, her visit to Mark Goddard and what he had told her about Porton Down.

'*How* many clickers?' Kit said, staggered.

'More than a hundred is what he said.'

Kit slid back under the water again. Held his breath. Fifteen this time. 'Well, what I have to do is easy,' he said on resurfacing, wiping his face with his hands again. 'I'm going to the hospital. The nearest one. Whether they have drugs or not, whether they work or not, that's where you need to be if you have bacterial meningitis. It's really quite simple. And I'm no use to you anywhere else.'

'But they're saying they can't . . .' she started.

Kit sat up. 'I'm going to bloody hospital, Lilly,' he said, his voice rising. 'What are they going to do, throw me out? "Oh, sorry, soon-to-be-deaf man with a deadly disease, you have to leave?" I mean, come on, Lilly. Christ's sake.'

Kit realized the whisky was talking, but he meant it. He would sleep – on the floor presumably – then get himself to the local A&E.

'I'll hand over the vaccine box,' he said, 'and they'll be so grateful someone will find one last bag of antibiotics.' He was joking, but it wasn't funny.

'And Rose?' said Lilly. 'What does she do?'

'I have no idea,' he said. His head swam. His world had changed and he didn't feel equipped to navigate it just yet. 'Literally no idea, Lilly. She's vaccinated. At least that's something.' He held out a hand. She reached and took it, kneeling by the bath. 'And I never said thank you. We drove all this way and I never said thank you.'

He started to cry.

At a White House press conference, the chief medical adviser to the president was recommending a return to mask wearing 'until we understand this new, frightening infection'.

South Wales Police were denying reports that as many as one in ten of their officers were reporting sick.

No buses were running in Birmingham, Brighton, Ipswich, Cardiff or Newcastle.

The day

6.25 a.m.

ROSE HAD ALL the information she needed. Now, she ran. She flew from the hotel, turned right, pounding the three blocks to the bus stop. A few heads turned as she passed. They saw a slight girl in jeans with a hoodie under a zipped parka. If they carried on watching, it was because of her speed. It was a sprint, for sure, but the sort of wild-eyed sprint you only hit when you are being chased. When you are in fear for your life.

Rose had woken at five. She had got up to use the bathroom and had been halfway across the room when she heard the first click. She froze, mid-stride. Waited. Breath held. She clicked again.

Rose started to shake.

'Daddy?'

She used the bathroom, then called again. Panicked. Terrified.

'Daddy!'

She found the adjoining door open, the room empty, a note on the floor. White hotel-headed paper, black biro. Her dad's handwriting. She knelt to read it.

Lilly dropping me at the hospital. Back soon. x.

She held the note in her hand.

On the brink.

'This is not OK. This is not OK. This is not OK.' She whispered the words, over and over. Rapid fire, a torrent of syllables. She rocked as she spoke, eyes squeezed shut, tears escaping anyway. 'This is not OK. This is not OK. This is not OK.' Slower now, and quieter. Eventually, she was still. Eventually, she was silent.

Back from the brink. She moved briskly now.

She showered, dressed, took all the biscuits from both rooms, put them in her bag. On her phone she opened her Discord server.

Anyone up? she wrote.

A flurry of replies. She pulled on socks and trainers.

So guess what, she wrote. *I click. I am clicking. I am a clicker. So that's that.* She put both her sweatshirts on, then the parka. The chat filled fast.

Need help. Best hospital nearest to the Wilson Spa hotel in Salisbury? Not Salisbury Gen. No car. Just cash. She ran to the bathroom, tipping out the contents of the basket of toiletries. She took shower gel, shampoo, then noticed a small cardboard box. Inside, two pink wax earplugs. She stared at them, put them in her jeans pocket.

On her phone she saw she had been tagged @Rose. *Get yourself to Southampton Gen. X7 bus from you. Pay on the bus. Just visited my mum in there. Not bad considering the heavy shit they're dealing with. They have drugs that work. Go for it.*

She hoisted her bag over her shoulders, took out the earplugs. Warmed them up. Shaped them in her fingers. She hooked strands of hair behind each ear, then pushed a ball of wax in as deep as it could go. Left, then right. She checked the mirror, turning one way, then the other. If the wax had been light brown they'd have disappeared completely. But they were pink. So instead, if you were looking hard, you'd see the plugs. Rose unhooked her hair, put her hood up. Now they disappeared. She found a glove in each of her coat's front pockets. Pulled them on. One more check in the mirror and she was gone.

The crowd around the bus stop was too much. Twenty, maybe more. Wrapped up against the cold, hands deep in pockets but eyes everywhere. Full of suspicion. Wariness. A new, uncomfortable caution at play. Rose saw the numbers waiting, pulled up. Consulted her phone. There was no way of telling how many were for the Southampton bus and who might be going to other destinations. The sign said six different routes stopped here. Rose ran on. Pavements, roads, kerbside, dual carriageway. The sprint eased off, but even the slower clip had a manic feel. An irregular pace, eyes wide and everywhere. She ran half a mile before she saw a deserted stop. A large Dior advertising hoarding, a shelter and a red plastic bench sat between the road and a grass bank.

She eased her speed, glanced over her shoulder. A dozen cars, no buses. She stumbled to the bench, then slumped. She sat for ten seconds, breathing heavily, legs bouncing. Agitated. She put a finger in each ear, pushed. Just to be sure. She stood, walked around the shelter three times then slumped again. Tugged at her hoody. Checked the traffic.

A bus. An X7. For Southampton. She stood up, put out her gloved hand. For a moment it looked as though it wasn't stopping, then it suddenly pulled over. The doors opened, the driver glanced up. Rose stepped inside, offered him a £10 note.

He frowned at her through the protective glass, held up his hand.

'Wait,' he said. 'It's not that simple.' He waved it away. 'Don't need your money. But I do need you to remove the hood.'

She screwed her face tighter, shook her head then re-offered the banknote.

'Please. To Castle Lane.' She coughed.

He frowned some more, deep grooves in his forehead. 'Hood down,' he repeated, his voice raised now. 'And you can keep the money.'

Rose looked around. Graffitied seats, unwelcoming passengers. Nine standing. One old lady sitting. A man with a mask under his chin stepped forward.

'Take off the hood or get the fuck off this bus.'

She took off the hood. Jaw set, eyes fierce.

The driver looked at Rose. He had a kind face, warm, smiling eyes.

'What's your name?' he said.

'Rose.'

'Rose, are you sick?' She shook her head. A shout behind them.

'Kill the engine.'

Rose put a hand on the driver's protective glass for balance, then jerked her head between the shouters and the driver.

'Yeah, kill the engine. And the heater. We need to hear her!'

The passengers edged closer. The driver reached for his microphone.

'This is my bus.' His voice blasted out of the bus's speakers. Harsh, distorted.

Everyone jumped. Everyone understood.

'I will decide who gets on and when the engine gets turned off. And the heater stays on. Please sit down.'

Most did, two remained standing. A bearded man and the man with the mask under his chin. The driver cut the mic.

'Rose, Castle Lane is the hospital,' he said. She looked at him beseechingly. He shook his head. 'And if you're sick like I think you're sick,' he said, 'you need to get off the bus now.'

Rose closed her eyes, appearing suddenly unbalanced. She took a step back, then collapsed down the steps, slumping against the automatic doors. She stayed down. A

Salvation Army woman ran forward, dropped to her knees. Her gloved hands reached forward and brushed Rose's hair away from her ears. She leaned closer, performed the briefest inspection, then scrambled back to lean against the driver's reinforced glass.

'Earplugs?' he asked.

The Salvationist nodded. 'Small and pink-skin-coloured,' she said, her words clipped, her breathing rapid. 'Pushed in deep.'

He nodded. 'We need to get her off. Now.'

Three of the men rushed forward.

'Just open the doors!' yelled one, a stabbing finger pointing at the driver. 'Get her off before she infects us all.'

The driver shook his head. 'If I open the doors, she'll fall into the gutter—'

'Where she belongs,' said the man, his words muffled only slightly by the fabric of the mask. 'Open the fucking doors.'

The Salvationist leaned towards the driver. 'Let me out by the back doors,' she said. 'I'll stay with her.' He mouthed a quick 'thank you' and released the back doors. He watched as she ran to the front, crouched ready to catch the girl if she rolled out, then raised her arm. 'Ready!'

He hit the door release. It hissed and began to open, then, sensing an obstruction, shuddered closed again.

'Jesus Christ,' muttered the driver.

'Try again,' demanded the masked man, and the driver obliged.

Rose was obstructing the door and, until she moved, or was moved, the door would stay shut.

'OK,' said the masked man. 'I've had enough of this. Ready?' His words were aimed at the driver, who shrugged.

'For what?'

Mask man made a show of holding his breath, then swooped towards the stricken Rose. Squatting on his haunches, he reached into the stairwell and grabbed hold of the girl's coat. With a noisy exhale he hauled her to her feet, Rose's head rolling uncontrollably.

'Hey!' The driver jumped from his seat. 'You can't do that.'

'Open the door!' yelled mask man. 'She's not blocking it now. Do it.' The driver hesitated.

'We do this gently,' he said. 'Hand her to the Sally Army lady, OK?'

Mask man nodded. The driver opened the doors. Mask man held the girl by both lapels, adjusted his grip, altered his stance, then threw her from the bus. She landed on top of the Salvation Army officer and they both hit the ground, hard.

Rose's fall was broken by the officer's body. The officer's fall was broken by the pavement, but she still came to first. Wincing in pain, she pushed herself up with bruised and bloodied elbows. She saw Rose lying across her, then fainted.

7.30 a.m.

The paramedic, gloved and masked, seemed as concerned for the Salvation Army woman, who had said her name was Dawn, as he was for Rose. He crouched in front of them, balancing every pitch of the speeding ambulance, riding the road on the balls of his feet. His eyes flitted between them. White, late twenties, a head of wild black curls.

'Tell me again what happened back there,' he said. An Australian accent. A breezy style.

'If it's concussion you're worried about, I think I'm fine,' said Dawn. Her face sported new dressings over her nose and left cheek. The man's smile was visible behind the mask.

'Maybe,' he said. 'Maybe you are. But you lost consciousness back there, Dawn. And that's a nasty crack to your head you've had. On top of the bruising to your back and ribs. So I need to know what happened.' He sat back on a wall-fastened pull-down chair, waiting. The blue-filtered skylight gave his face an unhealthy hue. The ambulance's drawers and monitors rattled as they tore along the dual carriageway.

Rose and Dawn, awkwardly balanced on the bed, exchanged glances.

'I was doing my job,' said Dawn. 'That's it, really.'

'Your job often involve getting thrown off buses?' he asked.

'Not normally.' A small smile lit up her face. 'But it's God's work, so I go where he wants me to go.'

The paramedic nodded, looked at Rose. Her cheeks and nose were grazed, a deep bruise forming above her left eye. 'And are you clicking, Rose? Is that why you're wearing earplugs?' She looked startled, reached for the woman's hand. 'You're not the first,' he added.

She nodded.

'I noticed them when I was dressing your cuts,' he said. 'Would you mind taking them out?'

Rose shook her head.

He nodded again. 'OK,' he said. 'How old are you, Rose?'

'Fourteen,' she said.

'So can we call someone? Let them know what's happened? Your mum or dad, maybe?'

Rose said nothing. Dawn prompted her, leaning closer.

'You need to say, darling,' she said. 'He needs to know something.'

Rose swallowed. 'My dad's clicking. Gone to hospital in Salisbury.'

'Just your dad?'

'He's with his girlfriend.'

'Understood,' he said. His eyes narrowed. 'Have I seen you before, Rose? You look familiar.'

Rose shook her head. He shrugged.

The ambulance slowed. A short blast of the siren, then it sped up again. Inside, the sound was deafening. Dawn flinched. Rose blinked. The medic resumed the questions. 'Do they know you were on the Southampton bus?' Rose shook her head. 'OK. Maybe send a text or something, just to let your dad know you're all right.'

Rose nodded. Retrieved her phone. 'Where are we going?'

'Same hospital as your dad,' said the medic.

Rose looked horrified, tried to stand. He eased her back down.

'But that's no good!' she said, her voice piercing in the enclosed cabin. 'They're out of drugs! It said so on the news. That's why I was heading to Southampton.'

The medic shook his head. 'Look, we go to the nearest hospital unless we're told otherwise. Their drug supply will be the same as Southampton. Don't worry. We've taken quite a few clickers like you there. They know what they're doing.'

Rose stared at the medic. Shifted her position on the bed. Her bruised eyes sparked to life. She had thought of something. He was intrigued.

'What?' he said. 'What did I say?'

She hooked hair behind both ears. 'I'll take out the earplugs if you answer a question,' she said.

He shrugged. 'Sure. If I can answer, I will.'

Using thumb and forefinger, Rose eased out each earplug. She held them both in the palm of her hand.

'So what's the question?' he said, amused.

'Have you ever been called to Porton Down?'

Whatever the medic was expecting, it clearly hadn't been that. He sat back in his seat, eyebrows raised. 'Have I what?'

'Have you ever been called to Porton Down?' she repeated. 'For clickers.' The paramedic looked between Rose and Dawn, as if deciding something.

'OK, well, I said I'd answer if I could. And it turns out I

can't, because I've been told not to.' He found a clipboard and started writing on a printed form.

Dawn leaned forward, closer to the medic. 'Why would that be? Who would tell you that?'

He shook his head, said nothing.

'You can say it's not true,' said Rose.

The medic carried on writing, said nothing.

'So I reckon it is true. And that you've been there . . .' Rose shrugged. 'Maybe twenty-five times.'

The medic didn't look up, but he had stopped writing. 'Less than that,' he said, his voice almost lost in the rumble and rattle of the journey.

They sat in silence.

Click.

The medic and the Salvationist looked at Rose. She put her earplugs back in.

Texted her father.

Kit was walking out of Salisbury General Hospital.
Lilly had found Trevor Littlewood.

9.45 a.m.

Lilly left Kit for a few minutes. She said she needed the bathroom, but the truth was she needed to walk. Even if it was
just around the swarming hospital corridors. Deep in her
coat pocket, she had found an old blue surgical mask. She
hooked it on, wondering about the last time she had needed
it. She hated the smell of dust, the musty fabric against her
mouth, the memories it evoked. It was, however, a barrier of
sorts against the overpowering smell of disinfectant. The
whole world now smelled of disinfectant. Every room, every
office, every shop. The one used at her father's morgue had
been eye-wateringly harsh but, as she remembered it, over-
laid with flowers. Christ, was she becoming an expert on
cleaning fluids now?

She understood the chemical process of disinfection. The
cleansing of a room, or a wound, of germs that cause disease,
was one of the first chemistry experiments that everyone
took part in. But at the morgue she had thought that the only
disinfecting she was interested in was a means by which she
could cleanse her mind of her father. A purification, if such a
thing was possible. Hopefully, the funeral, plus time, would
be the agent.

Lilly walked to think. She felt unmoored. Everything was
out of control. Kit's distress was profound and she felt totally
ill equipped to help. The vaccine for Rose was fine, but after
that? Where had been her wise words? What had she said
that had brought him any comfort? She wasn't sure she even
had any. Lilly had, increasingly, contemplated the possibilities

of a life with Kit, even found the horrendously loaded medieval word 'stepmother' occurring to her. Wondered too about Jess and Rose being stepsisters. She realized she liked the thought very much. But she knew the course of untreated bacterial meningitis. She wasn't sure if she had it in her to be a carer. Or a widow.

But she felt that Kit's pain had become her pain too (had she felt that way with Liam? She doubted it). When Kit suffered, she suffered. When he appeared with the vaccine box, clicking and exhausted, she had thought her heart would break. When they had held hands, Kit in the bath and in torment, she had contemplated what it would be like to lose him. And it was agony. Did that mean she loved Kit? She thought it probably did.

Lilly walked on.

The fast lane was the middle of the corridor; the slow lane was at the edges. If you hugged the wall, you were out of the way. Lilly hugged the wall. What she saw wasn't the panic she remembered from 2020, but it was certainly frenetic. She had paused by a stairwell when her phone rang. The old-fashioned American tone, shrill and piercing. She was momentarily embarrassed, then realized that no one had noticed. Even so, she stepped through the double doors. Her screen read 'Jeremy Casey'. She took the call. He was already talking.

'. . . strange one, Lilly, I must say,' he said. 'Sorry it's taken me so long to reply. But here's the truth. It's a nightmare. Yes, there's a shortage of antibiotics caused by a variety of factors – problems of supply, and so on. But the worst thing is that when we do use the cefotaxime or ceftriaxone, *it doesn't work*. In a few patients it works a bit, reduction in pain levels, for example, but essentially we might as well just give them paracetamol and send them home.' He paused for breath. Lilly jumped in.

'Wait,' she said, covering her mouth with her hand. She

spoke in a half-whisper, aware of the stairwell's amplification. Faced the wall, used it for support. 'To be totally clear. You're saying this new strain of meningitis . . .' She didn't want to finish the sentence out loud. Partly because of where she was, but mainly because its significance was so overwhelming.

Casey finished it for her. 'Is not responding to our antibiotics. Yes. And it *is* a new strain. Lab confirmed it once they sequenced the genes. So. Patients are diagnosed, admitted, hooked up to the drip. They click, they go deaf, and *then* come the traditional aches, neck stiffness and fever.'

The stairwell clattered with footsteps and conversation, but Lilly heard none of it. Her phone vibrated with a new message; she ignored it. Now it was her turn to finish a sentence. Head spinning, hands clammy.

'And deaths?' The palest of whispers.

'Sixteen,' said Casey. 'So far.'

'Dear God in heaven,' she muttered.

'Quite. The full implications haven't been announced just yet. Government will get involved, ministers will parade. That's when you'll know it's really bad.'

There was a pause in their conversation. Lilly knew what the next question should be but fought it anyway. She didn't want to know the answer. She leaned her forehead against the wall. Forced the words out.

'Average time between clicking and death?' she said. A few seconds of silence – what she presumed was a fresh calculation from Casey. More stairwell traffic, more chatter.

'On what I've seen,' he said, his tone still matter-of-fact, 'a few days. That's too vague, I know, but we have one case of three weeks and six of three days. A couple less than that. I'll do you a proper calculation, but that's a back-of-an-envelope job. It may well depend on your age. The younger you are, the longer you get.'

Three days?

'OK, thanks, Jeremy,' she managed, and hung up.

Lilly stood frozen in the corner of the stairwell. She knew the facts, of course. Everyone knew the facts. Rising rates of antimicrobial resistance across the world. An 'urgent threat', according to the World Health Organization. The search for new antibiotics that had been a huge priority and, so far, a failure. But that had all been, literally, academic. Now it was personal.

Three days.

She was about to push back into the corridor, already wondering what to tell Kit, when she caught words from a conversation a few flights above her. She froze, wondering if she'd misheard. Turned and looked up the stairs. Then she heard them again.

'Maddison and Bacon.'

'Hey!' Lilly yelled up. 'I know about Maddison and Bacon!' She leapt up the stairs three at a time. Wishing she was in trainers. 'Wait! Please stop!' She dodged out of the way of some running nurses. Accelerated past a slow-moving family. She glanced up. Two nurses, both women in scrubs and visors, peered over the railings. One raised a hand holding a notepad. Lilly jumped the final few steps.

'You know about this?' said the one with the pad. Brown skin, early twenties. She handed it to Lilly, who read as she caught her breath. An A4 pad. The top page had a series of lines of writing. Capitals, written with a black marker pen.

'What is this?' she said.

'One half of a conversation,' said the other nurse, black, older than her colleague by a few years. 'He's late sixties, a clicker. Lost his hearing. We're trying to talk to him, but his words aren't clear. We think he's trying to order food or something.'

She felt her phone vibrate again. She ignored it again.

The first line on the pad read 'MESS OF BACON?' Then

RASHERS OF BACON? Followed by RADISSON? MASON? Then, another hand. Neat, precise lettering. MADDISON AND BACON.

'He'd been muttering these words for ages,' said the older nurse. 'Like they were important or something. But then he wouldn't tell us why. He put a finger over his lips. And that was that.'

Lilly handed the pad back. 'They were soldiers who died at Porton Down. In the fifties and sixties. One got the plague, the other got Sarin poisoning. I forget which one is which.' At the mention of plague and Sarin, both nurses recoiled.

'Really?' said the older nurse. 'Why would he be mentioning them?'

'Plague and Sarin?' said the other nurse, keeping her voice low. 'This shit just got serious.'

'Quite possibly,' said Lilly. 'Where is he? Can I see him?'

The older nurse shook her head. 'Intensive care, so no. All the meningitis cases are on the first and second floors, but we are overflowing now so he could be moved anywhere.'

'Where was he when you had this conversation?' Lilly pointed at the pad. The nurses answered together.

'Latham ward.'

'Just below us,' said the younger nurse. 'His name is Trevor something. You know him?'

Lilly crashed through a few answers before telling the truth. 'No. I'm a vaccinologist. Dr Lilly Slater.' She produced her British Society of Immunology accreditation. 'I think he has some crucial information about this new strain of meningitis. I could write down some questions for him?'

The two nurses looked at each other. The older one nodded.

'Follow me,' she said.

In the deserted toilets by Latham ward Lilly stripped to her underwear, pulled on the blue scrubs she was offered. She handed her clothes to the older nurse, who in return gave her a full-face visor, an A4 pad and a marker pen.

'You have five minutes,' she said. 'Really. Then you leave. Agreed?' Lilly nodded.

'Of course.'

'And it's busy in there. Crowded. Way too crowded.' The nurse was matter-of-fact, but Lilly registered her stress. 'Plus,' she added, 'everyone in there has bacterial meningitis. You know the risks.'

'I do,' said Lilly. 'One question before I go in.'

The nurse nodded.

'Are the antibiotics working?'

The nurse blinked, shook her head. Shoulders dropped.

'That's why we're letting you in,' she said.

10.30 a.m.

Latham ward was a rough square. From the nurses' station, Lilly counted fourteen beds either side, guessed there would normally be room for eight. Each was surrounded with screens. Nearest to Lilly there was one empty bed without screens. Windows down the left side, weak sunlight falling on half the room. It was noisy. Three or four voices cried out for either attention or drugs. Probably both. In the few moments of quiet, clicking seemed to come from everywhere.

She walked the aisle. Each patient was attached to a drip labelled 'Cefotaxime'. Jeremy Case had said it alleviated some symptoms in a few patients. 'Some' and 'a few' seemed to be the key words. The bottom line was that a failing antibiotic was all these poor souls had. Then more beds would become available.

Three days.

They weren't the frantic scenes Lilly had witnessed on the Covid wards. But in its own, remorseless way, this was worse. The treatment wasn't working. The illness would run its course. It would let rip. They had painkillers, but that was it. The hope was gone. Four staff in scrubs and visors scurried between beds, adjusting a monitor or tucking in a sheet. They looked exhausted and helpless. All of them turned as Lilly arrived, then looked away as the older nurse, who had escorted her in, gave a pointed thumbs-up, followed by five fingers.

Five minutes.

Trevor Littlewood was in the end bed, on the right side. Drip, monitor. She wouldn't have recognized him from the funeral anyway, but this man was long and thin, with sunken eyes and thinning straw-coloured hair. His round, metal-framed glasses were folded on the bedside cabinet. He was in a feverish sleep, his forehead running with sweat. Lilly closed her eyes, took a deep breath. She hated to wake a dying man, but she had no choice. She touched him on the shoulder, then, when he didn't stir, prodded gently with her forefinger. His eyes opened. She stepped back, stood a metre away from him. She had the pad ready. She wrote fast.

MY NAME IS DR LILLY SLATER. I AM THE DAUGHTER OF ED SLATER. I SAW YOU AT HIS FUNERAL.

She saw him squinting, offered him his glasses. He hooked them on. Read, then re-read the words. He nodded. Gave a thumbs-up.

I AM SORRY YOU ARE SO POORLY.

He took his time reading. Then, another nod. Lilly wrote again.

ED SLATER WAS SACKED FROM PORTON DOWN IN 2005. DO YOU KNOW WHY?

Another long read and re-read, followed by a nod. They were getting smaller each time.

There was a shout from a neighbouring patient, a scurrying nurse. Lilly ignored everything but Littlewood and the pad.

DID AN EXPERIMENT GO WRONG?

He was straining now, slowing down, visibly weaker. She thought he had read the line but wasn't sure. She held up the pad again, but he had closed his eyes. She touched his shoulder again, then waited for him to focus. Time draining fast. She pointed to the words, tapping them gently. He mouthed the words.

'Yes!' Littlewood said, his voice slurred but clear. He tried to say more, but the words were indecipherable. He squeezed his eyes shut again. Lilly was sure he was suffering, but what choice did she have? She had one more question, one more minute.

Littlewood held out his hand, opened his eyes. For a moment, Lilly thought he wanted her to hold it, then realized he was staring at the marker pen. He wanted to write. She gave him the pen. Held the pad close. Angled it just so. She knew she was too close to him, but her time was running out. The older nurse had appeared at the nurses' station. Seconds, maybe.

Littlewood was writing. Big letters. A steady hand.

MEN-X.

Lilly felt the adrenaline rush. The prickly skin. The heart flutter. *Meningitis X*. They *had* been experimenting. But Littlewood was still writing. The strain of it etched across his tortured face.

The name JOE came first. The nurse was at her shoulder. TAYLOR came next. Each letter a struggle. The steady hand shaky now.

'Time's up,' said the nurse. Lilly reached for the pad, but Littlewood was writing one more letter. Sweat ran from his forehead into his eyes. He winced as he wrote. It was a letter S.

Littlewood tried to write more but he was spent. Lilly felt a strong hand on her arm.

'And now you go,' said the nurse. 'And you were never here.'

Lilly took the pad and pen. She bowed to Littlewood.

'Thank you,' she mouthed.

The nurse steered her away, moved her towards the doors.

Lilly's phone vibrated again. This time she checked her messages. 'Sweet Jesus,' she whispered. She read them again. Kit was clearly frantic.

'Your clothes,' said the nurse, holding out a neatly folded bundle.

'Come with me,' said Lilly, taking her arm.

'Wait—'

'Just while I put these on. Thirty seconds. I need to ask you something. Please.'

The nurse hesitated, then followed Lilly from the ward. In the toilets, one woman finished drying her hands and left. The cubicles were empty.

'Yes?' said the nurse. She folded her arms.

Lilly held her pile of clothes in front of her, eyes on the nurse. 'Honest opinion,' she said, her words bright in the restroom. Matter-of-fact. 'If your partner and their teenage child both had the new meningitis, were both clicking, would you bring them here? To this hospital? Would you leave them here?'

The nurse glanced around the room. She looked perturbed, unsure of herself.

'This is unattributable, obviously,' Lilly added. 'It goes no further.'

'But you're the vaccinologist . . .' began the nurse.

'And you're the senior nurse, here and now,' said Lilly. She waited. The nurse unfolded then folded her arms again. She was struggling.

'The usual procedure is . . .' she began again.

'I know the usual procedure,' said Lilly. 'And it isn't working. So. Your partner has it. His daughter has it. Do you bring
them to this hospital?'

The nurse took a breath. 'OK. So this is for now, for today.
Who knows what happens tomorrow? But if I had to make
that decision now, I would get them diagnosed. I would get
them a course of oral antibiotics – just in case they're the
lucky ones. I would get some strong painkillers.' She paused
as though unwilling to perjure herself. To blaspheme.

'And then?' prompted Lilly.

The nurse's shoulders sagged. 'I've never seen an antibiotic fail like this one,' she said, her voice quieter. 'Never.
So, to answer your question directly, I'd leave. After getting
all the drugs I could, I'd go home. And I'd pray.'

10.50 a.m.

Chasm and chaos. Both, Kit remembered, from the same
root. The Latin was *chasma*; the Greek *khasma*. Both meaning
a yawning hollow. He didn't remember a lot of his classical
studies, but when Rose's texts arrived 'yawning hollow' felt
about right. For now, they sat together on the floor, his arm
around her shoulders, her head on his. They didn't speak.
They had finished apologizing to each other. They had finished crying. Kit texted Lilly again. On his screen he saw
once more the three messages that had felled him.

Dad, I'm clicking.

I'm so sorry.

At your hospital in five.

He pocketed the phone.

They were in some kind of waiting room, a spillover from

A&E. Both wards were full. High, narrow windows, rows of plastic chairs, all taken. A large screen on the wall showed Sky News, sound off. They could be waiting for a flight in some low-rent airport. Sixty, maybe seventy distressed patients – or wannabe patients – each waiting to be seen. Some had family or friends with them, unsure how close to be, unsure who to complain to. Also, now, unsure whether anyone knew how to make them better.

On the row nearest Kit and Rose, an elderly couple sat in silence. Then, three students, on their phones. Behind them, a large, squabbling family, each taking it in turn to be more irate than the other. And on it went, for row after row.

'I was leaving,' Kit said. 'Actually on my way out. When your texts arrived.' His voice was cracked and rough, like he was back on the cigarettes. She didn't stir, her head still stuck on his shoulder. 'It was so shambolic, Rose. Everyone was losing it. I was losing it. Lilly pretended – I think – that she wanted the bathroom and disappeared. She's been gone ages.'

Rose stirred but said nothing.

Click – him.

He realized his neck had started to ache, and he worked his muscles by moving his head in a circular motion. He felt and heard the grinding of muscle, cartilage and bone. He hoped it was just his sitting position against the wall that was the cause, but he knew the symptoms.

'Think I need to stand up,' he said. He eased himself up just as Lilly arrived at a full sprint. She stopped in the doorway, looked up and down the rows. Kit raised an arm. She ran to their corner, dropped to her knees, threw her arms around Rose.

'Oh, Rose, Rose!' she breathed. 'I just got your dad's texts. I'm so sorry.' She pulled away.

Rose just nodded. Said nothing.

Kit, back on the floor, looked at Lilly, who was unsure what to say next. What do you say to someone who has just been diagnosed with a rare bacterial meningitis?

'The vaccine was too late then?' Rose asked Lilly.

Lilly nodded. 'Afraid so. You had the infection already.'

'And you?' said Rose.

Kit noticed the concern in the question. The briefest, tiniest moment of gratification.

Lilly shrugged. 'I guess I'm taking my chances,' she said.

'What's with the pad?' said Rose, pointing.

Click – her.

His own clicks he could deal with. His daughter's were tiny daggers.

'Ah,' said Lilly. Carrying on. She explained who Trevor Littlewood was. Rose sat bolt upright.

'You are actually kidding me,' she said, clearly astounded. 'My Discord and WhatsApp are full of Porton Down clickers. The medic in the ambulance admitted they'd been there loads of times.' She rubbed her eyes.

'They have over a hundred infections,' said Lilly. 'Maybe many more. And according to Littlewood, my father was sacked because of "MEN-X".' She pointed to the letters on the pad. 'I think that means there was a new meningitis strain there in 2004/5. They experimented with it. It went wrong.'

'I thought that was an X-Men thing when I saw it,' said Rose.

Lilly and Kit managed a smile.

'Not exactly,' said Lilly. 'All strains get a letter to differentiate them. X is mysterious, I suppose. So . . . that was that.'

Around them, the chaos of a struggling hospital. For the three hunched figures in the corner of the overflow A&E, the welcome distraction of a different story.

'So who is Joe Taylor S?' said Kit. 'Or is that supposed to be Joe S. Taylor?'

'Littlewood was determined to write it down,' said Lilly. 'He wouldn't let it go until he had written the "S".'

Lilly, Kit and Rose exchanged glances. A beat's pause.

Click – him.

'Well,' said Kit, 'we might well be up shit creek. And we might well be going deaf. But let's see if we can find Joe S. Taylor first.'

'From here?' asked Rose. 'Wifi sucks. Barely 3G.'

Lilly raised a hand, like she was in class. 'Kit, can I have a word? Want to ask you something.'

'Sure.'

'You can ask me too, you know,' said Rose, already back on her phone.

'May well do that.' Lilly scrambled to her feet. 'Literally one minute.' On the television, images of the chief medical officer giving a press conference.

Kit followed her into the corridor. Laminate floor, fading yellow-painted walls. The A&E waiting area was through steel and glass double doors twenty metres away. A steady stream of hospital staff exited and entered, the doors crashing and swooshing as they opened and closed. Kit stood where he could see Rose.

'The antibiotics aren't working, Kit. The drip they put you on, if you get admitted, is failing. I just asked the senior nurse on Littlewood's ward. She told me.'

'What?' said Kit. 'I thought it was a shortage they were worried about.'

'That too,' said Lilly.

'So there's a shortage of drugs that don't work.'

Lilly nodded.

'Your nurse say anything else?'

'Yes. "Go home. Get all the drugs you can, and go home." I didn't want to tell you in front of Rose.'

Click.

Kit could feel his anger rising now. He rubbed both hands together.

'So take a patient with bacterial meningitis away from all medical attention, away from doctors. Is that it? That's the advice?'

Lilly nodded. 'For now, yes. There's no point staying here if they can't make you better.' She managed the smallest of smiles. 'And on the way here from Latham ward, I passed four police officers. They were patrolling in twos.'

'Saw some earlier. A routine visit, I assumed. They must be here all the time.'

'But on patrol?' said Lilly.

He shrugged. There was a logic to Lilly's argument that made Kit feel suddenly weak. Of course, she was right; of course they should leave. In the waiting room he saw Rose get to her feet. Held her phone up. Kit nodded in her direction; Lilly turned.

In the corridor, she held out the screen.

Fresh concerns over antibiotics. Reports suggest that meningitis drugs are failing.

'That was quick,' said Lilly.

11.15 a.m.

The large, squabbling family in the waiting area had seen the news too. They were on their feet.

'The drugs are shit!' yelled one of the women, scrambling out of the row, tripping over legs and bags. 'Fuckin' drugs are useless!' They pulled and pushed each other out of the room, tumbling past Lilly, Kit and Rose in the corridor. Six of them, Kit counted. Three generations, he guessed.

A passing doctor in scrubs was instantly surrounded,

prodded and pushed. 'How can you give us this shit? You should be ashamed!'

The medic backed into the wall.

The tallest of the family, fifty-something, white, Crombie coat, bald, pushed his forehead against the terrified man. 'What are you doing to us!' he yelled into his face.

Kit pulled Rose close.

The doors from A&E crashed open, bouncing off the walls. Three security guards followed by two porters piled in, trying to reach the medic. As each member of the family was peeled away, they ran through to A&E reception. One of the guards rugby-tackled the man in the Crombie; the other two chased the running family. The porters helped the doctor to his feet. Two policewomen ran past, both reaching for tasers.

'OK, that's enough. Let's go,' said Kit.

In Germany, the Berlin Philharmonic Orchestra cancelled all upcoming concerts, as thirteen of its members reported 'hearing issues'. The Staatskapelle Dresden, the London Symphony Orchestra and the Birmingham Philharmonic followed suit.
Out running in Regent's Park, London, George Hall, athletics teacher at MCS, pulled up short. He had started clicking. Panicking, he called Aisha Khatri.

2.05 p.m.

In room 208, Lilly sat at the table, Kit on the bed. In room 209, Rose sprawled on the floor. Lilly and Kit had their laptops open; Rose worked her phone. Two plates of sandwiches next to Kit, one next to Rose. They ate and worked with a fear-fuelled ferocity. The adjoining door was propped open by Kit's trainers and a carrier bag full of medication. The hospital pharmacy had provided strong painkillers and, in case they got lucky, two courses of antibiotics. Stomachs lined with cheese, ham and bread, both Kit and Rose had taken their first dose.

They were looking for Joe Taylor.

'It's the most popular bloody name in the world,' said Kit, frustrated.

'And one of them seems to have had something to do with Taylor Swift,' said Lilly. 'Which means it takes up half the internet. So I've tried Joe Taylor Salisbury, Joe Taylor Porton Down, Joe S Taylor, dead and Joe Taylor meningitis. And all kinds of variations. None of it looks even vaguely right.'

'You mean they're all alive,' said Kit.

'I do mean that, yes.'

Kit looked at the bottom of the search page.

'And I know it always says "Some results may have been removed under data protection law in Europe", but it's never looked suspicious to me before. What if the Ministry of Defence guys wanted information on Joe Taylor to disappear?'

'Then it would disappear,' said Lilly.

'In which case, this is hopeless.' Kit reached for the A4

pad, read through Lilly's words again. He noticed the 'S' after Joe Taylor had a small mark after it. Held it to the light. Maybe a comma, maybe nothing. 'Your guy Littlewood. Was he trying to write more after the "S"? There's a mark here. Maybe the beginning of a letter?' He slid off the bed, held it out for Lilly. She peered at the page.

'It's possible. My time was up. I was being thrown out.' She looked at Kit.

'Another name? A title? "Sir", maybe?' she said.

Kit slumped back on the bed. He clicked, another spark firing in his head, and this time Lilly didn't look up. He thought that was the first time. They were roughly one a minute, occasionally two. The sound came from somewhere in the middle of his head. And now, stretched out between the clicks, a new sound. A high-pitched buzz filled his head, like a dying neon light. Nothing stopped it, quietened it or interfered with it. It was a relentless stream of white noise.

'Objective plus subjective,' he muttered. 'Quite the party.'

Now Lilly looked up, face drawn. 'Struggling?' she said.

'Imminent deafness focuses the mind,' said Kit, 'but this racket in my head blurs it all again.'

'You should be on the alert for the other symptoms—'

'If only I knew someone who used to have a meningitis poster on her bedroom wall,' interrupted Kit. She laughed; he smiled. It hadn't happened for a while. 'Muscle pain, rash, stiff neck,' he said. 'I remember.'

'And dislike of bright lights.'

'And that.'

Rose appeared in the doorway. She had changed back into her dungarees and bucket hat. She held her phone in her hand.

'Sergeant Joe Taylor,' she said.

Kit spun round; Lilly looked up.

'What?' said Kit.

'Sergeant Joe Taylor,' Rose repeated. 'I heard what you guys were talking about. I posted on my Discord server. Asking if anyone had heard of a Joe Taylor. Maybe a Sergeant Joe Taylor. This guy came back saying he was his uncle but that he had died when he was small, back in 2004. That's it.'

'Wow,' said Kit. 'Just like that.'

Rose shrugged.

'What made you think of sergeant?' he asked.

Another shrug.

'Been reading about Salisbury. Lots of army here. Thought it was worth a shot.'

'You thought right,' said Lilly, on her feet now. 'Can we meet this guy who responded, do you think?'

Rose shook her head. 'Nah. He's in Canada or something.' She disappeared back into room 209.

'In which case, Lils, why don't you ring?' said Kit. 'Actually call Porton Down. There must be a number, and it will doubtless lead to nothing, but you're a proper academic with a proper enquiry about a Sergeant Joe Taylor.' He waited for Lilly to look up. 'Worth a shot?'

She shrugged. 'Sure. You find me a number, I'll call. I imagine they'll have better things to do, but I'll give it a go.'

Click.

He found a number, airdropped it. 'There you go,' he said. 'The headquarters of the Defence Science and Technology Laboratory, Porton Down.'

Lilly shrugged, dialled, put it on speaker. Engaged tone. Tried again. Picked up on the fifth ring.

'DSTL.' A man's voice.

'HR, please. It's Dr Lilly Slater at GSL. Global Shield Labs.'

'What is it concerning?'

Lilly looked at Kit, pulled a 'here goes' face. 'I'm trying to find out about a Sergeant Joe Taylor. He died in 2004, I believe. I'm trying to find out more about the circumstances of his death.' She was about to add 'from meningitis' but held back. There was a brief silence.

'One moment, please,' said the receptionist. There was no 'on hold' music, just an occasional beeping tone. Kit realized he was staring at Lilly's phone, holding his breath.

The receptionist was back. 'Can I take your number, Dr Slater? Someone will call you back.' Lilly gave him the number and hung up.

'Somewhere,' said Lilly, 'I suspect a very big alarm bell is ringing.'

2.30 p.m.

Lilly asked for, and received, a lesson in Discord. Rose sat cross-legged in the middle of her bed, Lilly perched on the edge. Rose showed how her server worked, pointing out the count of 127,000 followers who had joined already. How they sent messages, live-streamed, had voice-chats. 'It's got ridiculously big, ridiculously fast,' she said.

Lilly read the messages Rose showed her.

'They all know you're clicking,' she said.

'I told them,' said Rose. 'Lots of them are too.'

'And all of this from the school strikes?'

Rose nodded. 'I've learned a lot from them.'

'Like what?'

'Like this town is nuts.'

'Because?'

Click.

Rose closed her eyes. Lilly, amazed at her calmness, wondered how she would fare if her time came.

Rose took a breath. Spoke fast.

'Stonehenge. Salisbury Plain. UFO sightings. The army

HQ. Porton Down. Novichok. The Skripal poisonings. Every-thing. All of it. The two main clusters of clickers are London and here. Why would that be?' Rose pointed at her screen. 'They all think that it's a Porton Down fuck-up. A "Maddi-son and Bacon", they call it, after two guys—'

Lilly jumped. 'The two guys who died!' she said. 'From Sarin and the plague. They call it a Maddison and Bacon? That's a thing?'

Rose nodded. 'Politer than "fuck-up", I suppose.' She pulled a pantomime wince. 'Sorry about that.'

Lilly smiled. 'I think, under the circumstances, you're entitled to use any language you choose,' she said.

Rose nodded, went back to her screen. Lilly returned to room 208. Rose was correct about the data. The last set she had seen had London and Salisbury as the worst, then Car-diff and Birmingham. Three big cities and Salisbury. Per capita, Salisbury would be the worst.

This town *was* nuts.

But she had forgotten the Sergei Skripal affair. The bun-gling Russian poisoners, the Novichok nerve agent left on the former spy's door handle, the near death of Sergei and his daughter, Yulia, the actual death of the woman who found the discarded poison bottle. She had listened to the *Newsnight* Diplomatic Editor saying it was an assassina-tion designed to be detected. That Putin owned it. She had watched the TV drama re-enactment with Anne-Marie Duff. Seen how Porton Down had solved, not caused, the problem. Then she had, like most of the uninvolved, forgot-ten it.

Momentarily, between rooms 208 and 209, she could hear both Kit and Rose clicking. The sadness was crushing. A countdown to deafness. And a constant reminder that they were running out of time. She walked back to her table, picked up the Post-it notes. One fact per page.

Sergeant Joe Taylor.
Men-X went wrong?
Where is Hugh Kerridge?
Deafness. How long?

She hesitated, then added: *Skripal/Novichok*
Maybe she'd gone nuts.
She considered the list. She called Mark Goddard.

4.15 p.m.

Lilly parked the Peugeot in the drive in front of Goddard's
house, as he had suggested. Taxis had all but disappeared,
the drivers spooked by the new meningitis, so the hotel had
rustled up a hire car. The hotel, too, was struggling. Fewer
staff, minimal service, worried faces. And no lobby or lift
music. Which Lilly thought a blessing.

Goddard was standing in the doorway as she exited the
car. Tan-coloured heavy corduroy trousers, plain dark blue
sweater over a light blue shirt, button-down collar. He nodded as Lilly approached.

'Good afternoon, Dr Slater,' he said. 'Come in.' That
voice.

'Good afternoon, Dr Goddard.' She stepped inside, turned
left into the lounge. Patterned rugs on polished floorboards.
A fire burning, freshly set, she thought. Curtains drawn, laptop open with a bouncing clock screensaver, pot of tea, two
cups and saucers on the Danish table. A small jug of milk and
a bowl of sugar.

'Please,' he said, indicating she should sit on the sofa. 'I
took the liberty of making some tea.' She thought of refusing.
There really was no time left for manners. Kit and Rose had

264

no time. The patients without effective drugs had no time. However, if it got her the answers, she would play along.

'Oh, thanks,' she said. 'Just black, no sugar.'

Clinking crockery, crackling fire, tight knot in her stomach. Goddard poured, slid a small wooden table to her side, placed the cup and saucer. He walked to his chair, pulled his trousers up at the knees, sat down.

Curtain up.

'So,' he said. 'You wanted to see me.' He sipped; Lilly sipped. Too hot, too strong; she placed the cup down. Half smiled.

'What can you tell me about Sergeant Joe Taylor?' she said.

She got two raised eyebrows. He sipped again. 'Maybe first you tell me why you are asking?' Stalling for time maybe, but the voice was flat, unemotional.

'Sure.' Lilly's hands were shaking again. She folded them together in her lap. Cleared her throat. 'I saw your colleague Trevor Littlewood in hospital. He has gone deaf, but we had a written exchange. He told me that a meningitis experiment went wrong. "Men-X" is what he wrote. That that was why my father was sacked. And then he wrote Joe Taylor's name down. You were there then, at Porton Down, I think.' She shifted position, leaned forward. '*That's* why I am asking.'

Goddard sipped some more. A prop, Lilly thought. A conjuror's distraction. Eventually, Goddard placed the cup and saucer on the table.

'It's a fair question,' he said, then paused. 'And I wonder if you might give me a moment? To check some files?' He pushed himself up, marched from the room, left the door open.

'Huh,' said Lilly to the empty room. Again, she felt the terrifying urgency of the hour clashing with this man's stately evasiveness. She stood up, wondering quite what files could be needed to answer a simple question. If Goddard had been working on the Men-X experiment, if that was what it was, he would have certainly known Sergeant Joe Taylor. And missing geneticist Hugh Kerridge. And dead whatever-he-was Ed Slater.

She walked towards the fire, its flames less fierce now but still strong enough to keep her at bay. The fireplace itself was Victorian, cast iron painted black, decorated with scrolls left and right. The mantelpiece's sole ornament, a blue enamel jug with a fake blue tulip inside. She paced the room, impatience growing with every step. Maybe she should call out that she had very little time? That it was a straightforward conversation she was after, not a multimedia presentation. She checked her phone. Nothing from Kit.

Another lap.

The room's only picture was the locomotive painting above the sofa. She leaned in to inspect. Long and thin, like an old, whole-school photo, acrylic paint on canvas. Thin wooden frame. The train was dark green with black-and-red trim, billows of white smoke trailing from its funnel. Travelling at speed. White numbers across its smokebox door and 'The Royal Duchy' painted in gold on the tender. It was good, she thought. Not her thing at all – too fussy, too ornamental – but well executed. If you liked that kind of thing.

Wait.

She'd seen another painting of a train somewhere. Her mind spun, her stomach flipped. Number 12 Clayton Drive. Her old house. The dining room. It had been askew after the break-in. Something her father would have put up, for sure. She tried to remember any details but failed. It was just a painting of a train. Or a photo. Whatever. And anyway, so what? Old men liked old trains. And that was that. It signified nothing.

Another lap.

She walked out of the lounge, stood in the hall. Three doors to the left, all closed. Stairs up were in front of her, front door to the right. Keys in the lower lock.

'Hello? Mr Goddard?' she tried. 'I really don't have much time.' She didn't want to shout, but she was agitated now. I'll give you sixty seconds, she thought.

Lilly walked two more laps of the lounge. The fire was dying; she didn't care. She checked her phone. Typed 'railway societies Salisbury' into Google, then, as an afterthought, added 'members'. Then selected 'images'.

The first face on her screen was Sergei Skripal.

She hoisted her bag.

Skripal?

From the hall she listened to the house. Goddard's voice was leaking from somewhere, it was impossible to tell where. A one-sided conversation. A phone call.

MI5? MI6?

She opened the front door, then closed it as quietly as two deadlocks allow. She stepped to her car, fumbled the remote unlocking with shaking hands, jumped inside. Ignition switched on, she crunched it into reverse. Arm across the passenger seat, she twisted to steer her way out of the drive.

KGB? GRU?

She'd eased the Peugeot back three metres when powerful headlights swung into her mirror. A large black Volvo had pulled into the drive, blocking her way. She, in turn, was blocking its progress off the road.

'Jesus, what now?'

Heart hammering, hands tight to the wheel, she waited for it to reverse. The driver would see what was happening, realize only they could solve the problem and reverse back to the street.

None of that happened.

The Volvo didn't move. It filled the drive. The driver's door opened. Goddard's front door opened. He appeared, saluted the Volvo. He motioned for Lilly to move her car forward to allow the new car room.

Lilly began to shake. It started with her hands, but in three heartbeats her whole body was trembling.

4.40 p.m.

Lilly is fourteen. She is wearing cut-off jean shorts and a paisley shirt rolled at the sleeves. She has new trainers and a new short haircut which she rather likes. She thinks it makes her look a bit like Gwen Stefani, but she definitely doesn't say that to anyone. Her mum approves too (that gentle smile she has!), but now she is asleep, in bed. Not well again.

It is a Saturday in May, the back door of 12 Clayton Drive is open. Lilly had been reading in the sun earlier but is now making herself sandwiches. The radio is on. The doorbell goes. Lilly thinks that it's Justine from school. They spoke on the phone about going shopping, but Lilly will have to tell her that her mum is unwell.

But it's not Justine. It's Lilly's father. She can tell it's him from the shadow through the front door's patterned glass. She stands still in the hall. She considers ignoring him but knows he'll make a scene like before and wake her mother. She is afraid to open the door in case he barges his way in. Storm upstairs. She calls through the glass. She hopes she uses enough volume to be heard, not enough to wake the sick. 'Mum's asleep. I don't think she wants to talk to anyone.' The shadow of her father says nothing, walks away. Lilly waits. Was that it?

She opens the door, steps out (should have checked from the lounge window!). His battered Toyota fills the drive. He is still here. She pulls the door to until it rests against her leg. She realizes with dread in her stomach that he is in the side passage, and she can't remember if she locked it. Because the back door is certainly open.

He appears from the side of the house. (She had locked it!) Suit trousers, black shirt, untucked. Short, greying hair that should have been shorter. Unshaven, unsteady. Lilly knew the signs.

He sees her and lights up. 'Ah! The mistress of the house is in!' he says. 'That must be because the madame of the house is out! And for the count most likely!' He manages to freight the 'madame' with both sarcasm and venom. He smiles, pleased with his joke. He peers at her. 'New haircut, I see.' She is surprised he noticed. 'You look like a boy.' She is crestfallen.

'I'd like a tea, if the kettle's on.' She knows she has to get him to leave, but she doesn't know how.

'It isn't,' she tries.

He is annoyed. 'Well, put it on then,' he says. Then adds: 'Boy.'

Lilly flushes with embarrassment. She thinks of running back inside. Shifts her weight. As her legs move, she hears the door click shut behind her. She feels the fear run up her spine, all the way to her newly exposed neck. Toyota and father in front, locked door and sleeping mother behind.

She is trapped.

4.41 p.m.

She was trapped.

Lilly watched the Volvo driver jump out of her car. She was late forties, powerfully built, barrel-shaped. Short brown hair, cut 1920s style with a side parting and wax which made it shine in the Volvo's headlights. She rolled to the front of her car, hailed Goddard. They both pointed at Lilly's Peugeot. A muffled exchange.

Goddard in front of her, bodybuilder behind her.

No way out.

The sequence of events was clear. She had asked to see Goddard. He had then called his muscular friend. Then, when Lilly had mentioned Sergeant Joe Taylor, bodybuilder got the 'step on it' call. And step on it she had.

Lilly had seen enough. She pushed her door open, climbed out. Goddard and bodybuilder stopped their conversation, turned to face her.

'Move your car,' Lilly said. There was a calm fury about her. Goddard noticed. 'Dr Slater, we just needed—'

Lilly held up her hand, palm out. 'I'm not talking to you, Mr Goddard,' she said. 'I'm talking to this woman here. Move your car. Please. I need to get back.'

The bodybuilder was still leaning against the Volvo bonnet, arms folded. She wore a military-style greatcoat. RAF blue. Black leather gloves.

'I was hoping we could have a conversation about Joe Taylor,' the woman said. Edinburgh Scot, patronizingly superior.

'Really,' said Lilly, boiling now. 'A conversation? Does this feel like a bloody conversation to you? I don't even know who you are. You haven't even had the courtesy to tell me your name.' She took a few steps forward, stabbing a finger at the front door. 'I know he is Mark Goddard and that he worked at Porton Down and went to my father's funeral. He has a nice house and a painting of a train on the wall.' Lilly hadn't spoken at this volume and with this fury since her divorce. Oceans of rage threatened to overwhelm her. Her hands were trembling again. She didn't hide them. 'But I left because I got suspicious. Ha! I wonder why! Well, now I want to leave. Now, I *am* leaving. I have two sick people to get back to.' The bodybuilder's eyebrows rose at that. Lilly walked closer to her. Two metres away now.

'So,' she said. 'Move your fucking car.'

The bodybuilder, still leaning on the bonnet, squinted at Lilly.

'Well, now, you're right, of course,' she said eventually. 'I'm Clarice Adams, Ministry of—'

'Pleased to meet you,' interrupted Lilly. 'Now move your fucking car.'

Goddard hadn't moved. The woman called Adams hadn't moved. At the end of the drive, two cars flashed past.

'Ministry of Defence.' Adams finished her own sentence. 'With special responsibilities for Porton Down. And I wanted to talk to you about Sergeant Joe Taylor.'

'Great,' said Lilly. 'Once you've moved your fucking car.' Adams looked at Goddard. Lilly took another step closer to Adams. Round face, no make-up. A face that had played rugby.

'Don't look at him. Look at me,' said Lilly. 'I'm the one you're threatening. You want to talk? You know what to do.'

Lilly imagined Adams and Goddard were surprised, because she was surprised. She had had no idea she was capable of such recklessness, such aggression. But it felt good and she didn't want to lose the advantage. They had misjudged her. She had misjudged herself.

Adams nodded, accepting the retreat. Hands up, patting the air. 'OK, OK. I'll move my fucking car then.' She climbed back into the Volvo, swung it round, parked parallel to the Peugeot, dwarfing it. Headlights stayed on. Lilly went back to her car. Feet crunching. Goddard watching.

'Hey!' he called, sounding alarmed. She ignored him. Under Adams's gaze, she three-point-turned, parked up facing down the drive, towards the road. Engine running. Just in case.

In room 208, Rose's click rate was two per minute.
In room 209, Kit's click rate was five per minute.
In London, Aisha Khatri, MCS head of science, had started to click.

4.44 p.m.

They were three points on a triangle: Lilly on the drive, Goddard on the steps, Adams in her car. Lilly was the apex, Goddard and Adams the base. Two equal sides made it an isosceles. Twenty metres from Lilly to Goddard, who was ten metres from Adams. Lilly and Adams exited their cars at the same time. Both stood waiting.

'Shall we carry on inside?' called Goddard.

'No,' said Lilly. 'Here is fine.'

It wasn't fine, of course. The temperature was falling again. Lilly was freezing but fired up. She would cope with the cold if it meant being out of the cage. She walked forward a few metres. Adams took a folder from her car, tucked it under her arm, then did the same. Goddard stayed where he was.

'So what was that then?' said Lilly, still mad. 'Because it felt to me like you were blocking me in.'

'Unfortunate optics, I agree,' said Adams. 'But we needed to speak to you, Dr Slater.'

There wasn't the time, Lilly thought, to point out that she had a phone, was staying locally and that 'unfortunate optics' was mealy-mouthed corporate bullshit. To the point, then.

'Why so urgent?' she said.

'Because,' said Adams, 'you've been asking about Joe Taylor.'

'I have,' said Lilly. 'But first, if I may, Dr Goddard, that painting of the train in your lounge.'

'What about it?' He didn't need to raise his voice by much; it seemed to roll along the drive. But his surprise was evident.

'Is that from the railway social club?'

'It is.' An upward inflection. Defensive now.

'Is that where Sergei Skripal was a member?'

'It is.' Still defensive.

'Did you know him?'

'I did. And do.' Past and present. 'Also,' continued Goddard, 'Hugh Kerridge and your father were members. We talk trains, have lectures, go on trips.'

'Was my father friends with Sergei Skripal?' asked Lilly, not quite believing she was saying the words.

'Not really, no. As far as I know.' He stepped out of his house now. 'You could have asked all this inside, of course—'

'And I would have done, but you had disappeared. As you well know.'

More cars out in the lane. A distant siren.

'Why are we talking trains?' asked Adams.

'I don't know,' said Lilly. 'You tell me.'

Goddard walked a few steps closer. 'Tell Ms Adams what you told me, Dr Slater. Let's start there.'

Fair, thought Lilly. 'OK,' she said. 'So Trevor Littlewood said an experiment was carried out at Porton Down in 2004 with what he described as Men-X. Meningitis X. It went wrong. Sergeant Joe Taylor dies, Kerridge and my father are sacked. Now there's a new, terrifying meningitis out there. There have been lots of cases at Porton Down. I'm just joining the dots.'

Adams pushed herself away from the Volvo. 'But you're joining the dots and forming the wrong picture,' she said. 'And, just to clarify, this is an off-the-record briefing. OK?'

'Sure,' said Lilly, shrugging. 'Whatever.'

'Joe Taylor died of a drug overdose in 2004,' said Adams. She gesticulated expansively as she spoke, arms and black-gloved hands working hard. 'The experiment in '04 was a continuation, a re-examining, if you will, of a US project the

273

Americans had sidelined some time in the mid-sixties. As part of their biowarfare programme, the US military weaponized a bacterium called Francisella tularensis. Infection with this bacterium results in symptoms similar to those seen in meningitis. Fever, mental disturbance, delirium, and so on.'

'I am familiar with the pathogen,' said Lilly. 'I've seen it in squirrel and rabbit carcasses. I didn't know it had been weaponized.'

Adams nodded. Goddard spoke. 'This is also off the record, Dr Slater. Some of us thought it was worth revisiting,' he said. 'In the, er, changed geo-political circumstances of the early twenty-first century.'

'To use as a bio-terror weapon?' said Lilly.

'To look at its possibilities, yes,' he replied.

'And against the rules,' Lilly said.

'Of course,' said Adams, both hands up, palms out. 'Totally against all the treaties we have signed. But the same as everyone else is doing. The Russians, the French and the Israelis, for certain. The Americans and the Chinese right behind.' Each country was mimed with a hand chop, each one a few centimetres along an imaginary line.

Lilly, Adams and Goddard had walked closer to each other. The triangle was tighter. Lilly still the apex, her back to the drive, Adams and Goddard the base, backs to the house, but now they were equidistant. Seven, eight metres apart. From isosceles to equilateral. Three clouds of steam merged between them.

'Sergeant Taylor volunteered,' said Adams. 'He needed the extra cash. He sat in a sealed, controlled glass booth. The tiniest amount of the tularensis was released via aerosol spray.' She held up the thumb and forefinger of each hand, like claws, a millimetre apart. 'The mix was one part pathogen to a million parts of air. Taylor received just enough to

274

infect him. He was sick for around six weeks, monitored closely. Then released. Seemingly healthy again.'

'I can guess what came next,' said Lilly.

'The mental disturbance I mentioned,' said Adams. 'The delirium. That's what did for him. Turns out he had hidden his drug use from us – amphetamines and ecstasy in the main – and the tularensis was the tipping point.' Adams stretched out both her arms in a gesture of despair. 'He overdosed with all of the above plus a litre or two of Jack Daniel's.'

The cold was seeping deep now. Lilly's ears and cheeks were numb. She kept her hands deep in her coat pockets, but they too were like ice. She had no idea of the truthfulness of what she was being told. But it sounded plausible. Coherent. One more question.

'And my father?'

Adams nodded, knew it was coming. She held out a manila folder.

'You can't take it away, but you can look at it,' she said. The triangle collapsed. Lilly stepped up, took the folder, stepped back. She walked until the Peugeot headlights were just enough to see what she needed. The folder contained just two sheets of A4 paper. One with 'Edward James Slater, dismissed' at the top, the other with 'Hugh Elliot Kerridge, dismissed'. A colour photo of each man was printed on the top-left corner. Kerridge had lost weight and the moustache; her father looked the same. Both men stared sullenly at the camera. Each page contained three paragraphs of type. The Kerridge sheet had a paperclip top left. Lilly flipped the page. Attached was a seven-by-five black-and-white photo showing three dark grey oval shapes against a lighter grey background. Each shape had a rough-edged, irregular black centre. Lilly took an informed guess. 'Bacterium tularemia?'

Adams smiled. 'Correct. Taken from the '04 experiment. And Goddard here took the photo.' Lilly didn't look up. The bacteria she was looking at were, as far as she could see, nothing like the image that Jeremy Casey had sent her. Even allowing for the huge advances in microscopic photography since 2004, it was clear that the image in her hand was not the new meningitis pathogen.

'Slater and Kerridge ran the questioning of Taylor,' said Adams. 'They didn't follow up, didn't check the medical records. They were culpable. They were dismissed.'

'How many others in the trial?' asked Lilly.

'No others,' said Adams. 'Just Taylor.'

'Bullshit,' said Lilly. 'One person doesn't constitute a trial.'

Goddard stepped forward; Lilly walked back. A new triangle.

'You are correct, of course,' he said. 'Human trials were an important part of our research from '49 to '89 but then had to be stopped. So this wasn't a trial as such.'

'What was it then?' said Lilly.

'It was an experiment that went wrong,' said Goddard. The words hung between them like the steam from his breath.

'So,' said Lilly, holding the folder out for Adams. 'It's Maddison, Bacon . . . and Taylor.'

Adams flinched, took the folder. 'That isn't how we see it. We can agree to disagree, obviously. But now you've seen the file we would ask that your partner's daughter stop her very public enquiries into Joe Taylor.'

So this was the point of it all, thought Lilly. This was the reason for this high-level visit.

'I'm sorry, *what* are you saying?' she said.

'Rose Chaplin, the daughter of Kit Chaplin, your partner,' said Adams, 'is on Discord and WhatsApp, asking about Joe Taylor. We'd like that to stop. Now that you know what happened you can tell her what she needs to know. And then she can stop.'

'Because?'

Adams scowled. The rugby face again. 'Because, Dr Slater, Sergeant Taylor's family were relocated. It was part of our arrangement. And these arrangements save lives.' Now Adams's hands flew like those of a street conjuror performing a cup-and-ball trick. 'Our enemies watch also, you know. And when they're done watching, they tap, hack, steal, poison and kill if they need to. The Skripals survived the Novichok poison – just – but Dawn Sturgess didn't. She found the bottle. Her dose was lethal.' Adams's right gloved finger jabbed her left gloved palm. Some close-up magic. 'Rose stops now, because lives are at stake. Any more posts and those accounts will have to disappear.'

The fumes from the cars hung low on the drive. Without even a whisper of a breeze they had formed a heady, heavy, toxic cloud. Lilly felt light-headed, exhausted and cold to her bones. She'd had enough. The warmth of her crappy little car was just a few metres away.

'OK, I'll tell her,' she managed. Walked to the Peugeot. As she opened the driver's door, Adams called out.

'And Dr Slater, you haven't seen Hugh Kerridge recently, by any chance?'

Lilly felt the blissful heat rolling from the car.

'No. Seen his son, but not him.'

'If you do see him, please tell us.'

'And how would—'

'I'll message you. I have your number.'

Of course you do, thought Lilly. 'You're my friend now?' she said.

Adams held out her palms. 'I can do that.'

And Lilly was gone. As she eased out of Goddard's drive, her skin tingling with the returning warmth, she reflected on the forced casualness of that last question. The Kerridge question. She had often observed how many conversations got to the nub of the matter only at their conclusion. How everything else was preamble and the real reason for the meeting was in the AOB. Any other business. The foot in the closing door. *Oh, just before I go . . .*

All of which made Hugh Kerridge, the frothing madman from her London reception, quite the enigma. The man of the moment.

In room 208, Rose's click rate was two per minute.
In room 209, Kit's click rate was eight per minute.
At the London Central Hospital, Harriet Teale had just died.

5 p.m.

Kit was sitting at the table, hands on his knees, eyes closed. The TV was off, curtains drawn, just one bedside light on. Rose was in 208, the adjoining door ajar. From the silence of his room, he could hear the clatter of hers. Laptop keyboard, music, snatches of phone chat. He had thought about calling her in. Decided no. He'd ride this one out alone.

There was a furious cacophony inside his head. Electricity ran through it now, 24/7. Sometimes it just hummed, but increasingly it powered what sounded like a head full of cheap, defective neon lights that were never repaired and were never, ever switched off. Maybe there wasn't an off switch.

He had been talking to Rose about shopping, or food, or maybe the news – he couldn't remember – but the words had this clanging cacophony running through them, on top of them. They swirled and crashed around each word and every sentence. He could hear what she was saying, but after a few minutes he didn't have the patience to care very much. He realized now that she might have been telling him something really important but, filtered through the tireless, out-of-control power station running in his head, her words lost any power.

Listening to her was exhausting. Listening to anything was exhausting. He kept still. Hands on knees, eyes closed.

The clicks cut through everything. Actually, he thought, they didn't so much cut through the bedlam as sit on top of the bedlam. Demanding to be heard. The headline act. The players of the power chords. Undoubtedly the drivers of the whole demented scene.

Hands on knees, eyes closed.

'Dad?'

Kit counted and timed. Everything was accelerating. When Lilly left, he had been two a minute, maximum. Now it was eight, minimum. The pace of change was greater than for any of his MCS students, some of whom had been clicking for over a week. Maybe he had a variant. Maybe he had got a bigger dose of whatever it was. Maybe he was just unlucky.

'Dad?'

He realized that, if he'd been driving, he'd have had to pull over. That if he'd been at the cinema, he'd have had to leave. That if he'd been teaching, he'd have had to stop. Normal life had disappeared. He wouldn't be able to hear the phone, watch TV, laugh with Rose. He wasn't in pain, not yet. But he was in anguish.

'Dad!'

Kit opened his eyes. Rose was in front of him, mouth open, eyes wide. Appalled. Horrified. Scared.

'Dad, what's wrong?' He heard her, as though through noise-cancelling headphones. A great muffling had taken place, a silencing of everything bar the clicks.

He took her hand. When he spoke, his voice sounded like it came from a thousand miles away.

'Rose,' he said, 'I think I've just gone deaf.'

5.19 p.m.

Rose wrote, *Oh my god, Dad, I don't know what to say.*

Kit shook his head. 'You don't need to say anything,' he said. 'Honestly.'

I am so so so sorry.

They were sitting on the bed in 208. Side by side. All the

lights on. Rose was writing on her phone, holding the screen for Kit to see. He was talking back. Hoping he still sounded like himself.

'Thanks,' he said. 'We'll get through this.'

Will we, though? Her eyes filled again, she wiped them with her sleeve.

Kit thought she looked utterly desperate. Red-eyed, exhausted and a face drained of colour. She slumped against him as she wrote.

Can you hear anything?

'Not much.'

You're shouting.

He gave a brief, sarcastic laugh. He'd said that to her so many times. Earbuds in, volume up, her voice was always too loud. He took her phone, typed, *Touché.*

Handed it back.

She put an arm around him; he rested his head on hers. So what happens now? he thought. If I die from this bastard disease, what then? What happens to Rose? He and Jody had written wills together, but the issue of Rose had been left unanswered. He had no siblings, no living parents. Jody had had a sister, but they disagreed on everything. 'She'd be better off in Barnardos,' had been her refrain. Jody's mother lived in New Zealand; her father was on a boat somewhere. He knew for certain Jody wouldn't want her daughter brought up by any of them.

Rose was writing again.

Does it hurt?

'Not at all.'

Will it hurt?

He shrugged. 'We have bags of drugs, remember?'

Rose hesitated, then wrote, *You can't die.*

'I have no intention of dying,' he said. Which, Kit thought, was honest, at least. He'd thought briefly about saying something more reassuring, but realized there really wasn't anything. When you've lost one parent, platitudes and misplaced optimism sound hollow. Even dishonest and dangerous.

More typing from Rose.

I don't want to die.

He felt it then. A gut-punch. Your kid should never have to say that to anyone, least of all a parent. And if they did, what did you say back? Knowing, as he did, that death was a possibility?

'I don't want you to die either,' he whispered. All he could manage. She put her phone down, embraced him with both arms. She held him tight around the neck, like he was falling overboard and she was his last hope. And maybe that was true. Her hair smelled of vanilla.

She disentangled. Wrote, *You're less than 24 hours. From when the clicks came.*

Kit had done that sum too. If telling the time and counting the hours could be called a sum.

'Fast, huh?' he said. 'Faster than the others, for sure. There's no logic there.'

I woke with it this morning. Before six.

Kit's heart was as heavy as when Jody had been near the end. He had no comfort to offer.

'I'm sorry, sweetie,' he said.

Gonna listen to some music, she wrote.

The unspoken words between them, *Before I can't.*

Kit nodded, then Rose added, *Are you sacred?*

He replied on her phone again. He typed, *I'm not SACRED. But I am SCARED!*

She punched his arm.

Still an English teacher then?

'Always,' he said. A reflexive response. Not true, though, he thought. Not any more.

Do we go to hospital now?

He shook his head. 'Nothing has changed, Rose. The drugs still don't work. When that's sorted, then we can go.'

Do we go home?

'Might be cheaper.'

Lilly is rich.

'You think?'

Richer than us.

'Everyone is richer than us.'

He had wondered about London. Everything was easier at home, though the thought of the journey was too much. He'd forgotten the car, parked God knows where. Lilly hadn't fancied it for her trip, found a rental. He had decided not to text her his big news, but Christ, he needed to talk to her. That was going to be bad too, but at least her cool rationality might serve them well. He preferred 'cool rationality' to 'emotional detachment'.

He realized Rose was staring at the curtains. A million miles away.

'What are you thinking?'

I was wondering what Mum would have done.

Wow. He hadn't seen that coming. 'Do you think that often?'

Every day.

'I never knew.'

You never asked.

Kit's phone rang. It was Lilly. Rose answered.

5.40 p.m.

The Peugeot swerved into the lay-by, braking hard. It crunched to a halt, gravel and trash spraying from under its tyres. The phone on the passenger seat was lit. It showed she was on the A354, had just gone through the village of Coombe

Bissett, heading into Salisbury. It was the same phone that had just brought her the news that her boyfriend had gone deaf. And that his daughter could be heading that way.

Both hands still on the wheel, Lilly stared dead ahead. The headlights picked out pot-holed tarmac and scrub. Cars flew past, a metre from her car door, but she wasn't looking. She didn't register. She didn't move. It was a full systems crash, and she'd had them before. They were always triggered by a sudden emotional overload. An empathy data dump that she didn't have the software to translate. She knew what was happening, understood it perfectly, just didn't react in the way others did. The way she was expected to. She processed differently. They might take the highway; she took the dirt track. They all got to roughly the same place in the end, as long as everyone else had the patience to wait for her. Which, in her experience, they usually didn't.

Everything together. The Volvo, the cage, Francisella tularensis, the deafness, the dead sergeant, the locomotive painting, the old house, the Novichok, her father, the Skripals, the hospital, the vaccine, the antibiotics, the meningitis. And the calamity of it all. The overwhelming, spirit-crushing calamity of it all.

Lilly opened both the front windows. Cold air and petrol fumes flooded in, she inhaled them both. The sweet, gassy smell fired some neurons. She called Jeremy Casey, he picked up.

'Thirty seconds, please, Jeremy. Has the new meningitis strain been confirmed?'

'Yes.' He was tired, his delivery slower. 'It won't be called Men-X, apparently, because that already exists, so it'll be called something else. Z, maybe. But whatever it's called, it's the incubation period that's the killer, Lilly. The clicking is what everyone talks about, but this fucker takes weeks to show its face. That's why it has spread so far.'

She wound up the passenger window. 'And any progress

at all with any antibiotic?' She tried to sound normal but knew she sounded desperate.

'None.' He paused, then added, 'You have skin in this game?'

'I do.'

'That young teacher fella?'

'And his daughter.'

'I'm very sorry to hear that, Lilly.'

There was nothing else to say. She realized he was waiting for her to hang up.

'OK, thanks, Jeremy.' She ended the call.

She scrolled her contacts until the screen showed *Professor Linda Harris, University of California, San Francisco.* Three rings, she picked up. An echoey and watery acoustic.

'Hey, Lilly. I'm in the bath, but it's fine, go ahead anyway.'

'I'm sorry, Linda, I'll call back—'

'No, no, really. Strange shift times here. You have to grab any time behind a locked door you can get. Particularly if the water's hot and you've got some Oliverum bath oil left.' The bathroom acoustic obscured only some of her old friend's exhaustion. The rest seeped down the phone.

'How bad?' said Lilly.

'Well, it's not Hilleman, at least,' said Harris. 'But that's the end of the good news. You've got it worse, but we have a couple of hundred or so cases in San Francisco, twenty-three deaths so far. Five hundred and counting nationwide. I lost three yesterday. And please don't ask me about them, as I won't make it to the end of the sentence.'

'OK,' said Lilly. 'Do the symptoms always follow in sequence there? Seems a bit erratic here.'

'Usually, yes. It's the clicks, then headaches, stiffness and deafness, but not always.'

'And the antibiotics? Anything happening there?'

A large exhalation. 'Nothing doing. We're working on some now, but almost all of our work for new antibiotics is aimed at tuberculosis and C. diff. And they'll take another three years at least. Maybe four or five. They're priority pathogens of course, but no one has been near meningitis for years.'

'No need,' said Lilly. 'Until now.'

More splashing sounds. From California to the lay-by on the A354. 'We're racing to divert resources, labs, staff, and so on,' said Harris, 'but unless we get lucky, we're going to be too late for this first wave, I'm afraid.'

'And what would "getting lucky" look like?' asked Lilly. She wound up the driver's window. Turned the heater up one notch.

'Oooh,' said Harris. 'I'd say finding out that one of the forty-something antibiotics the WHO says are in the pipeline is the perfect fit. By total chance. That does happen, and that would do it for sure.'

'OK, thanks, Linda—' said Lilly, but Harris was still going.

'Or that maybe some wacky lab in Wackstown, Arizona, has one on the shelf. Ready to go. We just have to pay. That would do it. Or, more likely, that Men-X just dies away. As soon as we're distanced, and it has nowhere to go. That's not a solution, but it would buy us time at least.'

Lilly heard the sound of knocking on a bathroom door. Muffled calls.

'OK, gotta go,' said Harris. 'Stay in touch.'

Lilly released her seatbelt, slid over to the passenger side, stepped out of the car. Her final call was to Jess. Who didn't pick up. She messaged *Call me when you can*, dropped the phone in her pocket.

She turned her back on the road, leaned against the car, folded her arms. No moon, no streetlights; the only illumination came from the Peugeot. She stared into the unkempt rubbish-strewn foliage of the lay-by. She knew she should be hurrying back to the hotel. Kit needed her. Even Rose needed her. But she had just a few seconds here. Three cars flashed past in quick succession. A Waitrose delivery van slowed, the driver peering across the lanes, then sped away.

Lilly closed her eyes. The traffic of the A354 became white noise and she filtered it away. She replayed her Goddard/Adams encounter, circling around the theatrics and the posturing. If Hugh Kerridge had been the point of the meeting – and she was sure it was – then Leon was her only contact. She needed to speak to Leon Kerridge.

A vibration from her coat pocket. A video from Rose. She had titled it 'ASAP!' Duration two minutes and seven seconds. The opening frame showed a white woman, early fifties. Black-and-yellow blouse, grey hair cut short, weathered skin. Lilly pressed play as two articulated trucks clattered past, a parade of cars following in their wake. The limited volume on her phone couldn't cope. She climbed back in the car.

Windows up, she rewound. Pressed play.

6 p.m.

'Hello, Rose. I'm Jenny Rosen, I live out in Winnipeg, Canada. Joe Taylor was my brother.'

Lilly inhaled sharply, paused the video.

'My God,' she muttered. The woman appeared to be filming at her kitchen table, a pine dresser laden with plates and hanging mugs behind her. Her hands were on the table. Fingers interlaced. Her voice was London, laced with Canada. She pronounced 'out' as 'oat'.

Lilly pressed play again.

'I've tried to record this four times. Hoping I can make it on the fifth.' A breath. 'So. You asked about Joe. Here's what I can tell you.' She sipped a glass of water, composed herself. 'This is hard,' she says. 'OK.' She goes again. 'It's hard because I never believed him at the time. No one did. Even our parents didn't really believe him.' She closes her eyes as if she is praying. Maybe she is. When she opens them again she glares at the screen. Then speaks faster. Getting it done.

'Joe was an addict. He joined the army to get clean and, for a while, it worked. But then he found the wrong crowd, or they found him, and he was off again. He hid it well – he was smart like that. Most folk thought he just drank too much, but it was worse than that. Much worse.'

More water. Another deep breath.

'So this is what Joe said happened in 2004. He said this to me. His sister. Who should have believed him. Anyways. After a particularly bad session, he was about to get thrown out. Joe said two plain-clothes at Porton Down told him they could get him off all the charges if he agreed to take part in an experiment. And they would pay him, too. Decent cash. They said it involved a tiny dose of a new meningitis strain, that he would be closely watched and given all the drugs – the medication – that he needed. That it was totally safe.' She unfolded her hands, covered her mouth with one, looked away. An off-camera voice, just audible in the car. 'You doin' great, love.'

She looked doubtful, Lilly thought.

'So,' she continued, 'Joe said that they told him they "got lucky".' She mimed the quote marks with her fingers. 'I remember the phrase specifically. They "got lucky". Something about an old woman, living alone. And that she . . . got infected somehow.' Jenny was waving her arms, moving her head in an 'I'm not sure about this' gesture. 'Maybe they got this disease from her. Anyway, that's it. That's all I remember. Joe got sick pretty quick. He lost his hearing, got headaches, all the usual things. I mean, it sounds a bit like this new disease, doesn't it? When I saw the news, I kept thinking of our Joe.'

She swallowed hard. Another sip.

'I can't tell you how guilty I feel.' On the verge of tears now.

'Mum and Dad have gone, so I have the full load. Their guilt and mine. Joe's hearing never really came back. The moods got darker. He overdosed December twenty-first 2004, died on Christmas Day.' She bit her lip, and her hand reached out to the camera to stop the recording. Then she was back.

'Sorry about that,' she said. 'I hope that helps, Rose. I don't know . . . I shouldn't be saying any of this, of course, as we got relocated with Joe's hush money. Promised to keep it all quiet. And I have done till now.' She managed a smile. 'But this feels like the right thing to do.' A pause. She was done. 'Bye then, Rose.' And Jenny Rosen signed off.

In the lay-by on the A354, Lilly clicked her phone off. Dropped it on the passenger seat. She had no doubt who the 'two plain-clothes' were. The men who had done the persuading of poor Joe Taylor. Ed Slater and Hugh Kerridge.

Lilly started the car, pulled back on to the road. 'Hugh Kerridge,' she said to the car. 'I do believe that you're a total shit.'

6.10 p.m.

Kit had read the hospital's advice again. Before he went on whatever hare-brained trip Lilly had come up with, he needed to know whether anything had changed.

It hadn't. The hospital was still full. The antibiotics still weren't working. He swallowed two co-codamol, put the packet in his jacket pocket, told Rose he was ready.

They locked up rooms 208 and 209, took the stairs. Rose hovered and worried around him.

'I'm not an imbecile, you know,' said Kit, his words a distant rumble. 'I can still walk down stairs.' She fell back, they walked normally. And while it was true that he had only lost one of his senses, his new shroud of silence had left him

289

feeling weak and vulnerable. He walked slower, he talked slower. To make sure he wasn't missing anything, he kept looking all round, turning, looking for danger.

Not knowing if he was being spoken to, not knowing if there was music, not knowing if his phone was ringing had left him feeling exposed. In an instant, Rose had become his carer.

She had given him earplugs to wear. *Just until we get in the car*, she had written, then pushed her own in.

Reception was deserted. Empty armchairs. No one behind the desk. No concierge. The always-burning log fire was out. Through the glass of the front door, an empty street. Lilly had said to wait here. He wondered if they were the only ones left.

Kit's head clicked away, though the frequency had slowed. He was glad of the earplugs. Rose put her arm through his. Took it away again. He felt a tug on his sleeve – a man was talking to Rose. He looked like the missing receptionist; his hotel badge said Pascale. Well groomed, mid-thirties. Creed aftershave. Black cloth face mask. He was explaining something, wringing his hands as he did so. Rose was nodding. Whatever it was, he was apologizing for it.

Rose grabbed a pad and pen from reception. Held it up for Kit. 'We have to leave.' She wrote fast. A large, loopy scrawl on an oversized white pad. 'They're having to close. We have two hours. He said he's very sorry.'

They stared at each other. Kit thought he could see pretty much everything in Rose's eyes, the set of her mouth, her posture. Fear and determination were most of it. But also sickness. An accumulating, relentless sickness that was in the process of wringing her out then stealing her hearing. Then it could come for her life. He needed to be here for her. He *had* to be here for her.

She was writing again. He thought his heart would break. *Stay here. I'll pack everything. Look for Lilly.*

Kit shook his head. 'Other way round. You wait here. I'll get everything. You can't pack, anyway.'

Outside, they both saw the Peugeot pull up. Lilly's beckoning hand. Kit raced up the stairs.

6.20 p.m.

It took Kit just ten minutes to pack everyone's stuff. Three cases, two carrier bags. Pascale delivered them on a trolley, loaded them into the Peugeot's inadequate boot. Kit and Rose thanked him, then got in the car.

'Sorry,' said Kit, his voice too loud in the small car.

Lilly put her index finger on his lips. Hugged him, both arms. She held it for a second, pulled away. He looked broken, she thought. Rounded shoulders, ill at ease, hair wild.

'*I'm* sorry,' she mouthed. He nodded. Removed his earplugs.

They sat, parked outside the hotel. Watched Pascale locking its doors.

'This is a shit holiday,' said Kit.

Rose laughed; Lilly didn't.

Rose removed her earplugs, leaned in between them. She pointed to her phone. The screen showed a WhatsApp account, labelled 'Solz', with Lilly, Kit and Rose named as the users. *Set it up an hour ago*, she wrote. *Thought we might need it. I've signed you both up.* Kit gave a thumbs-up.

Lilly talked. Rose typed and talked. Kit read what Rose wrote, then talked.

'Where are we going?' he said. Rose tapped him on the shoulder. 'OK, I'm loud. But still. What are we doing?'

'We're unlikely to find anywhere to stay now,' said Lilly. 'Everywhere will be closed, presumably.'

'So home then,' said Rose.

'Yes, that's one option,' said Lilly.

'We have options?' said Kit.

Click – Rose.

'Can we eat first?' said Rose. 'I'm absolutely starving.'

Lilly nodded, then Kit.

'Yes, please,' he said. 'Not that two clickers would be especially welcome in a restaurant.'

'Take-out then,' said Lilly, 'and it had better be me that does the taking. Just no complaints, whatever I bring back.'

'Fair,' said Rose. Lilly opened her door. 'Unless it's sushi,' she added.

Lilly left the engine running, the heater on. Rose put her hand on Kit's shoulder. He put his hand on hers. 'Clicks?' he said.

She typed, *2 or 3 a minute.* Then, *Headache?* Kit shook his head, held up the co-codamol box. She squeezed his shoulder; he squeezed her hand. They sat in their two versions of silence until food arrived.

Lilly arrived in a flurry of brown pizza boxes. The car filled with the heavy smells of freshly cooked pizza dough, melted cheese and the zesty tang of salami. The windows steamed up in seconds.

'First option was the best option,' said Lilly. 'Small place. Choice of four pizzas, that's all. So I got two with pepperoni, one without.' She handed over the boxes marked with a large 'P'. Paper napkins followed. And from her coat, two Coke Zeros. 'And yes, they're warm,' she said. 'Though God knows how.' Rose and Kit popped the cans. Chugged noisily.

Two slices down, Lilly wiped her mouth. Picked up the conversation. 'I guess we could stay at my old house,' she said. 'At Clayton Drive.' She knew she didn't sound convincing, because she wasn't convinced herself. And if they needed to go back to London, she was OK with that.

'The house where your father killed himself?' said Rose, mouth full, appalled. 'That's just the worst idea. Sorry, but home is good. Or the hospital. Or a ditch, to be honest.' She wiped her hands, typed fast. *L suggesting her dad's place! BAD IDEA!*

'Can we drive the hire car to London?' Kit said, Coke between his legs. 'Don't fancy the trip in mine.'

'No idea,' said Lilly. 'But before all that, I've had a visit from the Ministry of Defence.' She glanced at Rose in the mirror. 'They know you're asking about Joe Taylor and want you to stop.'

'What?' said Rose, outraged. Waving pizza. 'What happened to the "end-to-end encryption" that's promised?'

'You need to type and speak together, Rose,' said Kit.

'Oh yeah,' she said. 'Getting there.' She wiped the grease from her fingers, became the stenographer again.

'I have no idea,' said Lilly. 'But they said they wanted you to stop. Because it's dangerous, apparently. All part of that relocation deal, for the Taylors. The Russians, and other assorted enemies, could be following it all. The woman from the MOD was pretty pissed off.'

'Well,' said Rose. 'Imagine how pissed off she'll be when she watches the Jenny Rosen video.' Rose's fingernails tapped as she typed. She tapped and clicked. Tapped and clicked.

Kit's hand went up. 'Wait!' he said. 'Tell me what she says! Christ, this sucks. What's in the video?' He watched his phone for the answers.

'Well, I'll go first,' said Lilly, 'then you, Rose. At Mark Goddard's house, this big, aggressive woman from the MOD and Porton Down turns up, says Joe Taylor took part in an experiment using a bacterium called Francisella tularensis, which, she said, had been weaponized by the Americans in the 1960s and that can cause a type of meningitis.'

'Can't spell that bacterium,' said Rose.

'Doesn't matter,' said Lilly. She peeled another slice of pizza.

'Or meningitis,' said Rose. Then, 'OK, got it.'

'This MOD woman then says my father and Hugh Kerridge – who they're desperate to find, by the way – were fired for not realizing he was a drug addict and a liar. Also, sidebar, they all knew Sergei Skripal, S K R I P A L, in this railway appreciation club. So then this video arrives via Rose.' Lilly waves in Rose, who is still typing.

'Wait,' she says.

Kit catches up. 'How did this MOD woman know you were there?' A slice of pepperoni falls back into the box. He adds it to his next pizza slice.

'Goddard told her. They go way back. He called her in.'

Kit waits for the words to appear.

'And you know about this bacterium?' he says, pointing to where Rose had typed her version of 'Francisella tularensis'. 'This . . . whatever it's called?'

'In animals, yes. As a bio-terror weapon, no.' Lilly waited for the reaction. It was like speaking on a call with a massive satellite delay.

'Really?' Kit spluttered. Right on cue. *'Bio-terror?* Is that where we are?'

'But it *isn't* that,' said Lilly. 'Rose, tell him about the video from Jenny Rosen.'

Rose wrote fast. Kit read fast, hungrily waiting for each new word to appear. She explained the whole clip. The sister's guilt, the two men who had persuaded her brother to take part in the 'trial', the 'getting lucky' with a new meningitis strain, his overdose and death. Christmas Day 2004.

'If I had to choose,' said Kit once he'd finished reading, 'between the MOD woman and the Canadian woman, I'm going with Canada all the way.' He held up his last slice of pizza. 'Anyone want more?'

'Why would the MOD woman lie to you, though?' said Rose, ignoring him.

'Dunno,' said Lilly. Her phone buzzed. She wiped her hands again, read the text.

'What the hell is this?' she muttered.

Kit stared at her. Read her face. 'Well?'

She held up her phone screen for Rose and Kit to read. The text was arranged like a formal letter.

Dear Dr Slater,
I am fine.
My father is home now.
You can come round.

Sincerely yours,
Leon Kerridge
26 Salt Street,
Salisbury
England.

'Is this guy for real?' said Rose. 'Who doesn't know how to text?'

Kit read it again, then looked hard at Lilly. 'So,' he said, very slowly, 'the man you say came to your workplace last year, your father's friend, Sergei Skripal's friend, Leon's father, one of the men who persuaded Sergeant Joe Taylor to take part in this trial, the man the MOD are, apparently, desperate to find, is actually in his own house.'

Lilly nodded. 'Unless Leon has lost it completely, yes.'

She started the car, pulled away from the hotel.

'Twenty-six Salt Street?' said Kit.

Lilly nodded.

Kit finished eating, closed the box.

Rose clicked. Fourth in a minute.

295

7.08 p.m.

Lilly swung into Salt Street, parked in the first space she could find. She peered at a gatepost. They were outside number seven. The street was well lit, more elegant than Clayton Drive. Older, too. Early 1900s, maybe. The houses were terraced but set further back, with bigger windows and glazed front doors that sat in arched porches. It ran parallel with Clayton Drive, literally around the corner, but Lilly didn't remember ever coming here. She must have walked along it at some time, but she'd never had friends here. Lilly didn't think she'd ever used the phrase 'well-to-do', but there was no doubt that's what Salt Street was.

'What happens now?' said Rose. 'Do me and Dad stay here while you talk to your guy?' She hadn't typed, but Kit spoke anyway.

'I'm coming in with you,' he said. 'I'll mask up. Put the earplugs in. Whatever. But you're not doing this alone.'

Rose leaned forward. 'That leaves me on my own then.' Kit lip-read some, guessed the rest.

'Let's all do this,' he said. 'Go in together.'

'No, thanks,' Rose said. 'I'm good.'

'But that's just it,' said Kit. 'You're not good. You're sick. Come with us, Rose. We won't be long, will we?' He looked at Lilly.

I have no idea, she thought. 'Twenty minutes,' she said. 'Tops.' Rose slumped back in her seat. Kit and Lilly both swivelled to face her.

'I'll stay, really,' said Rose, already reaching for her phone. 'If I get bored or creeped out, I'll catch you guys up.' She looked up. Went from Lilly to Kit. 'What?' she said. 'I'll be fine. Engine running, heater on, doors locked and sweet music. Plus, if I'm here, it'll speed things along in there.' She gestured up the road. 'You'll be quick. Am I right?' She raised her eyebrows. The familiar challenge. Lilly began to type; Kit waved it away.

'I pretty much know what she said. I can see it.' A deep sigh. 'You win, Rose, you win.' Then to Lilly. 'We'll be quick, yeah?'

I hope so, she thought. 'Sure,' she said.

Salt Street was cold. As soon as they stepped out of the car they felt the ice cut through their clothes. A sleety drizzle had started, the almost-flakes settling briefly on their hair, melting on their faces. Not the weather for walking even ten paces, thought Lilly, never mind driving ninety miles. She took Kit's hand, trod gingerly as they counted the houses. Odds on the left, evens on the right. They stayed left until they were opposite number twenty-six.

There was no denying that the Kerridge house was shabby. By some measure, it was the least loved in the street. The detail of its neglect was illuminated by two streetlights which stood a few metres either side of its cracked path, and by what appeared to be every one of number twenty-six's lights. Two rooms upstairs, blinds up, lights on. One large box window downstairs, curtains almost drawn, lights on. Small, frosted hall window next to the front door, light on. The low terracotta-coloured garden wall had fallen inwards towards the house. In the front the grass was uncut, probably untroubled by a lawnmower all summer. Tall weeds sprouted from the broken slabs of the path. The house exterior was in urgent need of a painter, a roofer and anyone who could fix a gutter. The porch was running out of tiles. The black, plain front door just about held on to the brass numbers 2 and 6. The 2 had tilted slightly to the right, the 6 to the left.

Either side, the houses were well kept and modestly lit. The rest of Salt Street was well kept and modestly lit. Twenty-six was a blazing exception.

'It's like they've son-et-lumièred the wrong house,' said Kit. *Let's get this over with,* typed Lilly. Kit glanced back to the car. It was shielded from view by a line of parked cars, but he could see its lights even if he couldn't hear its engine.

'Agreed,' he said. They crossed the road. Now he could see Rose. The reflected Peugeot headlights showed her reading, head down, nodding in time to whatever music was playing in her earbuds.

At the path, he held back. Tugged at Lilly's sleeve.

'Look, Lilly. This is your thing,' he said. 'Don't bother typing everything. Just have the conversation you need to have with Kerridge. Find out what you need to find out. Include me if you need to, but otherwise . . .' He pushed his earplugs back in. 'Otherwise, I'll be your deaf and mute assistant. Or minder. Whichever you need the most.'

She wrote, *I'm glad you're here. I don't think H K is a very nice man.*

Words from Rose appeared. *Get on with it.*

Lilly nodded. 'Right then,' she said.

She stood on the cracked front-door step. Rang the bell. If it rang somewhere, she didn't hear it. She reached for the door knocker.

Her hand was shaking again.

His head was buzzing.

Rose was still rocking.

7.15 p.m.

The only unlit part of 26 Salt Street was the porch. Lilly stood just in front of Kit. From the step, their double shadows, courtesy of the streetlights, played on the front door. Jittery, skittish. Now the porch light snapped on, the door opened as far as the security chain would allow.

It was Leon Kerridge who answered the door. He looked neither surprised nor unsurprised to see her. Cap and jacket on.

'Hello, Lilly,' he said.

'Hello, Leon,' said Lilly. 'This is my partner, Kit. Might we come in, please? We won't be very long, I promise.' He moved his head to see Kit. Kit smiled, raised a hand in greeting.

'Is it about the text I sent you?' said Leon.

'Yes,' said Lilly. 'Yes, it is. You invited me round.'

'You have questions?'

'Yes, we do,' she said. 'If that's OK.'

Leon nodded. 'That's OK,' he said.

He unchained and opened the door, they stepped inside. The light and heat were both up full. Lilly and Kit squinted, undid their coats. Leon, in khaki cargo trousers and black hoodie, shuffled past them, throwing Kit a stare as he went. Kit gave Lilly a 'what's with him?' shrug, then they followed him into the lounge.

It would have been a fine room once. Maybe not so long ago. High-ceilinged, spacious, well proportioned. But it was the clutter that was in charge now. There was a sofa and an armchair, a coffee table too, but they had lost their battle with the junk. It was more of an outdoor yard than an Edwardian front room. It smelled of oil and paint stripper. Two ladders on their sides, metal and plastic buckets, an old racing bike with drop handlebars, a workbench with an open toolbox on it, a stiff broom, stacked wicker boxes in the fireplace, and a large, mouldy, possibly circular piece of cloth where a rug might have been. A garden parasol once upon a time, Lilly thought.

There were bookshelves either side of the fireplace, but most of the books appeared to be stacked in piles on the floor. Lilly noticed Kit tilting his head, reading the spines. Very few novels, as far as she could see. Top of the nearest pile was *Mendelian and Molecular Genetics*. A few general medical reference books she recognized. Then some railway books she didn't. *Weathered Steam Locomotives* by Andy Small. *Steam Locomotives* by Keith Moseley. *Guide to North American Steam Locomotives*, second edition, by George Drury.

'There's tea in the pot,' announced Leon.

'Tea?' Lilly asked Kit, exaggerating her lip movement.

Kit shook his head. Lilly said yes. Leon disappeared.

Kit typed, *All OK, Rose?* After a few seconds, *Yh.*

'This is weird,' he whispered. Then, 'Where's the dad?'

Lilly shrugged. Wrote, *Home improvements? Moving out?* She gestured around the room.

Now Kit shrugged. 'No idea,' he said. They inched their way around the room, taking care not to topple books or walk into buckets. 'Do we sit?' whispered Kit. 'Not sure I fancy it, really.'

They reached the sofa, an old leather three-seater with pillows instead of cushions. On one of its arms, a small white card. Lilly recognized it. She had one. Detective Sergeant John Appleby. Wiltshire Police. Two phone numbers, a landline and a mobile. A small, silver star crest with a red-and-gold crown on top, a cross in the middle. She showed it to Kit just as Leon returned. He handed a mug to Lilly, sat in the armchair without spilling from his. He stared at Kit. Kit stared back.

'So,' said Lilly, easing her way on to the sofa, 'the police have been, I see.' She pointed to the card.

'They have,' said Leon.

'Came to speak to your dad, I imagine,' said Lilly.

'Yes, but he wasn't here. They had a good look round, though. Took all our papers and computers. I gave them tea as well.'

'Really?' Lilly was amazed. 'Why did they take the computers, Leon?

'He is a very great man,' said Leon.

'I'm sure,' said Lilly. 'Why did they take the computers?'

'You met him once.'

'I did. We talked about that last time, I think.' Lilly was keeping her tone light, breezy, but it was fraying at the edges now. She rephrased. 'Why did the police say they came here?'

'Because,' he said, 'they think my father is a terrorist.'

7.23 p.m.

In the Peugeot, engine running, headlights and heater on full, Rose was reading. She clicked too, but was, for the moment at least, distracted. One of her playlists ran through her earbuds, but it was words that had captured her this time, not beats. There was still no word from Harriet or her parents. She was checking WhatsApp and her texts every few minutes, but there was nothing. She switched to Discord and noticed a link she'd been sent. Tagged her @Rose, said she'd be interested. She clicked through. It was the story of two murderers, Alexander Mishkin and Anatoliy Chepiga. The first man was a doctor, the second a colonel. It told of their trip to England, minute by minute. Of their weapon of choice, the deadly nerve agent Novichok. And of their poisoning of former Russian intelligence officer Sergei Skripal, his daughter, Yulia, and the passing stranger Dawn Sturgess.

Rose looked up the Skripals' address. Google maps said Christie Miller Road was ten minutes away by car, twenty-five if you walked. The story concluded with Mishkin and Chepiga's walk back to the station. A walk that took them sightseeing and window shopping in Salisbury city centre. Then a train to London and a flight to Moscow.

In front of the Peugeot was a Range Rover, then, at polite distances, a Tesla, a BMW, a Prius, a VW Scirocco, an old Saab, a classic MG and a Mini with a Union Jack painted on its roof. On the other side of the road from the Mini was a white van towing a trailer. In its shadow, by the passenger door, stood a man. Five ten, black cap, black woollen overcoat. Hands in pockets. Breathing hard. Looking through the van's windscreen and driver's window, he had a clear view of the girl in the car. The girl was busy. She didn't look up.

7.25 p.m.

Lilly typed fast. *He says the police were here today they think H is a terrorist.* Kit looked wide-eyed at her. She pulled an 'I know' face. He waved her on. Translating it into WhatsApp was holding things up.

His head was humming again. A steady electrical current now, like the fizzing you hear walking beneath an electricity pylon. The same key as the note Johnny Cash hums at the beginning of 'Walk The Line'. Or a buzzing fly. Something like that. He watched Lilly and Leon talk. Lilly was edge of seat urgent, frustrated. Leon was impassive, slow, occasionally puzzled. But Kit heard none of it.

If the police were saying Hugh Kerridge was a terrorist, Kit was inclined to agree with them. He couldn't really say why. But if a geneticist from Porton Down was being hunted for terror offences, it had to have something to do with Men-X. Which made the spread of the virus, or whatever it was, deliberate. Which made the Kerridge house a particularly dangerous place to be.

He WhatsApped, *Need to speed up. Getting nervous.*

Lilly gave a thumbs-up.

7.27 p.m.

The man by the white van stared at the girl in the Peugeot. Twenty metres, give or take. He leaned over the front wheel arch, closing the gap between them by a few centimetres. A closer look. He could see the hat, the hair, the concentration. She seemed to be reading. He peeled himself off the bonnet, glanced left and right, up and down Salt Street. He looked at the next car along, the one that would bring him closer to the Peugeot. A Fiat Uno. He stayed put. Three cars down, a seven-seater people carrier, sitting high in the road, casting a shadow that stretched to a garden wall. He hesitated, then walked the eleven strides to its protection. He found that if he stood by its petrol cap, he could see straight into the Peugeot. The girl had the reading light on now. Her seatbelt was off. The car was locked.

7.29 p.m.

Lilly realized that when Leon was upset or stressed, he clammed shut. She stopped asking why the police thought his father was a terrorist. Tried a different tack. He had stopped drinking his tea, though the mug was still in his hands. Lilly's sat untouched, at her feet.

'It was nice of you to text me,' she said.

'Thank you, Lilly.'

'Did you want to see me, Leon?'

'Yes.'

'Why?'

He looked uncomfortable now, glancing at the ceiling then all around the room. His eyes alighted on something moment-arily, then flitted away. She wanted to check on Kit but kept her eyes on Leon. Felt they were on the edge of something. That if she could just keep this moment going, it might lead somewhere.

'They think my dad is a terrorist.'

Lilly said nothing, waiting. She sensed Kit, in his new silent world, doing the same. Not breaking the spell. Not for a moment.

'But he's a good man, my dad.'

And so . . . thought Lilly. *And so . . .* She held her breath.

Leon opened his mouth then closed it again. That's some battle being fought in your head, she thought. When he did speak, it came fast.

'So, before I wiped my dad's computers, I printed an article. Would you like to see it?'

She felt a bolt of adrenaline. Typed. *He wiped their computers but printed something first.*

Kit looked worried, on the verge of leaving. He shuffled forward to the edge of his seat. Looking between Leon and Lilly.

'Can I see it?'

'Yes. I'll get it if you want.'

He says he's going to get it.

Leon put the mug on the floor, heaved himself out of the chair. He walked around the chair, stepped over the buckets, left the room. She thought of Goddard leaving, the MOD woman arriving. But this felt different – she could hear Leon clattering around in the kitchen.

Kit was wired. Stood up. 'What the fuck is this going to be?' he said. 'Lilly, this really doesn't feel good.'

7.30 p.m.

Rose, back on Discord, tried to message the story-sender. But her screen said, *Cannot connect to server.* Frowning, she switched to WhatsApp. An in-app message appeared. *Account temporarily suspended.* A timer underneath showed a clock counting down: *47 hours, 58 minutes.*

'Shit!' she yelled, kicked the front seat. She stared at her screen. Turned her phone off and on again. Same messages, same suspensions. She kicked the seat again. Looked up, looked out. She hadn't done that for a long time. Too long.

She caught movement. Across the street, behind the big people-carrier. She punched the reading light off. Checked the central locking. Pulled her legs up on the seat and tucked them underneath her. She stared at the car.

The blue Citroën Space Tourer was massive. It obscured at least half a garden wall. For the best part of a minute there was nothing. She was looking at a row of nice cars in front of a row of nice houses. Then the darkness shifted again. A head appeared briefly at the Citroën's rear, then ducked back to the dark. In the house behind, the porch light snapped on. It was enough to show Rose the outline of a man. A man who could have been watching her for a while.

Rose grabbed her phone. Called her father. Clambered into the front seat. Hit the horn.

7.31 p.m.

Three things happened at once. Leon walked back into the lounge, a wad of papers in his hand. Kit's phone vibrated. And the clear single tone of a horn came from the street. Kit stared at his phone, accepted the call, threw it to Lilly.

'It's Rose!' he shouted. 'Talk to her!' Lilly listened, to Rose and the horn together. She turned to Kit. Pointed to the front door. Mouthed, 'Go!'

He pushed past Leon, who dropped his papers. Out of the house in seconds, he sprinted down the middle of the road. He yelled as he ran. Rage and terror fired every muscle.

The Peugeot front passenger door opened. Rose tumbled out, ran the few steps to Kit, who hugged her hard. Dear God, he'd had enough of this. Too much sickness, too much fear. She pulled away. She looked exhausted, scared.

'There was a man!' she said, then slowed to a staccato so

he could follow. 'There. was. a. man. right. there.' She pointed to the Citroën. Kit ran around the car, waved at the woman who had appeared on her porch, who then went back inside. Without waving back.

'WhatsApp?' he said, puzzled that she wasn't using it.

'Blocked,' she mouthed, then resorted to a text. Typed.

My accounts are blocked. She held up her screen. He read, nodded.

Then, *A man was watching me. He ran off. Didn't see where he went.*

Kit grabbed Rose's hand. She tugged his. On her phone, she selected text, then clicked the microphone icon.

'Can we go home?' she said. The words appeared in the text box. Before he could reply, she added, 'I'm four a minute. Maybe five.'

Kit, deaf, sick and exhausted, embraced her again.

'OK,' he said. 'Well, here comes Lilly.'

7.35 p.m.

She knew they'd had enough. As Lilly ran from the house, she could see their pain and exhaustion. Rose's head on Kit's chest, his arms around her, they propped each other up. Swathed in steam, lit by sodium, close to collapse. The props were yielding. It was time to stop.

'He ran off,' said Kit as she approached, his voice abnormally loud again. 'Whoever he was, he's gone.' She looked around, up and down Salt Street. No one in sight, two faces at upper windows. That was it. An empty street. Left and right, parallel lines of frosted windscreens. The exception was the Peugeot. Engine still running, lights still on.

'What did he look like, Rose?' Lilly said, breathing hard. 'Could you see?'

'Not really,' said Rose, still holding on to Kit's jacket. 'Cap definitely. Dark one.' She trailed off, shrugged. 'Normal height, maybe? By the time I'd got into the front seat and hit the horn, he was gone.'

When she was close enough, Kit took Lilly's hand.

'And, Lilly?' he said. 'We've had enough. Home. Hospital. Either. Both. Rose's clicks are climbing. Let's get her safe.' He wasn't negotiating, just saying how it had to be. 'Plus, my head-aches are getting stronger now. We should just go.' He pointed at the car. Rose held her phone up. 'Just talk, Lilly,' she said. 'It writes it like a text.' She held the screen so Kit could see.

Lilly didn't know a phone could do that. 'Oh, OK,' she said. 'Well, yes, we can just go. I'll get whatever it was Leon was about to give me. Then we go. You want to stay here?'

Kit read the screen, shook his head. 'No. We do everything together now. No splitting up. Let's get whatever it is and go.'

They walked up the road at speed, Rose glancing behind her every few paces. Past the Scirocco, the Saab and the Mini. The door of number twenty-six was wide open. In the hall-way, Leon, his papers reassembled, stood motionless. Cap, jacket. Deep in Lilly's coat pocket, her right hand shook. She made a fist, calmed it down. They walked to the porch and stopped. Lilly, then Kit, then Rose.

'Do you know anyone who wears a dark cap?' Lilly asked Leon. 'On a cold night, you know. Maybe average height.' Rose and Kit glanced at her. She was clearly implying he did. Leon said nothing. 'OK, I'll be specific, Leon,' she said. 'Does your dad own a dark cap?'

'Yes,' Leon said. 'A navy one.'

'Is it hanging up here? Can you see it?'

Leon looked at the coat rack. Lifted a few. 'No, I can't see it.'

'Has he just come back?' she said. 'Maybe the back door?'

'No. I don't think so. I think he's gone to London.'

'You said he was back.'

'He is.'

'But now he's in London?'

'Yes.'

'Why do you think that?'

'He messaged me.'

'Do you know where in London?'

'I don't. The City Stay Hotel, maybe. He used to stay there.'

'Lilly—' began Kit.

'Well, I'll just take what you printed for me,' Lilly said. She held out her hand, Leon gave her the papers.

They all saw the top page. It was an A4 colour picture. The briefest pause before Kit shouted, 'What the hell is that?'

7.45 p.m.

It was a child's idea of a monster. The top sheet of Leon's document pile was in livid, trippy colours. Pinks, purples, oranges and greens. They adorned what resembled a six-legged spider that had grown a microphone for a head. It looked preposterous. The 'microphone' was shaped like a large egg, painted green and yellow and covered with purple spikes. Its 'handle' looked tightly wrapped in orange-and-red striped cable. The 'legs' appeared to be made from green plastic beads with red connection joints where the knees would be. A no-budget science-fiction television show from the 1960s would have laughed it off-set.

'It's a bacteriophage,' said Lilly.

Rose retrieved her phone. 'It's a *what*?'

'It's a bacteriophage,' Lilly repeated. 'A virus. It infects and replicates within bacteria.'

Kit leaned in. Watched Lilly's words appear in text form, then switched back to the image. 'That's for real?' he said. 'That thing *exists*?'

'For sure,' said Lilly. 'I haven't worked with phages before but, in the biosphere, they are everywhere.' She leafed through the other pages. Numbered one to thirty-eight. She caught key words and phrases, each one captivating. *Fermentation. Aqueous solution. Carbon source.* Now she was hooked. *Nitrogen. Metabolic cycles. Ammonia salt.* The skin from her neck to her scalp was starting to tingle. *Magnesium, zinc, anti-foaming agent. Starter culture.* There were diagrams of steel tanks and shake flasks. References to temperature controls and isolation processes. Her hands began to shake. 'My God. This is an antibiotic,' she said, her voice so quiet Rose's phone didn't pick up her words. Kit tapped her on the shoulder. Waited until she reacted.

'Lilly. What is it?'

Leon hadn't moved. No one had moved. They were all waiting, the cold temporarily forgotten. She glanced at each of them before returning to the pages. She took a breath, her hands calmed. 'OK. So, as far as I can see, this is the blueprint – no, actually more than that, it's a recipe, in effect, for an antibiotic, but using these' – she flipped back to the spider – 'using bacteriophages to fight the bacteria. It's a bacteria eater. "Phage" comes from the Greek word *phagein*, which means "to devour". They devour bacteria.'

Rose's phone was struggling with some of the running commentary, but Kit got the gist. 'An antibiotic for what? Does it say?'

She knew that it did. The image on page two, right after the spider/bacteriophage, was remarkably similar to the one Jeremy Casey had sent her two days earlier. Two round, joined bacteria. A diplococcus, covered in a dense mesh of straw-coloured hairs. Underneath the image were the words 'Neisseria meningitidis'.

She pointed to the words. Hand steady. Spoke clearly into Rose's phone. 'Neisseria meningitides is also referred to as meningococcus. So this document' – she waved the pages in her hand – 'claims to be an antibiotic for bacterial meningitis. But, crucially, a *different* antibiotic. One we haven't seen before. It's not claforan or rocephin. There is no reference that I've seen so far to penicillin. It uses phage therapy. And I've never seen that for meningitis. So this is either a clever fake from a science troll – quite possible, to be honest – or . . .' She looked between Rose and Kit, who stared right back, anticipating the end of her sentence. 'Or else, it's a treatment for your meningitis.'

Kit swallowed hard. Wiped his eyes. 'So a pile of junk or a bloody lifesaver.'

Lilly nodded.

'And,' he went on, 'if it *is* a new antibiotic, how long till that's . . .' He trailed away, not wanting to know the answer. And Lilly didn't want to tell him either. But she told the truth, gently.

'Six to nine months would be fast,' she said.

Kit read from the screen, closed his eyes. From a distance, somewhere in a Salt Street garden, a dog barked. Then two more joined in.

'No good for me,' he said. 'Six to nine days would be pushing it.' Rose looped an arm through his. 'And so I don't want to stay here a second longer. If you'll excuse us . . .' Kit turned, disconnected from Lilly, took Rose with him. They walked to the gate of number twenty-six, waited for Lilly. Back down the street, the Tesla doors slammed, then the car drove away. The Mini followed, then Salt Street was quiet again.

There was an added sharpness to the cold now, Lilly thought. Sleet turning to snow. Leon seemed impervious to it.

'We'll go now,' she said, holding up the document pages. 'Thank you for this, it might be important.'

Leon looked pleased. 'I thought it might.'

'And you say you wiped the computers?' she said. Rephrased: 'Why did you wipe the computers?'

'Dad told me to. He wasn't sure how to do it properly.'

'So you did.'

'I did. Yes.'

'But why did you print this document, Leon?'

'You don't like it?'

'No, I like it. But why this one?'

'I think that's obvious.'

Yes, I suppose it is, thought Lilly.

From the gate. 'Hurry up, Lil, for Christ's sake.'

'Yup, sorry! Ten seconds.' Then, to Leon. 'But your dad's OK, is he? You were worried about him. Not having his meds, you said.'

Leon smiled. 'I left them out for him and he took them. So that's OK.'

She nodded. 'Right you are. Thanks.' She turned away, then back again. 'Do you think your father has done anything wrong, Leon? Maybe something to do with this new meningitis?'

Leon frowned slightly. 'He's a great man.'

'Yes, but has he done something terribly wrong, Leon? Because if he's involved in this new disease in any way . . . well, he *is* a terrorist.'

Leon blinked, closed the door, turned the porch light off.

Lilly, Kit and Rose walked back to the Peugeot. Whatever the truth about what had happened here and how Hugh Kerridge had got the bacteriophage documents, she had to talk to Jeremy Casey. Because if it wasn't a scam, what she had in her hand was a medical revolution.

8.05 p.m.

Engine still idling, heater on max. Lilly sat in the driver's seat, Kit next to her, Rose in the back. Kit had just taken more painkillers. Rose had clicked twice before the ignition fired. Lilly held on to the steering wheel. Both hands.

'Thirty seconds,' she said, Rose's phone between her and Kit. 'This is why I need to speak to Casey. Before we go home.' She shifted position to face them, papers on her lap, one hand resting on the top page. 'I don't know what this is,' she said, tapping the documents, 'but I do need to pass it on. Fast. If someone who has worked in genetics, and at Porton Down, and who the police think might be a terrorist—'

'And who creeps around at night, peering at girls in cars,' interrupted Rose, her eyes closed.

'That too. For sure,' acknowledged Lilly.

'And who knew that Russian spy dude who got poisoned,' said Rose.

'All of that,' said Lilly. 'For all of those reasons, I need to photograph these pages and send them to Jeremy Casey, and he can take things from there. We've talked antibiotics before, he'll know what to do.'

Kit read the words as they rolled out on Rose's phone. 'I know you don't do gut feelings,' he said. 'But anyway. Gut feeling?'

It was a fair question. She ran the data again. Based on the information she had in her lap, the sheer weight of detail, the measurements for the intravenous bags, the description of the crystalline antibiotic solution, the images of gel capsules, the explanation of the entire process of fermentation, recovery and processing, she made up her mind. Reached the avocado.

'Gut feeling is this is genuine,' she said. 'It's something that *has been made*, not a speculative "this might work" piece.'

'Made by who?' said Kit.

'Well, indeed,' said Lilly. 'This is a big operation.' She tapped the pages again. 'A big *private* operation. Certainly nothing that we've come across. To get all this done in secret is extraordinary. Big Pharma, maybe. Probably. But very big and very secret. The World Health Organization would kill for this.'

Kit read then nodded. 'Better get going then,' he said. 'I'll hold 'em up, you snap 'em.' He took the pages from Lilly's lap, picked up the spider image. 'So this is what saves humanity. God bless the bacteriophage,' he said. 'Even if His design work here was a bit shit.'

At the back of the car Rose clicked, tapped and scrolled. In the front, Lilly and Kit photographed and emailed. When the last document had been sent, she texted Casey. She'd never used all caps before, but if there was ever a time . . .

URGENT. SENT DOC PAGES. READ AT LEAST TILL PAGE 8. CALL ASAP.

The Peugeot's engine ticked over, its heater just about keeping the cold at bay. She checked the fuel, put on the rear-screen defroster. She mouthed at Kit, 'Home soon.' He nodded, tried a smile, failed.

Casey called. Lilly put him on speaker.

'Hang on, Jeremy.' She turned to the back seat. 'Rose, will your dictation thing work with a call from another phone?'

Rose shrugged. 'Let's try.' She swiped some pages away, hit the mic icon. Handed her phone to Kit, who held it next to Lilly's.

'OK, with you, Jeremy. You're on speaker. Kit and his daughter, Rose, are here too. Go.'

'Lilly, what is this?' She heard exhaustion and a heavy dose of scepticism. Rose and Kit watched Casey's words appear as if he were there typing them in the car with them. 'What is it you've just sent me?'

'This is a document from the computer of Hugh Kerridge.

One-time geneticist and Porton Down man. Colleague of my father's. And he knew Sergei Skripal. The police have taken away his computers – they think he may be a terrorist of some kind. And I think he might be a part of this Men-X story somewhere.'

A few seconds of silence. Rose clicked again.

'Phage therapy is not my bag,' Casey said. 'My Russian ain't good enough.' He spoke carefully. With precision. 'But antibiotics are. There are currently forty-three new ones in clinical development around the world. A few might amount to something; most will disappoint. Twenty-seven of them are what you might call non-traditional. Antibodies, microbiome-modulating agents, immuno-modulating agents. File under miscellaneous.' His words swept across Rose's screen. Kit was transfixed.

'But none of them looks like this. It's a bacteriophage for sure, but I haven't seen this critter before. The sheath is shorter, the DNA head smaller. This is off-the-top-of-the-head stuff, you understand, Lilly, but I think it's what you wanted.' She let him carry on. Didn't want to stop the flow. 'Phages,' he continued, 'have been used for burns, eye infections, diarrhoea, sepsis, and so on, but never for meningitis.' There was a hint of excitement now.

'We find them, of course, wherever bacteria thrive. It's why some rivers, like the Ganges, are believed to have healing qualities. But this photo you sent, Lilly – well, my first stab is that someone has been engineering the phage genes.' He took a breath. 'And if someone has developed a phage that infects and replicates within meningitis bacteria, then I need to speak to him. Or her.'

Thank God for that, thought Lilly. 'Thanks, Jeremy,' she said. 'And consider the baton passed, please. This is me handing it to you. Get it to whoever needs to see it. I might be busy for a while.'

'Wait,' said Kit, leaning in. 'Mr Casey, this is Kit Chaplin. We met. I was the "civilian" with Lilly. And if my speech sounds a bit different it's because I've gone deaf and I'm reading your words from a screen. I need to ask. Why Russian? Why did you say your Russian wasn't good enough?'

'Ah,' said Casey. 'Almost all the work on phages has been done in Russia. There's a rich trove of research, but it's all in Russian. Polish, too, which doesn't help matters much. A lack of peer review, for certain. They seem to think of it as some kind of state secret. So the rest of us are all playing catch-up. That's it, really.'

'OK, thanks,' said Kit. 'Now, if you can go and make this antibiotic, Rose and I would be very grateful.'

A brief chuckle. 'Roger and out,' said Casey. Hung up.

8.20 p.m.

Rose leaned in, clicked. Her phone's digital EQ meter spiked. Kit winced.

'How's your head?' he said.

Her eyes narrowed. 'You know when you pull off a jumper or something and it crackles?' she said. 'And there's sparks in your hair? Like that. And fizzing. Lots of fizzing.' She laid her head against Kit's headrest. 'Driving me crazy,' she said. 'Oh, and you know Russia?'

'What?' said Lilly, surprised at the sudden topic switch.

'Why is it always them?' said Rose. Kit read her question.

'Why is what always them?' he said. 'Is this a Ukraine question?'

Rose sat back, tucked her legs under her. 'No, not that. It's what that old guy said. About the research. Then there's the poisonings here. Done by Russians. And old man Kerridge and Lilly's dad knew Sergei Skripal. He was Russian. Is Russian. And you know you asked Leon where his dad was, Lilly? Where in London he might be?' Lilly nodded. 'Leon said he used to stay in the City Stay Hotel. When he said it, I was like, that sounds familiar.' She held up a screenshot of the article she'd been sent by her Discord contact. Held it between them.

'So, these Russian agents have arrived from Moscow,' she said. 'Alexander Mishkin and Anatoliy Chepiga. They've got the Novichok poison in a perfume bottle, right? They get to Victoria Station. Then it says this.' Rose read from the article, pointing at the words as she went. Kit and Lilly followed her finger.

'*Friday 2 March 2018. Mishkin and Chepiga emerge from Bow DLR station, East London, and cross the road*' – now she stabbed each word – '*to the £48 a night City Stay Hotel*' – she looked at Kit, then Lilly – '*where they have booked a room for two nights.*'

The Peugeot was as silent as an old Peugeot with the heater blowing can be. Lilly's hands gripped the wheel. Kit stared at Rose.

'Bloody hell,' he said.

'So when Hugh Kerridge went to London,' said Lilly, speaking slowly, almost in wonder, 'he would stay in the same hotel as the one the Salisbury poisoners used. Really?'

'Yup,' said Rose.

'Which doesn't prove they met.'

'Nope.'

'But,' said Kit, 'the police idea that Kerridge might be a terrorist is sounding stronger by the minute.'

He's right, thought Lilly. No wonder they searched his house, took away his computers. Even if they were wiped. Which made the bacteriophage document feel even more important. She hoped Casey was already burning some ears with it. He was well connected. If he made a noise, a lot of people would listen.

316

The windscreen and side windows were misting up. Blooms of condensation crept across the glass. So much talking, thought Lilly. She used her sleeve to wipe herself a view, just in time to see Leon leaving his house. Cap, jacket. He looked up at the top windows as if checking something, looked right, walked left.

'Well, Leon's off somewhere.' She pointed across the road. Kit and Rose wiped their own windows, watched him draw closer. He had a small case in his hand, a briskness to his gait.

'Let's ask him,' said Kit. He hit the window button. As it lowered they all felt the chilled air roll into the car. Lilly shivered. Buttoned her coat back up.

'Hey, Leon!' he called. 'You OK?' Leon stopped, stared. Kit waved, leaned back. Lilly. leaned across Kit, waved. Leon walked over, stopping a metre from Kit's window.

'Look, Leon,' said Lilly. 'Sorry if you were cross about my questions just now. I had to ask, but I understand it wasn't what you wanted to hear.'

Leon, eyes everywhere but on Lilly, said, 'OK.' That appeared to be that.

'Well, have a good evening,' said Lilly. 'Going anywhere fun?' She winced at her own question. What a dumb thing to say. He's hardly about to go clubbing or to be propping up the bar at his local.

'No,' said Leon, 'just going home. Bye then.' And he carried on walking down Salt Street.

'What?' said Lilly. She jumped out of the car. 'Wait, Leon.'

He stopped again. She walked around the car. He waited for her to speak.

'What do you mean "going home"?' She pointed back up the street to number twenty-six. 'You've just been at home.'

Leon adjusted his grip on the suitcase, shuffled uncomfortably. His cheeks were already red with the cold.

'I live at 12 Clayton Drive,' he said. He turned, walked away. 'No, no, Leon.'

Lilly ran after him. Kit climbed out of the Peugeot, Rose close behind.

'No, Leon,' said Lilly. 'That's my old house. Remember? You live at 26 Salt Street. Up there.' She pointed back up the road. 'Remember? You put that address on the text you sent me.' They were both in the middle of the road, Kit and Rose hanging back by the car, passenger door open. A fox appeared briefly by the bins opposite. Slunk into the shadows. Leon stared straight at Lilly. Chewed his lip.

'I live at 12 Clayton Drive,' he said. 'My father and your father lived at 26 Salt Street. It was on my text because that's where I was when I sent it. Goodnight, Lilly.'

Leon walked to the end of the street. Turned left. Towards Clayton Drive.

8.40 p.m.

Kit knew he'd missed something important. He read it in Lilly's face, felt it in the urgency with which Rose thrust her screen at him. He felt the percussion of the door slam and the air pressure pulse on his face. But his head was a sandstorm now. A wind whipped grains around his head. He felt every grain. Knew there was no shelter, no dune whose lee could provide respite. Calm and quiet was not something he expected. The headache had worked its way up from the back of his neck to the base of his skull. The car's headlights were definitely brighter. When had that happened? He wanted to switch them off but just covered his eyes with his hands instead. Knew it was him, not the halogen. He was adrift. Signals were down. Communication was lost.

Rose, in the back again, had written out some of the Lilly/Leon exchange for Kit, but he had pushed it away. Lilly was in her default position of driver's seat, hands on the wheel, eyes straight ahead. Processing the data but struggling. She hadn't noticed the trouble Kit was in. Rose got her back.

'Lilly,' she said. 'Look at Dad.'

It was like coming round from a dream. Re-focusing after a faint. *Her father had been living with Hugh Kerridge.* Presumably having booted Leon out to live in her old house. Had her father been gay? If so, what did that explain, if anything? Or maybe it was nothing, just some old-age flat-share arrangement?

'Lilly, look at Dad.'

That was why those books at number twenty-six had looked familiar. They were her dad's books. Books she remembered from Clayton Drive now resident at Salt Street.

'Lilly!'

She was back. Turned to Rose.

'Sorry . . .'

'Look at Dad. He's worse.'

Rose was right. Kit looked terrible. Greying skin, a sheen of perspiration, a pulsing vein in his neck. She should be focusing on the father who cared and loved, not the father who had never managed either. She didn't really care who he had lived with, even if it had been a Russian-loving, meningitis-spreading mass murderer. Her father had been a callous bastard, and that was the end of it. Lilly felt Kit's forehead, took his pulse.

'Pain is bad,' he said, stirring. 'Noise is bad.' On his fogged-up side of the windscreen she wrote with her finger. *Home or hospital?* He focused.

'Both,' he said. 'I dunno, Lilly. Maybe hospital. Stronger painkillers would be good.' He closed his eyes. 'Where was Leon going then?' She spoke into her text app, hit the mic icon. The way Rose had shown her.

319

'He said he lives at my old house in Clayton Drive. And that Kerridge and my father lived together. Here in Salt Street.'

Eyebrows raised. 'Really?'

She shrugged. 'So when I was outside the Clayton Drive house, after the break-in, and Leon had already set up tea, that wasn't such a big deal, as *he actually lives there*. Also, he just walked in once the copper had left. It's his bloody house – of course he walked in!' Lilly went over the last forty-eight hours. 'And the smell in the main bedroom must have been Leon, not my dad.'

She wondered what else she had missed. She had sat in Leon's kitchen, not her father's. She and the old-fashioned copper had walked around what had become Leon's house, not her father's. Why her father had killed himself there could wait. Kit and Rose needed to go. She buckled up.

Lilly U-turned in Salt Street, stopped at the end of the road. A thought. Foot on the brake. Car in neutral.

'Rose,' she said, 'the man in the cap. You say he disappeared when you hit the horn.'

Rose leaned forward. 'Yes, when I looked up I couldn't see him. Why?'

Lilly checked the mirrors. No cars behind her. Nothing moving at all.

'The gardens of Salt Street back on to the gardens of Clayton Drive,' she said. 'And some of the fences are pretty rickety. Hugh Kerridge would know how to get to his house that way. Because if he wasn't running up or down the street, he must have gone left or right. And right is Clayton.'

The windscreen wipers brushed away the few snowflakes that had settled. Kit was still covering his eyes. The words were scrolling but unread.

'So . . . Leon and Hugh Kerridge are now both in your old house?' said Rose.

Lilly nodded. 'And isn't that quite something?' she said. It was time to go.

First gear, indicator, foot off the brake. Turned left. Then left again.

Clayton Drive.

8.51 p.m.

It was the type of snow that would settle. Large flakes fell on frozen ground. The Peugeot's headlights caught them as they came to rest. The black of the road shone as the car crawled towards number twelve. Lilly parked up.

'Really?' said Rose.

'Really,' said Lilly.

They were outside number eight, tucked into a space behind an old jeep. Lilly peered through the windscreen. Around the cul-de-sac, all the houses were the same. Eight was a copy of twelve. Low brick wall, short path to the front door, side passage to the rear garden. Every house she could see had lights on, including number twelve. Upstairs was dark, downstairs was lit.

'Well, someone's home,' said Lilly. She killed the headlights, then the engine. Kit stirred, removed his hands from his eyes.

'Doesn't look like the hospital,' he said.

'They're both in there, Kit,' said Lilly, again speaking close enough for Rose's phone to take dictation. 'Leon *and* Hugh.'

'Do they have industrial-strength painkillers? You know, like a hospital?'

Lilly leaned across, took his head gently in her hands. 'Kit, listen.' Here it was then, the moment of truth. And she'd say it out loud, not just think it. She let him go, held Rose's phone

321

between them. 'There must be a possibility, given what Leon printed off, that in there' – she pointed at number twelve – 'that in there, we can do better than that. Because if Hugh Kerridge has the antibiotic recipe, maybe, just maybe, he has the actual antibiotic as well. Maybe he's been taking it – who knows?'

Kit watched the words roll across the screen. Lilly watched him read them. He shook his head slowly, pointed at the screen. 'Those "maybe"s are working very hard in that sentence,' he said. 'Carrying a lot of weight.'

Lilly smiled. 'Agreed, Mr English Teacher.'

'And you think what?' said Kit. 'That they'll just hand it over when you ask for it?'

'Leon might,' said Lilly. 'He really might. If he can.' She could feel the seconds ticking away. 'And look, you drove from London to get the vaccine into Rose's arm. Let's at least walk a few yards to see if they have the antibiotic. We can go to the hospital for sure. And we will. But isn't it worth just trying?'

Kit read.

If I were you, I'd gamble, she thought. 'And we might not have long,' she said. 'I don't suppose Hugh Kerridge will hang around. Even in his son's house.'

'Your house,' said Kit. 'It's your house. Whoever happens to be in it.'

'Legally true,' she said. 'Just doesn't feel like it at the moment.'

Kit rolled his shoulders, rubbed his neck. 'Who was that copper who showed you round?' he said. Lilly rummaged in her coat pocket, produced his card.

'DS John Appleby,' she said, showed Kit.

'Was he nice? Did you like him?'

'Yes and yes.' Without the heater on, the temperature in the car was falling rapidly.

'Then call him,' he said. 'Tell him what we're doing.' He undid his seatbelt. '*Then* we can do it.'

8.55 p.m.

Appleby didn't pick up, Lilly left a message. They all climbed out of the car, shut the three doors as quietly as they could. They stood briefly, gazing up the road to number twelve, the Peugeot's cooling engine ticking fast.

'That's not me,' said Rose, pointing at the bonnet. 'In case you were wondering.' She hoisted her rucksack over her shoulders.

'Much room in that?' asked Lilly. 'In case . . . you know.'

'Plenty,' said Rose.

Number twelve was the last house on the left before the semicircle arced around to the other side. Lilly walked on the pavement with Kit, Rose just behind. Music and shouting came from number nine. The sound of a television from number ten. Kit took Lilly's hand past eleven. And then they were at twelve.

The downstairs bay-window curtain was roughly drawn, light leaking through. The hall light was on, the front door's stained glass glowing red and green. The police incident tape was gone but the side door was still broken, hanging unhappily from one hinge. Whenever in their forty-eight-hour window her 'emergency' builders had been planning to repair the damage of the break-in, they clearly hadn't found the time yet.

Rose clicked. '*That* was me,' she said. 'Ring the bell? Use your keys?'

'Round the back,' said Lilly.

'Wait,' said Kit, tugging at her sleeve. Keeping his voice down. 'Call Leon. You have his number. Ask him if he has the antibiotic.'

It wasn't a bad idea, Lilly thought. He responded to direct questions. She scrolled through her texts.

'Good idea,' she said. She called. Put the phone to her ear.

They stood by the low wall. Rose held on to Kit. Kit held on to Lilly. Snow settled on Rose's cap. Kit brushed flakes from his face. The TV was still blasting from ten and they were still shouting in nine, but outside twelve, the first ring leaked from Lilly's phone. *What do I say?* she thought. Second ring. *Does your dad have any antibiotics?* Third ring. *Because we really need them.* Fourth ring. *How did he get it anyway?* Fifth ring. *Can we come in?* Sixth ring. Seventh ring. Eighth ring. Kit looked at Lilly. She shook her head. Hung up.

Inside twelve, an upstairs light came on. The main bedroom, curtains closed. She'd slept in there herself, on the few occasions that her mum had let her. Scared or sad, sometimes both. They had been the conditions of entry. Once granted, she would climb into her mum's bed and fall asleep in seconds. That was how she remembered it. Presumably it then became her father's bedroom. And now, unbelievably, Leon Kerridge's bedroom.

'Lilly,' said Kit, his voice a pained whisper. 'If they have the drugs that we need, we're going to have to take them. Steal them. You know that, don't you?'

Lilly wasn't sure that she did. But now Kit had said it out loud, it seemed obvious.

'But they're in my house,' she said. 'I might just assume everything in it is mine.'

DS Appleby has picked up his messages. Alerts the nearest CBRN (chemical, biological, radiological and nuclear) team. They are thirteen minutes away.

9 p.m.

Lilly first, then Kit, then Rose. They walked to the side door, stopped. Getting past it wasn't going to be difficult, but getting past it quietly certainly was. Broken open in the break-in, it had been pushed back, almost shut. The top hinge had given way and the door had sagged away from its frame. It sat at an angle, its bottom-right edge rubbing hard against the path. Moving it would be noisy.

Lilly pointed at the bottom hinge then see-sawed her hand, shook her head. They got the message. This could fall apart. The door was weathered pine, heavy enough for two. Lilly stooped, gripped the edge. Kit took the handle. A passing car or a barking dog could have masked the sound. But none came; the drive was quiet. Lilly nodded at Kit: they couldn't wait. They both lifted. One, maybe two centimetres. The bottom hinge creaked but held. Now they needed a gap of maybe thirty centimetres between jamb and latch. They went slowly. The hinge protested low and long, each brass catch and croak sounding deafening on the silent path. Rose gritted her teeth, glanced nervously behind her. She stepped closer as if she could shield the sound from the world.

They stopped short of the thirty. Lowered it again. They both brushed their hands on their clothes. Lilly slipped through. Kit pushed Rose through next, then held his breath as he stepped up. He wasn't going to make it, that much was clear. Lilly moved to adjust the door again. Kit waved his hands, shook his head. He took off his coat and jumper, handed them to Rose. He'd lost three centimetres and he scraped through. Dressed again hurriedly.

Six steps to the garden. Lilly paused at the corner of the house. She held her arm out. Kit and Rose pulled up behind her. She waited for her eyes to adjust to the dark. The back of the house, in contrast to the front, was in darkness. She could make out the high fence at the end of the garden, but it was largely silhouetted. The buildings of Salt Street stood the other side, and Lilly realized she could see the Kerridge house from where she stood. Number 12 Clayton Drive and number 26 Salt Street. In full view of each other. It creeped her out.

Kit nudged her. She edged her way around the corner. The makeshift repairs to the kitchen door had held. Blue tarp and plywood, maybe some new nails to hold it all in place. She knew it opened; Leon had opened it for her. Made her tea. But now, with Kit and Rose close behind, it felt like a threshold about to be crossed. Real and metaphorical. The house was hers, but it felt owned by the Kerridges. Possessed by them. And before them, her father. It was the repository of everything bad in her life and she couldn't wait to get rid of it. And if she couldn't sell, she'd burn it down.

Lilly balled her fist. Her hand didn't shake. She opened the door.

Counter-terrorist specialist firearms officers receive a briefing from their team leader. A CBRN tactical adviser is alongside him. They have pulled on quick-don hazmat suits with respirators.

9.03 p.m.

Kit couldn't hear the outside world but his inside world more than made up for it. Every heartbeat, every millilitre of blood that rushed through every vein, pounded in his head. As they stepped into the darkened kitchen, it all kicked up another notch. He could hear the danger.

Lilly in front, Rose tucked in close behind him, her hand hooked on his belt. Three torch phones lit. Darting search-lights in the dark. The place was still a mess, with unwashed cups and plates in and around the sink. A half-eaten meal of sausages and peas on the table. Packets of food scattered on workspaces. A pantry door open, a fridge, an old gas stove, two chairs around the table, another on its side. Blinds at the window pulled shut. Closed door to whatever was next, pre-sumably the hall. Light shone under the threshold. Lilly typed.

Someone upstairs. Noises.

He nodded. The smell of the cooked food lingered. He picked up one of the sausages. It was still warm. Either a hor-rible meal or an interrupted meal. Maybe both. He glanced at Rose, still hooked to him. He tried to look reassuring; so did she. They both failed. She pointed at the ceiling. He nodded again. Lilly opened the fridge; he peered over her shoulder. Eggs, butter, a supermarket tray of sausages with three miss-ing. In the door, a plastic carton of milk and a silver screw-top flask. Lilly glanced at Kit, reached for the flask. She put one gloved hand on the case, the other on the screw cap. She tightened the seal. Removed the flask.

'Probably soup,' he whispered in Rose's ear. 'But in case it isn't.' Like maybe Novichok, he thought. Rose turned; Lilly unzipped the rucksack, placed the flask inside. 'I'll take the rucksack now,' he said. Rose shook her head. 'Too small for you,' she mouthed. He shook his head. She pulled away. Rose kept the rucksack.

Their three beams searched every corner. Lilly crouched and shone her torch into the cupboards. Kit checked the pantry shelves, then swept his across the windowsill. Rose tapped his shoulder, pointed. He followed her finger to a metal box tucked up against the fridge. The size of two stacked shoe boxes. A bread bin, he thought. But who knows anything? He leaned in, lifted the lid, shone the torch. Three bagels, two flasks. Another notch on the sound levels. He waved Lilly over. She was the one with the gloves. Rose turned; two more flasks in the rucksack.

'Heavy?' he mouthed. He mimed holding a weight in his hand. Lilly shook her head. Wrote, *Empty, I think. But fridge flask heavy.* He nodded. Why anyone needed three flasks, two of them kept in a bread bin, would have to go unexplained for now. The lids were on, and would stay on.

He wanted to leave now. Make a run for it, take their chances with the flasks. *Shall we go?*

Lilly shook her head. *Not yet.*

He sat on one of the chairs. Everything he didn't want to hear, he could. Everything he wanted to hear was lost. He was sure three people searching a kitchen were making way too much noise to stay undetected. But he didn't know that. He didn't know anything. Two Kerridges in the house, or just one? Might Hugh Kerridge have some antibiotics or vaccine? Did he have anything to do with anything? Kit didn't know. Lilly was in charge. He would leave it all to her.

Lilly had moved to the door. The one he had assumed led to the hall. Her gloved hand on the handle. She lowered it slowly. All the way down. Opened it slightly. The tiniest of cracks, but the thin shaft of light was enough to illuminate most of the room. Christ, what a dump. Rose moved to Lilly's shoulder. Together they peered through into the hall.

Lilly's hand flew to her mouth; she spun and pushed Rose away. Kit jumped up, caught her. Another notch. The door swung open. He stepped in front of Rose, hand on her arm. All the lights in the hall were on. By the front door, Leon Kerridge lay face down, head on the doormat, right arm folded beneath him, the other outstretched in front. Reaching for the door. His hoodie was lacerated, slashed open in four places, soaked in blood.

Kit held on to Rose. His head screeched. Lilly walked into the hall. He saw her freeze, stab a glance up the stairs. He lip-read.

'He's coming.'

The CBRN Method of Entry (MOE) team is four miles away. CBRN commander has alerted the military, the ambulance service and the fire brigade.

9.11 p.m.

The footsteps on the landing stopped abruptly. Lilly moved away from the stairs. If Kerridge were to look over the banisters, he wouldn't see her. In the kitchen doorway, Kit and Rose held up their phones to her: 999 dialled on both. He pulled Rose into the kitchen, pushed the door shut. She heard the whispers, not the details. She presumed 'ambulance', 'police' and 'Hugh Kerridge' would be part of it.

She crouched by Leon. Four deep stab wounds. They formed a diamond shape. One near the lumbar vertebrae, left and right to the seventh and eighth vertebrae, one between his shoulder blades. She tried for a pulse from his left wrist, knew there'd be nothing. Leon's left eye was half open. Blood had run on to the floor, pooling under his left arm.

He could have been dead for only minutes. He had walked past them, they had spoken. Thirty minutes ago, maximum. His father must have been waiting. Maybe he knew about the bacteriophage document, knew his time was up. Had he watched the handover? Had he seen Leon with the documents? Something must have driven him into a frenzy. She remembered his mania when he had turned up at her work. The shouting. The aggression. He must have become unstable. No wonder Leon had moved out.

More sounds from upstairs. A rustling, crumpling noise, followed by a metallic click. A closing. An end of business. Lilly knew it was time to run. The car was in the street, just a few metres away. They could be gone in seconds. But so, too, could Hugh Kerridge. He would disappear with whatever

330

drugs and information he had in his possession. He was just one old man. They had to stop him. Delay him, at least until the police arrived. Kit and Rose emerged from the kitchen. She pointed at herself, then at the stairs.

'I'm going up,' she mouthed. Then she pointed at Kit and Rose. 'Go to the car.' She pointed to the street.

Kit shook his head. Waved his arms in a big circle. 'All together.' He repeated the mime.

More shuffling steps from the main bedroom.

'Wait,' said Lilly.

9.13 p.m.

Lilly went to the first stair, twisted her head up. Eyes on the top landing. It was clear, but she would be fully visible from now on. She climbed two steps backwards. The main bedroom door was open. She held on to the banisters. Four more steps backwards. She saw movement, a flash of yellow in the bedroom, and froze. Five more to the half-landing. She crouched. Right hand on the bottom railing. Kit stepped on to the first stair.

'Wait,' she mouthed, palm of her left hand pushed out. It started to shake. Kit waited.

Ten steps to the first floor. Bathroom, her room, main bedroom. Her head dropped. She took a breath. She knew she should be terrified. Part of her *was* terrified. But mostly she realized she was angry. She glanced at poor Kit and a wide-eyed Rose. Thought about all the misery they represented. The sickness and the death. The boy who had run out into the road back in London. Then Leon, downstairs on the carpet. Also, her mother, who had died in that room. And that was enough. She pointed at Kit and Rose, first and middle finger splayed, then to her position on the half-landing.

'You, here,' she mouthed. Then she stood, walked up the final ten stairs to the first floor. Then ten steps to the main bedroom. She trod lightly. She heard Kit and Rose following her. Knew they'd be watching her, that they had her back. In the doorway, she paused.

Kerridge, dressed in a yellow hazmat suit, was crouched in front of the large fixed wardrobe, its sliding doors open, his back to Lilly. He had a toolbox beside him and was filling it with items that appeared to be buried underneath the floorboards. When he leaned forward, his arms disappeared deep beneath them. The angle was so precarious it looked as though he might topple over. When he righted himself, gloved hands slipped a small silver flask into the toolbox. He bent for another. With the full hazmat, he was oblivious to her presence.

Lilly had worn four types of PPE in the past; this looked like Type One. The Americans called it a Level A. Internal breathing apparatus, fully fitted face piece, and maximum protection against everything. Gases, dangerous chemicals, particles, spores. She knew from painful experience that it took at least thirty minutes to get into one. So he must have murdered Leon while he was *in the suit*. Maybe Leon had surprised him. Maybe Leon hadn't even known who was attacking him. But Level A was the highest-grade protection. And Lilly had none. She had maybe thirty seconds before he was done and his toolbox was full of flasks.

The risk of contamination was obviously extremely high. Kit and Rose were already infected, but how certain was she that all Kerridge had here was Men-X? Why wouldn't he have other toxins? If the Russians were involved, and Kerridge had stayed at that hotel in London, there must be a possibility of Novichok. She pulled out her phone. Removed a glove with her teeth. Selected the camera. Her hand shook. She tried to steady it with her other hand, but that shook too. She stepped back, leaned her arm against the door jamb. He was in the frame, so was the toolbox. Seven or eight flasks were in shot, some with silver caps, some with grey. Room for two or three more. She pressed the white circle button. Took the picture.

The phone clicked.

And flashed.

The police have cordoned off Clayton Drive, Salt Street and four other adjoining roads.

Clarice Adams and three MOD colleagues have left Porton Down for Clayton Drive. They are twenty-five minutes away.

9.15 p.m.

Kerridge spun round, fell back against the wardrobe base. Lilly slammed the bedroom door shut, heard a muffled roar from the other side. Kit and Rose climbed three stairs. Lilly stood outside her old bedroom.

'I'm going in here. Let him follow me,' she hissed, 'then bolt the door.' She pointed at the bolt locks, top and bottom. Kit stared, turned to Rose, and mouthed, 'It's a trap!'

Rose nodded her understanding. 'Go!'

Lilly ran to her old room, stood in the far corner. Heart thumping in her chest, she found Appleby's number. Scrolling was easy. She steadied her hands as best she could. At the fourth attempt, she sent him the picture. If the police were coming, they needed to know what they were facing.

She heard Kerridge's boots on the landing. Then the shouting started. From the stairs, Kit and Rose started to yell at him. It was hard to believe it was only two voices. The wall of furious invective was terrifying in its intensity. Their words were weapons and wielded by a father and daughter in fear of their lives. And this man was the cause of it all. Their voices overlapped and amplified each other. Every curse word she had ever heard was thrown. A broadside of hatred.

Lilly needed Kerridge to know where she was. She ran to the window, noisily undid the bolt, opened the sash. Kerridge and the freezing air tumbled in together. Lilly retreated to the corner, pressing herself against the wall to control her shaking. She faced a man in a voluminous yellow gas-tight suit, oval face piece, heavy boots. Under the face piece, the white cotton hood, goggles and mouth mask. No weapons that she could see.

He spun sharply to the door as Kit was swinging it shut. One gloved hand got caught, the wood slamming with force against his fingers. Oak door edge to oak door jamb. His index and middle fingers snapped at the distal joints below the nail. The skin tore, bleeding into the hazmat gloves. Kerridge howled, fell to his knees. On the other side of the door, two bolts slammed home. With his good hand, he reached for the handle. It turned, but the single-throw steel bolts were solid in their strike plates.

'So that's you fucked,' Lilly said, and started to laugh. Kerridge pushed and pulled at the door. She hit the mic icon on her phone. 'The simplest of traps. Got you hook, line and sinker. That really is you done, Kerridge, isn't it? It's all over. One door, two bolts. How much did they cost? Ten pounds each? To stop Leon coming in, presumably?' Her mouth was dry and she swallowed twice. Imagined Kit and Rose listening on the other side of the door. 'He's dead. As you know,' she said. Lilly knew she shouldn't get too close to a used hazmat suit. That it should be decontaminated carefully before studious removal. That she shouldn't even be in the same room as it and him. But the fury was in charge. It overrode the training. 'What did it feel like to kill your own son? How much money or power makes you do that?'

She could hear his breathing now, harsh and fast. It was amplified somehow. Presumably there was a comms system attached to the internal breathing apparatus of the hazmat.

'I really hope that hurts,' she said, pointing at his fingers. 'And when you finally get someone to help taking the suit off, man, that's going to hurt even more.'

From the window, sirens. From the landing, Kit and Rose.

'The police are coming, Lilly!' There was a metal-on-metal

scraping sound from the bottom of the door. Kerridge heard it, spun round.

'No! Lock it!' Lilly yelled. 'Don't come in!'

'Dad has a knife!' yelled Rose. 'He can help!'

Kerridge looked at the window. Sash half open.

'Yeah, you could jump,' said Lilly. 'I'd think about it too. In your predicament. Might not kill you, though. So . . . quite a risk. Old man hits concrete from twenty feet . . . could be nasty.' The sirens were closer now. She forced herself to focus. The clock was ticking for her too. 'Or you could help,' she said. 'Even now. I'd say ninety seconds till the police are here and this all ends for you. So before this all gets messy . . .' She took a deep breath. 'I'm a vaccine researcher. I know my way around pathogens. Those flasks you have out there. The ones in the box and in the fridge downstairs. Do any of them have a vaccine or an antibiotic to deal with this new meningitis? I've seen the bacteriophage recipe. Is that what's in the flasks?'

The hazmat breathing got heavier.

'My partner and his daughter out there are sick. The way so many are sick. Dying, probably. If there is anything you have that could help them, please tell me now. The police will take it all away. You know that. It's over. But please . . .'

His breathing rasped on the inhale, rattled on the exhale. She'd give it one more try, then open the door.

'No one else has discovered what you have. If it works, you know there'll be a medical revolution. The Kerridge name—'

A cough from the hazmat speaker, then, slurred and slow, 'You got that wrong.'

Lilly was startled. 'I got what wrong?' Alarm bells ringing.

'Oh, Lilly.'

A poor-quality microphone and speaker – little more than a walkie-talkie set – but the two words landed in the room like a gut punch. She caught her breath, winded. She felt light-headed, unstable on her feet. Her skin crawled. She backed away to the far corner. She was losing her mind, or her hearing, or both.

'Lilly,' he said again. 'You got everything wrong.'

And there it was. Now she knew. She gave in to the shaking, her knees collapsing under her. Lilly allowed herself to slide down the wall until she was slumped on the floor. It wasn't Hugh Kerridge. It was Edward Slater.

Her father.

9.20 p.m.

By the time she had taken her head out of her hands he had somehow removed the yellow hazmat hood, the white cotton hood and goggles. Left hand working, right thumb and little finger. Grunting, grimacing. He peeled away the mask. Dropped it to the floor. He was almost bald, a few wisps of hair plastered to his scalp, grey skin. Haggard and gaunt, pale blue, bloodshot eyes. Thin, almost non-existent lips. He leaned against the far wall, opposite Lilly. Slid until he too sat on the floor. She thought he was actually trying to smile.

'Hello, Lilly,' he said again.

She felt sick. 'I went to your funeral.' Lilly's voice was a harsh whisper. 'I saw your body in the morgue. I read your suicide note.'

'Ah. That was Hugh's funeral.' A tired voice; tight, restricted throat. '*His* body with the face blown off. It's what happens when the gun is placed just so.' He mimed a gun at ninety degrees to his chin. 'And when the bullet is a frangible one. Maximum impact, nothing left. He had lost his hair. We were the same height. He was wearing my clothes. So . . .'

Lilly retched, then vomited. Once, twice, and she was

done. Eyes on Slater. She spat the last of the bile at him, then wiped her mouth with her sleeve. Her head was ringing. Beside her, her phone transcribed everything. Transmitted everything. Scrolling fast. The cursor was flashing, waiting.

'Did you fire the shot?' she said.

He was cradling his right hand with his left. ''Course not,' he said. 'Someone else.'

'Was Hugh your . . . partner?' Lilly's head was spinning.

'We lived together, if that's what you mean. But he got sick, you see. So that was that.'

'Your suicide note said, "I'm sorry. I made so many mistakes. I'm sorry." '

'Now I *did* write that,' he said. 'If there's a note, there's no coroner. So that was neat, I thought.'

'I'd been wondering about that,' Lilly said. She paused. 'Wondering if you'd realized what a monster you'd become.'

He shrugged. Said nothing.

'I should have known.'

'You made your mind up about me when you were two.'

She nodded. 'I did. And I was right. The cold-hearted, evil fucking monster then is still the cold-hearted, evil fucking monster now.'

He shrugged. 'Whatever you want to think,' he said. Then a frown. Deep creases in his forehead. 'Are you clean?'

'What?'

'Are you clean?' he repeated. 'Or sick? With the meningitis? You said your partner and his daughter were dying . . .'

'They're clicking, yes. They have your meningitis.'

'And you?'

She shook her head. 'No, I don't think so.'

He smiled, nodded. 'Didn't think so.'

'Why?'

'If you've had it once, it seems you are immune to this strain.'

Lilly was flabbergasted. 'I've had meningitis?'

He nodded. 'When you were tiny. Nasty, it was. Your mother got you that poster, remember? To make sure you never got it again. You stuck it up there somewhere.' He pointed at the wall.

Lilly was overcome. All these years, she had assumed it was him and it was actually her. Her mother had bought her the meningitis poster.

'"Meningitis! Know the symptoms!"' she muttered.

'That's the fella.'

She glanced at the WhatsApp scroll. Kit had written, *Gun?! Knife?! FFS!*

'Who was the "someone else"?' she said. He looked blank. 'Who killed Hugh?'

A brief pause. 'They sent someone. From the same unit.'

A hammering at the door. Rose's voice. 'We're coming in. Dad and me. The police are outside, Lilly. Is that OK?'

'Wait!' she called. 'The hazmat might be contaminated.' Then, to Slater: 'What's in the flasks? There's grey and silver tops. What's the difference?'

'Grey is the vaccine. Silver is the antibiotic.'

'That's it?' she said. 'In which case, why the hazmat?'

'Because the black tops are new meningitis bacteria.'

'Men-X?' Lilly was incandescent.

'As it has been incorrectly labelled, yes.'

'You've got more?' she said, her voice rising. 'Christ! Haven't you done enough damage?'

'Like I said. In the black tops.'

'I haven't seen any black tops.'

'You haven't looked.'

'But nothing else? Any toxins? Any Novichok?'

He raised what was left of his eyebrows. 'You think that's likely?'

'Yes, I do.'

Slater thought about it. 'I don't think so, no.'

'You don't *think* so?' Then, a thought. 'Wait. But if there's no Novichok and it's just Men-X, why are you in a Level A haz-mat suit? Surely you're fully dosed up on the new antibiotic.'

His face softened. 'The chemo kills it, I'm afraid.' There was a moment of what passed for silence. More sirens, and much closer. Lilly stared at her father.

'You're dying anyway?'

'So it would seem.'

'How long?'

He shrugged.

'Well,' she said, 'you deserve a long and painful death. I hope that's what you get. I'm ashamed to be your daughter.'

'You always were.'

'And with good reason.'

Lilly heard crying from the landing. Rose. She sounded hysterical.

'And might there be a reason for all this suffering you've inflicted?' Lilly said. 'Do you want to have a go at that one?'

Car doors slamming. Shouted instructions. More sirens. Kit calming Rose.

'It wasn't supposed to be like this.'

'Oh, really? What was it supposed to be like?' Lilly pushed herself up, leaned against the wall.

He took a beat. 'The meningitis bacterium fell into our laps. Mine and Hugh's. We got lucky. Bacteria constantly mutate and swap genes. One of these changes created a strain that was stronger. More able to survive. It had developed in someone who lived alone, who then presented themself to a quick-thinking doctor. Porton Down got hold of it. We ran an experiment.'

'On Sergeant Joe Taylor,' said Lilly.

'Someone like that. Anyway, it all went wrong, but when we got fired we kept a sample.'

'And sold it to the Russians.'

Slater nodded, smiled again. 'Eventually, we did. That was Hugh's idea. He'd worked with a Spanish geneticist who was SVR. The re-branded KGB. They arranged a pick-up. Here in Salisbury. Paid us well.'

That was the connection, thought Lilly. Of course it was. Now it made sense. 'March 2018,' she said. 'Mishkin and Chepiga.'

He nodded, pointed at her. 'Smart kid.'

'I got it from my mother.'

He swatted her words away. 'As it turns out, they had . . . other work that day.' He waved his two arms, still encased in the hazmat. A 'how were we to know?' gesture. 'The Novichok was a sideshow. A drop-off. Their main work was the pick-up. We met in the city centre. Entrance of the coin shop. Very brief. We disposed of their perfume bottle for them; they took the meningitis from us. Said they would play with it. Come back to us when they were done.'

'When they were *done*? When they'd genetically engineered it?'

He nodded slowly. 'The long incubation period wasn't a surprise – they'd worked on that. But the clicking and tinnitus-like side effects certainly were. But it had been weaponized. In an aerosol. We wanted revenge on Porton Down; so did they. Hugh got himself a pass, sprayed it in a couple of places. It should have been more controlled. Should have been tighter! But the stupid bugger got himself infected. Then he spread it everywhere. That's when it got out of control.'

Lilly was grateful she was still propped up against the wall. The realization of what had happened was as clear as it was sickening. Hugh Kerridge had come to London, ranted and raved *over her*, and then *she* had passed on the infection to Kit and Rose. And they had infected the school.

341

'Hugh got scared. Became . . . unstable.'

'So you killed him.'

'So he was killed.'

'Did you watch?'

Lilly knew there was drama outside. Knew that an elaborate operation would be needed to retrieve them and the flasks. Specialist police teams, backed up by the other emergency services. Possibly the army. Who knew what the threat was? Certainly she didn't. But here, in her old bedroom, with the taste of vomit in her mouth and its stench in her nostrils, she saw her father clearly. Saw madness in his dying eyes.

'No,' he said. 'I did not. I stayed clean.' His eyes widened. Sat up a few inches. 'I watched Porton Down suffer. *And* I stayed clean.' He sounded so pleased with himself Lilly felt nauseous again. Her phone still scrolled. Kit had written, *Police and ambulance here. Kitting up. Not long. Stay cool. We're just outside the door. Police know everything.* She was sure there were police in the garden but avoided looking for fear of disturbing the equilibrium. Her father wanted to talk, seemed proud of what he'd done. She wanted to hear him. This last time. Then he could rot in prison.

Outside 12 Clayton Drive the MOE team are assembled. Behind them, the CTSFOs (counter-terrorist specialist firearms officers). Behind them, public order officers, also in hazmat suits and respirators, warn neighbours to stay inside.

9.35 p.m.

'Are you armed?' asked Lilly.

Slater had barely moved since slumping to the floor. He still cradled his damaged hand. He snorted briefly. 'If I was, I couldn't use it. If I had a gun tucked in my belt it would take me ten minutes to reach it. And my fingers are broken, so . . .'

Lilly and Ed Slater stared at each other for some time. She saw nothing in his face. No sadness, no pleasure, no emotion at all. He hadn't moved since sitting down, hadn't glanced at the open window. She was freezing but knew the end was imminent. She typed, *Come in. Slowly.* In a few seconds, both bolts were drawn back.

'Wait!' she called. Watched him. He still hadn't moved. Like he hadn't heard. 'OK,' she said.

Kit came in first, then Rose. Both holding phones. Rose, distraught, tears running freely. Kit ran to Lilly. She held up her hand.

'I'm fine,' she said. 'Meet my father.'

Slater looked terrified. 'But they're not clean!'

Heavy boots on the stairs, then silence. Movement in the main bedroom. The clanking of metal. Dragging, slamming, closing. Making safe.

Lilly crouched in front of Slater. Lifted his head with her fingers. 'I'll ask them to leave. But first. The antibiotic. In the silver-topped flasks. How do you take it? What's the dose? Come on, *Dad*, what's the dose?'

'I don't know,' he whispered. 'You just drink it from the

343

bottle.' Lilly scrambled for Rose's bag, removed the silver-topped flask. She unscrewed the top, poured ten mils into the cap. Kit made Rose drink first. Lilly poured again. Kit drank second, licked it clean.

'Just the one?' he said.

Slater was horrified. He stabbed glances at Rose, then at Kit, then back. Lilly gestured to Kit to remove his earplugs. Placed her right index finger over her lips. It didn't shake. Kit removed his plugs, placed them on the floor between them. He clicked immediately. Slater gasped. Rose removed her plugs, flicked them at Slater. They hit him in the face, he gave a little scream. Terrified, he pushed himself against the wall. As far away as he could get. Which wasn't far enough. Rose, Kit and Lilly knelt in front of Slater.

'This is for my friend, Harriet,' said Rose, tears falling from her face.

'This is for Rose,' said Kit. Glazed eyes, body shaking.

'And this is for Mum,' said Lilly. 'Every droplet. Every particle. Every molecule.'

They opened their mouths wide. Took deep breaths. Exhaled until there was no breath left in their lungs.

The spore was shaped like a ball, dull grey and seventeen microns in length. That is to say, seventeen thousandths of a millimetre. It spun as it drifted. The spore cloud of which it was a part was buffeted by eddies of breath, draughts from the open window and the heat of nearby human bodies. The cloud floated past two mouths, then spun faster as breath was exhaled, blowing the spores away. Then a third mouth opened, breathing in sharply. A sudden intake, and the air was sucked inside at a speed of two metres per second. The spore was pulled in through the mouth, through the fibrous muscle of the pharynx and past the open epiglottis. In the larynx it was bounced further by the tens of thousands of identical spores in the cloud, all of which had made the same short journey. The ball spun faster.

At the end of the inhale, the spore was pulled down the trachea, a straight drop to the bottom of the windpipe. As it fell, the cloud rotated anticlockwise and the spore funnelled through the tubular branches of the left lung. It slowed as the tubes constricted then stuck on the wall of one of the smallest. There, it waited for germination.

Programmed.

Coded.

Under orders.

In twelve weeks, its hard keratin shell will break and its bacteria will be released. They in turn will release auto-inducers – tiny molecules that signal to each other. Once they message that they have the numbers, the bacteria will attack.

Until then, the spore cloud's cargo of lethal toxin will have to wait.

Two months later

IN LILLY'S KITCHEN the blinds were open and the sun threw stripes across the room. Rose sat at the table, head in her hands. A new dressing gown, untied, had fallen open. An oversized T-shirt of Kit's came to her knees. She had barely moved for five minutes.

The house was silent. On the table in front of Rose, her laptop and phone. Both switched off. From her dressing-gown pocket she took a small, plastic oval case. She held it in her palm, placed it on top of the laptop. She rearranged the three items absent-mindedly. Laptop, phone, case. Each repositioned, played with. She stood up, filled the kettle, took some paracetamol. From the cupboard she found her mug and a teabag. She waited by the kettle, watching the steam curl from its spout.

Rose walked to the table, picked up the case. Popped it open, removed a tiny, acorn-shaped, white earbud. With her left thumb and forefinger she twisted it into her left ear. Tapped it twice. She tugged some curls of her hair as low as they would go. She sat drinking her tea, checked her reflection in her phone screen. Pulled at some more strands until her ear was covered.

'Hey,' said Jess, wandering in. Hair down, black pyjamas, laptop.

'Hey,' said Rose.

Jess made a cafetière of coffee. Took her time. Shuffled between fridge and worktop. The kitchen filled with the smell of the ground coffee. She turned to Rose.

'Can I play music?' she said. 'Do you mind?'

''Course not,' said Rose, not looking up. 'It'll sound shitty with this thing . . .' She pointed at her ear, shrugged. 'But I haven't got the settings right yet. So my bad. And it's your place, so . . . your rules.'

Jess pulled her phone from a breast pocket, swiped and pressed. Some beats began to play, but she kept the volume low. Sat opposite Rose. Studied her screen. Occasionally she raised her gaze to Rose, then looked away.

'Did my mum tell you about the whole surname thing?' she said.

Rose looked up, frowned. 'No,' she said. 'What surname thing?'

'She doesn't want to be a Slater any more.' Jess looked as though she was about to say some more, then changed her mind.

'And what do you think? You're a Slater too.'

Jess shrugged. 'I mean, I get it. Her dad was a total shit, but it would be weird for sure. Maybe it would be just her that changes. Her mum's maiden name was Wilson. But I don't really fancy being Jess Wilson.'

'So you'll stick?'

'Probably.' Jess started typing. Turned the music up.

Lilly winced. 'Ouch,' she said.

'Oh,' said Jess. 'Sorry. Was that me?' She turned the music down again.

Rose nodded, hand over her ear. 'Sounded all distorted.'

'Well, it's only been a couple of days. I'm sure you'll get it right.'

Rose shrugged. 'Maybe.'

'Can I see?'

Rose hesitated, then tucked some strands of hair behind her ear, revealing the hearing aid.

'Looks exactly like an Apple AirPod from here,' said Jess. 'I thought it was a light brown colour when you got it.'

'I painted it white,' said Rose.

Jess smiled. 'Perfect camouflage.'

10.35 a.m.

Lilly hesitated by the kitchen door. She knew Jess and Rose had got up before her, had heard them talking. They seemed to be fine with each other now. It all seemed to become calmer after the funeral somehow. The pain and grief of the last few weeks would last a lifetime but, for now, if the two girls could find a way to live in the same space together, everything would feel easier. They could stay for the meeting or not; it was up to them. She hoped that they would, and had told them as much, but that she would understand if they bailed.

Lilly was dressed and ready. Old agnès b jeans and an oversized brushed cotton, powder-blue shirt. She had thought, briefly, of power dressing, but changed her mind. Her Saturday clothes were always the same, whoever was visiting. Even if they were from the Ministry of Defence. She pushed open the door.

'Morning,' she said. 'Any coffee going spare?'

Jess waved her hand in the direction of the cafetière. 'Yes, but it's blow-your-mind disgusting.'

'Too strong again?' said Lilly.

'It's my signature brew.'

Lilly poured, laughed. She sat at the table; neither girl looked up. She sipped, gingerly.

'God,' she said. It really was as bad as Jess had said.

'Told you,' muttered Jess.

Lilly wondered if drinking rocket fuel was wise with the MOD woman about to arrive. Her heartbeat already felt raised. She didn't want to push her luck. But her daughter had made it, so a few more sips would be fine. She glanced at her watch.

'So this Ministry of Defence woman is here in a few minutes. Are you in or out?'

'In,' said Jess and Rose together.

'Definitely in,' said Rose. 'But I'm not getting dressed for her, because she's a bitch.'

Jess glanced at her mother. Lilly nodded affirmation.

'You wait till you meet her,' she said.

Lilly tidied the kitchen, wiped surfaces. 'She asked me to go in to their offices. In Whitehall. I refused.' From a cupboard she produced a dustpan and brush. 'So that's why she's coming here. And I wanted you guys involved.'

'Is this for her?' asked Jess. 'The sweeping and everything.'

'It's for me,' replied Lilly. 'Also, it's what you do.'

The doorbell rang twice. The woman was early. Before Lilly could react, Rose ran from the kitchen.

'Rose, I'll—'

Lilly heard the door open until it hit the end of the safety chain. She heard Clarice Adams's voice.

'Oh, hello, I'm—'

Rose interrupted. 'I know who you are. Before you come inside . . .'

Lilly walked into the hall. She was about to interrupt, but Jess held her back. 'Let her say this,' she whispered.

'. . . there's one rule,' said Rose. 'You speak to Lilly with respect. You treat her with respect. Always. Or you don't come in at all. How's that sound?'

Lilly covered her mouth with her hand. Sudden tears.

Christ, she thought, she's doing this for Kit. It's what he would have said.

10.55 a.m.

Around the kitchen table, Jess and Rose, then Lilly and Clarice Adams. The MOD woman was wearing black trousers and a black jacket over a grey shirt. Fresh wax in her hair. She looked sharp, thought Lilly. Not *her* Saturday clothes.

'First week back at work?' said Adams.

Like you care, thought Lilly.

'Yes,' she said. 'GSL have been very understanding. And Rose went back to school on Wednesday.'

Adams nodded, took a sip of coffee. She pushed her chair back. That was the pleasantries over and done with. She looked at Lilly, Jess and Rose in turn. She opened her mouth to speak.

Lilly jumped in. 'First,' she said, holding her hand up. Adams closed her mouth again. 'Before you give us your talk. You lied to me. You lied about Sergeant Joe Taylor. About Porton Down and who knows what else. So my starting position is that you are about to lie some more. Your department lies. The government you work for lies.' She dropped her hand. 'But carry on. Please.'

Adams tried again. 'OK, well. First, everything I tell you – whether you believe me or not – stays here. In this room. It will be easy to trace any leak, as so few people know what happened. Is everyone clear on that?'

'Are you threatening us?' said Lilly.

'I am here to put the fear of God into you,' said Adams. 'So yes. And I don't really give a fuck whether you like me or not either. That's not my concern.' Her rugby face was back. 'I just want you to understand what is happening here.' She turned to Rose. 'I know you still have a huge following on social media, but there will be nothing that I say *here* that ends up *there*.' Her right index finger stabbed the table. 'Do you understand?'

Rose nodded. She looked startled, pale. 'I know that you shut me down before. Just when it was getting dangerous.'

'And I'll shut you down again. Just so we're clear.'

Rose went quiet. Adams nodded. Gathered herself.

'It is true that my job requires me to be somewhat economical with the truth,' she said, 'particularly when national security is involved.' Rose rolled her eyes. 'So let me tell you what I can. Tell you what I think we know. Then, it is obviously up to you whether you believe me or not.'

Lilly nodded. 'We got that bit,' she said. 'Carry on.'

'And you know some of this already, Lilly. Your father and Hugh Kerridge were lovers. Off and on, but mainly on. And they were traitors. Kerridge was recruited in Spain by the SVR, the Russian Foreign Intelligence Service. This was 1994, 1995, we think. They had a microbiologist by the name of Cardoso – a very successful one, by all accounts.'

Lilly nodded. 'I found a photo of him with Kerridge. They were studying DNA. Quite a big team.'

'Indeed,' said Adams. 'He wasn't just a successful scientist; he was a successful agent too. We think he recruited four others in his time at Alicante and Oslo. There is, as you can imagine, a lot of catching-up going on. Not just here, but in Spain and Norway too.'

'Did you not know about Cardoso then?' said Lilly.

Adams shook her head. 'We did not.'

'Why did he pick Kerridge?' said Lilly. 'He wasn't exactly a high-flyer.'

Adams nodded. 'We don't know for sure. Best guess? He was impressionable. Influenceable. Also, poor. He might have seemed a reasonable investment.'

'Is that the same as weak and greedy?' said Lilly.

'It is,' said Adams.

'No wonder he and my father got on so well.'

Adams nodded, her hands palm up, acknowledging the point. Lilly glanced at Jess and Rose. They were both staring at Adams, open-mouthed.

'So when did Kerridge recruit my father?'

'We don't know that he did,' said Adams. 'Not at the moment. But then Cardoso died and the SVR lost contact. Or lost interest – who knows? It all goes quiet till Kerridge turns up with SVR operatives in Prague, at the Best Western Hotel in 2014. We think this is where Major General Sergeev, one of the Salisbury planners, asks about Porton Down. And Kerridge mentions the meningitis trials that went wrong.'

'And that weren't even trials,' said Lilly.

Adams ignores her. 'We think when Mishkin and Chepiga came to town to pick up the vial, they took the opportunity to plant Novichok on the Skripals' front door. Two ops for the price of one. They doubled up. But the meningitis was the main job. The Novichok was the icing on the cake.' Adams's hands were conducting again, sweeping gestures followed by intricate pointing. Lilly had never seen anyone use their hands so expressively.

'When the Russians realized what they had they instigated an extraordinary plan. They had a new, if wild, biological weapon – the meningitis. But that was only half the story. Now they wanted a vaccine and an antibiotic.' A left-hand chop to the table, a right-hand chop to the table. 'Their plan, as we understand it, was to use your father and Kerridge as useful idiots. To pay them handsomely. Let them be the cause of the outbreak. Give them small amounts of vaccine and antibiotic for their own protection. Then the Russians would ride in as the saviour of the world. And deny any link to their agents. They would deliver the drugs, take the acclaim and the thanks of grateful nations.' Adams tried a smile. 'And, as you might have noticed, that's something they don't have a lot of right now.' She took a short breath. 'Pariahs on the world stage. Evicted from most international organizations. Guilty of countless war crimes. Chechnya, Syria, Ukraine.' Adams had the room. Lilly, Jess and Rose were rapt. 'And after the embarrassment of their Sputnik V Covid vaccine roll-out and the exposure of their state-sponsored doping programme for their Olympic athletes,' Adams continued, 'this was a *gift*.' Both hands in the air, hallelujah-style. 'Their history of phage-based medicine gave them credible cover. Everyone knew the Russians were obsessed with phage research. Now we would know why. It all fitted.'

'Until my father and Kerridge fell out,' said Lilly. 'And my father got cancer.'

Adams nodded. 'They got greedy and careless. Then it all fired half-cocked.'

'What does that mean?' said Jess.

'It means it was a shit show,' said Adams. 'Before they could spin their story, we knew what they had been doing. And could prove it.'

'So all the drugs being used to combat this meningitis strain are Russian,' said Lilly.

'Either made in Russia or from a Russian design. Yes.'

'And how many dead?'

'Can't tell you that.'

'And how many deaf?' asked Rose, leaning in. Her eyes glistened.

'Can't tell you that either.' Adams's eyes flicked to Rose's ear.

'Humour us,' said Lilly, sharply. 'Ballpark. More than a thousand dead?' Adams nodded. Lilly clasped her hands in her lap. 'And how many deaf? Ten thousand? More?' Adams nodded again.

Adams shifted in her seat; Lilly jumped in.

'So, presumably, this must count as a biological weapon attack on the UK. On a NATO country. Doesn't it?' The contrast between the domesticity of her surroundings and the apocalyptic nature of her language was not lost on her. But the logic seemed unmistakable, the implications unavoidable.

'It is true,' said Adams, 'that the price Russia will pay for this will be . . . profound. However' – both hands flat on the table, she spoke more slowly now – 'they have let it be known that China is now the major investor in their chemical industry. In the research, the development and the manufacture. All of it. We are not sure how true this is, but the possibility of a Chinese connection complicates matters. Profoundly. It muddies the waters. Makes clarity well-nigh impossible. Unwise, even. There is a certain . . . nervousness about how that particular relationship could develop.'

Adams paused.

'So who goes to jail?' said Rose, her throat tight. 'Who goes to jail for murder? For the murder of Harriet Teale. For mass murder. Who gets punished?'

Adams shifted her balance. 'No one, Rose. I'm afraid the answer is no one.'

There was silence in the kitchen. The sun had gone in. The coffee was cold. Lilly felt a chill.

'So, the bigger the crime, the smaller the punishment,' she said. 'If any punishment at all.'

Adams spread her arms. 'Above my pay grade,' she said. 'Prime ministers and presidents will decide what happens next.' She leaned in, put both arms on the table. Steepled her fingers. 'I can, though, offer you a financial package. In recognition of all that you have been through. All that you have lost. And everything you did to bring the story to a conclusion that could have been so much worse.'

'To buy our silence,' said Lilly. 'Like you did with Joe Taylor's family.'

'Effectively, yes. As your story will need stay a state secret. But it is a genuine attempt to compensate you. In some small way.'

Lilly gripped the table, closed her eyes. She thought back to that first text message from Kit about tinnitus. The meeting in Pret. His terror at becoming sick and his fears of losing Rose. The last few moments with her father. It all seemed a lifetime away. But now she would have a cheque from the government to make it all better.

From the hallway, the sound of careful footsteps. The kitchen door opened. Kit was wearing pyjamas. Bed hair. He blinked. Lilly beckoned him in. Wrote on the pad.

We've been talking about you.

Rose ran to her father.

Led him to the table.

Acknowledgements

With grateful thanks to Dan Kaszeta at RUSI, 'King of Nerve Agent Twitter' and author of *Toxic: A History of Nerve Agents, From Nazi Germany to Putin's Russia*; Mark Urban, *Newsnight*'s Diplomatic Editor and author of *The Skripal Files: Putin, Poison and the New Spy War*; and Jonathan Mayo's *Daily Mail Online* article 'The Novichok files', quoted by Rose here (yes, he's my brother). Also to Mark Honigsbaum's *The Pandemic Century: A History of Global Contagion from the Spanish Flu to Covid-19*; Paul A. Offit's *Vaccinated: One Man's Quest to Defeat the World's Deadliest Diseases*; Arthur Allen's *Vaccine: The Controversial Story of Medicine's Greatest Lifesaver*; Mary Davies and *The Economist*'s always excellent Science and Technology section. My son Joe gave me lessons in Discord, former Chief Superintendent (now top author) John Sutherland advised on police ops, and hospital manager at Addenbrooke's, Daniel Northam Jones, advised on hospital matters.

All mistakes will be mine, of course.

Also thanks to my fellow 'We also have day jobs' trade union members, brothers Tom Bradby and Jonathan Freedland.

Bill Scott-Kerr and Eloisa Clegg provided the inspired Transworld editorial guidance, as ever.

Most public buildings described here are fictitious. If bad things are going to happen, it's just easier that way.

Also thanks to the fabulously helpful experts at the Meningitis Research Foundation whose vital work you can find at meningitis.org. Their aim is to defeat meningitis – which remains a universal public health challenge – by 2030.

This book is dedicated to the memory of Alan Mayo, my father's brother, who died aged one from meningitis. Also to the memory of Mary Bird, my mother-in-law, who was always an enthusiastic reader of my books.

About the author

Simon Mayo MBE is a writer and broadcaster. His previous books include the *Sunday Times* bestseller *Knife Edge, Mad Blood Stirring, Blame* and the *Itch* trilogy, filmed for TV by the ABC. He hosts *Drivetime* on Greatest Hits Radio and the film-review podcast *Kermode and Mayo's Take* with Professor Mark Kermode.